Darker Than the Starless Night

THE NUMENBORN SAGA

DARKER THAN THE STARLESS NIGHT

by

REBECCA BRODKEY

The Vibrant Machine Press

Developmental Editor: Kit Haggard (www.kithaggard.work)

Line and Copy Editor: A.J. Peterson (author.ajpeterson@gmail.com)

Cover Illustrator: Emily Nolan (millyillus@gmail.com)

Interior Illustrator: Rin Varga (rinvargaillo@gmail.com)

*For anyone who has ever felt like their mind is broken.
I promise, your mind is wondrous. And powerful.*

—

And for Aaron, my bringer of dawn.

IN THE YEAR OF OUR QUEEN CCXXII
Touching Rocks
Inisfail
Panchaia
IBERNIA
Northumbria
ALBION
Caerl Tui
LE
UNKNOWN
Traiana
DRESSEN
OKEANUS
uncharted
ISPANA
Traiana
N
W
E
S
IN THE YEAR OF OUR QUEEN CCXXII

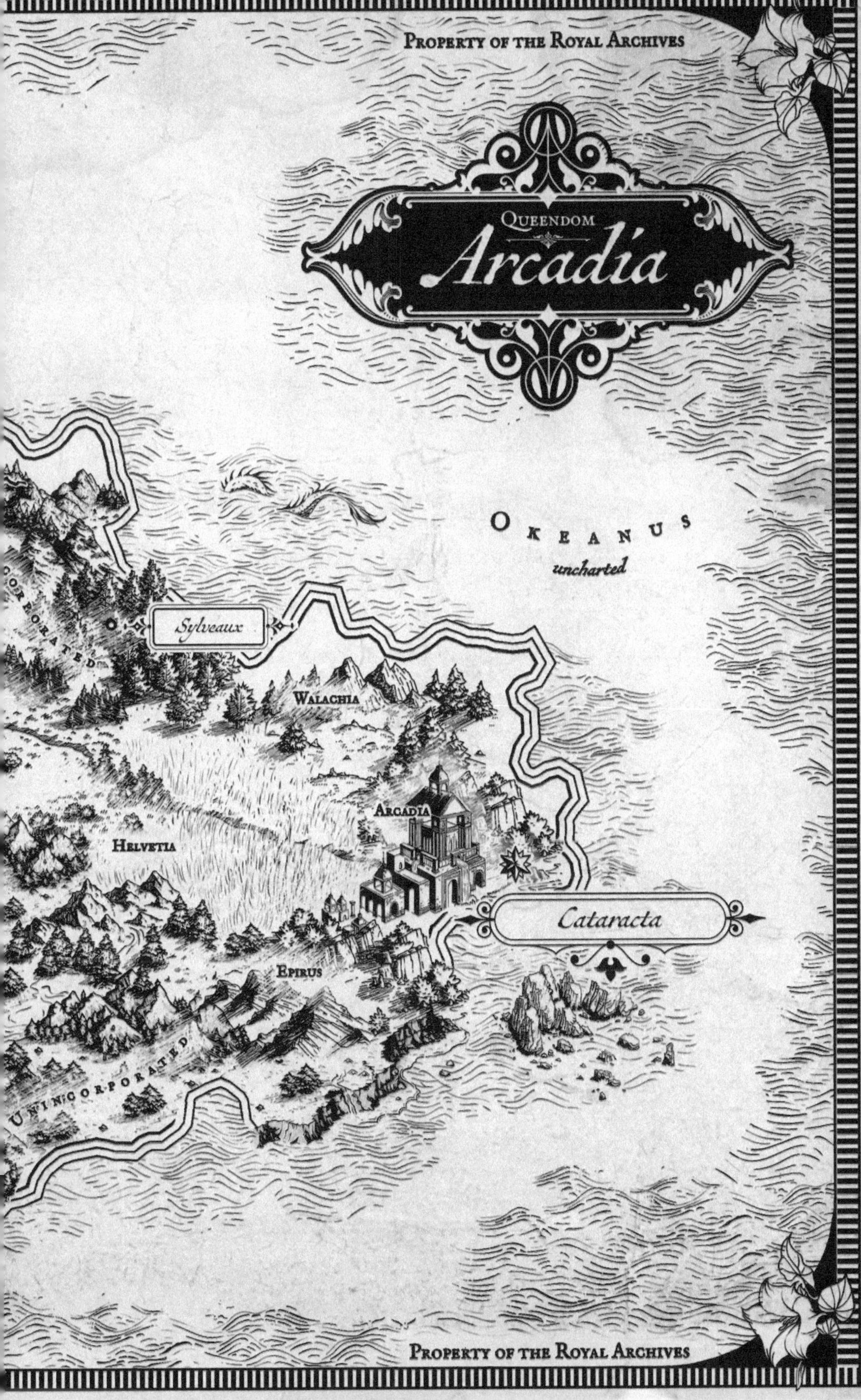

PROPERTY OF THE ROYAL ARCHIVES
QUEENDOM
Arcadia
OKEANUS
uncharted
CORPORATED
Sylveaux
WALACHIA
ARCADIA
Cataracta
HELVETIA
EPIRUS
UNINCORPORATED
PROPERTY OF THE ROYAL ARCHIVES

PRONUNCIATION GUIDE

Yom	YAHM
Lior	LEE-OHR
Lucan	LOO-KIN
Quia	KEY-AH
Misho	MEE-SHOH
Cernunnos	KER-NOO-NOHS
Triarii	TREE-AHR-EE
Amaurosis	AHM-OR-OH-SIHS
Numen	NOO-MEHN
Wacachan	WAH-CAH-CHAHN
Arcadia	AHR-KAY-DEE-UH
Panchaia	PAN-K-AYE-AH
Inisfail	IHN-IHS-FELL
Ibernia	EE-BEHR-NEE-AH
Traiana	TRY-AH-NAH
Renos	REE-NOHS
Arduinna	AHR-DWEE-NAH
Ardennes	AHR-DEHN
Cataracta	CAT-AH-RAK-TAH
Quetzal	KET-ZAHL
Tezcat	TEHZ-CAT
Thoth	THOHTH

TABLE OF CONTENTS

PROLOGUE

Yom sometimes became so entranced by the twisting, curling vines of Moonflower in her guardian's laboratory, that she swore she heard it whispering to her. It wasn't the only plant that seemed to murmur; many of them had at one point or another, as if secrets pumped through their veins rather than water. And sometimes, Yom attempted to whisper back.

"What are you doing?" Lior startled her, sneaking up from behind to pinch Yom's hips, which had lately been taking on an unwieldy width. Lior's blue eyes, true as cobalt, blinked at her expectantly, a wry grin spreading across her face. Her dark hair unfurled in waves, framing fine features and pale skin, a whisper of pink coating her cheeks and nose. While Lior's features made her unquestionably beautiful, it was her unflinching spirit, her magnetic essence that drew Yom to her, like charged air pulled towards lightning.

"Nothing," Yom said a bit too quickly, heat racing to her cheeks at the absurdity of being caught speaking to plants. "Just the exercise your mother gave us." Lior was the daughter of Yom's guardian, Eden. Despite this biological connection, she was utterly uninterested in the inheritance of Eden's extensive knowledge of the chemical arts. Yom supposed Lior burned too brightly to be kept squirreled away in a laboratory.

Lior laughed at the clear fib, twirling back to her own workstation with the grace of a dancer, while Yom followed her movement hopelessly. They played a game of pretend often, that Lior was a beautiful heiress and Yom her dapper and chivalrous suitor. Lior primped herself with Eden's beauty powders—crushed pearl on the cheeks, beetroot stain on the lips—and Yom donned a borrowed, fraying waistcoat and millworker's boots. They promenaded down the city's crooked and dreary avenues, arm in arm, Lior holding a lacey fan over the lower half of her face and Yom deepening her voice into something gruff and—she hoped—sultry. The game started as Yom's way of protecting Lior from the leering eyes of their city, Inisfail, but lately, Yom had been clinging to it rather desperately. It was the only time she didn't speculate about whether she was succumbing to these confusing and weighty feelings by herself. It was the only time it was easy to imagine that Lior felt the same way.

"How are my little chemists?" Eden returned from the apartment they shared upstairs. Her eyes crinkled in a smile as she smoothed away the wisps of gray hair clinging to her cheeks. Lior and Eden were almost spitting images of each other, though Eden's features were given more definition over time, and her eyes were brown rather than Lior's striking blue.

"I finished the sleeping draught," Yom said brightly. They had advanced far enough in their schooling that Eden allowed the girls to have independent study in her laboratory. Yom usually finished Eden's assignments within the first fifteen minutes, and spent the rest conducting her own experiments, or helping Lior complete hers.

Eden hummed with a nod, and Yom bathed in the glow of her approval.

"And you, dove?"

Lior held her hands behind her back and remained silent, trying to look contrite.

Eden sighed. "Come here, sit."

Yom and Lior dutifully took stools that circled the central hearth, and Eden pulled up her own stool across the fire from them.

"Every living thing is animated by the same force. It beats steadily, in the truth of a being. This is all the chemical arts are," Eden paused to gesture at the laboratory surrounding them, dim light flickering over hundreds of small glass bottles and jars lined up neatly on shelves. "Accessing these hidden truths of every living thing. It's an art that dates back to the Ancients," Eden watched her daughter, but Lior merely yawned. Yom hung on each word.

"Can you tell us a story?" Lior leaned her head on Yom's shoulder. "It's getting late, I'm sure it won't kill us to pause lessons until tomorrow."

Eden pursed her lips and tried to look stern, but she always struggled to say no to Lior. The chemist seemed to accept that this was a battle for a different day.

"Alright, one story. But you must promise never to repeat it outside of this circle."

Yom and Lior nodded eagerly. The fire crackled and licked their faces with warm light as Eden's hands poised in the air like a conductor of music. Eden had only begun to share her stories recently, once she had deemed them old enough not to slip up and repeat them. Yom didn't understand why, they were just stories after all. Stories unlike anything they had been taught in school.

"Which one do you want to hear?"

"The Separation of Arcadia and Panchaia," Lior said decisively, another thing Yom admired about her. Of course every child in Arcadia was told the bedtime story of the Separation. But it was simple and plain, the story of an ancient people engaged in an ancient war, and the calamitous earthquake that forced its halt. It did not glitter in the same way as when Eden told it.

"Very well," Eden winked at Lior. "The story of the Separation begins in the shade of the World Tree, Wacachan, at the meeting of sea and sky." The laboratory around them faded away and Yom was transported elsewhere, to a great tree surrounded by water, an eternal reflection of the star-littered sky above it. "The gods sprouted from its branches, and the titans from its roots. I like to think it was the World Tree's own sap that animated them, gave them their lifeforce." Yom saw spindly branches and their delicate buds twist into svelte limbs.

"The immortals were young and brash then, drunk on adolescent power. The gods watched their titan cousins use mud and silt to shape rolling hills, form rivers, raise lush mountains. The titans filled these gardens of creation with intricate beings that had horns and fangs and wings to tend to their paradises. 'We must create something,' the gods said to each other hungrily.

"It was the two eldest brothers, constantly fighting, who banded together to create the first human. They shaped her from mud and sticks, and breathed a little of their own lifeforce into her. She bounded the land in exuberance, beautiful and fickle and fragile. Their siblings saw what the two eldest had created and felt a jealous hunger open inside them. They wanted to create something. To leave their own mark. To prove that they themselves were worthy of creation.

"One by one they shaped their own humans, and exhaled a bit of their lifeforce into their creations. But soon the humans realized they could create their own life, without the help of the gods. They left, and settled far and wide through the lands of the titans. And then, something strange happened." Yom snuck a peak at Lior and saw she was listening just as raptly. "The power they felt dissipated. 'This cannot be possible,' the gods whispered to each other. 'How can our own creations control us so?' It was as though the very act of creating these humans had twined their fates together.

"The gods unleashed rain and thunder, brutal heat and fire, until the humans crawled back, begging for mercy. The humans offered their own blood as worship, and the gods felt the power condense on them once again like dew.

They knew then that whatever the humans could give, they could also take away. The World Tree was the endless axis around which even the gods must turn.

"Like their cousins, the titans found themselves bound to their own creations, unable to leave the realms that they had built. The immortal beings had to strike an agreement with each other in order to survive.

"Humans explored and settled into the titan lands, and the titans allowed them, expecting them to care for their paradises. But the land did not need the humans as the humans needed the land. Humans destroyed and reshaped areas of titan land to create their own settlements. The titans attempted to control them, but they remained under the authority of the gods. The titans grew resentful. Discontent festered to a boiling point."

Yom held her breath. Any child in Arcadia knew enough to fear what came next.

"The war lasted decades." Eden looked between Yom and Lior, the Ancient War surrounding them in the flickering shadows of the laboratory.

"Legions of human and animal warriors died, entire realms were razed with fire and battered with torrential rain. Anything the war touched, it destroyed. Until the unthinkable occurred: the gods killed a titan. These immortals did not even know yet that they could die. That even they were not endless.

"In the wake, Wacachan itself interceded. It saw total annihilation, if the war continued. The World Tree created a great rupture between two halves of the world. The enchanted waters that circled the earth—"

"Okeanus," Yom whispered. Eden smiled and nodded.

"—filled in between the two halves, making the crossing between them impossible. The gods were confined to one side and the titans to the other. But the lines were not clean. Warriors of both factions were trapped on either side. Generations, then centuries, then millenia passed as each half picked up the pieces of their world.

"To this day, both the gods and the titans fear that the other side will discover how to cross the enchanted waters of Okeanus and return to finally finish the war." Eden smiled and sat back.

"That's it?" Lior whined.

Eden raised her eyebrow, knowing what she withheld. "What more is there?" she asked, feigning ignorance.

"Which half became Arcadia?"

"That is a story for another night," Eden leaned over to tap both their noses affectionately. "Time for bed."

Yom basked in the grandeur of the story, held it close to her chest like a fine jewel.

"Do you think the stories are real?" Yom whispered once they were alone in their room, having snuck from her own bed into Lior's after Eden left. Their quarters were illuminated by a single lamp as they huddled close.

"The Ancient War was just a war amongst the ancient peoples." Lior scrunched her nose. "There were no gods or titans." She took one of Yom's curls between her fingers and twirled it. "Do you think it's true that Panchaia is trying to make the crossing and restart the war one day?"

Yom contemplated for a moment. Even in the farthest reaches of the provinces, the shadow of Panchaia loomed from across the waters of Okeanus. The fear and distrust was woven deep into the fabric of Inisfail, as it was everywhere in Arcadia.

"I don't know. But if they do, I'll protect you." Yom hardened her features for a moment to show Lior how menacing she could look.

Lior laughed and leaned over to kiss Yom's cheek. But instead of a short peck, her lips parted ever so slightly and lingered on Yom's skin, soft as a rose petal. When she pulled back, Yom saw nothing but openness and trust in her eyes. The breath caught in Yom's throat, and the words hung on the tip of her tongue, itching to be released. Words expressing how beautiful and in awe of Lior she was, how she would like to always be the one whose arm Lior held as they walked through the city, how it felt like a whole life could be passed with nights like this, together. Lior always leapt into something right away with her full force, while Yom got there eventually, in her own time.

But before any of those words could be given form, a strange sound from the laboratory below stole their attention. A splintering, followed by a sharp crack.

"Mother?" Lior shot up and called out. When she did not hear a response, she raced out of bed.

"Wait—" Yom tried to stop her, "Don't go down there alone—"

Lior was already padding down the steps by the time Yom pulled herself up to follow her. From the top of the stairs, Yom could see a light on in the laboratory. Its door was ajar, broken glass scattered on the floor. Her mind raced through the possibilities: corrupt royal legionaries, midnight robbers, or maybe the thugs she heard whispers of prowling the edges of the city, known only as Stags. Lior turned back to Yom with eyes widened in panic before she broke into a run towards the laboratory. Yom tried to reach for her, not ready to rush anywhere she didn't yet understand, but Lior fell through her hands like water. Yom whispered after her, begging her to wait, but Lior did not look back before slipping inside the laboratory door.

Yom tip-toed down the steps, and crouched against the wall next to the laboratory's opening. Slowly, she peered inside.

"Who are you?" Eden's voice carried from the far side of the room. She backed up towards her workbench, groping for something behind her. Her hand found a stone pestle and clutched it behind her back.

The edge of a cloak came into view. Two cloaks, Yom realized. She squinted to make out the color in the dark but could only see fine gold thread stitched around the edge.

"You don't recognize us?" The voice crawled under Yom's skin and chilled her bones. It was like no voice she had heard before, and even in that moment she knew it would etch itself into her memory. The hair on the back of her neck stood up, sensing a dangerous predator. Eden was struck silent. The two cloaks inched closer. Yom spotted Lior crouching behind a bench, just out of Yom's reach. She willed her to stay there.

"What do you want?" Eden's face was guarded.

"We heard you have a very special girl." A different voice now, a woman, but with the same crawling effect.

Lior blazed into their view, stepping up to stand next to her mother. She acted with the confidence of someone who always had a home, always had arms to run into. Defiant and fearless and beautiful.

Eden cursed and pushed Lior to stand behind her.

"You can't take her," Eden's voice was steady, but the hands holding Lior were shaking.

"We can do whatever we want." One of the cloaked figures crossed the room impossibly fast. Yom only saw a flash of light reflecting on metal before the figure stepped back, and drew a knife from Eden's chest coated in crimson. It slid out of her far too easily.

All the warmth flooded from Yom's body. Lior was screaming and holding her mother, her howls deep and bright.

The sound severed Yom.

The laboratory stretched away from her, as if through the opposite end of a tunnel. Yom continued watching the scene, but suddenly she was looking through the eyes of a stranger. Her limbs were heavy and unfamiliar, no longer attached to her mind. As Yom watched the woman who had treated her like a daughter crumpled on the floor, she stretched further and further down the tunnel, the space between before and after becoming an uncrossable chasm. The parts of herself that basked in Eden's story and felt the warmth of Lior's kiss on her cheek needed to be locked away, or they would consume her whole. She withdrew into herself, meticulously tucking these memories—and the pieces of herself embedded in them—into the crevices of her mind, to places where they would not hurt her.

From an impassable distance, Yom watched the second cloaked figure approach Lior and ever so gently blow a gust of purple powder into her tear-streaked face. Yom squeezed her eyes shut, trying to regain the tether to her body. Steps creaked over the wood floorboards as the two cloaked figures approached the door Yom hid behind. Paralyzed by fear, she sank into the shadows of the hallway and curled into a tight ball. She rocked there silently, willing herself to stand up, to go after them, to protect Lior. When she was finally able to open her eyes, nothing of her former home remained but the faint, metallic smell of powder and smoke.

I

The Binding

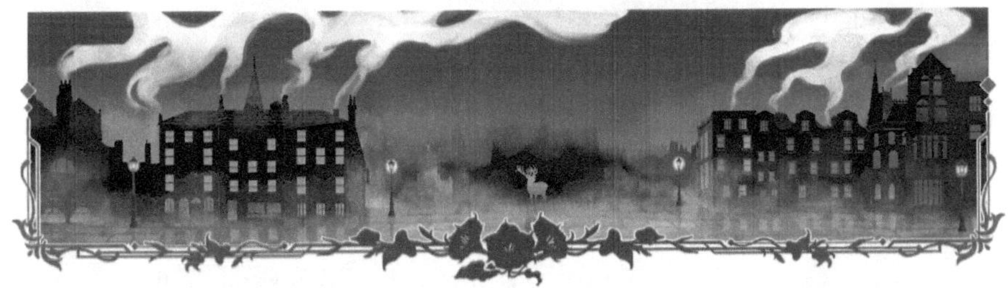

YOM'S THOUGHTS GNAWED AT HER, SHARP AS TEETH. They flashed reminders of death where it had no place lurking: in alleyways during routine errands, in the eyes of children, in the mirror on the rare occasions Yom looked. In the cage of her thoughts, memories warped into nightmares. Her most reviled mistakes replayed over and over until it was Yom whose hand withdrew the blood-soaked knife from Eden's chest. Her mind warred with itself the hardest after the lights went out. Often, she felt she was one dark night away from being ripped apart. The only thing she had found over the years that quieted these marauding thoughts, was powder. Which was rather convenient, as Yom was quite talented at making powders. Powders that could kill a person, and heal them. Make them feel nothing, and everything.

Yom was fortunate she hadn't taken a mind dulling powder this particular morning. The euphoriants coursing through her made her awareness sharp enough to pick up on a surreptitious hand snaking around her partner Lucan's waist, lifting the purse off of it. The purse that was distended with coins from a full morning of collecting tributes.

"Lucan!" Yom barely had time to shout before taking off after the thief, who slipped into the traffic of soot-coated workers filing towards the mill. The only identifying feature Yom caught was a dandelion yellow jumper.

The air smelled of wind and salt and metal as the labor yard rushed by on either side of her in a great blur of brick and stone. Yom shoved her way through the crowd just in time to see the yellow jumper slip into Butcher's Row. It seemed the thief wanted a chase.

"This way," Yom hollered at Lucan as she lurched left into the narrow avenue lined in blood and dust. Large men in grime-covered aprons waved their cleavers at Yom in admonition, but she ignored them. She would have her own cleaver to deal with if they didn't get that purse back.

The yellow jumper veered right as it left Butcher's Row, racing past the crowded stalls of the freeman's market. Yom was only able to close a few feet of distance. She admired the thief's speed for a moment before following the miscreant into the merchant district. She barreled through merchants and their harried associates arriving at their grand offices in three piece suits and stiff hats, almost knocking over a few.

"This kid is fast," Lucan huffed as he finally caught up to Yom.

The thief had managed to stay out of reach for too long now. No one could outrun Yom in her own city.

"Steer them left," she said as she dodged an indignant baker dumping a drum of water on the cobblestones. "I'm going to cut them off in that alley." Lucan dipped his head.

Yom bounded up a staggered pile of crates outside a produce seller until she reached the canvas awning over its door. She propelled herself forward, swinging from the support beams until she righted herself overtop the awning. She leapt between awnings towards the thief, feeling fearless and indestructible, soaring on her powders. Lucan inched up on their right and swung his arms out to force the thief left just as Yom turned the corner down the same alley.

She swung down to land in the thief's path. Even the impact of the cobblestones beneath her boot felt dull behind the cloud of her powders. Yom got her first look at the thief's face. It was a young boy, who startled and skidded to a stop but didn't look as scared as he should. Almost like he was enjoying this. The boy whipped around to see Lucan pull up behind him.

"Nowhere to go, kid." If Yom had been dry, she would have been embarrassed by how heavily she was panting.

She saw the gleam in the boy's eye right before he turned and spun underneath Lucan's arms and then somehow through his parted legs. Before Lucan realized what happened, the boy had given him the slip and taken off on the same crowded road they were just on.

Yom swore and ran after him but didn't see a trace of yellow in the direction he had gone. She hunched over to catch her breath when it was clear they had lost him.

"He's going to be pissed," Lucan said gravely as he pulled a hand-rolled wand from his waistcoat. He scraped a match against the brick and lit the wand, taking a long drag and exhaling minty smoke in a cloud around them.

Yom reached into the small leather pouch on her powderbelt that she kept stocked with rotating powder experiments. The current iteration was a strong euphoriant she had dubbed Aetherium. She pulled out a small pinch and held it up to her nose to inhale. "We'll find the kid before he has time to throw a fit."

"How do you know he'll be here?"

"I know where someone on their own ends up at that age." Yom leaned back on the brick wall lining the freeman's market yard. Lucan was smoking another wand, his third since they had lost the boy. He never listened to her when she told him the sandberry made him irritable. His thick brows pushed together as he glared at her, his pale blond waves oily from raking his hands through them. "He looked hungry," Yom added as she scanned the market stalls.

"Kid could be halfway to the Albion border by now. And you know when *he* finds out—which he will—he's going to blame me—like always—and—"

"The boy is lost, not stupid. He's not leaving Ibernia." He may well have left Ibernia's capital city, Inisfail, but she wasn't going to stoke Lucan's fire further with that possibility.

The smells of the market taunted Yom's empty stomach. She had to close her eyes so she wouldn't be too tempted to abandon their task. Meat pies, seared fish, buttery pastries, and the sweet perfume of flowers. She tried to remember the last time she had eaten. Or slept. The early morning collection shifts were the worst, and no matter how far Yom advanced in rank, she was never able to escape them. She didn't sleep well at night; everything the daylight dulled came back with a vengeance. Last night she had whittled away the hours experimenting with her Aetherium formulation, testing out birch leaves to bind the mixture better and extend the release of its effects. Just as the first rays of light had slipped through the seam in her curtains and exhaustion finally weighed down her eyelids, Lucan had banged on her door to pick her up for their shift.

One aroma caught her attention: freshly baked bread. "Over there." Yom edged the wall until they stood behind the baker's stall.

"We should just tell him, he can put out a signal to keep all eyes—"

"Quiet."

"Come on, he'll be angrier if the kid escapes the city."

Yom held up a hand to shush him.

"Bluefingers." Lucan muttered the name she was known by throughout the provinces. He did it to remind her of the stakes; he was one of the few people who normally used her given name.

Before Yom could hiss at him to be quiet one more time, she caught the flash of yellow. The boy was crouched between the skirts of a few young ladies. A small but confident hand reached up and snatched a half loaf, and then a pastry. *He's not spending the purse in the city*, Yom realized. *So he's not a complete idiot.*

"Antlers up," she whispered as she elbowed Lucan and nudged her head towards the boy. Lucan's eyes lit up and he ground the remainder of the wand under his boot as he pulled a copper wire taut between his fists. Yom snaked through the market, eyes not daring to leave the yellow of the boy's jumper now that she knew how slippery he was. She stepped in front of him and spun to face him, grasping his shoulders at the same instant Lucan wrapped the wire around his wrists, pinning them behind his back.

"Remember us?" Yom smiled like a cat.

They led the boy into a narrow gap between buildings. Lucan's tall frame blocked the light of the entrance, casting a shadow over the boy as he held him. Yom patted around the boy's middle and then down each leg until she felt the hard lump of the purse tied around his ankle.

"Didn't your mother teach you not to steal?" Yom pulled the purse out from under his pant leg and knotted it onto her powderbelt.

"My mother is dead," The boy replied tersely. Yom stood back up and took a longer look at him. He couldn't have been older than thirteen, with round cheeks and floppy, sand-colored curls draped in a curtain around his face. The yellow jumper was roughly knit and unevenly dyed, surely not a mother's touch. He met her eye, a resilient set to his features.

"Do you know what the punishment is for theft?" Yom asked him, exasperated. The boy looked at her meekly. "You'll hang from a post with a nail through your hand."

The boy's eyes widened in horror.

"You'll be cut down at the wrist."

The boy shook his head vehemently. "I have young sisters, they can't feed themselves without me. I only stole to buy food for them." He searched her face for a shred of mercy.

"Doesn't matter who it's for. You can't steal from Cernunnos." Yom took a breath. "He won't let something like this go unpunished."

"But you've got it back now!" The boy insisted. "No harm, right?"

"Cernunnos already knows." Yom didn't like to spend too long thinking about it, but it was like he had spies in every corner of the city. If a pin dropped in Inisfail, sooner or later, he knew about it.

"Cernunnos?" The boy asked, face screwed up in concentration as he put together the full picture of where he had found himself. His face changed the second he noticed the bronze torc around Yom's neck.

"You're a Stag," he said, awe in his voice.

Yom thumbed the delicate stag horns molded into each end of the torc. She brushed the scar underneath before dropping it back onto her collarbone.

"Please," the boy begged, "I didn't know. I need to get back to my sisters and our farm. I can't till our fields with one hand. We'll starve!" The boy craned to look back at Lucan, eyes registering the same torc wrapped around his neck. "Please just let me go," the boy begged.

"We can't." Yom pinched the bridge of her nose. *Or it will be our hands he cuts off.*

"Please, I'll do anything!"

"He is fast." Lucan raised a brow.

"Don't," Yom warned.

"What is it? Whatever it is, I'll do it."

"Trust me, kid." Yom grabbed the hair on the crown of his head and forced him to look at her. "Take the punishment."

"It's his decision," Lucan said evenly. "Cernunnos will pardon the theft, and give you a loan to feed your family."

"Lucan—"

"In exchange for Binding yourself to him."

"I'll do it." The boy nodded eagerly.

"Not so fast." Lucan clicked his tongue at the boy. "We'll take you to see him, and he'll decide if you're worth Binding."

"And if he decides I'm not?"

"Then he'll name your punishment, or make you another bargain for the pardon."

Yom's stomach turned at the idea of the other ways Cernunnos allowed people to earn a pardon.

"I'll do it," the boy said resolutely.

"What's your name?" Lucan steered the boy out of the alley, one hand on his shoulder and the other gripping the copper manacles.

"Murtagh," he said as he looked between the two of them. "But you can call me Moss." Moss was too excited; Yom resisted the urge to smack some sense into him.

"Is it true you have more money and lovers than you know what to do with? That you can take down a man twice your size? That Stags rule every inch of Inisfail?" The questions spilled out of Moss in a torrent. *Yes*, Yom thought. *All it costs is everything.*

"Sure is, kid." Lucan winked at him. "Ain't nothing better than being a Stag," he said stonily.

They walked down the main avenue of the city, mid-morning traffic creating a river of people to wade through. Yom stayed silent and fell behind them, struck by an image of Lucan leading this boy through the city not as a thief, but as a Stag, newly gleaming torc bouncing around his neck with each step. Her hand drifted to her belt and she raised another pinch of Aetherium to her nose to drown out the image. She lost awareness of the people who cowered as they passed, lost awareness of Lucan and Moss walking ahead of her, lost awareness of herself, if only for a moment.

They turned down a narrower street lined with downtrodden shops, mirthless except for the Green Demon glowing at the far end. Green strips of fabric yawned over the door, and red hyde lanterns floated out front. Inside the fogging windows, the patrons already started to indulge, though it was barely past midday. The tavern was surrounded by a cluster of unassuming brick buildings that had become Yom's stomping ground in the six years since she became a Stag.

Moss' childishly high-pitched voice interrupted the silence. "Whoa. What's this?"

"The Cut," Yom said brusquely as she shouldered past Lucan to step into the narrow alley to the right of the tavern. She tilted one shoulder forward to fit through, and held her breath to avoid the smell of stale piss and hops. Along the brick wall halfway down the alley sat a rusted door with a faint carving of a stag head. Yom knocked roughly, and the door whined open. A hand creased with grime waved them in. The straw-haired twins were standing guard that day, both massive, with their arms crossed and shirts rolled up over forearms the size of Yom's head.

"You're late," one of them said in a deep voice. Their names were Castor and Lock but Yom could never keep straight which one was which. In her head she just called them the bollocks.

"Got distracted," Yom waved vaguely in Moss's direction.

"Fresh meat?" A bollock asked, half-amused.

"We'll see." Lucan flashed a smile. Sometimes Yom thought he looked like the buzzards that trolled the hills outside the city, with their sharp beaks, beady eyes, and wings that they spread to fly but also to puff out their chest and prove they existed.

"He is displeased with your tardiness," the bollock said, opening the door straight ahead of them. A narrow tunnel stretched out behind it.

"Cheers." Lucan nodded at them, smile gone, as he and Moss passed.

"Bite me," Yom muttered at the bollock and closed the door behind them.

They walked through the tunnel in silence but Moss's breathing quickened in the cramped space. The tunnel was dim, small flames flickering inside lamps to illuminate their step.

Yom leaned down to whisper in Moss's ear, "You can still take the punishment and leave with your life."

Before Moss could reply, Lucan wrenched open the door at the end of the tunnel and flooded them with bright light. He walked through and gestured for Moss to follow, the boy's hands still bound behind his back.

The other side of the tunnel always felt like an optical illusion. Beyond the door, an expansive greenhouse opened up in the hollowed-out shell of the building. The top of the building's brick walls had crumbled and been replaced with a domed glass ceiling, bathing the room in the soft light of Inisfail's perpetually overcast and drizzling sky. An enormous oak tree in the center almost reached the glass ceiling, its canopy towering over most of the room. Even from far away, Yom could see the first buds sprouting from its branches like nails on a thousand-fingered hand. They took the small path edged with celandine that led through the greenhouse to a clearing under the tree's shade.

At the base of the tree, cross-legged and barefoot, Cernunnos sat facing away from them. His broad back was covered in his typical dark green tweed jacket, and his thick mane of peppercorn black hair cascaded over his shoulders. Yom knelt down a few feet from him with her head bowed, and Lucan quickly unwrapped the wire from Moss's hands before joining her. Moss stood there for a second too long and Yom tugged him to his knees.

"Why is the thief here, and not nailed to a post?" Cernunnos asked in his deep voice, rough and blunt, without turning to look at them. Yom's toes curled in her boots at the reminder that Cernunnos always knew what was happening, as if he had spies constantly whispering in his ears about everything that went on in Inisfail.

"We chased him through four districts, sir." Lucan spoke.

"You're getting slow?" Cernunnos's voice held a sneer.

"No, sir, he's fast. He's interested in a bargain. Needs money to feed his family."

At this, Cernunnos turned his head slightly and let his cold, gray eyes drift over his shoulder. Yom shook her head to herself. It was almost laughable how predictable Cernunnos was when he smelled a weakness he could exploit.

"You think he could be a half decent fighter?" He stood, his three piece suit with hardly a crease out of place. Large, weathered hands braced Moss's shoulders and stood him up. He turned his chin side to side to look at his face and weighed Moss's comically skinny arms between his hands.

"He's got potential," Lucan offered.

"Parents?"

"They're dead," Moss spoke.

The sound of Cernunnos's backhand striking the boy's face cracked through the air. Yom bit her tongue.

"First lesson of being a Stag, boy: you'll speak to me only when spoken to. And you'll address me as 'sir.'" Moss nodded, managing to keep his hands at his side and not touch his reddening cheek.

Cernunnos raised his brow at him.

"Yes, sir," Moss said quietly.

Cernunnos nodded and paced away from them to face the tree. Yom tugged on Moss, gentler this time, to return him to a kneel.

"It could be of use, sir." Dougal's voice rounded the tree before he did, his deep blue satin robes swishing along the base of the oak as he walked. He was the Principal Archivist of Inisfail's branch of the Royal Archives, and Cernunnos's steward. He kept every single book and ledger in the Stag operation from his privileged position in the Queen's service. "You're running lower in numbers on the southeast line because of that skirmish at the Albion border."

"How many died?" Cernunnos asked as calmly as if he asked whether it would rain later.

"Ten, sir." Dougal cleared his throat.

Yom blinked. Lucan had mentioned something about this, but Yom hadn't asked for too many details, opting for powder instead. The possibility of dying while Bound to Cernunnos was a weight in her gut that she preferred to leave be.

"Shame," Cernunnos remarked without feeling. He turned back to the three of them. "I'll make the bargain. I will Bind him tonight." Moss exhaled next to her. "Bluefingers, mind the boy. Return him at dusk."

"Yes, sir," Yom grumbled, wondering why she had to watch him when it was Lucan and his snake mouth that had offered Binding up to him in the first place.

"You're dismissed." Cernunnos flicked his fingers at them. Yom stood and pulled Moss up with her.

"Lucan," Cernunnos added. "A word."

Yom led Moss back down the path, not able to stop herself from peeking over her shoulder at Cernunnos and Lucan conferring privately, their backs turned to her.

"*You're* Bluefingers?" Moss asked her after they had entered the tunnel once again.

Instead of speaking, Yom held up her hand as they passed a light, her fingers stained blue from an especially messy accident she'd had toying with a rare cobalt alloy without gloves. She could feel Moss gawking.

"But you're so—" the boy paused on a sharp inhale.

Yom looked back at him right before wrenching the door open into the landing where the bollocks stood. "Yes?" she asked dryly, prepared for the usual reactions people had to her when they learned that Cernunnos's infamous chemist was just shy of twenty years, and female at that. *But you're a woman,* was usually the first. Too young, too attractive, not attractive enough. Someone could always find a fault in her when they learned who Bluefingers really was. She pulled Moss along by the scruff of his neck without acknowledging the twins.

"Have fun babysitting," one bollock snickered as she deposited Moss back into the alley. Her head was beginning to pound.

Yom reached into her pouch but found it was empty. She leaned her head back on the damp brick wall and rubbed her temples, watching the clouds rolling past the slit between buildings.

"You're so young," Moss finished his thought, eyeing her as if just her presence could suck him into a deep powderhole if he wasn't vigilant.

"Older than you." Yom sniffed. The residue of her last dose haunted her senses.

"Yeah, but I'm nobody."

"I was nobody when I was your age too." Yom pushed herself off the wall. "I need more powder."

Yom opened the door behind the crowded bar of the Green Demon and took the stairs up to the second floor. She assumed Moss was still following her but wouldn't blame him if he tried to run. The stair whined with a telltale creak of Moss's steps behind her. To the left of the second floor landing was the thick red curtain that led to the pleasure rooms, and to the right, the black door that closed off the Powder Parlor.

Yom opened the Powder Parlor door and nodded at the Stag watchman who stood on the other side of it. The room was windowless and dark, filled with smoke and the remnants of powder clouds. Sparse lanterns drifted through the air, lighting up the low couches and pillows with husks of life draped over them. Languid, glassy-eyed patrons looked in awe at the ceiling or at each other. The room was filled with the low whispering of people lost in their own world, and vague moans of pleasure as the powders pulled the room into an abyss.

The feeling of Moss following close on Yom's heels was almost a comfort. Perhaps if he was frightened enough to cling to her, he would come to his senses and leave while he still could. A young powdermaid worked behind the mirrored bar that ran the length of the room, and Yom parked Moss on a stool in front of her.

"Elise." Yom tapped the countertop. "Watch him." She pointed at Moss, who was gaping at the shelves of countless glass vials that lined the wall in front of him. "He's got sticky fingers."

"Hi, honey." Elise's voice turned sugary when she spoke to Moss. Yom rolled her eyes. Elise never sucked up to Yom like that, and Yom was the one who hired her and divvied out her weekly earnings. "I think I have something I can give you back here, give me a minute."

Yom ducked beneath the bar and grabbed a few jars of raw compounds and extracts. She grumbled to herself about being sidled with an annoying, immature kid incapable of making decisions while she combined the formula for Aetherium in a mortar and ground it into a powder. She could vaguely hear Elise laughing with Moss about something inane.

"I need something that dulls pain," a voice spoke from the other side of the bar. Yom knew most of the regulars in the parlor, and could easily recognize the husky voice of someone who frequented powder. This voice was crisp and clear.

"Let me see what I have for you, honey." The powdermaid twirled to survey the shelf behind her.

Yom turned around to see Dougal's apprentice. Despite Dougal's deep involvement in the Stags, somehow his apprentice at the Royal Archives remained distanced from it all. She couldn't remember his name, although she recalled it was something strange sounding. He wore the same satiny blue robes as Dougal, the uniform of those dedicated to serving the Queen, and a pair of delicate reading glasses perched on the bridge of his nose. In the dim lantern light of the parlor, shadows danced over strong cheekbones, plump lips, and shrewdly thick brows. The apprentice met Yom's gaze, his eyes narrowing as she took a pinch of her powder mixture and inhaled.

While the Aetherium clouded around her, Yom reached back and plucked a mild painkiller off the shelf. "This will do the trick." She pushed it across the bar to the apprentice. "What's it for?" Yom generally didn't ask questions about where her powder ended up, but she couldn't help her curiosity this time. She had never seen him in the Cut before. "Nasty paper cut? Big bad books finally get you?"

The apprentice was wholly unamused.

"It's for Dougal. Cernunnos is working him to the bone."

"Same as the rest of us. Not everyone gets to sit in a library all day." Yom studied him. His posture and apparent discomfort said he considered himself above all this. Above Yom.

"They're Archives, not just a library. We protect the history of all of Arcadia."

Yom snorted. The apprentice opened his mouth to continue his tirade.

"Give me a break. You protect the history of whatever the House of Flowing Waters decides is worth protecting. Which is anything that supports the rule of the Queen." Yom gave him a mocking salute.

"You work at the Royal Archives?" Moss piped up next to them.

Yom refused to be the first one to break the apprentice's gaze.

"I do," the apprentice turned to him. "I'm Quia." He offered his forearm to Moss.

"Moss." The boy grabbed onto his forearm and they held each other for a moment. "I've never been to the Royal Archives."

"You can come anytime. I'll show you around. We have a lot of fascinating history." At this, he glanced pointedly at Yom. "Important to pass on to future generations."

"Thanks." Moss smiled brightly. Yom almost envied how quickly this boy's mood could lighten. "Can we go after I'm Bound?" he turned to Yom.

Quia and the powdermaid both stilled at the mention of it, and Yom cursed this boy and his casual repetition of words he could not comprehend.

"He's being Bound?" Quia whipped back to Yom, outrage twisting his features.

"It was his choice. He stole from Cernunnos. It's this, or lose a hand."

"He's too young."

"I was his age when I was Bound."

"And look where that's gotten you."

Yom let his judgment roll off her. He knew nothing. "It's his choice." She held up her hands; it was out of her control.

"Why are you all acting like it's such a bad thing?" Moss asked. He looked around all of them.

"Honey," Elise reverted to her sugary voice. "It's painful. And it's... permanent." She looked at Moss with pity. Yom rolled her shoulders and straightened her spine. She would take fear over pity any day.

"It's barbaric," Quia said under his breath.

"I want to be a Stag. I don't want my sisters or I to worry about money ever again. And I want to be feared." He puffed out his chest. Yom couldn't help but huff a small laugh.

"You will be, honey." Elise patted his hand. "You'll be the scariest Stag that Inisfail has ever seen." Moss twisted his face into something goofy and turned to the powdermaid. She laughed.

"He's just a kid," Quia spoke softly, only to Yom.

"Not all of us have people in our lives to protect us from making bad choices," Yom replied, annoyed that he was allowed to voice all of her concerns and she could do nothing to change it.

"I'll see you at the Archives sometime, kid." Quia brushed Moss's shoulder. The boy beamed at him. His royal robes shimmered in the dim light as he walked out of the parlor.

Yom emptied the bowl of her mixture into the pouch on her belt and sealed it. She looked back at the spot the mild painkiller had filled, and saw the more intense version next to it. Slipping the heavier painkiller into her belt, she hopped over the bar and tugged Moss behind her.

"Bye!" He waved over his shoulder at the powdermaid. Yom heard a soft, forlorn *goodbye* from behind the bar.

"Where are we going?" Moss asked.

"Back to the Green Demon. You'll need some liquid courage for tonight."

"Sounds fun," he said cheerily. Hopefully the Binding would cure some of the kid's incessant need to befriend everyone. It was quite good at that.

DUSK HAD COME FAR TOO QUICKLY FOR YOM'S LIKING. She had pushed a glass of strong spirits into the boy's hand and thrown back a few glasses herself while she found the hardest Stags at the tavern for Moss to talk to. She put the boy in front of seasoned enforcers and he didn't bat an eye. No matter what anyone said to him, Moss was set on being Bound. Of course, they were forbidden from sharing the one thing that might dissuade him from going through with it. The process of the Binding was a staunchly kept secret, one you were only privy to if you had gone through it yourself. One of the many paradoxes of being a Stag that made Yom want to rip her own hair out. She downed the rest of her drink and pulled Moss up by the collar.

"Time to go," she said simply, her limbs heavy with the prospect of what was to come. Moss had managed to charm every Stag he had talked to, and he received a pat on the shoulder or a ruffle of his hair from all of them as they walked out.

Yom took a generous inhale of powder as she guided Moss back through the alley to the side door, and back through the tunnel into the greenhouse. Lucan waited at the base of the tree, hands clasped behind his back. Yom stared straight ahead and refused to meet his eye when he nodded at her. At least after this she would be rid of the boy, she comforted herself. Things could go on as usual.

Walking around the base of the tree, she descended the hidden staircase. The steps wound through the tree's root system until they came to a heavy wooden door, surrounded by earth.

"You're sure about this?" She turned to Moss one last time. His nerves were finally starting to show but he nodded. Yom pushed open the door and entered the familiar room.

The ceilings hung low, and the fire in the hearth burned bright. The walls were stained with sandberry and soot, the rugs worn down to their threads by a thousand nights just like this one. The room was lined with Stags, with Cernunnos standing in the center. Dougal stood immediately to his right, his face unreadable. Cernunnos held out his hands in welcome, his teeth bared in a grim smile.

"You've made an excellent choice," he boomed in the otherwise silent room. "Kneel before me." Cernunnos swept his hands in front of him.

Moss slowly but steadily stepped forward, and Yom took her place among the ring of Stags. The boy sank to his knees in front of Cernunnos.

"For the crime of theft, your debt is ten years, to be paid in my service."

Moss swallowed.

"Do you accept this Bind, only to be removed when your debt has been repaid?"

"Yes, sir," Moss spoke.

The debt will grow every day you spend in this prison, Yom fought the urge to scream. Her knuckles turned white gripping her powderbelt, tamping the urge to pull him to his feet and shove him into a run.

Cernunnos turned and walked towards the fire. Two Stags stepped forward and knelt down next to Moss to clasp his arms. Moss looked at them, confused. Cernunnos bent over the fire and when he stood back up he held the white hot torc between two clamps.

Moss took one look at it and jerked his head around to find Yom, his eyes full of fear. He began struggling between the two Stags who held him, trying to push away.

"No—wait," Moss cried, "I don't want—" He was cut off when a third Stag came behind him and put a leather belt in his mouth, muffling his words into grunts. He tried to push up but the Stags kept him on the ground. As Cernunnos stepped closer with the torc, now burning a bright orange, he smiled at Moss's reaction. As the torc got closer to Moss's neck he devolved from grunts to blood chilling screams in protest.

Cernunnos circled the torc behind Moss's head, and drew the clamps together.

Moss's screams turned guttural as the superheated torc was tightened around his neck, and the room filled with the smell of burning flesh. Yom could feel the pain of her own Binding still seared on her skin, a phantom that never truly went away. Her own screams from her Binding filled her ears on top of Moss's.

Cernunnos removed the clamps and let the torc fall to rest around Moss's neck. Normally Yom turned away for this part, but she felt compelled to witness it this time. Moss had spit streaming down his chin but hadn't bitten off his tongue thanks to the gag. His face looked like he had gone elsewhere, a place Yom remembered well. Where the mind took you in one last act of self-preservation, where things like this didn't happen to a person. But it was Cernunnos's reaction that caught her off guard. He almost seemed to stumble on his feet. His gray eyes blinked and looked faraway, like he too had gone somewhere else.

The Stags let go of Moss, smoke still floating up from his neck. He collapsed onto the ground, out cold from the pain and shock.

"Get him a bottle and a girl and he'll sleep it off," Cernunnos said as he wiped grease off his hands, already back to his state of complete composure.

Yom recalled her first night, thrown into a cramped room in the Cut with just a bottle to help and a thin mat to sleep on. The pain had made her feverish and delirious, the only comfort coming in the form of restless sleep. She tried to turn and walk back the way she came, tried to remain unaffected by the events of the day. But her legs refused to move. She cursed to herself before turning back to Moss.

"Leave him," she barked at the Stag who was about to throw him over his shoulder like a sack of flour. The Stag backed off without a word.

Yom gently pulled Moss's arm over her shoulder and lifted him to stand. His head lolled onto her chest. She walked them back up the stairs. At the base of the tree, the garden was dark, and Lucan was nowhere to be found. Yom shook her head. *Coward.*

The walk through the Cut to her quarters was slow-going. Moss came in and out of consciousness, only moaning and dragging his feet when he was awake. Finally she reached her door and pulled Moss over the threshold. Her quarters had upgraded since that first night in the Cut. Her talents as a chemist—which were sorely needed in Cernunnos's then heavily agricultural, and thereby outdated, operation—had made her quite important to him.

Yom laid Moss down on a lounge by the fireplace and rested his head on a pillow. Digging through her cabinet, she found antiseptic powder and strips of cloth. Moss groaned as she elevated his head and moved the still hot torc out of the way to dress the wound. She sprinkled the antiseptic before wrapping it tightly with cloth. Streams of tears shined on his cheeks and Yom felt something being tugged in her chest. She took the painkiller off her belt and sprinkled some in her hand.

"Moss," Yom said softly. He groaned in response. She held the powder up to his nose. "Moss, take a big breath in through your nose." Just lucid enough, he followed her instructions and breathed in the powder. He let out a dreamy sigh as his body slowly went limp.

Yom stood, took another pinch of Aetherium and yanked the stopper off a bottle of cheap barley spirits with her teeth. As she took a long pull straight from the bottle, knuckles rapped on her door.

Yom cracked the door, bottle still in hand.

Lucan stood on the other side, and as Yom opened the door fully, she saw a girl next to him wrapped in the red silks of the pleasure room.

"I'm sorry," Lucan murmured, with the smile that only came out in the little hours. As if a midnight apology could make up for the fact that he was the reason Moss had entered an indefinite servitude. This smile was different from his buzzard smile. It was the smile Yom had first seen when they met on the streets of Inisfail six years ago, just before Yom became a Stag. It made Lucan look younger, like he was someone still capable of being happy.

"You're wasting your breath. I'm not interested tonight." Yom swung the door closed again, but Lucan braced it with his slender hand.

"Don't be upset. The boy wanted a way out, and I provided it."

Yom recalled how Cernunnos had spoken to Lucan privately, likely giving him a reward for recruiting a new Stag. Ever the altruist, Lucan was.

"I brought you a treat." Lucan's eyes danced to the girl who stood next to him. "We can share her." He took a step forward, already expecting Yom to say yes. She had a moment where she saw herself clearly: she would allow Lucan and this stranger to come in, would drown herself in bodies and powder, and she would continue on tomorrow as if today had never happened. Because the alternative—being alone with her thoughts, alone with the echo of Moss's screams, alone with herself—was far more dangerous.

Yom wordlessly stepped aside to allow them in.

II

Loyalty

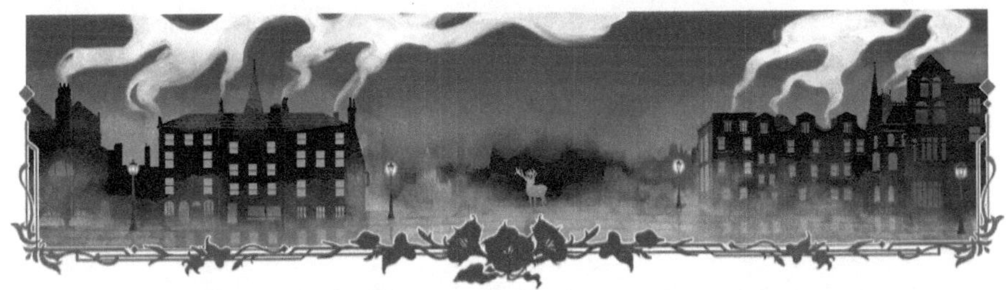

YOM TOOK A JAB TO THE FACE. She wiped away a glob of blood and wrinkled her nose to right the feeling of it. The Cut's training room was full of its usual grunts and the salty odor of sweat mixed with leather. But across the gymnasium, three figures wrapped in black armor prowled the edge.

"Why are they *here?*" She held up a glove to stop Lucan from continuing his assault so she could catch her breath on the sparring mat. The armored figures were recognizable anywhere: triarii. The Queen's elite warriors, who served as both her envoys and her personal guard, stood out like oversized beetles in the training room. They were covered chin to toe in black chitinous armor, only their faces exposed with their armored hoods pulled back. An unnerving sight even for the most hardened fighter.

Lucan shrugged. "Checking on taxes, negotiating export cuts? Who cares?"

"Yes, but why are they here?" Yom motioned around the training room.

"Perhaps they are looking for wives," Lucan offered smartly. Yom shoved him and he stumbled back a step, laughing.

"They don't take wives, imbecile."

"Perhaps they will make an exception for an especially agreeable exemplar of womanhood like yourse—" He didn't get the chance to finish his glib comment before Yom socked him in the jaw. It would have hurt more without the padded gloves on, but she would settle for small victories.

When Lucan's head snapped back, his blond tendrils escaped their knot and fell around his face, framing eyes that had the twinkle of a tempted beast. He countered by ramming her in the torso and leveraging his foot to trip her to the ground. It was a good move; Yom filed it away for later use. They wrestled for control before Lucan had his legs wrapped around her middle and a thick arm caging her neck from below.

"I always win, remember?" he panted out under her. His arrogance gave Yom the opportunity to elbow him in the ribs, which allowed her to wiggle around enough to get a knee to his groin. His arms loosened and he doubled over, groaning. She pulled his arm behind him and used the threat of dislocating his shoulder to get him to roll over, then perched on top of him, pinning his arms.

"First time for everything," Yom whispered in his ear. He bucked beneath her, and she let herself be shaken off, laughing.

"Very impressive." Vague clapping echoed along with a voice she didn't recognize. After she stood up, she realized it was one of the triarii, and he was walking straight towards them.

"So it's true," she muttered to Lucan as they watched the triarii approach, his armor utterly noiseless as he walked. The armor had a faint glisten from closer up; it was made of interlocking pieces that glided together in perfect harmony. Legends of the triarii armor were as exaggerated as they were ubiquitous. That it could withstand the direct stab of a knife, that it allowed them to walk through fire, that it contained a myriad of hidden weapons at the triarii's disposal. The noiselessness seemed to be one of the more believable fables about the armor, providing a tactical advantage but also unsettling opponents. Very few people went up against a triarii and lived to share the story, but those that had whispered that it was like fighting something inhuman.

"It's not often we see women in a training room," the triarii said. His voice was smooth and harsh at the same time, like smoke.

"They only bring me in to fight the weaklings." She nudged her chin back at Lucan. He kneed her in the back of the thigh. The triarii tipped his head back and laughed. Now that he was closer, Yom saw that the left half of his face was covered in knotted scars, as if it had been burned systematically. The scars shone blue on his dark skin, spreading up into his short fuzz of hair. But when she looked closely at the right half of his face, she could make out a broad set nose and high cheekbones that couldn't belong to someone much older than her.

"Misho." He extended his forearm.

"Bluefingers." Yom grasped it, and the pads of his fingers almost felt like a shock when they touched Yom's skin.

He looked at her curiously. "The famed chemist. What an honor."

Yom dropped his forearm, still feeling a tingle on her skin. "The honor is mine," she said. "It appears the legends of triarii armor being impervious to flame are a bit exaggerated." It slipped out before she could stop it and she instantly regretted it. Mouthing off at a triarii could have deadly consequences.

Misho was unfazed. "Not everyone is born into their fate; some of us have a winding path there." He motioned to his face. "The Stags, of all people, should understand this." Yom recoiled from the suggestion that it was her fate to be a Stag. She had to hold onto the hope that a better ending awaited her somewhere, free of Cernunnos's Bind.

"Perhaps one day you will do me the honor of a spar. That is, if you take a break from training weaklings."

"Name the time." Yom looked between him and the two triarii flanking him. Suspicion kept tugging at her, the niggling question of why they were here in the first place.

Misho nodded at her and started to turn.

"You've already met Lucan?" Yom asked. Misho halted and turned back to them.

"No, I haven't had the pleasure." Misho extended his forearm. Lucan's expression revealed nothing as he reached around her to grasp it. "I've certainly heard of Cernunnos's best fighter."

Lucan grunted in response. This coming from the boy who had dragged her halfway across the city years ago to watch a triarii procession from the edge of the Queen's Square. For a fighter, there was no idol like the triarii in all of Arcadia. Yet Lucan was expressionless.

Misho nodded at them and turned to leave, the other two triarii flanking him.

Lucan hardly waited a second before pulling Yom into a tight headlock.

"Weakling, huh?"

"The truth hurts," she gasped out.

YOM COULDN'T STOP THINKING ABOUT THE STRANGE INTERACTION with the triarii as she walked back through the Cut with Lucan.

"Odd that the triarii would even be in the training room, isn't it?" she fished.

Lucan shrugged. "You know the Queen does business with Cernunnos, unofficially."

Yom adjusted her attack. "And you've never met that one before? Surprised you weren't more excited given how pathetically obsessed you were with—"

"No," Lucan cut her off, his eyes focused straight ahead. "I haven't met him before."

Yom's gut folded in on itself. Lucan didn't often lie to her, and when he did, she usually understood why: either he spent the night with someone else, which she didn't care about, but he seemed to try to keep from her in some misguided act of chivalry; or he was sneaking around on special errands in hopes of a promotion. And he was always quite bad at lying, at least to Yom's trained eyes. She doubted it was the former, and she wracked her brain to try to understand how it could be the latter. What task could Lucan have that had any overlap with the triarii? Even seeing them in the Cut was strange. Like Lucan said, it was well known among the Stags that Cernunnos maintained certain business arrangements with the Queen, but it was all off the royal record, and usually something straightforward like taking a cut of the Stag exports. Certainly not worth hiding. But here he was, lying to her face, and somehow involved with the deadliest warriors in the entire queendom. Yom took in the sharp line of his jaw, the tension it held. He was keeping something from her. Something big.

WHEN YOM PUSHED OPEN THE DOOR TO HER QUARTERS, SHE WAS surprised to see Moss awake. He had spent the last week sleeping like the dead on the small lounge by the fireplace, barely moving other than to drink water and nibble on food she brought. Yom had been helping him keep a steady high on painkilling powders as well, but he had the occasional bout of lucidity. *Why did no one tell me that was what it would be like?* he would mumble, only half awake. *Cernunnos has forbidden us from speaking of the Binding,* Yom would tell him each time as she sat by the fire, watching the smoke create and destroy shapes. *I tried to tell you*, she wanted to add but knew it would mean nothing. The truth is that the pain of the Binding faded over time, but the reality of being indentured to Cernunnos was harder to come to terms with. *Money has been sent to your family*, was the only comfort she could offer him. At hearing this, he looked almost content.

"Do you need more powder?" she asked as she closed the door behind her.

Moss looked at her thoughtfully before shaking his head. "When can I see my family?" he asked.

Yom's stomach dropped. "It will be a while before you're allowed to leave the city alone."

Moss's face fell.

"But you will be given a wage. It won't be much to start, but you'll earn more as you become more skilled."

"We weren't always poor, you know." He wrung his hands together, as if he was concerned about her opinion of him. "Our farm made a decent living when I was young. Then business changed, and my father only had a fraction of the demand in the last several years. He started drinking and died trying to mount a horse when he was piss drunk." Moss sounded bitter. "My mother didn't live much longer after that, it was like she just gave up after he died. Then it was up to me." Yom swallowed. The timeline he mentioned coincided with the shift in Stag operations towards powder as their main export over agriculture. Farmers who didn't switch to growing raw ingredients for powder saw huge dips in their business.

"I'm sorry," Yom offered as she rubbed her jaw.

Moss shrugged. "Today is a new day."

Yom nodded numbly.

"What was *your* life like before the Stags?" Moss asked.

Yom's heart lurched as the distant memories of Eden's laboratory, and Lior dancing around it, beckoned. Even in memory, Lior was a magnetic force that captured anyone who traveled too close in her orbit.

"Nothing special," she rasped.

"Then why did you join the Stags?"

This kid didn't know how to pull a punch. The unwelcome feeling of sitting in the empty rubble of the laboratory surfaced, and the endless loop of days that followed, when Yom wandered the streets: hungry, alone, and rudderless. Until a few roughneck pickpockets cornered her in the very market they had found Moss in, and only the appearance of a brash and foolish bystander created enough of a distraction for her to run. And run she did, straight into a gangly-limbed blond boy with a shining new torc around his neck, who promised her that there was someone who would be happy to provide food, shelter, and protection. In exchange for a measly debt, of course.

"I was hungry," Yom said flatly, shoving the entire cascade of memories away. Moss saw right through her but didn't press any further.

"Speaking of that, can we get some hot food? I don't think I can eat any more cold leftovers."

Yom shot him a glare.

"I'm grateful you've been bringing them. But still." He clasped his hands together and stuck out his bottom lip. Yom rolled her eyes.

"If the Stags see you hanging around the Green Demon, they will start putting you to work." Yom stretched her sore limbs, wondering if she would regret what she was about to offer. "But if we go to the Powdery, I keep some food there."

Moss jumped to his feet.

Yom sighed. "Try to look less...chipper."

A CUTLET SIZZLED ON AN IRON PAN ELEVATED OVER ONE OF YOM'S chemical burners. Moss practically drooled as he watched.

The Powdery was quiet, most of the morning shift powdermaids gone except the unlucky two that remained to clean up. The space was stripped back to brick and windows, lacking all of the finery of the lavish floors below it. Wooden workbenches stretched out in rows, each station equipped with scales, crank grinders, and a supply of essential chemistry. This space was occupied by bookkeepers and grain traders before Yom discovered it and showed Cernunnos the potential. Mass production of powder, the first of its kind in the provinces. It quickly became the most lucrative output of the entire Stag operation.

"Is this where you spend most days?" Moss asked as he munched on a raw potato wedge. Yom slapped his hand away as he reached for another, firing up a second burner to fry them.

"Less now. I used to spend all day every day here, when I wasn't on collection shifts." This was why she kept a small pantry stocked with essentials. And became quite adept at pilfering cuts of meat from the Green Demon kitchen when they weren't looking. "It runs pretty smoothly without me these days." Yom still planned and approved production runs, but she had a few powdermaids who had been working with her long enough to take over the direct supervision. It was fine by Yom, it just gave her more time to develop her experimental offensive and defensive powders. The best of which, she kept to herself.

Yom lifted the cutlet onto a plate and piled some potatoes next to it. "It's ready." For a second she couldn't find Moss; he was wandering around the nearby workbenches.

"Can I try one of these?" Moss picked up a vial of white powder from the table.

"No," Yom said sharply as she grabbed it from his hands.

"But you take powder all the time."

"And that's why I'm qualified to tell you that you shouldn't. Go eat your food." Yom uncorked the vial, finding it strange that there was a random powder laying around when all the production runs this week were supposed to be Furoris—a mania-inducing powder they gave to fighters and foot soldiers. She dumped a small amount into her palm. There was one plant it looked like, but Yom hadn't worked with it in ages. The plant she was thinking of was a heavily controlled substance, only legally grown and handled by royal chemists and botanists. The only reason she had seen it before was that Eden kept a consistent growth of it, in secret of course. She rubbed it between two fingers and brought a pinch up to her nose to smell without inhaling it.

It was a powdered extract of Moonflower. And even the sooty smell of its ash thrust Yom back in time, to Eden's laboratory.

"Careful with that!" Eden admonished. Yom giggled as she handed back the tincture bottle she had been about to drop into another beaker.

"We don't play with Moonflower." Eden took the dropper bottle from Yom's hands. "It's a very important plant."

"It's illegal," Yom said. Eden had always told her their Moonflower stores were a secret but only recently in school had she learned why.

"That's because the people in charge have small minds." Eden slipped the bottle into her red apron. "This plant has been sacred for longer than the House of Flowing Waters has been in power."

Yom leaned in, hoping Eden was about to tell another story.

"It's powerful for its gift of—"

"Suggestibility," Yom jumped in, always wanting to show Eden how well she listened.

Eden smiled and nodded. "Which also makes it dangerous. Its effects are... intense, and even the slightest improper dosage could be lethal. But it's also been sacred for as far back as the Ancients. It is a symbiotic spirit, one half of a whole. If this flower is the moon, then Darkness is the great sky that it shines within."

Yom yanked herself out of the memory, pushed it a safe distance away.

"You," Yom growled at the powdermaid sweeping several tables behind them.

"Me?" The girl looked quite frightened as Yom stormed towards her.

"What in the bloody Okeanus is this?" Yom held up the vial.

"I-it's from this week's p-powder run," the girl stammered.

"No, this week you're making Furoris."

"There was a change of plan," Cernunnos interrupted. His hulking, green-suited frame filled the Powdery entrance. Everyone in the Powdery stopped what they were doing and stood at attention, eyes cast down.

"That's not a problem, is it, Bluefingers? This is, after all, still my Powdery."

Yom wanted to snort at his words. This was the first time she had seen him here in years. "No, sir," Yom gritted out, studying the floorboards. "It's just that—it's illegal. If the Queen—"

"Let me worry about the Queen, Bluefingers. She is not your concern. All you need to do is follow orders. Can you do that?"

This was strange, even for Cernunnos. Why would he keep his chemist in the dark about his own powder operation? Normally Yom called the shots, and now he wanted her to fall in line and follow orders? And this happening while the triarii skulked around their training room couldn't be a coincidence. Yom needed to figure out what was going on, even if she had to go behind Cernunnos's back to do it.

"Yes, sir."

Cernunnos crossed the room to stand closer to Moss. Yom prayed the boy was keeping his cool, this being his first interaction with Cernunnos since the Binding.

"I see the boy is ready to be put to work."

Yom's breath stopped. "I need his help." She strung words together as she went. "I have to do a supply run to the other side of the city for a new knock-out powder I'm developing, sir."

"Very well." Cernunnos held Moss's chin, examining him like a hog at auction. "I expect a sample tomorrow."

"Yes, sir."

Cernunnos left with slow, purposeful steps and Yom didn't inhale again until he was out of sight.

"We get to leave the Cut?" Moss asked excitedly.

Yom had made up the knock-out powder excuse. Her real plan was to visit the Royal Archives, to investigate any history of business the House of Flowing Waters, and thereby the triarii, would have in Inisfail.

"Yes." Yom pulled him towards the exit.

"But my meal," Moss whined.

"Bring it."

Moss trailed Yom out of the Cut, scarfing down potato wedges and bites of meat while they walked.

"What kind of supplies are we getting?" he asked as he chewed.

"None. We're going to the Royal Archives," Yom said under her breath.

"To see Quia!" Moss grinned. Yom was confused for a second but then remembered the snarky apprentice they had met in the Powder Parlor.

"Right, to see Quia." *Not to secretly investigate what Cernunnos and the triarii and possibly even the Queen are up to.*

Yom held onto the brass railing of the streetcar as it rattled on its tracks towards the city center. Moss looked over the railing at the passing city with a wonder that almost made Yom envious. The Stag presence did not have much overlap with the streetcar lines, so the areas they passed through were filled with pedestrians milling by, most of them blissfully unaware of the underworkings of the city. When they neared the Queen's Square stop, Yom pulled Moss to the back of the car and they jumped down onto the uneven cobblestone.

The Queen's Square was packed with hawkish vendors peddling wares, streams of people crossing from one end of the city to the other, and young children running around wreaking havoc. The façade of the House of Flowing Waters was maintained here, the Queen and her various Lords governing the province of Ibernia, and all of Arcadia. In these areas of the city, Cernunnos and his Stags were nothing but a frightening bedtime story told to keep children from misbehaving. Royal legionaries were sprinkled throughout the plaza in their northern uniforms of thick blue coats with gold trim, plates of brass armor hidden beneath. The legionaries trolled the square with a supreme self-importance, though they were nothing more than brutish foot soldiers next to the triarii. In Yom's circle, they were known as blackcoats.

The plaza was lined with majestic edifices: the Archives, the Institute of Medicine, the Embassy of the Queen. The white marble structures gleamed in the sunlight and glowed in the shadows. Each had grand steps leading up to fifteen-foot tall bronze doors, closed in by towering pillars with intricately carved capitals that corresponded with the use of the building: scrolls for the Archives, medicinal herbs for the Institute of Medicine, and scales for the Embassy. Supposedly, the square was just a taste of the decadence found in Arcadia's capital, Cataracta, the home of the Queen.

In the middle of the plaza stood the statues of Queens past carved in stone, the rule of the House of Flowing Waters stretching back centuries. The statues grew in height towards the center of the plaza, each Queen having commissioned one larger than her predecessor. At the center, the Grieving Queen Andromeda towered over the plaza in her larger than life effigy. Her moniker derived from the violent passing of her mother, Queen Cassiopeia, and Andromeda's subsequent thrust into ruling at an unusually young age. She was carved with the delicate silks and chains that were said to adorn her most striking beauty, a steady torrent of water carved across her body and washing over her feet. As Yom approached the base of the statue, she spotted the singular tear carved into her face, the only symbol of her grief.

Yom led Moss on a jagged path through the crowd, until they were within spitting distance of the Archive steps. Royal flags billowed between columns, and scholars strolled up and down the steps, arms laden with scrolls and large leather bound volumes. Despite Quia's offer for Moss to visit, Yom was under no delusion that they would be welcomed if they walked in the front door.

"This way." Yom tugged Moss away from the front steps. She navigated through the crowd to the side of the building, finding a modest path that led to a servant's entrance. Yom gave the handle a gentle tug, and it swung open. The hallway beyond the servant's entrance was cramped and lined in wood. Yom traversed it quickly with Moss in tow, acting like she had been there many times. At the other end, they opened a similar door into a tall, domed atrium. Marble staircases curved around it on either side and colorful light flooded from above. Yom walked into the center and stood, looking down at the four pointed star inlaid in the floor and then up at the stained glass dome, seeing a pattern centered around a similar shape above.

Yom's reverie was interrupted by an older woman marching towards them in satin blue robes.

"What are you doing? How did you get in here?" She grabbed Yom's arm, and Yom tried not to laugh at the attempt to manhandle her.

"We're here to see an apprentice, his name is—"

"Quia!" Moss pointed to the upper level, where Quia stood at the railing watching the scene unfold.

"Hey, kid," he called down. "It's alright, Maeve, they're with me."

The woman reluctantly let go of Yom's arm and harrumphed before walking away, grumbling to herself.

"Enjoying the show?" Yom called up to him. She could have sworn she caught an eye roll as he stepped away from the railing and waited for them at the top of the stairs.

Yom walked up the steps, the Archives silent except for faint rustling of paper and the sound of their boots brushing the marble floor. When they reached the top, Yom could see the four pointed star more clearly. At the tip of each point there was a subtle inlay of metal, a sun and a moon across from each other, and a rain cloud and fire.

"Glad to see you made it through, kid." Quia braced Moss's forearm with a warm smile. Moss smiled back but winced for a split second. "May I?" Quia asked, motioning to the collar of Moss's tunic. Moss nodded. He snuck Yom a look that said, *See? I'm hard to forget.* Yom suspected he was right.

Quia gently inspected Moss's neckline and peaked under the bandages Yom had dressed the wound in.

"Looks like you'll make it." Quia managed a half smile at the grotesque sight.

"Didn't realize you were a doctor too," Yom muttered.

"Who's been taking care of it?" Quia asked Moss, but Yom knew the question was directed at her too.

"Do you see anyone else here?" Yom looked around pointedly. "Just me." Quia stared at her. Not that she needed it, but she wouldn't have minded the tiniest bit of recognition.

"Well, kid. I told you I would show you around. What do you want to see?" Quia's voice brightened as he spoke to Moss.

Yom cleared her throat. "Is there somewhere we can speak in private?" She knew even the Queen's Square wasn't safe from Stag ears, especially with Dougal playing both sides of the line.

Quia pursed his lips before turning on his heel. He led them through tall stacks of volumes that reeked of dust and old paper before he opened a door to a small, windowless room. The room was lit only by lanterns and contained nothing but a worktable with a scroll unfurled on it. Yom glanced at it, expecting a stuffy record or history, but it was verse. Metered lines surrounded by intricate and faded watercolors. Quia had been reading poetry.

"Secretly a romantic?" Yom asked with a soft snort.

Quia speared her with a look, moving to stand between Yom and the scroll. "Might you get on with your business? So I can be rid of you faster?"

Yom breathed in and out, trying to remember she needed information from this infernal apprentice. "Are there any records of less than official business of the Queen in Inisfail? Business with the Stags?" she asked in a hushed voice, despite being in a sealed room.

"In our records, the Queen collects taxes from all citizens of Arcadia. And in return she provides protection and order." Quia's voice was formal.

"And off the records? What business would she have with Cernunnos?"

"You know who this is a good question for? Dougal." Quia grabbed for the handle of the door. "I'll go—"

Yom stopped him with a firm hand on the door.

Instantly Quia looked intrigued. "Interesting, doing some snooping behind Dad's back?"

Yom felt nauseous at the implication that Cernunnos was her father. "Just answer my question and we can get out of your hair."

"Why would I endanger my apprenticeship for a criminal like you?"

Yom stepped closer, waiting for fear to enter Quia's eyes, but he stayed infuriatingly calm. "I'm happy to tell Cernunnos exactly what you think of him. I'm sure he won't take it out on Dougal."

Quia blanched.

"I'm waiting." She tapped her foot for emphasis. "Dad really is sensitive when he finds out someone doesn't like him." Yom pouted.

"You're unbearable." Quia glared at her. Yom winked at him. "You know the business she has with Cernunnos," he said quietly. "She takes cuts of his exports in exchange for immunity from the usual tariffs and business permits the merchants need."

"Yes." Yom dismissed that with a wave of the hand. "That's ordinary. I'm talking about something out of the ordinary."

"Why?" Quia narrowed his eyes.

"Nothing that concerns you."

Quia's eyes vacated for a moment; Yom could practically see the idea sparking in his mind.

"What is it?" She stepped close enough to see the flickering lantern light in the whites of his eyes.

But Quia's face grew stony once again, shutting her out. Yom's gaze darted around the small room, looking for something she could use to be more persuasive. He had brought them to the barest room in the archive, with nothing but the scroll and an inkwell on the lone table. But Quia seemed like a true stickler. Someone who didn't like messes.

Yom took two self-assured steps to the table and picked up the full inkwell to hold it over the open scroll of verse. Before Quia could register what she was doing, she slanted the inkwell over it.

"What are you—" Quia reached out but stopped when Yom tipped the inkwell a little closer to spilling.

"What is it?" she repeated.

"That scroll is a three century old original," Quia gritted out.

Yom shrugged. "Sounds like a good time to replace it."

Quia made a frustrated noise in the back of his throat. "The Queen is concerned with two things: maintaining the rule of the House of Flowing

Waters over Arcadia, and war with Panchaia." Quia didn't break eye contact with the inkwell as he spoke.

"But there are no internal wars happening in Arcadia. The rule of the House is more secure than it's ever been," Yom pressed. Even in Inisfail, they had felt the ripples of Queen Andromeda's loss when she first took the throne. The rumors were that it was Panchaian sympathizers who had launched an attack from inside her own palace, an attempted coup. The collective grief and outrage had united the queendom and the House of Lords beneath her, an excellent political device it turned out. Yom hardly kept up with the politics of a state that had no bearing on the underworld she inhabited, but sometimes from the outside it was hard not to see right through some of the larger plays.

Quia watched Yom as if he was waiting for her to understand something.

"You're saying it has something to do with Panchaia?" she asked incredulously.

"I'm not saying anything. I am telling you that those are her two interests. And that the people in power will not be satisfied until one side loses."

People in power, as in more than just the Queen. Could he be implying Cernunnos? What interest would he have in Panchaia? Since joining the Stags, Yom had noticed that most of the war paranoia was fear mongering from the House of Flowing Waters to strengthen its own rule.

"So if it's not an internal struggle in Arcadia, you're saying it has to do with Panchaia. But how would either side accomplish anything when it's not even possible to cross between them?"

"The Panchaians know how to make the crossing." Quia smiled as if he knew something Yom did not. "And again, for the record, I'm not saying anything."

"Those are just stories."

"What are stories?" Moss looked between them hungrily, soaking up their words. Yom had forgotten he was with them, so absorbed in sparring with Quia.

"Some think there are Panchaians living among us already." Quia widened his eyes at Moss like he was starting a ghost story. Yom watched him skeptically.

"It's absurd," Yom dismissed. "If that were true, they would have attacked Arcadia already."

"Making the crossing is different than being able to sail an entire army across it."

"Even if they haven't attacked yet, the Queen would still be hunting down any Panchaians who step foot in Arcadia." Yom spoke and then paused, realizing what she had just said. "Are there any records of ever capturing a Panchaian in Arcadia?"

"No." Quia shook his head. "Not that I've ever seen. But not every event is added to the Archives." Something heavy settled into his gaze.

"But you think it's possible? That they've captured Panchaians before? That they're hunting them now?" Yom pressed.

"Anything is possible. But like you said, they're just stories. Right?" Now it was Quia's turn to press her. Yom ignored him, lost in thought. "Do you mind?" Quia nudged his chin at the inkwell perched precariously over the scroll, and she narrowed her eyes at him before returning it to the table. He exhaled.

"Quia, are there any records of how Stags are able to repay their debt?" Moss asked.

Quia looked at him with sympathy. "We don't have physical records of it. But Dougal has told me stories of Stags being Unbound. It either requires a repayment of debt in coin, or a new bargain be made." Yom wanted to tell Moss that the debt would continue to accrue every day he spent in the Cut. A bargain Cernunnos was willing to make for a Bound Stag was near impossible to find, and deserting to seek a new bargain in another province was far too risky. The provinces were a dangerous place, especially for someone as naive as Moss. She stayed silent.

Yom patted his shoulder. "You'll repay the debt one day. I know it." Moss looked a bit comforted by this. There was a third way that a Stag could be Unbound: one that demanded the ultimate price. But this third way was a path you could not return from, and Yom refused to plant the seed of it in his mind.

"Hey." Quia nudged him. "Do you want to see the weapons archive room?" Moss's eyes widened and he nodded enthusiastically. Quia laughed. "It's this way."

As Yom followed behind them, a warm feeling seeped into her, something like gratitude. Gratitude towards Quia for trying to cheer Moss up, she realized, before berating herself for becoming so attached in the first place.

When they returned to the Cut, bells were ringing through the halls. She pulled a junior Stag aside.

"What's going on?"

"It's a gathering in the greenhouse. They announced it an hour ago."

Right on cue, Dougal's voice projected through the copper pipe amplifier system that ran throughout the Cut. "Cernunnos requests your presence in the greenhouse. All Stags not in the field must attend." The message was repeated several times before the projection ceased.

Yom kept a firm hand on Moss's shoulder, letting them be swept into the procession of Stags headed through the long tunnel to the greenhouse. Cernunnos's gatherings were wildly unpredictable, especially an impromptu one like this. She tried not to jump to conclusions but suddenly felt wary of their trip to the Archives.

Yom stood close to the center of the crowd of Stags all gathered under the oak tree. Moss stood next to her, looking a bit green around the gills. The crowd murmured as they waited for Cernunnos to arrive.

"I heard a Stag stole from him."

"No, I heard he's giving everyone the day off to attend the Feria."

Yom snorted to herself at the ridiculous idea that Cernunnos would ever give a day off. And to the flower-ridden festival of spring? Fat chance.

"Hey." Lucan tapped her shoulder and stepped in next to her. "Where were—"

"It's time to speak on a grave matter." Cernunnos's voice immediately hushed the din, and a circle gathered around him at the center. "Who can tell me what the most important quality of a Stag is?" He scanned the crowd, his gray eyes boring into each Stag whose gaze he crossed.

After a few seconds, someone piped up behind Yom. "Strength!"

"Ruthlessness!" someone else offered.

"Loyalty," Lucan said just loud enough to be heard. Cernunnos swiveled around and pointed at him.

"That's right. Loyalty. The world out there is changing." Cernunnos swept his arms at the lot of them. Yom's jaw ticked. Perhaps Quia wasn't completely full of it, and Cernunnos was making some shadowy reference to Panchaia. "And I need to know that my Stags will do what needs to be done, *no matter what.*" Heads nodded throughout the crowd. "This goes for every single Stag." Cernunnos found Yom in the crowd, and her stomach dropped. "Where is the boy? Our newest Stag."

Yom's hand found Moss's shoulder. He looked up at her, clearly nervous. "It will be fine," she whispered, though unconvinced herself. She pushed him through the crowd with a nudge. His body shook.

"Don't make him come up alone, Bluefingers. Join us."

Yom wished she could say she was surprised. She nodded and followed Moss until they were both in the clearing with Cernunnos. He clapped a heavy, ring-laden hand on each of their shoulders. She should have taken more powder before this.

"Since you seem to have taken a shine to the boy, you'll show everyone how simple it is to not let emotions get in the way of following orders." He was speaking to Yom but addressing the crowd. "Draw your knife."

Yom's head snapped up and she looked to him for a sign that this was some kind of joke.

"I won't ask twice."

Her fingers fumbled to draw out the knife from her powderbelt.

Cernunnos nodded imperceptibly. "Good. Now kill him." As he said this he stepped away so that Yom stood an arm length away from Moss.

The boy looked at her with unchecked fear in his eyes. She wanted to believe this was just a test, but also knew Cernunnos was perfectly capable of killing someone to make a point.

"I'm waiting." Cernunnos's tone was so calm he could have been talking about supper.

Yom's hand twitched, but she couldn't raise the knife at Moss. He already looked ready to piss himself.

"This is your final chance." Cernunnos watched her, challenging her to disobey a direct order.

She swore and pulled Moss into her in one swift motion, one hand holding a tuft of his hair to pull his head back and expose his neck, and the other holding a knife at his throat.

"Good. Now finish it."

Moss trembled in her grip. Yom saw every step that had led her here, to this moment, like a staircase that burrowed into darkness. She turned a blind eye to the powders she knew were being sold to dubious buyers. She watched in silence as kid after kid Bound themselves to Cernunnos with promises of riches and power. She shook down innocent shopkeepers for their last few coins in the name of corrupt protection tributes.

Yom dropped the knife with a soft thud onto the grass. "I won't," she said quietly.

Cernunnos stepped to stand so close that Yom should have been able to feel his breathing, and the fact that she couldn't made his presence even more ominous.

"I knew it." His voice was coldly soft, speaking so only Yom could hear him. "I've given you everything, but you're still the same little girl who came running to me all those years ago. Broken and alone. And that's all you'll ever be." His words rang through her as if she were hollow.

"Lucan," he bellowed.

Lucan stepped forward and Cernunnos turned away from her to nod at him. Lucan drew his own knife and wound back to deliver a stab to Moss's gut. Yom watched frozen as he jabbed it forward. In a flash Cernunnos stopped his hand as the knife was an inch away from piercing Moss's skin. Moss's eyes were screwed shut, and they slowly opened when he realized the knife had never finished its path.

"See how easy that was?" Cernunnos clapped Lucan on the back, but then his icy gaze turned back to Yom. "Consider this a warning. For now, I will only strip you of your rank. Pray that one day, I will give you the opportunity to earn it back."

Yom's jaw dropped. Years of working her way up, of practically building Cernunnos's powder operation from scratch, of following orders that made it difficult to look herself in the eye, gone in the course of a minute. Her face burned.

"Lucan will take over powder production from now on."

Yom's eyes shot to Lucan, but he looked just as surprised as her.

Cernunnos looked around the crowd once again. "Let this be a warning to all of you ratbag Stags. I have no use for soldiers who can't follow orders," he boomed. "Dismissed."

The crowd stood in shocked silence for a moment. Lucan moved first, heading in Yom's direction. "Antlers up, yeah?" he said to the Stags he passed, receiving some grunts of ascent. No one looked Yom in the eye, murmuring among themselves.

Yom shouldered her way through the crowd, trying to get to the exit. *Soldiers?* Stags weren't soldiers. Lucan was calling for her, caught behind the tide of people.

"Oi, Bluefingers!" The bollocks trailed her on either side.

"So we figure, if you're no longer his favorite little chemist," one bollock began.

"You'll need to start pulling your weight in other ways around here," the other bollock continued.

Yom tried not to listen to them but the blood rushed to her face.

"And there's always a need in the pleasure rooms," one of them smirked.

A steady hand grabbed her arm. "Piss off, cocks." It was Lucan's voice coming from behind her. Yom could feel the bollocks sneering before they peeled away.

"I'm sorry," Lucan said softly as he tried to hold her arms.

Yom elbowed him off. "Did you know that was going to happen?" She tried to keep the emotion out of her voice.

"I knew he was going to give a speech about loyalty. I didn't know he would ask to kill the boy."

"What about loyalty to other Stags?"

Lucan remained stone-faced.

"Would you have done it? If he hadn't stopped you?" She met Lucan's eyes, looking for something she already sensed was gone.

He stayed silent.

"You disgust me."

"Hey," he held her arms forcefully now, "You're no better than me. We've both done worse. I'm just trying to make something of this." He motioned to both their torcs.

"What is there to make of these beyond freeing ourselves of them?" She tugged on hers for emphasis.

"You heard him. The world is changing. I want to make sure I have a place in it."

His words illuminated something. Connections shimmered between all the separate incidents. The triarii lurking in the Cut, the secret production runs, the speech about loyalty. In hindsight, they were all engineered to test her. To see if she would follow orders, if she could be controlled. And she had failed. Now Lucan, who had clearly met the scarred triarii before the training room, who was willing to do anything Cernunnos ordered him to, was situated at the head of powder production.

Lucan noticed the gears turning in her mind. "Do not push this, Yom. Keep your head down and show Cernunnos you'll do what it takes."

Yom tried to glean if he really believed what he was saying. The saddest thing was, it seemed like he did. There was a hunger blooming in him, leaving less and less of the gangly boy she had met, who had first brought her into the Stags. She felt like she had been asleep for years and was just now waking up.

"You are weak," she said softly, her fury giving way to resignation. "Don't even think about coming to my quarters again."

"You'll come around." His hand brushed her cheek as she turned away, and for the first time, his touch felt like nothing.

III

Wall of Moonflower

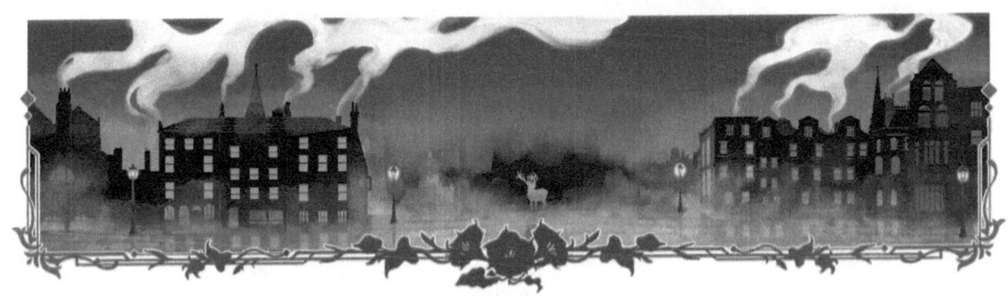

YOM BARELY LEFT HER QUARTERS FOR THE NEXT WEEK, INTENDING TO enter a powderhole and stop coming up for air altogether. Cernunnos could take away her access to the Powdery, the Powder Parlor, and her dominion over the powdermaids who worked there—all of whom she had found and trained herself—but he couldn't take away her mind. She had created almost every powder recipe in circulation, and many more that she had kept for her own personal collection. She held this truth close to her chest as she whiled away the nights alone in her quarters, surrounded by a cloud of various powders, waiting for someone to tell her that these rooms would soon be taken away as well.

Managing to avoid Moss so far, Yom eavesdropped enough to learn he was ramping up on Stag duties, shadowing collection shifts. Whether he understood it or not, associating with her would put a target on his back. The rest of the Stags understood that all too well, leaving Yom alone during the rare occasions when she left her rooms to trudge down to the Green Demon for a hot meal and a glass of spirits.

It was Moss who Yom thought of one morning as she sat in the Green Demon, alone at a table next to the bar. The tavern buzzed with morning traffic and the air reeked of eggs and sausage. She wondered if her avoidance of him would make Moss think she blamed him for what happened. It wasn't true of course, the object of her blame sat across the tavern from her, playing cards with a few other Stags, laughing over a breakfast ale. Lucan had grown quite comfortable in his new standing.

The bell over the door jingled and two Stags walked in, with a timid Moss in tow. Yom clenched her jaw and sank down in her chair, holding her forehead in her hand in the hopes she would go unnoticed. With a furtive glance, she saw Moss looking right at her. He was raising his hand to wave but she stopped him with a curt shake of her head. His face fell. Then, a sweep of distinct blue robes covered her view of Moss. She sat up a bit to see it was the snarky Archive apprentice, who stopped to talk to the boy. *Quia.* She wished she could march over there and deliver a retort about how much time he seemed to be spending at the Cut for someone who looked down so haughtily on the Stags.

"You're doing the right thing, avoiding the boy," a voice said softly.

Yom snapped upright.

"Don't turn around," it added. It took her a second to recognize it as Dougal's voice. She sat back, closer to the direction it had come from.

"I'm sorry for what happened," he said. He sounded sincere, but Yom had no intention of letting her guard down enough to believe it. She could see now how every situation had been calculated to test her. To see if she would fall in line, or ask questions. And this was likely no different.

"I'm sure you helped him plan it."

"I didn't know what he was going to do."

Yom shook her head. Doubtful.

"You're not the only one who is experiencing a change in...responsibilities."

At this, Yom hesitated. "What do you want?"

"Same thing as you. Answers."

"Didn't you hear? The world is changing. That should bode well for someone like you, no?" *Someone who can walk between the Queen's world and Cernunnos's world with ease,* Yom thought.

"I don't think it bodes well for anyone."

Again, the sincerity in his voice gave her pause. The stool scraped behind her and Dougal stood, clothing rustling.

Dougal bumped her shoulder as he passed. "Pardon," he said without a second glance at her, but something that had a pointed corner had been pushed into her hand. His blue robes swayed as he walked away, and Yom saw Quia tracking his movements as he left. Then, Quia swiveled to look at her.

Yom kept her hand clamped over what Dougal had given her and downed her spirit in one gulp. Pushing away from the table, she noticed Moss was looking at her again, and she gave him a small smile before slipping out the backdoor of the tavern, into the alley. After a deep breath, she looked at what was in her palm.

It was a wrinkled and folded piece of paper. When she opened it, elegant script scrawled over a few inkspots.

The scarred triarii crosses the Queen's Square every day at midday.

The scarred triarii—the one Yom had met in the training room. She hadn't seen him again since that day, but she had never gone looking. Distrust roiled inside her. Why would Dougal drop something like this in her lap? She supposed if the note was true, looking into it presented its own dangers, and better a disgraced chemist than the head of the Royal Archives. If she could figure out what was happening, surviving it was more likely. And whatever Dougal's motives were, it was the only lead she had. Besides, she had so little left to lose.

Yom stuffed the note in her pocket and tightened the powderbelt around her waist. She guessed by the height of the sun she had about two hours until midday, and it would take an hour to get to the Queen's Square on foot. Taking the streetcar would be too conspicuous after what happened last time. She buttoned her coat and unfolded the collar to cover her neck, stuffing her hands in her pockets. Setting off at a brisk pace, she took a back route through the city via the narrow network of alleyways, avoiding crowded avenues and keeping her head down.

Roughly an hour later, Yom emerged into the crowded Queen's Square. Queen Andromeda's statue loomed at the dead center of the plaza, and she headed straight towards it. Climbing up onto the pedestal of the statue, she crouched in between her legs and the wave at her feet. From here, she was at eye level with the top of the crowd but remained hidden. The clock mounted at the top of the Archives showed a little under an hour until midday. She settled into her roost and scanned in all directions every so often, watching the crowd move like a turbulent pool of water.

An hour and a few inhales of powder later, she looked around once again for a sign of the triarii and still found nothing. The first brushes of doubt touched her; had her trust in Dougal's note had been misplaced? But there was no reason to draw her away from the Cut. All she had left to be taken away were her quarters. Her stomach dropped as she thought of Moss, alone surrounded by Stags, and now halfway across the city. The boy was a nuisance, but she cared about him. And Okeanus knew he was too naive to fend for himself among the Stags. She began to hurriedly climb down from the statue's pedestal, just as movement caught her eye.

Halfway between the Queen's statue and the Royal Archives, a wave of people were parted by a flash of black moving through the crowd. The glistening black of triarii armor. Relief washed over Yom but only for a brief moment before she jumped down from the pedestal and made her way through the crowd, tracking Misho like a wildcat in the weeds.

Tailing him became easier once he left the throng of the central plaza, but Yom had to be more discreet in her pursuit. She stayed a safe distance away, along the edges of the avenues he took. He walked with sure steps and people cleared his path as he moved. A thought struck her that he was like Dougal. Able to walk between the Queen's and Cernunnos's world with ease.

A green door stood out ahead, the recognizable symbol of the Stag posts that were dotted throughout the city. But Misho walked right past it. He kept going for a ways down the same avenue, the width becoming narrower and narrower as they went, making it more and more difficult for Yom to remain unseen. Finally he turned into a door on the left side, just before the street forked in two.

Once he was out of sight, Yom situated herself across the way behind a cluster of barrels outside a pub, watching the door. The windows surrounding the door were dark, with faint shadows of large leaves and a film of humidity creeping in around the edges of the glass. An herb shop?

"What are you doing?" A whisper from the side startled her.

Without thinking, she drew her knife and lunged towards the source of the voice, nearly knocking the barrels over. When the shock subsided and she processed whose neck was now pressing into her knife, she saw Quia, garish blue robes and all, pinned against the wall.

"What are you doing here?" she hissed back at him.

"Following you," he said simply, no alarm about the knife. Her eyes bulged, expecting a better answer. "And you?" was all he added.

"This is Stag business. You could be killed for interfering." Yom pushed the knife harder against his throat.

"I don't think it is."

"Excuse me?"

"I don't think it is Stag business. I saw you sneaking through the city, and I know your rank was stripped."

Yom pursed her lips. "Dougal should watch how much of Cernunnos's affairs he shares with you," she said icily. "Wouldn't want you to learn too much and have to be silenced."

"Dougal refuses to tell me anything." His annoyance was clear. "I had to ask around myself."

"Maybe he's protecting you."

"I don't need protection."

"Clearly," Yom snorted. Despite having a knife at his throat, Quia looked frustratingly poised. His dark hair was combed back, falling around his shoulders, and his copper skin was quite luminous up close. His spectacles had slid so far down his nose there was nothing blocking her view of his dark lashes and eyes that looked like barley spirits swirling in a glass. He was too pretty for his own good, Yom decided. As he squirmed beneath her knife, she caught the metallic scent of lampblack ink, and something harder to quantify. Something that smelled like wind and the bits of earth it carried. They stared at each other, both unblinking for a beat, until she reluctantly withdrew her knife.

"If you're so knowledgeable, then you must know I'm completely in the dark." Yom turned back to watch the entrance of the shop.

"You know something. Otherwise you wouldn't have come to the Archives with those questions." Quia cleared his throat. "And Dougal slipped you something this morning. I saw him."

"Jealous?" Yom smirked. "I don't want to get involved in whatever lover's quarrel is going on between you and Dougal. I'm just here for answers."

"Me too."

"If someone catches us, I won't stick my neck out for you."

"I can take care of myself," he said simply.

She shook her head. His funeral.

They sat in silence, watching the shop for a sign of the triarii. Minutes stretched into an hour before Yom spotted movement through the window. She elbowed Quia. Misho pushed open the door and locked it behind him, looking quite the part with his armored hood pulled over his eyes. He resumed his jaunt back down the avenue in the direction of the Queen's Square. Once he was out of sight, she stood.

Yom walked over to the door and crouched down in front of it. Quia followed her, but it was as if he walked on air; his footsteps didn't make a sound. No wonder she hadn't heard him following her. *Too light on his feet to be trustworthy*, she thought as she plucked her pair of hooked tongs from her belt. She jammed them into the lock and began fiddling.

"Interesting skill," Quia commented from behind her.

"I'd recommend being quiet if you want to leave here with all your fingers, Princess. I'm not quite as nice when you don't have Moss as a human shield." She hazarded a glance back at him and her annoyance skyrocketed at the amusement on his face. As if he thought he could take her. She would have him knocked out before he could say *mercy*.

"You're welcome to try," he said lightly, reading her intent.

Lucky for him, the faint clicks of the lock disengaging saved further discussion.

The door swung open, and Yom stepped into the dark shop. Quia followed, closing the door behind him, and took in the room intently, a slight bend in his legs as if he were preparing to pounce. Yom dismissed the thought, no doubt imagining it.

The smell of mint and sage was thick, and the air was heavy with moisture. Yom led the way, knife in hand, wading through the dense foliage of herbs and blooms. It was standard stock, several varieties of milder nightshades and medicinal herbs.

That is, until she reached the back of the shop and saw an entire wall of blooming Moonflower. Its sharp-edged leaves and pointed white petals were unmistakable. As she stepped close to it, the perfume of its flowers brought back more haunting, vivid memories of watching Eden work it into tinctures and verjuices. *If this flower is the moon, then Darkness is the great sky that it shines within.* The longer she stared, the more she became aware of a faint buzzing emanating from the wall of Moonflower. She stepped closer, a dull weight gathering in her limbs. The buzzing morphed into something more rhythmic, something that almost sounded like words—

"What business would Cernunnos have with an herb shop on the other side of the city?" Quia stepped up next to her. "Let alone the Queen?"

Yom turned her attention away from the Moonflower's sounds, and they returned to a faint buzzing. She felt along its vines, refusing to believe this was all there was to the shop. Her knife was clutched in one hand, but she took care not to knick any of the vines. She had this feeling that she shouldn't disturb it, that its dew shouldn't be spilled carelessly. As she moved along the wall, the buzzing seemed to grow louder. She twitched, trying to ignore it, until finally she found a crease in the wood behind the leaves. The buzzing halted, as if she had found what she needed to find. Her hand felt a notch and pulled. As the door creaked open, the Moonflower vines slipping over it, the buzzing returned to its low volume. Yom braced herself as she peered inside.

It was a tunnel. All Yom could see was an archway that opened into somewhere light and densely green at the end. Padding through the darkness, the arch of green grew larger and larger. She crossed the threshold at the end of the tunnel into a room full of neatly tended rows of a plant she had never seen before, with thin aisles between each row and a perimeter of space around the edge. Light streamed in through opaque glass along the ceiling and the humidity in the air was suffocating. She walked along one edge of the room, glancing between the rows of plants on her right and a workbench that stretched along the wall. There was a thick book splayed open on the bench, and when Yom looked closer, it seemed to be an observation log of some sort. Its first entry was a little over a week ago, the day before she had met Misho. Each line item showed a date and a number, and some had symbols scribbled that she didn't recognize.

Yom turned her attention away from the log to scan the plant again, but she still couldn't identify it. She had gotten a little rusty identifying plants on sight since she switched to working with extracts and refinements, but for a plant to register no familiar characteristics was hard to believe. Then she spotted the faint purple vein running through the center of its leaf. Kneeling down, Yom grasped the leaf in her hand and turned it over. The leaf's edge was faintly serrated and a purple vein that snaked through it. She rubbed it between her fingers to massage out some of the oil and lifted it to smell. The aroma was intoxicating, sweet and dark. Pulling out a match, she struck it along the floor and held it to the base of the leaf. Sure enough, the flame burned with a distinctly violet hue at the base.

"This isn't possible," Yom said. She let go of the burning leaf and the sweet smell of the smoke overwhelmed her.

Quia had rounded the room and stood next to her. He whispered the name Yom knew it by as he inhaled the smoke and closed his eyes. "Amaurosis." *Darkness.*

Violence flashed through Quia when he opened his eyes.

"I've only ever read about it in the oldest records of chemical arts, and even those accounts were based on secondhand legends. It's been lost since the Separation," Yom babbled, at a loss. The accounts of the mythical plant were scant, but it was a powerful ally in the war, to both sides. Supposedly it submerged the user in a semiconscious state with hyper-strength. It was dubbed Victor's Root. "It's not possible," she repeated again, to herself. "It was lost." Whole fields of it were razed towards the end of the war, each side sacrificing their own access to it in order to keep it from their opponent.

"It was not lost everywhere," Quia said quietly.

"But if this truly is Amaurosis, there's enough here for an entire–"

"Legion," Quia finished.

But something else clicked, too. *If this flower is the moon, then Darkness is the great sky that it shines within.* No, it wasn't possible. There's no way Eden meant that this plant was the symbiotic partner of Moonflower. This mythical plant that didn't even *exist* in Arcadia to her guardian's knowledge—

The door hinge creaked. Quia moved first, spotting a pile of discarded crates in the corner and yanking Yom with him into a sliver opening behind them. She was piled in next to him and the hard edges of the metal equipment in the crates cut into her skin.

"It's maturing well." Cernunnos's rich, husky voice commented from the entrance.

Swallowing her shudder, Yom squirmed to see through a crack between slats of wood. Cernunnos paced down one of the rows of plants, his suit perfectly in place and his thick hair combed back. Quia crouched, tense, next to her.

"It will be ready to harvest in a month," another voice spoke. A triarii emerged from the shadows behind him and walked parallel to Cernunnos's path. His armored hood was still pulled over his eyes, but Yom recognized him as the scarred one she had followed.

"Yes, it will." Cernunnos plucked a leaf and rubbed it between his fingers, holding it up to his nose and inhaling deeply before smiling. "But will your master's end of the bargain be kept?"

"The Queen plans to demonstrate at Lupercalia."

What could this have to do with Lupercalia? Yom thought, confused. It was a ceremony they knew little about in the provinces; it marked the end of the eight days of the festival of Feria. The Queen hosted the Arcadian elite at her palace, the House of Flowing Waters, in the capital city of Cataracta, on the other end of the queendom. What would Inisfail have to do with it?

"Then there should be no issue sending one of my emissaries to observe the ceremony."

"Do you not trust my master?"

Cernunnos let out a great laugh. He continued walking further through the short stalks. "Your master has had six years with nothing to show for it. What's changed now?"

"His other half has returned. She has accepted the role she is destined to play. I can assure you, you and your siblings will be quite pleased, come Lupercalia."

His other half returned, accepted the role she is destined to play? Yom couldn't imagine who Misho spoke of. She wasn't familiar with Lords outside of Ibernia, and the Ibernian Lords were all but figureheads being stationed this far from the capitol.

Cernunnos grunted.

"But I can also assure you, if anything gets in the way of your end of the agreement, or any*one*, you won't enjoy your position in the new order."

Cernunnos whipped around. "You dare threaten me in my own realm?" His voice changed as he spoke, it heightened and multiplied throughout the room, carrying the girth of a stag's roar. The hair on the back of Yom's neck stood at the sound of it.

"I am just the messenger." Misho held up his hands, washing himself of responsibility. He stepped closer to the crates. Yom's breathing stopped altogether. "It is merely a reminder that whatever can be given, can also be taken away." Misho surveyed the wall that Yom and Quia clung to. She thought he even paused for an instant on the crates, before continuing to turn on his heels.

Cernunnos's voice returned to its normal tenor. "Your master would do well to remember who holds the power on this side of Wacachan," he growled. *Wacachan.* The name echoed in Yom's ears. It felt as if it had stretched across time to be spoken at this moment, both ancient and familiar. But she could not place it.

Misho walked back towards Cernunnos. "For now," he said, and left the room.

IV

Wacachan

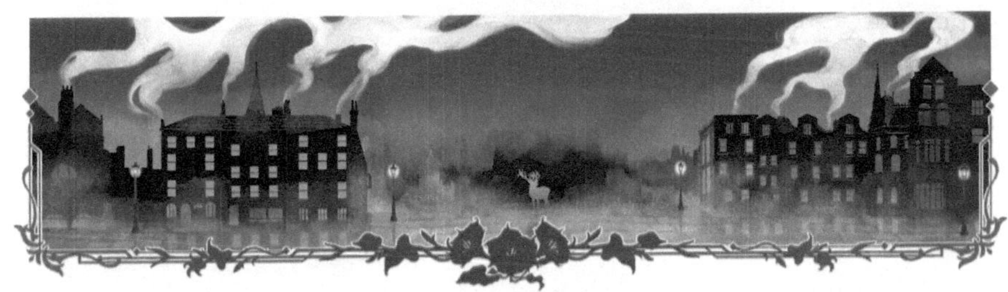

Yom did not dare speak until they slipped out of that cursed greenhouse the way they came. Cernunnos stormed out in a rage, and the triarii had slunk off as well to Okeanus knew where. The rational chemist in her considered that it would be prudent to examine the Amaurosis later—when she was alone. But in truth, a far more irrational thought clawed at her. *If this flower is the moon, then Darkness is the great sky that it shines within.* If Eden truly did have some knowledge or connection to the plant, then perhaps she could glean something of her former guardian from it. The violet-veined plant had beckoned her, scratching at her until she could do nothing but listen to it. Tucked inside her waistcoat, burning a hole of violet fire, was a stalk of Amaurosis she had cut just before they left.

Her head spun. Only when she and Quia were tucked safely in an alleyway did her breathing return to normal. She leaned against the brick wall and looked up, trying to fight a wave of nausea. The sky in the slit between buildings had changed from cerulean blue to a dark gray. A storm was coming.

The world tilted as she considered she knew nothing of Cernunnos, of the triarii, even of Quia. The sheltered Archive apprentice, witnessing the shady dealings between the Queen and Cernunnos. She expected him to react with shock and horror. When she turned to look at him, his brow was furrowed with worry, but he was calm. Calmer than her.

"Why aren't you more surprised?" She tried to glare at him, but it was half-hearted. "What do you know?"

"More than you," he said offhand. "You should run along back to the Cut, bury your head underground as usual."

At this, Yom opened her eyes. "Run where? What did you say to me?" Indignance swelled over her nausea.

"You've never cared about the truth of your master before, and now is no time to start."

"He is not my master." Still at a loss for everything else, of this she was certain.

"Could have fooled me." Quia gestured at the torc around her neck.

She was about to fire back at him when she realized what he had said. "What truth?"

Quia shot her a dark look before turning away from her.

"Don't you walk away," she whisper-shouted at his back. Shoving down the nausea Yom, did the only thing that seemed to make sense. She followed him.

"Go home." Quia's command repeated several times as Yom followed a few steps behind him through a winding maze of narrow avenues. For a royal apprentice golden boy, he was certainly skilled at navigating the city's labyrinthine back routes. She thought they were going in the direction of the Queen's Square but was having trouble keeping her sense of direction in this part of the city. Without warning, Quia turned into a narrow crevice between buildings and Yom followed. She had absolutely no idea where they were.

"Quia."

Yom spun around, knocking her shoulder against one of the walls, to see Dougal standing inside a door cracked open along the alley, hurriedly waving them inside.

"Did you find something?" Dougal asked, looking at Yom.

"Why would you go to *her?*" Quia fumed.

"Let's do this inside." Dougal turned to open a space in the doorway for them.

Yom looked between Quia and Dougal for a moment, seeing anger in Quia's face and concern in Dougal's. This was Cernunnos's steward, his right hand. How could she trust him? Following his note was one thing, but what it had uncovered was far bigger than she was prepared for. *What if Dougal already knows about the Amaurosis?* Yom considered. *What if he's just as in the dark as you were?* she countered herself. Uncertainty felt like a shroud over her mind, and something told her there would be answers inside. She nodded and entered.

Inside was a cramped apartment covered floor to ceiling in haphazardly piled books and scrolls. Dougal led her to a modest kitchen with a small wooden table.

"What is this place?" She hesitated next to the table.

"This is my private residence." Dougal set a mug with steaming liquid onto the table and gestured for her to sit. His voice was comforting, and when Yom met his eyes, they were gentle. This was not the Dougal she knew.

Yom sat on the edge of the seat, keeping her arms crossed in front of her. "I don't know where to start." What she had heard and seen was replaying in a violent loop in her head, and louder than all of it was the grotesque version of Cernunnos's voice. Inhuman was the only word she could conjure for it.

"Tell me what you saw," Dougal prompted.

"They're growing Amaurosis," Quia muttered as he watched the tea swirl in his own mug. Yom glared at him. Perhaps he didn't understand the significance of Dougal's relationship to Cernunnos. "A whole room of it," he added.

Dougal collapsed into his seat, shock and horror flashing across his face. He was a better actor than Yom thought.

"Cernunnos?" he asked.

Quia nodded. "And the Queen," he added, referencing Misho's words. *My master.* "Together."

"His lap dog is probably well aware already," Yom cut in.

Dougal turned to her. "I understand why you're hesitant to trust me, Yom, but everything I have done has been for the good of Arcadia and the people in it."

"Offering Moss up was for the good of Arcadia?"

Dougal winced. "I have to do things I am not proud of to prove myself to Cernunnos, even after all this time. It's difficult to live with, but the alternative—not being able to keep tabs on what he does, on what they all do—is worse."

"Who is 'they all'?" He couldn't mean Stags, or he would have included Yom in that group.

Dougal ignored her question and turned back to Quia. "I thought they were searching for Panchaians. How could they have gotten Amaurosis seeds?" Yom realized with a start she was hearing words taken straight from her visit to Quia at the Archives.

"A traitor could have brought them across from Panchaia. In exchange for asylum." Quia considered.

Panchaians know how to make the crossing, Quia had said before. And now he talked about it not as if it were an urban myth, but as if it were true. Yom's head pounded. It had been too long since her last dose of powder.

"Do you have any spirits?" she asked, a hint of desperation in her voice.

Dougal nodded and stepped away to return with a bottle of something amber. He poured a healthy amount into Yom's mug. She drank down the scalding liquid edged with fire in one long sip and then motioned for another pour, sinking into her chair as the spirits numbed her.

"They could be looking for the numenborn," Quia said.

"Or they've already found them."

"Looking for what?" Yom struggled to follow. "I thought Amaurosis was used to create supersoldiers."

"It has many uses." Quia spoke about it with suspicious familiarity.

"If I'm not mistaken, Eden shared some stories with you before her passing," Dougal said softly. His hand found Yom's shoulder, but she jerked back, scraping her chair on the floor as she pushed away from the table and stood. It was like the breath had been punched out of her. No one in her world knew of Eden, not even Cernunnos.

"What?" Yom's voice was shrill. "How do you—"

"I was a friend." True sadness weighed down Dougal's voice, but Yom still couldn't believe it.

"No," Yom shook her head vehemently, "That's not possible." Eden didn't know anyone who worked in the Royal Archives; she had hardly even visited the Queen's Square.

"Those few of us who came from a certain...background had to maintain completely separate lives, outside of the rare occasions we were able to meet." The idea that Eden knew and conspired with the head of the Royal Archives against someone like Cernunnos was far-fetched and absurd. If it was true, it would have very real consequences. *Like punishment of death.*

"Do you know," Yom cleared her throat, vulnerability leaking into her voice, "what happened?" It was a question she had never dared to ask.

A light went out behind Dougal's eyes. "Eden became quite secretive in the years before her death. I think she had learned something, something dangerous. I tried to find out what it was, but she wouldn't confide in me. And then it was too late." Dougal looked down. "I did all I could to investigate what happened. All I could find out was that whoever did it was an outsider. It wasn't a Stag. And whoever it was, they were either very good at covering their tracks or had some very powerful friends."

"And her daughter?" Yom's voice was low. She couldn't bear to say Lior's name.

Dougal shook his head. "They covered Lior's tracks as well. She left the province without a trace. And you—" When he met Yom's eyes, his were glassy. "You had already been Bound by the time I found you. But at least you were under the protection of Cernunnos."

Anger ballooned in Yom's throat. There was a world where she could have been saved from being Bound.

"In telling these stories, Eden tried to prepare you without putting you in danger." Dougal leaned towards her but did not stand, looking at her as if she were a frightened animal.

Yom took another step back. Eden's stories had been locked away since that night. Enshrined in her memory by the loss, and shunned for the same reason. Some part of Yom believed that Eden was killed for telling those stories, and that made her death partially Yom's fault for listening to them.

"It's dangerous to know the truth of this world. Certain...powerful beings have gone to great lengths to keep it a secret," Dougal pressed on. There it was again, a cryptic reference to the truth, except this time, it had something to do with Eden. The memory of Cernunnos's voice, how it had morphed and curled in around Yom's very soul, still brought back chills. Underneath the fear and guilt that came with thinking about Eden's death, there was an insatiable urge to understand.

"She won't be able to handle it," Quia interrupted. "She should never have been involved in the first place."

Quia's doubt lit a fire in her.

"I've handled worse. Tell me," Yom commanded, pushing aside her fear, slowly returning to her seat at the table.

"Eden told you of the World Tree and the immortal beings born of it?" At the mention of the World Tree, pieces of Eden's story revealed themselves like pearls in the sand. She was once again on the cusp of adulthood, sitting by the laboratory hearth, imagining a great tree surrounded by water on all sides. The name floated to the surface again. *Wacachan.* That was where she had heard it, the name of the great tree sitting at the center of the world. Everything flooded back. She saw the creatures that sprouted from its branches and roots, beings with the power of creation in their fingertips. The two sides of the Ancient War, the gods and the titans, and Lior's question that Eden had intentionally left unanswered: *Which half became Arcadia?* Interwoven with the memories of the story were her last moments with Lior and Eden. Hiding under the covers with Lior by candlelight. The sound of Eden's gasp as the knife was drawn from her body. Lior's howls. They too came back in a torrent, uncontrollable.

Yom shook her head. "It's not real. It was a bedtime story."

Dougal's expression hardened. "The story they told you in school of the Ancient War is only a shell of the truth. Every warrior who fought in the war did so on behalf of one of these immortal creatures. Immortal beings turned on each other and the world was almost destroyed because of it."

"It's not real—" Yom insisted.

"The war was never won, the conflict never resolved between the immortals. By splitting the world in two, Wacachan merely made it impossible for the immortals to bring their legions across Okeanus to restart the battle.

"Do you recall how the war ended the first time?" Dougal watched Yom patiently as she realized the question was addressed to her.

Of course she remembered the history she had been taught in school, that an earthquake of unprecedented size had ruptured the very ground in two, and the treacherous waters of Okeanus had done the rest of the work of separating the two halves. But Dougal was asking about Eden's story. Yom's brow furrowed as she tried to remember the details, the drops of the story dangerously close to slipping through her hands. It was something unthinkable, Eden had said.

"The gods killed a titan." Dougal pressed on in her silence. The mention of gods and titans took Yom by surprise each time she heard it. "And the titans have never forgotten. They have been biding their time, calculating a way to bring legions across Okeanus and seek their revenge."

The distrust of Panchaia had been sewn deeply into the fabric of Arcadia, and it had always seemed like a tool to keep the House of Flowing Waters in power, but it could also push Arcadians to support a war they had no personal stake in, if for no reason other than to stop Panchaia from doing the same. Yom leaned forward on the table with her head in her hands. Gods and titans, improbable yet menacing, swirled together in her mind, visions of Amaurosis-fueled legions and killing fields strewn with bodies.

"I told you she couldn't handle it," Quia said softly.

Yom poured herself another mugful of the spirits, and sprinkled a pinch of powder in it for safe measure. "If what you're saying is...real, even if they can create a legion with it, they have no way to get to Panchaia." Okeanus remained, the notion of crossing it still unimaginable.

"One of the uses of Amaurosis is that it can reveal certain...abilities." Dougal spoke slowly.

"Dougal," Quia warned.

Dougal ignored him. "Occasionally a human is born with an echo of a god's original lifeforce. The ancient name of this lifeforce is *numen*. These rare humans are known as numenborn."

"What kind of abilities?" Yom narrowed her eyes.

"Several. The main one of them being access to the god's power whose numen echoes in their own. It could be influence over the weather: wind or rain, for example. Or influence over the mind and body: sexuality, sorcery."

Yom snorted. "That's nonsense." If there was someone with those kinds of abilities, Cernunnos and his Stags would have more resistance controlling Inisfail, and the entire province of Ibernia.

"Another ability that I don't think even the World Tree anticipated is that numenborn are able to navigate the crossing of Okeanus."

Unable to hold back any longer, Yom laughed. "Where are they?" She looked around emphatically. "There's no one in Inisfail who can control the weather. Let alone sail across Okeanus."

"The right person has not tried yet," Quia muttered.

"I assure you, they are real," Dougal said. "The titans have cut off Arcadia from the gods completely. The humans who grow up here know nothing of their origin. Numenborn live and die without ever knowing of their true nature."

"Except now they need one," Quia muttered darkly. "It sounds like there is a deal between the House of Flowing Waters and the House of Oak. He grows Amaurosis, and the Queen provides the numenborn. It sounds like—" Quia sucked in a breath. "They've *already* found the numenborn," he said through his exhale.

Dougal put a hand on Quia's shoulder.

"It's all my fault."

"There's no point in dwelling on the past. What matters is what we do about it now."

Quia shook his head. "The exchange sounds like it will happen at something called Lupercalia. Do you know what that is?"

Yom rolled her eyes. How could a royal apprentice not be aware of one of the Queen's longest standing traditions? But something else he had said caught her attention. *House of Oak.* As if the House of Flowing Waters was not the only dominion in Arcadia.

"Yes and no. Lupercalia is a ceremonial feast held on the last night of the Feria inside the House of Flowing Waters. But the House has always kept it secretive."

Yom processed everything they said. If the House of Flowing Waters was the House of the Queen, that meant the House of Oak was the House of Ibernia, of Inisfail. Of Cernunnos.

"Wait." The room around Yom threatened to spin. "You can't mean that Cernunnos is one of these—"

"Titans." Dougal nodded firmly. "They have grown adept at hiding themselves among the humans. They have learned over many centuries that Arcadia works better for them when they govern from the shadows."

"And the Queen?"

"The Queen is human. The House of Flowing Waters united Arcadia under a human government."

The time before the House of Flowing Waters was a dark patch of Arcadian history. Under constant threat of barbarians and marauders, warlords provided safety in urban strongholds in exchange for an absolute and bloodthirsty rule. Yom realized what Dougal was implying.

"The warlords—"

"Titans," Dougal confirmed.

"No." Yom spoke mostly to herself as her world spun out of control. "No," she repeated without conviction as she combed through it. Cernunnos, centuries—millenia—old, if this was to be believed, ruling over them like cattle.

It was too ridiculous to entertain, but certain truths could not be ignored. The voice he had used in the room with the triarii, sounds no human could make. The way Cernunnos seemed to know every going-on in the province without being told.

"This is a lot to take in." Dougal's voice was gentle as he watched Yom, but she was drifting further away. "But we need to get to the numenborn before Cernunnos's and the Queen's deal comes to pass. It's the only way to—"

Cernunnos knows everything without being told. Which meant he might already know where she had been that day, where she was at that very moment. Yom stood suddenly. The ground was unsteady beneath her. "I need to go."

"You can't leave, you're a part of this now." Dougal held her forearm.

"I'm not a part of anything." She sounded less forceful than she wished. "I wanted the truth, and if what you told me is true, I am getting as far away from it as possible."

"Let her go." Distaste was thick in Quia's voice. "She can bury her head underground until she suffocates from it."

"However it came to be, you can help us do something about this." Dougal kept a firm grip on her arm.

"We don't need her help," Quia insisted.

"Quia is right." *For once,* Yom added in her head.

"You can't run from this." Dougal spoke with certainty. "If they have the numenborn already, then it's a matter of time before they gather legions. The Stags that are Bound will be the first to be enlisted."

Soldiers, Cernunnos had called them. Yom wrenched her arm out of his grip, refusing to listen to any more.

"What about the boy? The one who was just Bound?" Dougal pressed. "Is he to be used as a pawn in a war he has no part in?"

Yom's shoulder twitched at the mention of Moss. "I'll take him with me. We will find asylum in another province. Commute our debt."

"And when they start growing Amaurosis there? When that province turns over its people and the Amaurosis legions are assembled? Where will you run then?" Dougal questioned. "You can't just turn away from learning something like this."

Yom had been running away from far more than this for a long time. The world had turned its back on her, and she intended to return the favor. "I can and I will." She twisted her arm out of his grip.

"Eden would have wanted you to help us." Dougal's tone was beseeching.

"Let her go—" Quia insisted.

"You can't do this on your own!" Dougal raised his voice for the first time at Quia. "And one of us needs to stay here to keep an eye on Cernunnos." He turned back to Yom. "There are so few of us left who have kept the truth alive. You've seen what happens when people cross the titans. Do you really want to leave the fate of Arcadia up to them?" Yom knew it was Eden he meant, when he spoke of people crossing titans.

"You've already admitted you don't know the first thing about what happened to Eden," Yom said with as much venom as she could muster.

"I am so sorry I couldn't protect her. But if she were here, she would do everything in her power to prevent thousands of innocents from being led to slaughter."

"Lucky for her she didn't live to see it," Yom said coldly. She yanked the door open, and ran.

YOM RACED THROUGH BACK ROUTES TOWARDS THE CUT. She cataloged everything she needed to pack before leaving, and rehearsed the reason she would give to allow an opening long enough for her and Moss to stow away on a transport that would cross province lines. As long as they crossed the Ibernia border, Cernunnos could not follow them into another province without inciting war. He may send Stags after them, but Yom knew how they operated. She could evade them long enough to figure out a new plan.

Her hands shook as she pulled out her set of keys and looked for the one that fit the rusted side door. Just as it was squeaking open, a strong hand grabbed her shoulder and spun her around, directly into a cloud of powder.

The last thing she heard was a voice sneer, "Antlers up, Bluefingers."

Yom woke to the harsh smell of smoke and the crackle of fire. She opened her eyes and saw the tree roots that snaked through Cernunnos's private study beneath the oak tree. Pushing her hands into the rough wool rug, she sat up.

"Thank you for joining us, Bluefingers." Cernunnos's hulking frame stood straight ahead of her, silhouetted by the fire. The three black triarii stood with their hoods drawn to Cernunnos's left. And in front of Cernunnos, gripped by his gnarled hands and barely reaching his torso, was Moss.

At the sight of Moss, the contents of Yom's stomach suddenly traveled back up and she lurched onto all fours, heaving.

Hands yanked her up to standing from behind. "Sorry about the sickness," Lucan's voice slithered into her ear as he pulled her back against him. "Unfortunate side effect of the powder I gave you." His voice raised another urge to heave, but she swallowed it down, clutching her stomach. Lucan left her standing there and took up his place on Cernunnos's right.

"You've been very curious lately," Cernunnos said lightly. "So I wanted to invite you here, for this demonstration."

"I don't know what you're talking about." Yom spoke even though she knew it was pointless. Whatever was about to happen was past negotiation.

Cernunnos squeezed Moss's shoulder even tighter. "Allow me to show you. Since the boy has recovered so quickly from his Binding, he'll start to make himself useful to me." Cernunnos pushed Moss down to his knees. Moss's eyes shined as they looked up at Yom.

"Wait—" Yom's voice broke, "He hasn't done anything, just let him go."

"Perhaps he has done nothing, but it appears you require a more forceful lesson in disobeying me."

Yom's stomach dropped, her worst fears unfolding before her eyes.

"Lucan." Cernunnos jerked his head at him.

Lucan opened his coat and pulled out something green and white. As the firelight danced on it, Yom realized it was a stalk of the young Amaurosis, bundled with a vine of Moonflower. She moved to step forward and intervene, but two of the triarii had moved behind her, and suddenly her arms were pinned behind her back. Lucan handed the stalk to the third triarii who remained by Cernunnos's side. The third triarii pulled back his hood and the dim light illuminated the ridged surface of his scars.

Misho stepped up to the hearth and let the stalks be licked by the flames until they caught fire. The room was silent as the bundle burned with a violet flame, the remains gathering in the triarii's outstretched palm. In seconds, it was nothing but ash.

"Please don't," Yom begged. "Please, I'll do whatever you want." No one turned to her.

Misho walked to kneel at eye level in front of Moss.

Yom was shouting now, telling Moss to close his eyes and hold his breath, but she could no longer see him.

Misho held his palm up in front of the boy and blew the ash into Moss's face. Yom's limbs were heavy with dread, her weight held up almost entirely by the triarii behind her. Misho leaned back on his heels and Yom finally saw Moss. His eyes fluttered open but his pupils were dilated, almost his whole eye engulfed in black. Misho trailed his thumb from Moss's forehead down his nose and over his lips. Moss looked at the triarii like the entire world existed in Misho's eyes.

"Hello," Misho gripped his chin. "Stand." Moss stood with unnerving calm. Misho drew a knife from a sheath hidden somewhere on his leg and handed it to Moss.

"Draw blood from yourself," he instructed.

Moss held the knife and drew it in a delicate line up his forearm without breaking eye contact with the triarii. Yom watched in horror, and spared a glance to Cernunnos to see a look of smug satisfaction on his face.

It came to Yom with a sickening lurch. The reason they grew the Moonflower. *It's powerful for its gift of suggestibility.* What good is hyper strength without the ability to control and direct the one who wields it?

"Very good. Now, attack." The triarii turned and motioned towards Yom. The other two triarii dropped her and she collapsed onto all fours again. Moss gripped the knife and walked towards Yom.

"Moss, don't do this," she pleaded. "It's me, Yom." Moss twitched but continued walking towards her. Yom repeated his name over and over until he was in striking distance. Moss swiped the knife through the air, and Yom flipped backwards out of the blade's path.

"Moss, this isn't you, this is Amaurosis. It's just something they've given you!"

Moss jabbed the knife at her gut. Yom dodged and pulled the hand with the knife behind his back, putting enough pressure on his shoulder that he had to drop it.

"Moss, please," she whispered desperately. His other hand swung back, and Yom didn't move quick enough to miss it. His nails cut into her cheek. The scratches burned, and Yom felt a warm trickle of blood. He whipped around and clawed at her with his bare hands. She blocked him with her forearms and tried to get behind him again to pin both arms. After dodging a few more blows she got a good foothold behind him and brought them down to the floor, one arm holding both of his and one arm squeezing around his neck just tight enough to cut off his circulation.

Moss thrashed, but she kept hold of him until his movements slowed and his body went limp. Yom rolled him off of her and caught her breath.

"Beautiful," Cernunnos said from the other side of the room.

"Imagine what it will be like when it's fully matured."

Misho began walking towards Moss's still unconscious body, and Yom leaned over to shield it.

"Enough," she huffed, meeting Cernunnos's eyes. "You've had your demonstration."

"Yes, I have." He jerked his chin at Lucan.

Lucan pulled her to her feet and restrained her against the wall as the scarred triarii examined Moss more closely. Misho felt for the boy's pulse and his breathing, and opened his eyelids to see his pupils.

"He's still alive, but his pulse is slow," Misho addressed Cernunnos. "We will have to test the dosage again at full maturity."

Cernunnos nodded.

Moss began to groan and squirm but Misho shushed him, hands still holding his head. Misho's face flashed with remorse.

"And now, Bluefingers, it's time for your demonstration."

Yom watched in a daze as Misho twisted Moss's head to an unnatural angle. With a faint crack, the triarii unceremoniously snapped Moss's neck. Yom gasped as her body went numb, and she felt herself tunneling away from it, retreating to a place where something like this could not hurt her. She was in her body and she wasn't, seeing someone who couldn't be her hunched over on the floor. But when she looked out, it was through the eyes of this broken shell of a person.

"You think I don't know you've been sneaking around?" Cernunnos's voice boomed over a wailing sound. It was sharp and anguished. "I know everything." Cernunnos's voice morphed again, and Yom could hear its truth. The roar of a stag, the pounding of hoofs, the rattling collision of antlers. "Do not cross me again."

Yom slid to the ground, guilt drowning her. The ghost of something broken reawakened in her, its jagged edges demanding to be felt. *Your fault your fault your fault.* Vaguely, she realized that the wailing noise was coming from herself.

Two of the triarii began to drag away his body, but Yom lunged for it. She tried to keep a hold of him, but he was slipping right through her fingers. Desperate to hold onto anything, she latched onto the sleeve of his tunic, the same yellow one as the day they met. The hem ripped, a fragment squeezed in Yom's hand, as the triarii hoisted his body off the floor, and carried it out of the room.

Cernunnos stepped directly in front of her. She looked up to meet his cold gray eyes. "Your powders make you too valuable to kill, for now," he said softly, in his normal voice, "but there are other ways to make you obey if needed." He began to step past her but paused. "Don't even think about going near the boy from the Archives." Cernunnos sauntered out of the room, hands clasped behind his back, as if he hadn't just executed a boy.

Someone picked Yom up off the ground and led her up the stairs. When she registered a hand holding her arm, she looked back to see Lucan.

"How could you?" she hissed.

"This will pass," he said simply. "He's just one boy."

"It's not just about Moss." Yom pulled her arm out of his grip. "This whole thing is wrong."

Lucan nudged her to keep walking up the stairs until they reached the top and rounded the tree. The garden was dark, a faint outline of the night sky visible through the glass roof.

"You've completely lost your mind." Yom shoved him. "Whatever he's promised you isn't worth it."

"I honestly thought you would be excited. This would have been a huge opportunity for us." Lucan steadied her and squared his body to her. "We could have made a place for ourselves in the world. Together." Somehow the way he said it made it sound like he still believed it was possible.

"I don't want a place in the world Cernunnos is offering." As the words left her, she realized she meant them with every fiber of her cursed being.

"Have it your way then, stay at the bottom. Just don't get in my way." Lucan shouldered past her.

"Where are you going?" Yom shouted after him.

"Gotta take care of your little boyfriend." He smiled cruelly. "If you wanted more attention, you should have just said so."

Yom's stomach threatened to turn again. The crack of Moss's neck was still ringing in her ears, the wound of Lucan's betrayal still fresh. And now, he threatened Quia. The apprentice was a pain in her ass, but she didn't want anything to happen to him; she couldn't handle another life on her conscience. Quia seemed to be the only person who would do something about the Amaurosis—Amaurosis that would turn kids like Moss into soldiers. The sound of his neck snapping rang louder and louder in her ears as Lucan walked away, until it was all she could hear. Until it was a thousand necks snapping, of a thousand kids that were her age when she was Bound: pawns in a war they had no part in. The sound was a thundering roar, rushing all around her, breaking down every illusion that she could run away from this. In its wake, it illuminated the boundary between before, and *after*. And now, wading through the murky after, all she knew for certain was that it was time to run towards something.

Going after Lucan—after Quia—would be crossing a line. She would be a deserter. The only way she would be able to return to Inisfail—to the Cut and the home she had created there—would be in chains. *I'm already in chains*, she thought bitterly about the warm metal that circled her neck. But there were other provinces—friendlier ones to the south, according to the interprovincial travelers—if Yom could stay alive long enough to reach one. There was one thing she knew for certain: if the war reopened between Arcadia and Panchaia, no one would be safe. Especially not someone Bound.

Yom counted each breath after Lucan's tall blond head disappeared into the tunnel, waiting until it was safe to break into a sprint, and head him off at the Archives.

YOM WATCHED FROM SEVERAL LENGTHS BACK, PEERING AROUND A stone corner, as Lucan banged on the servant door of the Archives. A female apprentice opened the door and jumped when she saw Lucan's frame looming in the doorway.

"C-can I h-help you?" she stuttered.

"Just here to see Dougal's apprentice," Lucan pushed the door open, knocking the woman off balance in the process. Yom followed with the lightest steps she could manage, getting the toe of her boot in between the door and its frame before it closed behind him.

"Where is he?" Lucan asked from the other end of the hall.

The door squeaked, and Yom barely slipped inside an open chamber before Lucan turned to look behind him.

Yom followed from a safe distance as he took broad strides down the hall of office chambers. Lucan silently drew his shortswords from their leather scabbards. So this was to be another execution, without a chance for Quia to fight. Yom tried to formulate a plan, but her thoughts were flitting about too quickly. It was like trying to catch a fly. Her hands fiddled with her powderbelt, and she realized her answer was right in front of her.

At the end of the hall, she saw an office with a light on, the door cracked. Lucan opened it and stepped in, Yom hovering just out of sight on the other side.

Quia stood next to a table, tying off scrolls before slipping them into a pack using only sparse lantern light.

"Going somewhere?" Lucan asked.

"What are you doing here?" Quia asked, surprised, but the candlelight was already reflecting off Lucan's shortswords.

"You've been poking around in Stag business," Lucan sneered. "You're going to regret it. Or, I guess you won't feel much of anything when I'm done here."

Yom tipped the door open, vial of powder ready in her hand. But instead of attacking Quia, Lucan whipped around and pinned Yom to the wall, knocking the wind half out of her.

"Ah ah." He pushed into Yom's wrist, the tip of his shortsword inches from her cheek. "Just couldn't stay out of it, could you?" Lucan muttered bitterly.

"I'm just doing what you're too weak to do," she huffed through gritted teeth.

Lucan pinned her harder, leaning in so that their faces were only a few inches apart. "You're throwing everything away! You'll be hunted down for this. There's no going back." Yom heard the turmoil in Lucan's voice, saw that on some level it was hurting him that she was doing this. But he was right, there was no going back. No going back to a time before the triarii skulked around the Cut, before she discovered the Amaurosis and Cernunnos's plans for it, before Moss—

Yom bit her lip and stayed limp in Lucan's hold. She would have one instant to put all of her strength into an attack. "I can't go back," she whispered, one last unspoken entreaty for him to understand. Then, she gathered her strength, and thrashed her captive wrist.

"Quia, look away!" Yom shouted as she smashed a vial of powder into Lucan's cheek and closed her eyes. She had dubbed the powder Luminix, and designed it to explode with light upon contact. Even through her eyelids the world turned a hot white, and Lucan let out a mangled scream. Her wrist was released and the shortswords clattered to the floor as the light dimmed. She squinted her eyes open to see Lucan holding his own face, blood trickling through his hand. She had about three minutes before he would regain his sight.

"Quia, now!" Yom waved for Quia to follow her. Quia, looking sufficiently confused and startled, slung his pack over his shoulders and started to round the table.

"You little rat, you'll pay for this," Lucan seethed, reaching a hand blindly out towards Yom. She took the opportunity to pull Lucan to the ground using his own maneuver.

"What do you think of my little powders now?" Yom wrestled to keep Lucan contained, her knees digging into each of his arms. His blond hair was disheveled and his eyes were vacant, two tracks of tears spreading from them. She groped on her belt for another vial with her free hand, hoping she counted correctly to identify her Somnarium, instant sleep powder. Holding the vial up to her mouth, she yanked the cork off with her teeth and emptied it in a slash over Lucan's face, the dark blue powder coating him as Yom held her breath. He twitched for a moment as it invaded him, but then his movements slowed and eventually ceased.

Yom's body relaxed and she pushed herself off of him. Scrambling to stand, the full weight of what she had done hit her. Lucan, slippery and conniving as he was, had been her oldest ally in the Stags. Now, she had no one, and she had just crossed Cernunnos again, to save someone who was practically a stranger. She looked over her shoulder at Quia, who watched her with a hint of shock, and she saw the path in front of them take shape—the only path she could take—now that she had set her entire world on fire.

Quia brushed off his shock and extended a hand to help her up. She gripped it and felt soft skin, but with faint callouses. Not bothering to let go, she pulled Quia behind her as she hurried down the corridor they had come in, bursting out the servant door of the Archives into a mist-filled night.

"Can you get a message to Dougal?" Yom asked, yanking Quia into a run. She led them through the back routes until she could taste blood in her throat, attracted like a magnet to the one place she was confident Cernunnos knew nothing about.

"Ask him to meet us at Eden's laboratory," she said softly as Quia kept up with her. For all his previous skepticism and snark, he merely nodded.

THE PLAIN RED DOOR WITH THE FAINT GOLD PAINT OF A CHEMIST'S symbol was covered in ghostly white cobwebs. It was situated on an unassuming stretch of cobblestone in the artisan district, though for Yom everything about it was riddled with memories. She batted the webs and their spiders away as she thumbed through her keys for the one she had kept all these years. It fit the lock of the door with an easy click and the door swung open without a fight, as if it hadn't been six years since she had left without any intention of ever returning.

The dust kicked up in a cloud when she stepped inside. It was only lit by faint moonlight passing in through the grime coated windows, but the place was just as Yom had left it: a mausoleum. Before she had too much time to think, a shadow passed in front of the windows. Yom opened the door before Dougal even had the chance to knock.

"You were right," she told him, once the door was shut again. "Finding this, this—" she paused, still unable to say the word.

"Numenborn," Dougal offered.

"Yes. Finding them. What do you need me to do?"

"What about Moss?" Quia asked.

Yom pulled the rip of yellow linen out of her pocket. Quia took a step back, and Yom met his eyes. They were full of condemnation.

"It was my fault," Yom said shakily. "If I hadn't been sneaking around, sticking my nose where it didn't belong, he would still be alive. Cernunnos killed him to punish me."

"It's not your fault." Dougal's hand braced her shoulder. She looked up at him to see the sadness she had noticed before etched into the fine lines of his face. It seemed like it was a permanent part of his expression, the more she understood this side of Dougal. "This is Cernunnos's doing."

Yom shook her head. "No, it's my fault he was Bound. I should have tried harder to stop him. I thought he would settle into the Stags and still have at least half of a life. Now he has nothing."

"Not everything is in our control." Dougal's other hand found her shoulder, and he held her steady. It suddenly struck Yom what it must be like to be in Dougal's position in the Stags, never committing violence but forced to witness it, because no one else would. "I should have come up with an excuse not to let Cernunnos Bind him. I am as much to blame. I was too busy protecting my own position in his organization."

Yom shook her head and looked down, resolute. "He was killed because of me. But I won't allow his death to mean nothing. I won't allow any of their deaths to mean nothing." The memories of the last evening Yom spent in this laboratory threatened to surface, but she pushed them down, rubbed Moss's linen between her fingers to distract herself.

Yom knotted the scrap of yellow around her wrist, and asked, with a determination boundless and steady like the night, "What's the plan?"

V

All aboard the Morningstar

DOUGAL REACHED INTO HIS ROBES AND HELD UP TWO GOLD-FOILED tickets. "I hoped that was what you were going to say."

Yom gaped at him. *"You* have Morningstar tickets?"

"Morningstar?" Quia asked.

"I've been saving them for something important. I think this qualifies," Dougal said. "Cernunnos will be checking every transport and caravan that leaves the province. This is the best way out."

Yom swallowed. She still didn't understand the limits of Cernunnos's influence, the boundaries of his power. "And if he already knows?"

Dougal put the fine cardstock of the ticket in her hand. "He limits his own power by cloaking himself as mortal. He knows only what his servants tell him, and what he can sense through his muffled numen connection." Dougal tilted his chin down, and something passed between Yom and him. "If you can make it onto the train undetected, by the time he puts the pieces together, it will be too late to catch you. He's a titan, but even his power is not endless."

Yom nodded slowly, gaze drifting down to the tickets now sitting in her hand like a promise. The gold foil gleamed in the faint light, the Morningstar's name written in grand lettering, with the symbol of the traveling star embossed lightly. She had only taken the Morningstar a couple times, and only for Stag business, paid for by Cernunnos. The tickets cost a small fortune. It was a brilliant idea; the interprovincial train was the transit of choice for Lords and wealthy merchants—no one would be looking for a disgraced, fugitive Stag on it.

"What is a Morningstar?" Quia repeated, then turned to Yom. "And I still don't trust you."

"Quia, hush. We're all on the same side." Dougal sighed.

"Were you not paying attention when I saved your ass from Lucan?"

"He only came after me because of you!" Quia shouted before Dougal shushed him again. "And I easily could have taken him."

Yom snorted. "Doubtful."

"Enough," Dougal silenced them both. "You two will board this train at first light. Yom, you will help Quia make it to Cataracta safely, and once you're there, Quia will intercept the numenborn at the one place we know they will be: Lupercalia."

"I can get there myself—"

"You don't even know what the Morningstar is. You've probably never left Inisfail."

"You have no idea where I've been."

Dougal huffed in exasperation. "Quia, the provinces are a dangerous place. You need to go with someone who knows how to navigate them."

"And all I have to do is get him to Cataracta, before Lupercalia?" Yom asked Dougal. He nodded. She leaned back on her heels, satisfied. If they were lucky, the journey would only take a week. Then, she would find a friendlier province willing to commute her debt. She could start over with a clear conscience, and a hopefully boring future ahead of her. No legions, no wars. Perhaps she could open up her own laboratory.

"And if Cernunnos comes looking for her? You know, since she is Bound and all?"

"I'll worry about that." Yom dismissed him with a wave of her hand. Once she crossed the Ibernia border, she just needed to evade capture—and stay alive—until she could strike a new bargain, in a friendlier province. Simple, she assured herself.

"I must leave you two." Dougal abruptly pulled Quia into a crushing hug.

"What will happen to you—" Quia paused as Dougal whispered in his ear.

"I'll be just fine, son." Dougal said loud enough for Yom to hear as he pulled away and squeezed his shoulder.

"And you." He turned to Yom. He approached her for a hug and Yom tried to back away, but his hands caught her first. "The Bind is a double-sided coin," he whispered as he reeled her into an embrace. Yom hardly had time to question what he meant.

With nothing more than a curt nod, Dougal slipped out the door onto the empty street.

"Strange guy," Yom muttered, looking down at the gleaming foil of the tickets. "If we're leaving at first light, we need to change clothes."

YOM STEPPED INTO THE VAULTED GLASS AND BRASS ENCLOSURE OF THE train station with a disgruntled Quia at her side. She had swapped her waistcoat and trousers for a flowing skirt and petticoat that had belonged to Eden, with enough room to keep her powderbelt buckled underneath. She wore a light camisole and a lace smock on top, with her coat fastened over it. The collar just managed to cover her torc. A quick application of the beauty powders that had remained untouched in Eden's room hadn't hurt either. Crushed pearl powder for the cheeks, beetroot stain for the lips and a sweet perfume of lady's mantle had transformed her into someone almost unrecognizable. That along with black lace gloves to hide her stained fingers, and she was satisfied she would be able to board the train unnoticed.

But as she walked through the station, Dougal's strange whisper repeated itself in her ear. *The Bind is a double-sided coin.* It had been so quick she couldn't be sure she hadn't imagined it. She hardly knew anything about the foreign piece of metal molded around her neck, other than it indicated to the world that she wasn't much more than Cernunnos's property.

Quia plodded along next to her, a spare inky velvet cloak from the laboratory fastened around his neck, comically short on his taller frame. Yom had given him the buttoned shirt she had been wearing beneath her waistcoat, and found a red silk scarf to tie around his neck to make him look wealthy enough to blend in on the train. Yom had insisted that their best cover would be as a merchant's son and his female companion. She had spent more than enough time with the girls who worked in the pleasure rooms to pull off the act.

The station was still waking up, full of early morning commuters leaving and arriving to the city for work, as well as various wealthy merchants in their heavy silk coats and robes. The first drops of light were seeping in through the glass walls, the world outside a soft, deep blue. The station contained five tracks: four that spanned each direction through Ibernia from Inisfail, and the fifth for the Morningstar, the only interprovincial line that came this far north.

"You don't have anyone else you need to say goodbye to?" Yom asked Quia through a falsely cheery smile as they walked through the station, standing closer than either enjoyed.

"No," Quia said gruffly. "Why do you care? I don't see people lining up to hug you goodbye either."

"No reason, just think it's odd that your only friend is an old man."

Quia stopped her with a prod to her collarbone. "Let's get one thing straight: we're not going to become friends. I meant it when I said that I still don't trust you. You just keep up your end of the deal and we will go our separate ways as soon as possible."

Before Yom could snipe back, a high-pitched whistle interrupted the quiet shuffle of feet and early morning whispers.

"We're going to be late for our train, *Princess*," Yom sneered as she started walking again.

"Don't call me that," Quia bit out. Yom relished his look of annoyance. About to poke him further, she noticed a cluster of royal legionaries prowling the edge of the hall.

"Stay close," Yom whispered, weaving her hand through Quia's arm. "Without the royal robes, you're a fair target for blackcoats." She nudged her head towards them. "It's a matter of time before Cernunnos realizes we left the province and puts out a bounty on our heads."

"Why do you call the legionaries blackcoats?" Quia asked under his breath.

"The fact that you don't know just shows you wouldn't last one day on your own in the provinces." She gave his forearm a condescending pat and noticed that it was quite toned. Archivists shouldn't get much exercise beyond carrying large tomes around the Archives—an activity that wouldn't produce that kind of muscle.

All aboard the Morningstar, repeat all aboard the Morningstar, destination Traiana, an amplified voice echoed through the hall's pipe system. The fifth track came into view with the Morningstar sitting in it, steam already billowing from its head. A large brass lamp adorned the helm, the oil inside already lit and casting shafts of light over the silhouettes of its boarding passengers. The train was at least twice as big as the trains that ferried people through the province, lacquered black with gold detailing and two levels of wide open windows. The symbol of the morningstar that was on the ticket was also painted in gold on the steam engine car in larger-than-life size. The Morningstar would take them about a third of the way through the provinces, to Traiana. From there, Yom didn't know the route as well but figured they would find a transport with the modest purse Dougal had given them. Traiana was a notoriously ruthless city that made its wealth through the trade of men as fighters, entertainers, and slaves; it was not a place she planned to spend any length of time.

They entered the line of passengers waiting to board, inching towards the conductor, who was punching the same gold-foiled tickets she had in her pocket. She casually scanned for the blackcoats and saw them huddling now. A glance in the other direction almost made Yom's heart stop. The hulking Stag bollocks entered the far side of the station.

"Put your arm around my waist," Yom said through a smile.

"Why?"

Yom was ready to strangle him. In a move that she hoped appeared more natural than it felt, she reached back and guided his hand to wrap around her waist. His hand was broad and warm, his fingers flexing the only sign of his resistance. Yom leaned into him and prayed they blended in.

As they approached the conductor, Yom focused on the gold buttons and piping on his black uniform. She met his eyes and attempted a friendly smile as she handed over the tickets, but her palms were sweating and her heart was beating too quickly. She comforted herself with the knowledge that at this point, she had nothing left to lose but her own life. And she had stopped caring much for that a long time ago.

The conductor smiled at her beneath a thick white mustache as he punched their tickets, the same way he had done for every other passenger. "Welcome aboard," he said pleasantly as he handed them back their tickets.

Yom dipped her chin and walked up the steep steps to board, Quia right behind her. As soon as they were in the hallway of the car, she exhaled and shoved his hand off.

They shuffled through the car, surrounded by shining lacquered panels and gold trim, crystal chandeliers twinkling above them and illuminating the upper level of compartments. Quia gawked as he took in the spectacle, and Yom elbowed him.

"At least try to act like you've been here before," she hissed.

Yom looked on each side for an empty compartment, also using the opportunity to look through the compartment doors, out the train windows to make sure no blackcoats or Stags were nearing the train. Because she was focusing all of her concentration on the flashes of the station outside the window, she didn't notice the person in front of her turn around.

"Hello there, sweetheart, are you lost?" A young man with light brown hair slicked neatly back and tanned skin stood in front of her. He wore elegant black robes that hung open, a dark gray waistcoat beneath with a rose gold pocket watch tucked into it. His brows were thick and his nose long and curved down at its tip. If Yom had to guess, she would say he was nobility. The merchants preferred gaudier clothes.

"Just looking for an empty compartment for my companion and I." Yom stalled in the aisle and felt Quia bump into her, also distracted.

"How delightful. I'm Damian." The nobleman held out a white gloved hand to Quia. Quia looked at it as if it was a foreign object and not an outstretched hand. Yom elbowed him again. Quia finally reached out and gave it a brief shake.

"Smart of you to bring a snack." Damian was clearly speaking to Quia, but he looked at Yom as if she was a roast pig laid out for him to eat. "That's an interesting necklace you have there, sweetheart—" he reached a gloved hand out to touch the tip of her torc peeking out from the lapels of her coat, but Quia stepped in between them.

"She's not available," Quia said firmly. The steam engine let out a distant roar and the machine came to life beneath them. The whistle rang and the train chugged forward with a jump.

Damian removed his hand in surrender. "My mistake, friend. But don't hold it against me. This train travel is unbearably droll. I can always use company." At this, he snuck a glance back at Yom.

"No harm, no foul," Quia said with a tight smile before reaching for Yom's wrist and pulling her with him around their new friend Damian.

Once they had passed into the next car, Quia dropped her wrist and Yom took the lead again, relieved to see them pulling out of the glass enclosure of the station. Finally, she found an empty compartment, and yanked on the lever to open the door with a whine. Holding the door open, she waved Quia inside. As he passed, she noticed three burly figures lumbering on the other side of the car in their direction.

"Bloody Okeanus," Yom muttered and launched herself into the compartment behind him, yanking the door closed with her and huddling beneath the door's porthole. She knew these men. The three Bears—as large and hairy as their namesake—worked for Coventina, Cernunnos's sometimes ally, sometimes rival in the neighboring province of Albion. They were her enforcers, and often traveled to negotiate her export of steel and steam power with their words and their fists. Yom tried to slow her heartbeat, and convince herself they were only in Inisfail for trade reasons.

"Something wrong?" Quia asked, amused.

Yom stammered, "Ah—nothing, no—just some—old friends." Quia stared at her. "We didn't part on the best of terms." This was putting it mildly. The last time Yom had seen them there had definitely been some death threats, which had made her grift all the more satisfying. It wasn't her fault they had taken one too many hits to the head and lost a few too many critical thinking skills. Anyone traveling with that many gold pieces on them was asking to be conned.

"The three men," Yom whispered, "the ones that look like bears, can you see if they're still in this car?" Quia stood and leaned over Yom to press his forehead against the glass.

"I think they kept walking."

Yom exhaled and stood up.

"Care to explain?" Quia asked.

"Not really, no." Yom brushed off her skirt and sat down on the burgundy velvet bench opposite Quia. Hopefully those three men would be getting off in Albion's capital, Northumbria, the second stop of this train. Although with their jobs, they could be going anywhere. She swore again to herself.

Quia shook his head and muttered something under his breath.

"Yes?"

"Nothing. Just wondering how many people we're going to run into that you haven't screwed over."

"How do you know they didn't screw me over?"

"Because I've met you." Quia looked at her like he truly despised her. He thought she could be broken by his opinion of her, but she would prove him wrong.

"Alright, let's hear it. Tell me what you think of me. Clearly you need to get it off your chest."

Quia stayed silent for a moment. Yom challenged him with her eyes.

"You're a powderhead and a thug. You only care about yourself."

Yom laughed. "That's all you got?"

"You're the reason Moss is dead."

"I know that," she snapped before she could catch herself. One thing she would not do was let Quia see any of his words affecting her. "It's going to hurt one day."

Quia looked as if he was trying hard not to take her bait, but his curiosity got the better of him. "Hurt when?"

"When you fall off your high horse. You're quite judgemental for someone who knows so little about how the world works. I'm sure even your beloved Dougal has his vices."

"No, he doesn't." Quia's tone was sharp.

Yom shrugged. "He has to have one. He couldn't have gotten that close to Cernunnos without a weakness. He likes to have control over you. *All* of you."

"What's your weakness then?"

"I thought you had me all figured out?" Yom smiled wickedly before turning to look out the window. They traveled on elevated tracks through the city, the ride bumpy and a bit dizzying as the train hurtled forward, twenty feet above the ground.

"I'm sure I could guess."

"I'm sure you couldn't." Yom closed her eyes and rested her head on the padded bench behind her to quell the dizziness.

"I get five guesses."

She opened one eye to see if he was serious. "Three."

"Four."

"Fine. If you can't guess in four tries, you're not allowed to speak for the rest of the train ride, unless I ask you something."

"And if I win, you're not allowed to take any powder for the rest of the ride." Yom grunted. This train ride would last two days. She hadn't gone that long without powder in years. Luckily she didn't think he had any chance of getting it right.

Yom nodded. "Out with it. What are your guesses?"

"You're a powderhead." Quia studied her.

"Wrong. Powders fill a void. They don't create one on their own."

"Parents?" Quia asked as a question.

Yom shook her head. "They're dead." There was a hint of pity in Quia's eyes and she resented it. "Happened a long time ago. Cernunnos knew nothing of them."

"Gambling debt."

Again, Yom shook her head. "I don't make bets I won't win. Which reminds me, you have one more guess." She smirked, already imagining the blissfully silent train ride ahead of them.

"A sibling." Quia paused. "A sibling who got in trouble and needed you," he pressed.

Yom couldn't stop her shoulder from twitching. "No one needs me anymore." She pulled her gloves tighter on her hands.

"That's it." Quia snapped his fingers. "Someone did need you, and you let them down."

Instead of answering, Yom leaned in. "You're out of guesses."

"But my last one was right?"

"Guess you'll never know. Now that's the last I want to hear from you until we get to Traiana," Yom commanded as she brought a pinch of powder up to her nose.

THE TRAIN'S FIRST STOP WAS JUST BEFORE NIGHTFALL, IN ALBION. This was the province Yom was most familiar with, outside of Inisfail, seeing as they shared open trade routes for the most part. It was also the province where her three ursine friends were from, and where she hoped they were leaving. As each figure stepped down off the train and dispersed in different directions on the platform, she scanned for the hulking trio of Bears. To her annoyance, the new passengers boarded and the train pulled away from the platform without any sign of those three having left.

Stomach growling but unable to leave, and too proud to ask Quia to help her get some food, Yom slumped into the seat. She draped her coat over herself as a blanket and tried to find a comfortable position to sleep.

A knock on their compartment door startled her upright. Smiling broadly on the other side of the porthole stood Damian. Quia looked up from the tome he was reading, glasses perched on the bridge of his nose. The gold spectacles framed his eyes well, though Yom decided pointedly not to notice this.

"He's making a scene out there, let him in." Yom sat back and braced herself.

"One stop down, two to go," Damian said as he sat down rather close to Yom. "So, what brought you to Inisfail?" Damian spread out on the bench and stretched an arm behind Yom. She kept herself calm by imagining breaking each of his fingers, slowly.

Quia looked to Yom for a moment before speaking, and she gave a slight nod. She was impressed he still respected the terms of their bet.

"I'm apprenticing to take over my father's merchant business," Quia enunciated each word, managing to sound rather elegant. "I was negotiating powder shipments."

At this Damian leaned forward. "I've heard the stories about the powder from Inisfail, the strongest in all of Arcadia." He licked his lips. "Do you have any with you?"

Quia's eyes flicked to Yom before he spoke. "Afraid not, everything is on a transport. It's meeting me in Traiana." Damian slumped back, disappointed for a moment before he turned his attention to Yom.

"I see, powder isn't your vice. But it seems the Inisfail women have caught your fancy? I've been to every province now, and I can safely say the women in Cataracta are the finest."

Quia looked surprised at his blatant words, as if Yom was not sitting right there. But then he seemed to realize something in what the arrogant lordling had said.

"You've been to Cataracta?"

"I live there. The only reason I'm in these dirty provinces is because my father insisted I travel to all of them before I take over his Lordship."

Yom's ears perked up. A lordling from Cataracta would be a perennial guest at Lupercalia. "Did someone ask for powder?" Yom interrupted, surreptitiously reaching inside the waistband of her skirt to pull out the pouch she kept the Aetherium in. "Silly me, I forgot I brought this."

Damian clapped his hand onto her knee and squeezed. "Atta girl!" he cried. "Great choice." He winked at Quia. Yom poured out a large dose of the powder into her hand and held it up to the lordling.

"What is it?" Damian hesitated a moment.

"Does it matter?" she countered. He smiled deviously and held her hand tight as he inhaled it straight from her palm. The effect was instantaneous. His eyes glazed over and his jaw slackened. Yom sometimes forgot how potent her powder was, having become quite accustomed to its effects.

"Now you were telling us about Cataracta?" Yom pulled Damian's chin to look at her.

"I was?" Damian asked through a haze. Quia was watching the scene on the bench opposite him unfold, almost looking impressed.

"You were." Yom used her most soothing voice as she stroked Damian's hair. It was too fine and a bit oily. "You were just about to tell us about Lupercalia. We heard that the Queen is bringing a special guest this year."

"What guessst?" he slurred.

"The special guest." Quia had caught on to what Yom was doing. He leaned forward with his elbows on his knees. "The one who is doing the demonstration."

"There isss no demonssstration, isss the same asss alwayss."

"What happens during Lupercalia?" A hint of Yom's own curiosity bled into her words.

Damian held a clumsy finger up to his lips. "Iss a sssecret." Yom rolled her eyes. Even gone on powders, the nobility were bred to keep the secrets of the House of Flowing Waters.

"But someone new is joining this year?" Yom pressed.

"No." Damian pushed that same finger against Yom's lips. She tried to pry his hand away but he was surprisingly tense. "This year isss the Queen. She hass never done it before. Hecctorrr takess sssomeone in her place. But not thiss year." He slid his hand over her cheek and dug it into her curls. "You're pretty," he said with a dopey smile spreading on his face.

"Who is Hector?" Yom looked at Quia, who seemed to be weighing this name as well.

Damian's head lolled and his eyes had turned to glass. Yom pulled away and moved to stand up, but before she could lift off the seat, Damian's arms snaked around her and held her as if he was a child and she was the stuffed bear on his bed. From close up his brandy and thyme cologne drenched her nostrils, and the pimples that lined his jaw came into focus.

Quia held in a snicker. Yom sent him a glare that promised death.

"Help me get him off."

Quia shook his head and pointed to his mouth, reminding her of her wish. *I will kill you*, she mouthed. He shrugged and returned to reading his tome.

Resigning that she would be dealing with the drugged lordling on her own, Yom snuck her hand into his robes to check his pockets. She found a heavy purse and a metal flask. Ever generous, she lightened his purse by several coins and tucked it back into his robes. A quick sniff of the flask and she recognized it was a much more expensive spirit than what she normally drank. She took a swig before pushing it into her pack.

The train hit a bump in the tracks and everything jolted. Damian grumbled and adjusted his grip on Yom, but she used the break to slip away. He reached blindly for something and Yom pushed Quia's cloak into his arms. Pulling the balled up cloak close to his chest, he settled back into the seat with a dreamy smile on his face.

Turning in the small compartment, Yom saw Quia had taken up his whole bench with scrolls. Without asking, she pushed a few to the floor to make room for herself. He was about to say something, but instead made a dramatic show of picking the scrolls up and tucking them back into his pack.

"Who is Hector?" Yom asked as she balled her own coat up and shoved it between her head and the corner of the compartment.

"I'm not sure. It could be another Lord..." Quia trailed off.

"Or?"

He turned the tome he was reading towards her. The text was small and cramped on thin, waxy pages. He pointed to an etching of an angular face inlaid in a column of text.

"The inner proceedings of the House of Flowing Waters are kept quite secret," Quia's finger dragged along a line of text as he spoke, "but when the House was first established as the ruling body, the Queen often operated through her procurator." Yom stared at him blankly, not recognizing the word. "A proxy of sorts," he explained. Beneath the etched face, the label read: *Tarquin, procurator of Arcadia's founding ruler, the Virtuous Queen Lucretia.* "Not much is written about them beyond the first few generations of rulers, but it's possible the procurator still exists and maintains a strong presence in the House of Flowing Waters."

"Can I?" Yom reached for the thick volume. Quia shrugged and handed it off to her. She checked the spine and saw *Decisive Battles of Arcadia* foiled in silver on faded navy linen. Flipping through the area near the etching of Tarquin, she vaguely scanned the text and found another inlaid etching of a beautiful woman, with similarly angular features. *The Virtuous Queen Lucretia, founding ruler of Arcadia.* In the paragraphs below the etching, the mention of Lupercalia caught her eye.

It is said that the Virtuous Queen Lucretia, accompanied by her brother Tarquin, walked directly between the two Houses in the midst of battle, dressed in all white with flowers in her hair. Each side was so captivated by her beauty that they ceased their fighting, and not a single sword tainted her with its touch. The Head of each House approached them and they parlayed in the center of the battlefield for eight days. The soldiers on each side feasted and celebrated during the ceasefight. The small buds of the battlefield were given the chance to bloom, and by the end of the eighth day, the field was ripe with the blossoms of new life. The Heads of Houses each addressed their soldiers at the end of this eighth day. They announced that from this moment on, Arcadia would no longer be torn apart in war, but united under one ruler. A Queen who would allow for the independence of each of these Houses, but unite the network of them under the common banner of a new House. She would never marry, as she belonged to the people of Arcadia, body and soul.

It was then that the Queen's companion Tarquin, her future procurator, enacted a ritual, with everyone present as witness, to seal this agreement. This eight day long festival was repeated each year to celebrate the incorporation of

Arcadia, adopting the name of the Ancients's celebration of spring, the Feria. At the end of the eight days, the Queen and her procurator held their same ritual, a reminder of the promise made to Arcadia, and a rejuvenation of its life. Known from then on out as Lupercalia, a time of growth and fertility.

Yom grunted, seeing the sibling familiarity between the two etchings the longer she looked. *Body and soul*, she repeated to herself. What kind of ritual would demonstrate that promise? And who would promise something like that in the first place? Though she supposed it wasn't much different from the torc around her neck.

"What did he mean about someone being taken in the Queen's place?"

Quia glanced at Damian as he started to snore lightly. "I think we need to learn more about what actually happens during Lupercalia."

"Then we're screwed," Yom muttered as her eyelids finally drooped closed.

YOM'S SLEEP WAS RESTLESS, AND SHE WAS PLAGUED WITH THE FAINT feeling of something crawling on her skin. In a half lucid state, she was sitting next to Quia in the train compartment, but looked down to see a small horde of spiders scuttling over her body. She woke with a startle, slapping at her arms and legs for a few adrenaline-filled seconds before she realized there were no spiders.

Next to her, the bench shook, and she looked over to see Quia holding in a laugh. He returned to what he was doing, reading yet another scroll of paper, by now only with candlelight. Yom stretched and rubbed her neck and shoulders to ease the stiffness. Across from her, Damian still slept, a prominent stream of drool escaping down his chin.

Her hunger had turned to a dull ache. She searched the pockets of her coat for any errant food. There were spare pieces of lint, fragments of minerals and the occasional empty vial, until she found something damp and fuzzy, with prickly sharp leaves. It was the Amaurosis stalk she had snipped before they left the herb shop. Heart thumping, she angled away from Quia to extract it. It felt like holding a weapon in her hand, after what she had seen it do to Moss. It almost seemed like it was whispering to her, a scratchy undertone she could barely make out. Yom's hands trembled, and she rushed to open the journal she kept for her formulation scribbles, pressing it between the pages. Instantly the scratching whisper ceased, and Yom breathed a sigh of relief. But a second later, her stomach growled like an angry cat.

Quia grunted and held something up to her. It was a mince pie, sitting primly on a handkerchief. Her stomach bellowed at the sight, and she wasted no time inhaling it in only four bites.

"Thank you," she said mid-chew. Quia nodded without looking up again.

Yom stood and looked out the window, seeing nothing but pitch black, and a quick glance through the door's porthole showed nothing but the dim flicker of the candles illuminating the hallway. Now was as good a time as ever to risk venturing outside the compartment.

"Come on," she grunted as she pulled Damian up and draped his arm over her shoulder. "Time to go back to your compartment." He stirred and pulled against her.

"No," he grumbled. "I want to stay with my friends."

"I don't think they're your friends," Yom muttered under her breath, feeling a drop of pity for the lordling. "Let's go back to your compartment. Your friends will come find you after you've gotten some sleep."

"Hmmm, that sounds nice," Damian sighed.

Yom pulled him along the train car, scanning for an empty compartment. The faint hum of metal on metal and the twinkle of the train's extinguished chandeliers were the only sounds. She had to walk halfway into the next car before she found an empty compartment with an expensive looking leather satchel that matched the elegance of Damian's attire.

"Here we go," she whispered as she ever so gently clicked open his door and guided him inside. "You'll sleep it off and barely remember a thing."

Damian settled onto his bench, splaying his limbs across it.

"Thank you." He reached for Yom's hand before she could leave. She wanted to tell him that he shouldn't be thanking her, but incriminating herself further wouldn't be worth it for a moment of honesty. He let her hand go and fell back into a light snore before she clicked the compartment closed.

Yom stood in the center of the hallway, looking in the direction of their compartment. But morbid curiosity pulled her in the other direction, towards the three Bears. If she could figure out why they were on the train, she could get some reassurance that it had nothing to do with Quia and herself.

Creeping down the hall in a crouch, she heard only sparse whispers about wanton governesses and woeful royal tax policies. She made it to the last passenger car without hearing anything useful, when a hushed voice a little further down the aisle caught her attention.

"The conductor said a passenger with a Stag torc boarded the Morningstar. And she was traveling with a boy who matched the description."

"Well why haven't we seen them yet? Bluefingers don't know we're here." This voice Yom recognized. It was of the leader of the group, who had a special reason to hold a grudge against her.

"The conductor didn't see any stained fingers, maybe she's in disguise."

"Or maybe we're following the wrong Stag," a third voice grumbled.

"No," the leader growled. "She's here." A beat of silence passed before he spoke again. "Tell me again, how much?"

"Five hundred denarii." The voice that answered was smiling.

Yom balked. If she had any doubt of how much Cernunnos's legion of Stags was worth to him, five hundred of Arcadia's solid gold coins settled that.

A whistle of admiration rang out from inside the compartment.

"What I could do with five hundred denarii," the leader mused. "I'd take my lady all the way to the eternal city with that much."

A throat cleared. "But, boss, won't we split it?"

"Yeah, yeah, you'll get your share of the bounty." Yom could practically see the leader waving his hand in dismissal. "I won't lie, boys, I'm going to enjoy this. That two-faced bastard Bluefingers has had it coming. No-good, lying thief." Yom checked off in her mind that some hostility remained from their last run-in. "And what kind of person forces another man's wife?" There it was: the tiny misunderstanding that had come to light during their last run in.

Yom was fuming. She couldn't believe the nerve to say that Yom ever forced herself on anyone, man or woman or else. As if she would ever need to. She had never found gender to be a limiting factor in attraction, and years of experience had taught her how to recognize women who did not feel the same. Yom recalled this Bear's wife had been extremely interested in anyone who *wasn't* her husband, the brute.

After a few seconds, she realized the compartment was silent. Then shuffling and a grunt.

"Of course, boss, it's disgusting."

"She was forced," the third voice confirmed hesitantly. Yom couldn't help letting a muffled snort escape.

"What was that?" The leader growled.

Yom shot from the floor and sprinted through the dark train.

"Remember that bounty I mentioned?" she spoke to Quia in a rush once she clicked the compartment door closed again.

"Tell me again what you heard." Quia tapped his foot.

Yom recounted the overheard conversation again, leaving out the details he had no concern with.

"You're sure they're looking for both of us?" Quia asked. It seemed like he was still coming to terms with being an official enemy of the Stags and a wanted fugitive.

"They're looking for two passengers. Which means you, unless it was someone else who Cernunnos sent Lucan to execute back in Inisfail?"

Quia leaned back and scrubbed his face. "I'm not in the mood for jokes," he said through his hands. "Do you think they will go after Dougal?"

"He has high ranking in the Stags. That status won't count for nothing."

"But?" Quia winced.

"I don't know what Cernunnos will do, but Dougal knew what he was doing. He made his choice. You have to honor him by respecting it."

Quia made a surprised noise. Yom raised an eyebrow.

"Just shocked that something wise came out of your mouth." Quia's lips twitched like he was fighting a smile.

"I have my moments." Yom sat back and looked out the window, the rolling hills of Inisfail having given way to the craggy terrain of Albion. Dawn seeped into the sky like a bleed of ink.

"This changes nothing," Yom decided. "I'll figure out a way to sneak us off the train in Traiana, and we will pick up new identities there."

"And until then?"

"We don't leave this compartment."

The faraway screech of train brakes roused Yom from another bout of restless sleep. They were arriving at the next stop. She tried to regain her bearings by looking out through the sheer curtain they had drawn over the window, lost in thought as she considered possible exit routes. When Yom refocused on the scene outside the window, three familiar men prowled the platform, brushing shoulders and checking the hands of all the passengers that exited.

"Shit." She sank down into the seat until her eye level was just above the edge of the window.

Eventually all the passengers left the train and the new ones boarded, forcing the three Bears back on before it departed, looking even more frustrated. After the train chugged back to life, in the distance, she heard knocking. Followed by muffled words.

The Bears were scanning compartments one by one, and by the sound of it, they were starting uncomfortably close.

Quia's eyes widened and met Yom's. Her mind whirred, trying to come up with a plan. Making it to another empty compartment further away was out of the question, and the compartment they were in offered no hiding spots large enough for a person. She needed a way to hide herself, or slip further into a disguise—

"I'll not have you harassing our patrons," the conductor's voice scolded. "You'll return to your car at once." There was grumbling, but the three Bears obeyed, their sounds moving further away from Yom and Quia's compartment. The conductor could have them thrown off the train, after all. Or worse, call in blackcoats.

"That was too close." Quia let out a long exhale.

"Relax. Traiana is next and I'll get us past them. We'll be on our way before you know it."

Quia grunted and sat back across from her.

The train continued on through the morning into the afternoon. The land outside blurred into one green and gray mass that lulled Yom back into a half awake state. That is, until a harsh screech of the train jolted her back. She scrambled to look out the window, but nothing indicated they were at Traiana already. Then she saw it. Two six-seater transports of blackcoats pulling up to the train, ominous plumes of rose steam rising from their engines. The transports were using powder fuel, in addition to steam. They were in a hurry.

"Shit shit shit," she hissed. Quia was still sleeping, and she shook him roughly.

"What?" Rubbing the sleep from his eyes, he looked where she pointed, and saw the blackcoats for himself. Their coats billowed as they jumped down from the leather seats that lined the transport's glass enclosure.

"New plan, we're getting off early. You're about to find out why they're called blackcoats."

VI

The blackcoats are coming

the harsh wake up.

"They're here for the bounty." Blackcoats were corrupt thugs, without the honor code of the Stags.

"They're probably just checking people's papers," Quia said, still confused.

"You don't understand—" she said angrily as she leapt up to the compartment door to make sure it was pulled as tight as it could go and the lock securely turned. "Since you have no idea how things actually work—" she drew the opaque shade down over the window and crouched underneath the porthole. "But blackcoats are corrupt. Half the underground bounties in the provinces are collected by them." She yanked Quia off the seat to crouch next to her.

"That can't be right, they're royal legionaries. The Queen would never allow it."

"Has it ever seemed like the Queen gives a flying bollock what happens in Inisfail?" Yom hissed. "As long as she gets her taxes and the nicest cut of exports, she couldn't care less what happens within the province borders. The blackcoats outside the eternal city are nothing more than mercenaries."

Muffled voices sounded from the hallway, accompanied by heavy footsteps. Then, the train lurched back into motion. Of course, the blackcoats board and then trap them on a moving train, no doubt giving the conductor a perfectly official-sounding reason for the stop.

"Pack up. Now." Yom hoped Quia would choose this moment to heed her, for once.

Heavy, metallic footsteps passed their compartment. "We're looking for two people we suspect of traveling without their papers," a voice spoke from the hallway.

"Thank gosh you're here," a harried voice projected from the other side of the train car. "Two passengers drugged me yesterday. Then they stole from me." It was Damian.

Yom rolled her eyes. It was a flask and a few coins. She could show him real theft if that was what he really wanted.

The clock was ticking. Their best chance would be to get further down the train, away from the blackcoats before they started scanning compartments.

"Sir, we're here on official business. We don't deal with petty crime."

"I *am* official business!" Damian's voice raised. "Do you know who I am? Do you know who my father is?" Yom would have to thank Damian later for creating such a useful diversion. She slid open the compartment door as quietly as possible and pulled Quia, who was still fastening his cloak, behind her.

Yom walked with a deliberate but calm pace down the hall, keeping an ear on the conversation.

"Sir, I will only ask you once. Step aside."

"Not until you apprehend the thieves and return my items!"

"I gave you a warning, sir." The blackcoat turned. "Shackle him. Get him out of the way."

"EXCUSE ME?" Damian screamed, clearly unaccustomed to not getting his way. *"I am a VICTIM!"* He continued shouting as metal cuffs rang through the hallway.

"Conductor?" The blackcoat called as Damian continued grunting curses and threats about his father. Yom was almost at the door between cars. "We're looking for a young man and a woman. The woman has fingers that are stained blue and a Stag torc around her neck."

"A what?" Damian screeched. "The whore who stole from me had a strange necklace on, is she wanted for other crimes?"

Yom reached the door and opened it with calm haste, not waiting to hear what they were about to figure out. The blackcoats were walking towards their now empty compartment. Yom pushed Quia further into the next car.

"What are we going to do?" Quia whispered.

Yom studied the hallway in front of them. "I'll figure it—"

"BLUEFINGERS!" The gruff voice of the leader of the trio of Bears shouted from ahead of them. "I knew you was here."

All three bearlike men gathered on the opposite end of the aisle, faces rabid. "I was right, wasn't I?" The leader stood in the center and clapped his companion on the chest. Just as hairy as she remembered. They muttered, *You was, you was,* and, *Let's get her!* before catapulting towards Yom and Quia in a half sprint, voices crescendoing with grievances. Incoherent rage about denarii she owed, honor she had stolen, limbs they would be severing, et cetera.

Yom backed up towards the door between cars, whipping around to see the blackcoats standing outside their empty compartment. Then one blackcoat caught sight of her through the door's foggy window.

"There!" the blackcoat called out.

"You," the blackcoat pointed at her, "stay there," he commanded. A blur of blue coats began hurtling towards them from the next car.

"OI!" The Bear trio's leader shouted from the other side of Yom, *"THEY'RE OURS!"*

"In here." Yom pulled Quia into an open compartment with a very proper looking couple inside who watched on in horror. She locked the door and drew her knife. "Not a word," she tapped the base of both their throats with the knife's tip before crouching with Quia underneath the porthole.

"What now?" he whispered.

"I'd say we have about one minute before they get through that lock." Right on cue, someone began banging on the compartment door. The couple, now huddling together as far away from them as possible, whimpered.

Quia examined the rim of the window opposite. He shook his head just as the banging on the door increased its fervor. The window to the outside was sealed tight. No other exits.

Yom surveyed her powderbelt but didn't see any offensive powders she could use in such a small space that wouldn't be dangerous to Quia or her. She switched to defensive powder options and plucked a vial of Tenebrax, her shadow powder. The banging outside sounded like it was accompanied by a skirmish between the blackcoats and the Bears. Perhaps if they fought each other long enough, it would give Yom and Quia time to escape.

"Hold this." Quia shoved his cloak into her arms and pulled his pack in front of him.

"What are you doing?" Yom hissed. "This is no time for reading!"

He ignored her and dug into the pack until his entire forearm was buried, pulling out an instrument wrapped in leather. Unwrapping it from one side revealed a white blade that went yellow at the edges. Once the compact knife was unsheathed and only the leather handle remained, Quia stood up in the center of the compartment. He faced the porthole window that was now beginning to crack under the weight of the banging fists. The sound was punctuated by the quiet whimpers of the two bystanders trapped inside with them.

"You're going to get yourself killed!" Yom tugged to pull him away from the window. He seemed completely unaware of the splintering glass as he readied himself into a stance in the crowded space, knife poised. She heard him whispering something under his breath, with his eyes closed. Yom couldn't make out what he was saying, and paused her movements in confusion. She was about to tell him there were better ways to get himself killed if that's what he wanted, when his eyes reopened.

"On my signal, open the door." His voice was eerily calm.

"Wait, Quia—"

One glance from him shut her up. There was something in his face, a fierceness that had not been there before. Yom didn't understand how the change had occurred, but when she looked at him, she was looking at a warrior.

Quia turned back to face the porthole, and its glass finally cracked. "Now."

Yom inhaled as she opened the compartment door, and Quia pounced. He leapt between blackcoats and slashed his knife with a graceful ferociousness she had never seen in a fighter. He moved so quickly Yom felt gusts of air echo from his strikes. One second he was crouched on the ground slashing behind someone's knees and the next he was latched onto someone else's shoulder, severing the tendons that connected it to their arm. She rubbed her eyes to ensure she wasn't hallucinating. There was nothing to compare it to, other than the mountain cats she had heard stories about in the southern reaches of Arcadia.

The blackcoats and the Bears had begun taking each other out as well, and Quia was able to incapacitate everyone frighteningly fast. The hallway was strewn with blood and twitching bodies.

Yom's words were caught in her throat. "What—"

Quia grabbed her wrist and pulled them into the hallway before she could finish her thought, yanking her from a stupor. He took surefooted, graceful steps over the limbs of the men, while Yom stumbled after him. As they stepped over the groaning bodies, she realized he had methodically disarmed each one without causing any mortal injuries.

"What's happening over there?" Damian's voice carried from the car behind them, clearly still cuffed. "Did you apprehend the thief?"

They raced through the rest of the cars until they reached the back of the train, where there was a heavy steel door with a large handle barred closed. Quia wrenched the handle back and the door swung open. The blur of tracks raced beneath them and a ravine yawned to the left, with a steep slope down and a river rushing at the bottom. The train's speed and the depth of the ravine triggered a wave of dizziness in Yom.

"Absolutely not," Yom said flatly. "I'll take my chances with the blackcoats." Right on cue, someone groaned from the direction they had come, followed by the slow shuffle of someone trying to get back to their feet.

Quia pulled Yom in to fit snugly against him with an arm banded around her waist. She was shaking her head and trying to wriggle away when he took a great inhale and launched himself over the edge of the train, aiming for the ravine, taking Yom with him.

The freefall caused an immediate lurch in Yom's stomach that swallowed her yell. Quia's grip on her was an anchor as they soared through the air, his tight hold the only reassurance she had. She screwed her eyes shut, waiting for the impact, but it felt like they took longer than they should have to reach the ground, like their trajectory slowed mid air. She didn't have much time to think about it as the ground came up to meet her feet with a crack. Quia's grip jolted and they separated.

Her knees screamed at the impact, and Yom was thrown into a violent tumble down the ravine. The breakneck momentum made it impossible to catch her feet, so she rolled into a ball and let the ravine toss her down its slope. Each new impact with the ground was painfully amplified by stones and sticks and tree roots in her path. The sound of rushing water approached and Yom strained her spinning tunnel of vision to get sight of it. The water grew to a roar and Yom felt the spray on her back just in time to grab onto a tree root at the bank. Her feet and calves plunged into the water with a slap and she fought her own momentum, holding onto the tree root until her hands lost sensation. Hanging from a root, legs being tugged by the current, her head spun endlessly and her stomach felt ready to purge itself. When her aching arms were finally able to pull herself up out of the water, she sprawled out on the bank, chest heaving.

Yom took inventory of the sharp pains and dull aches now dotting her body. Her immediate relief of having survived the plummet gave way to disorientation, which snowballed into anger. Anger directed at the person whose fault it was they were now laying at the bottom of a ravine, instead of a comfortable train compartment. When she had built up enough fury, she finally sat up and saw Quia several feet away, plunged into the river from his torso down, eyes closed. His cloak being snagged on a root seemed to be the only thing keeping him from being swept into the current. Yom took a good few seconds to weigh the pros and cons of freeing his cloak and allowing him to be taken by the river. Her need for him to receive her verbal beration outweighed the opportunity for revenge.

With unnecessary roughness, Yom dragged him up from the edge and dropped him at a safe distance on the bank. She kneeled over him and considered the least pleasant ways she could wake him up.

"Wake up, you son of a bitch," she said as she slapped his face, taking no small enjoyment in it. Quia's eyes shot open, disoriented and annoyed, and he managed to grab her wrist before the next slap could land.

"What in the bloody Okeanus was that?" Yom said sharply.

Quia rubbed his eyes. "What?"

"The train? The fighting, the…" Yom waved her hand, unable to finish her thought without sounding ridiculous. *The fact that you fight like a wild animal on powder?*

"You're welcome." Quia closed his eyes.

"You expect me to thank you?" Yom sat back in disbelief. "I could have gotten us out of there without creating that kind of scene. You just tripled the size of the target on our backs. And for what? For us to land at the bottom of a ravine? Without any access to transport and no way to get back on the train!" Her words gradually increased in volume until she was shouting. A loud bird cawed at the intrusion and faint rustling started somewhere to their left. She fisted Quia's shirt and pulled him towards her, watching him carefully.

"You're no Archive apprentice," she whispered, an inch from his face, as menacing as she could. "Who are you?" Moments replayed over and over, begging to be strung into an answer. *Panchaians know how to make the crossing,* he had said. The odd familiarity he had with a mythical plant that had not been seen in Arcadia in millenia. *It was not lost everywhere.* The way he fought, like no person she had ever seen in Arcadia. Not even a triarii shared that fighting style.

"I think you already know." Quia's voice was resigned. Yom's fire of rage was smothered a bit by the gravity of the truth he was leaving unspoken.

"Tell me." She gripped his shirt tighter and held her breath.

He nodded and was quiet for a moment. "I am from Panchaia."

Misho's boots fell softly on the Morningstar train's steps. His two triarii companions followed him to create a triangle, their standard formation.

The legionaries had sent up powder signals for reinforcements, and their faces had paled when they saw the beetle black of triarii armor glistening in the sun. Misho surveyed the state of the legionaries: some standing holding their shoulders and arms, and some seated, presumably rendered unable to stand. Sprinkled along the edges were a few other bounty hunters who seemed to have gotten caught in the scuffle.

Misho padded down the aisle, the movement of the interlocking pieces of armor quieter than a whisper. He nudged his chin at the leader of the company, a captain, and led him into an empty compartment. The triarii removed his hood, and sat back onto the cushioned seat, motioning for the captain to do the same.

The legionary captain sat down, still skittish, remaining on the edge of his seat.

"Tell me what happened."

"We were checking the train for passengers we suspected of traveling between provinces without documentation." The captain's voice was practically shaking, "We found—"

"Captain," Misho interrupted him, "let's cut the shit. This will be much easier for you if you tell the truth."

The captain swallowed.

"We know about the bounty," Misho added for good measure.

"Yes, we were looking for those two," the captain said hesitantly, as if he expected Misho to inflict punishment. "It was the boy, he–he attacked us."

"One boy took on ten blackcoats?" Misho's voice was calm, guiding the captain along.

"Yes," he said slowly.

"How."

"He," the captain glanced back at the door, "he moved like an animal, I–I've never seen anyone fight like that. Like he wasn't—" the captain paused.

"Human?" Misho offered. The captain nodded.

"Thank you for the information," Misho stood and opened the compartment door.

The captain muttered something under his breath.

"What did you say?" Misho turned back, hands bracing the doorframe.

"I said he moved so fast you could feel the air coming off his strikes."

Misho gripped the wood so tightly he could feel it splintering under his fingers.

YOM LET GO OF QUIA'S SHIRT AND FELL BACK ON HER HEELS. The spinning that had subsided after the tumble came back with a vengeance. She looked at the boy she now found herself trapped at the bottom of a ravine with, and realized she knew absolutely nothing about him. He could be a Panchaian spy and need to kill her now to keep his cover, for all she knew. She was already under a death sentence if it was discovered she had helped a Panchaian travel through Arcadia. But how would anyone be able to tell he was Panchaian? Nothing was suspicious in his appearance; he looked like any other Archivist: no scars, no permanent marks painted on his body, no gruesome expression that promised death to Arcadia. There was no resemblance to the illustrations from scraps of ancient codices that lived on in history books about the time before the Separation. Anyone could be from Panchaia, and she would have no idea. This notion settled like a stone around her neck.

Yom scrambled to put some distance between them. "Is anything you've told me true?"

"Yes." Quia looked at her earnestly. "My name really is Quia. Everything you know about me is true, I only hide who I am because it's not safe for me here."

"But why—why are you here?" Yom decided keeping him talking would give her a chance to form a plan to get away from him.

"I traveled here with a small exploration company several years ago. My whole company was killed besides me. I had to go into hiding."

"Are you going to kill me?" The question slipped out. Yom hated how small it made her sound.

Quia laughed; it caught Yom off guard. "Wouldn't I have done that already if that was my plan?"

Yom stared at the ground, parsing through whether this logic was sound. "Maybe you still need something from me?"

"I have no intention of doing anything to you, Yom, let alone killing you. This changes nothing." Quia wrung his hands. "Can we go back to hating each other?"

Yom looked up the steep walls of the ravine, and at the swiftly moving river. If she continued to question him and she was right, no doubt he would grow weary of it and decide to finish the job early. If he was telling the truth, then they needed to keep moving.

"I have questions." Yom eyed him.

"I would be shocked if you didn't." Quia stood and brushed himself off. "I'll tell you anything you want to know." He held out a hand to help her up, but she wasn't quite ready to take it.

Yom stood on her own. "We need to keep moving."

Quia nodded wordlessly, and motioned for her to lead.

"I'm not walking in front of you. You go first. We're going to follow this river to Traiana." Quia sighed in exasperation but started walking. Yom took up a stride a few paces behind him.

"Let's hear it." Quia turned and walked backwards in front of her. Yom saw up close how light on his feet he walked, as if he barely needed to touch the ground. Not to mention how gracefully he stepped over the roots and rocks that lined the river without even looking down.

"Why did you come here originally?"

"Like I said, exploratory mission. Panchaia deems it important to keep tabs on Arcadia. Government systems, weapons development, popular sentiment."

"Why not go back?"

Quia cleared his throat. "Remember I said my whole company was killed? The numenborn who led us through the Okeanus crossing died. I had no way to do it on my own." Yom grunted. She had to admit that his story added up.

"Can everyone in Panchaia do what you did back there?"

"No. I am part of the warrior caste. There are several castes."

"That was a bit more advanced than what I've seen of fighters here."

"Children of Panchaia are more connected to their numen, with that comes more acute skill."

Quia held up his palm. At first, Yom didn't see anything, but when she was closer, she saw a hairline white scar sliced diagonally across his palm. She grabbed it to examine it more closely.

"It's a mark every child of Panchaia bears. We receive it during the Trials, when we first open the connection to our numen."

"I thought only certain people have numen?"

"Only certain people have *excess* numen." Quia pulled his hand back and turned to look around the river. "Everything has numen. The river, the plants on its bank, you, me, even the words we're speaking. All of it comes from the World Tree, therefore all of it contains some of its lifeforce."

Yom looked around the river and down at her own hands. "If that's true, how were the Panchaians in your company killed?"

"We merely have an advantage in a fight against someone without numen connection, it doesn't make us immortal." Quia looked at Yom for a minute before continuing, as if he was deciding what to share. "And looking back on it, I suspect we were not the only ones here using a numen connection to enhance fighting skill."

Yom's brow wrinkled as she considered his words. "What do you—" Then it occurred to her. The greatest fighters on the continent, who had near inhuman ability as well. "You mean that's the reason the triarii have the skill they do?"

"I can't be sure. If it is true, I have no idea who has trained them in that way. I've tried to look more into their order and the House of Flowing Waters, but the official records are suspiciously incomplete."

The mention of the House of Flowing Waters raised questions that had never occurred to Yom. "What is Panchaia like? Is the ruler similar to the Queen? The House of Flowing Waters?"

Quia's eyes grew distant. "Panchaia lives and dies on the whim of the gods. In exchange for divine favor they have sacrificed all of their own will. I didn't even realize it until I came here, and saw what it was like for people to live without knowing a thing about Wacachan, the Immortals, any of it."

"But they—we—are living a lie. The Immortals *do* exist. Cernunnos controls every inch of Inisfail, of all Ibernia."

"I'm not sure what's better anymore. Living inside an illusion, or dying in the name of truth."

They fell into silence as Yom thought more about the lies that had ripped the very earth from under her. The far reaching echoes of that implosion. The question that had been nagging her more and more. Yom could not contain it any longer.

"What do you know of the Binding?"

Several more steps passed before Quia answered.

"Nothing of the act of Binding remains in Panchaia, being that all the titans have been here in Arcadia for millenia. The gods have their own rituals of servitude, but they look quite different and give a different kind of control. All that is known is that titans bind their servants to themselves, and act through these servants. The titans first bound their animal servants to create stewards of their realm when the humans began settling. They created envoys by interlocking their numen with that of their animal servants. In the days of the Ancients, you could think about it as..."

"A leash?" Yom offered up sardonically.

"A bridge."

A bridge, a double-sided coin, a proper pain in Yom's ass. She pursed her lips and continued walking. It might have been all the times she hit her head tumbling down that ravine but his answers felt sufficient, for now. She was already on the run from one titan, and now inadvertently she risked the wrath of the House of Flowing Waters itself. If Quia was telling the truth, and he didn't plan to kill her, then what else was there to do but keep going?

Yom decided to give him an answer of her own. "Yes," she said into the void between them. Quia looked confused. "Yes, Princess, we can go back to hating each other."

He smiled.

"How far until the next stop?" Misho asked the conductor, who was looking at him like he had a dagger to the conductor's throat.

"I–it's about an hour more to Traiana."

Misho nodded and motioned for the conductor to restart the train before stepping into an empty compartment and clicking the door shut. From a pocket behind his leg armor, he withdrew a bundle of dried leaves mixed with fragments of yew. He arranged the yew fragments into a small pile in his gloved palm with the leaves resting on top, and scraped a match along the underside of the compartment bench. It sparked brightly blue-orange before he nestled it underneath the yew. The sticks caught fire and the flame licked its way to the leaves, the fire taking on a green hue.

"I'm in the middle of something." A silky smooth voice floated out from the plume of smoke.

"A Panchaian is here," Misho spoke. The voice through the smoke remained silent. "He is traveling with the fugitive Stag." Misho could feel the rage even through the smoke.

"The Amaurosis?"

"It's still safely growing in Inisfail."

"So that beast managed to do one thing right." A pause. "What do they know?"

"They know of the Amaurosis growth, but not of her. It's not clear yet if they are evading capture or looking for something."

"I want that Panchaian. But the Stag must be returned to him. That is a law I cannot afford to violate."

"We will head them off in Traiana." Misho hesitated. "How is she?"

"She is not your concern," the voice snapped. "You have no idea how long I've waited for this. I will not have one of Cernunnos's brats get in my way." The voice spoke more to itself than to Misho.

"I won't fail, master."

"For your sake, I should hope not." A wave of chills passed through Misho. He swallowed it away. "The runaway Stag, who is she?" The leaves were almost all burned, the plume of smoke almost gone.

"She was nobody before Cernunnos. An Inisfail orphan he took in."

"Find out everything you can about her," the voice growled from the fading smoke. "Make her regret this."

The Gutter

THE LATE AFTERNOON LIGHT SLANTED THROUGH THE TREES, shattering into tiny pieces on the surface of the river. After an almost sleepless night on the riverbank, listening to every ripple of water and snap of a twig, Yom and Quia had started moving again the moment dawn broke the horizon. They walked in a tense silence at odds with the music of bird calls and the gentle splashing of fish racing down the river. Yom had decided to accept his story for the time being, but something had shifted between them, some trust lost on both sides. They walked side by side, neither allowing the other to take up the rear. After a particularly obvious twitch from Quia when Yom raised her arm to roll it in its socket, she decided to put a stop to it.

"What is it?" she asked flatly.

"What's what?" Quia kept his gaze focused straight ahead.

"Why are you acting strange?"

"I'm not."

Yom drew her knife and in the blink of an eye Quia had taken it and turned it back at her. She raised an eyebrow.

"Fine. I'm anxious. You're the first person besides Dougal on this entire continent who knows who I am. And you're...you."

"What's that supposed to mean?" Yom grabbed the knife roughly out of Quia's lowering hand and slid it back into the sheath on her belt.

"You're a criminal, how do I know you're not plotting for a way to exchange me for a purse ten times larger than the bounty on our heads?"

Yom stroked her chin. "You know what? That's actually a great idea." Quia shoved her and she cursed as she tripped over a root. Quia, as Yom was growing used to, had no lack of grace while walking. He could probably walk across hot coals blindfolded and make it look like a purposeful dance.

"This is the part where you say, 'You have nothing to worry about.'"

Yom regained her stride next to him. "Relax, princess. If I turn you in, even if I get that kind of bounty, you would be imprisoned and I would have no idea how to find this...magician by myself, and the war would happen anyways. All the money in Arcadia wouldn't be able to keep someone out of a world war."

Yom knew it was cruel not to give him the assurance he was looking for, but doing that felt like the beginning of an allyship she was not ready for. The last ally she had trusted had ended quite poorly.

Quia, as was becoming typical, seemed to read her thoughts. "What happened with you and that other Stag?" Yom had the urge to dismantle the question with something sarcastic, but her retort was stopped in its tracks when she tripped over another tree root. Or this time perhaps it was a stone. She growled in frustration and cursed the middle of nowhere they had found themselves, Okeanus knew how far from civilization, let alone how far from Cataracta. For a moment she felt a pang of longing for Inisfail. Not for Cernunnos or the Stags, but for the rain-bloated skies and the grey stone of the city. The warmth of the Green Demon just after nightfall with a hot bowl of stew and a fresh ale. The comfort of her Powdery, all her tools and stock and scribbled notebooks of different formulation experiments. The brightness of the stars during the witching hour of a clear night, when all the lamps and torches of the city had been extinguished. And the enveloping velvet of a starless night, those endless, molten depths that made Yom feel for the slightest moment that perhaps she was not alone.

But Yom knew—no matter whom they succeeded in finding in Cataracta— it would be a long time before she was able to return to *that* city.

"Lucan." She answered Quia's question, her voice rough and her hands gripping her powderbelt tightly. "He made his loyalties clear. I suppose I'm not surprised but I wish it was someone else who had decided to sell out."

"Because you two were together?"

Yom snorted humorlessly. "No." She cleared her throat when she realized Quia was watching her, still waiting for more. "We were friends, sure, and we had our fun, but we both knew what it was."

"So you slept together but didn't love him?" Quia said this with an air of judgment, like he was identifying a paradox.

"Bloody Okeanus you're nosy." Yom pinched between her brows. "Maybe when you grow up, and actually sleep with someone, you'll understand that love has nothing to do with it."

"I have slept with people!" Quia snapped.

"You're going to need to work on that before we get to Traiana. No one will believe you, and virgins are extra valuable."

The ravine was finally flattening and the terrain began to pitch down. Yom hoped that her estimation was correct and that they would make it to Traiana by nightfall. The province they were trekking through, Dressen, was notorious for traffickers. Another night stranded on the riverbank would be pushing their luck.

"Wow," Quia uttered and stopped. He stared straight ahead, at the broad sprawl of a city at the base of the hill, nestled at the confluence of two rivers. Traiana.

"Pretty, right?" she asked, returning to her descent.

Quia nodded. "Wait, what do you mean that virgins are extra valuable in Traiana?"

"This is one of the most violent provinces in the queendom," she called over her shoulder.

"What?" Quia caught up with her quickly.

"Drugs, sex, gambling, you name it you can find it in spades down there. But the province's economy is mostly supported by the buying and selling of people."

"No that can't be right, in our records it's a—"

"Fishing town?" Yom laughed. "Renos sure has done a good job covering it up. Excellent way to lure naïve people like you in." Yom looked Quia up and down. "Maybe you would get lucky and they would take you in as a fighter. Their arena is legendary. People travel all the way from the eternal city to watch fighters compete in it."

"I thought the enslavement of Arcadian citizens was outlawed?"

"There are many ways around that law." The torc weighed heavily on Yom's neck.

"Wait a minute, who's Renos?"

Yom noticed a boat moored several yards down the river. Strange that someone would just leave it there. "She's—"

"Going to be very happy to hear we have two unannounced guests," someone said from their left. Yom jumped, but before she could draw her knife, two sets of hands took hold of her arms and wrenched them behind her. A cloud of coarse powder burst in her face. She tried to spit it out, but it was too late. It was a hack's Somnarium, lacking Yom's touches of lavender to cushion the belladonna's steep fall. As the powder dragged her down, a young girl's face swam in her vision. For a split second, the girl's face was the spitting image of Lior, at the exact age that Yom remembered her.

YOM SWORE GROGGILY AS SHE CAME TO, A DULL ACHE SETTING INTO her limbs. Her arms were glued to her sides and she couldn't separate her legs. The roar of the river returned; she was eye level with the reedy mud of the riverbank, her arms and legs restrained with thick rope. She squirmed until she found Quia, equally restrained a few feet away. Her gaze wandered up from the ground and she registered three sets of slender legs, all strapped with various leather weapons holsters. Two girls—sisters, likely—had scrunched up faces, like they had just eaten a lemon. Standing behind the pair was an even younger girl, whose eyes were widened and whose stance was defensive, as if she wasn't sure to be wary of Yom or her own companions. She had the exact same coloring as Lior: pale skin, dark hair, and blue eyes. And she couldn't be a day over thirteen.

"Sorry about all this, there's a couple fugitives on the loose and we can't be too careful." It was the same self-assured voice that Yom had heard before the powder. From behind the three girls, a woman emerged with a shock of bright reddish orange hair and freckled skin, swaggering towards them. She wore slim-fitting trousers held up by braces, similar weapon belts strapped up and down her legs, and a simple, oversized morning coat that swayed as she walked. Slung over her shoulder was Yom's powderbelt.

Yom held in a groan. Their captors must have searched them while they were unconscious.

"A whore who's Bound? You must be special," the woman remarked as she came within a foot of Yom. Around her neck was a silver torc with the head and tail of an eel molded into the ends.

Fantastic, Yom thought dryly. They had run directly into Renos's Eels.

"Or perhaps you're more than a whore, from the looks of this thing." Rye held out the powderbelt between them, and Yom swallowed. "Strange thing for a whore to carry, isn't it?"

"I'm an exporter. Those are samples of our powders."

Rye examined the belt again, weighing this story.

"And we prefer the term escort."

The woman watched her for a moment before laughing. "I like you." She kneeled down and snaked her hand around Yom's wrist, holding up her lace-gloved hand and the shred of Moss's tunic tied around it. Yom held her breath, hoping the lace was thick enough to hide any traces of her blue fingers. "Shame you had to trespass on Renos's land. You're not going to like the punishment."

"We're here to see Renos, actually." Yom lifted her chin. "We're emissaries of Cernunnos." It struck her. Renos's Eels. Cernunnos's Stags. Coventina's Bears, even. How many of the cutthroat leaders she had heard stories of in the provinces were titans?

"Oh?" The woman raised her eyebrows and looked at Quia, seeing no torc around his neck.

"He has to maintain his status as a merchant's son." Yom glanced at Quia. Miraculously, his expression gave nothing away.

"What would Cernunnos have on a merchant's son?" The woman asked, clearly humoring Yom for the sport of it.

Yom shrugged as best she could while tied up. "Who knows. Probably just trying to stick it to his dad." She did not chance another look at Quia. "Doesn't matter. We've traveled a long way to bring valuable cargo through here."

"What cargo?" The woman's tone turned serious.

"New powder. First round of production." The woman scanned Yom's face. "I can prove it. If you'll let me." A slight nod from the woman and Yom continued. "The leather pouch, there," Yom nudged her chin at the pouch that hung from the front of the powderbelt.

"Do you mind?" Yom asked the woman, hoping she would release the ropes around Yom's arms.

"Not at all," the woman drew a small dagger from one of her belts and cut the pouch loose. She sniffed the contents before extracting a fingerful and inhaling it. As she exhaled, she moaned.

"That's good," she said breathily. "You have more?" Her gaze turned greedy.

"It's in a safe place." Yom jerked her chin behind them. "Didn't want to risk any misunderstandings before we negotiated a deal for safe passage with Renos."

Yom held her breath as the woman stared at them a moment, sizing up everything Yom had said.

"Fine. I'll take you to see Renos. No guarantees she agrees, though."

"No guarantees you get any more of that then," Yom nodded at the pouch still clutched in the woman's hand. She knew a powderhead when she saw one.

The woman made quick work of the rope around Yom's legs and looped the remnants onto a hook on one of her holsters. The two lemon eaters picked Yom up and set her on her feet with her arms still bound. Now upright, she could feel the absence of the powderbelt. It sunk in that not only had she lost her personal supply of Aetherium, but also every other powder weapon on that belt.

"This boy's a merchant alright. Look at his bag." The younger, timid girl showed Quia's bag full of scrolls that she was haphazardly repacking with its contents. Quia looked quite contrite about the state of it. The girl found Quia's leather-wrapped knife and looked it over, but didn't say anything.

"What's that, Citrus?"

The girl hesitantly looked up at her leader, and the knife was snatched out of her hands before she could say a word.

"And who shall I tell Renos has come to see her?" The woman asked as she examined the knife closely, not thinking to unwrap it.

"Lior." Yom said the first name that came to her head and instantly regretted it. "And this is Damian," she nudged her shoulder at Quia.

"Rye," the woman responded in turn, tucking Quia's knife into one of her weapons garters. When Rye's mouth tipped up in a sly smile, Yom realized she couldn't be more than a few years older than her.

Rye turned her attention to Quia and stepped up so her face was only inches from his.

"Damian," she said the name as if tasting it. "What a pleasure."

Yom had to look twice to be sure she wasn't imagining the look in Rye's eyes. She wanted him. *Just wait for him to open his mouth*, Yom thought.

"This is Agathon and Aurele." Rye gestured at the sisters. Yom looked beyond them, to the last of the party, with her matted brown hair and blue eyes. A wave of guilt threatened to crash over Yom at the girl's resemblance to Lior, but she kept it at bay, resolving to find more powder as soon as she could.

"And her?" Yom gestured at the girl.

"Oh, and that's Citrus," Rye said offhand, as if she hadn't thought the girl important enough to share her name.

"Clementine," the girl corrected softly.

Rye turned around, her long hair whipping Quia in the face, leaving little else in the way of introduction. "Let's go. I want to be back for a hot supper." She began walking up the hill without a second look. Yom and Quia stood, a bit dumbfounded, before they received a nudge and an authoritative hand on the shoulder, guiding them towards the boat Yom had seen moored. *Of course,* Yom kicked herself. She should have hidden them the second she noticed it.

As they were corralled onto the boat, which was especially rickety and cramped with six people on board, Yom chanced a look at Quia. She tried to warn him what they were walking into, but his expression seemed to be concerned with something else. Before she could decipher it, he turned back to look straight ahead, and the boat was released from the tree root it was moored to. They began to float down the river.

They descended in silence and the trees thinned. Hillside dwellings began popping up on either side of them. The city expanded in front of them as the sun glowed gold on the horizon. The lamps of the city came to life and the sprawl turned into a constellation of twinkling lights. Eventually they found themselves floating on flat water, wrought iron posts on either side of the river marking the city entrance ahead of them. Rye sat at the bow, without turning to check on them once. Her hair moved with the rocking of the boat, a bright red harbinger swaying in Yom's vision.

Yom had to admit that Traiana kept to its reputation as a small fishing city upon first glance. The buildings were mostly built of wood and stone, the main avenues concentrated along the two rivers that met in the center of it. Rye and the lemon eaters roped the boat to a hook on the stone river wall, looking utterly at ease as they leapt onto the ledge. Clementine's small hands appeared at Yom's back, pushing her to a stand with her arms still bound. Rye pulled her with surprising strength onto the ledge, and Yom awkwardly rolled herself to a stand on the stone walkway, teetering a bit on her feet. Quia was extracted in the same deranged way, and they found themselves walking down what seemed like a central thoroughfare of Traiana.

Fishing boats lined each side of the river and the city buzzed with activity. Burly looking men staggered down the avenues, already slowed by ale, stumbling and tripping over themselves to avoid Rye as she cut straight past them. As they followed the river deeper into the city, and as the twilight progressed further into night, the people they passed on the avenues grew more menacing. Men were passed out on the street, or rutting into women without bothering to go somewhere private. Jaded eyes followed their movements closely. Yom noticed some even turned their direction to follow them. Rye paid no mind to it, but the girls behind her were not so immune. They bumped up closer against Yom's heels to keep up with Rye. Next to her, Quia grew more agitated.

"Make sure you don't vomit before we get there. You're looking a bit peaky, and they won't let us in if you smell any worse than you already do," Yom whispered to him. While she said this in complete seriousness, Quia snorted.

A dilapidated old boat house came into view at the nexus of the rivers. More of a miserable shack than a house, but an eel wound itself inward in a carving on the door. *This is it.* Yom took a deep breath and braced herself.

Rye marched up and banged her fist on the door.

The wooden door creaked open and a huge man who would have given the bollocks a run for their money stood in the frame, blocking the light of the lanterns inside. He gave them a look up and down. A memory resurfaced, with frightening clarity, of when they first returned to the Cut with Moss. Guilt reared with it, punctuated with the memory of Moss's floppy hair bouncing as he walked through the Cut. *Your fault your fault your fault,* Yom's mind shouted at her. Every hour that passed reduced the effects of the powder Yom had in her system, and a dark pit threatened her if she completely dried out. A craving for more hit her so forcefully she felt lightheaded.

"Tourist attractions are that way," the hulking giant pointed a jaundiced yellow fingernail caked in dirt behind them. "Unless you're looking for another kind of attraction," he directed a greasy smile at Yom.

"Don't be crass, Killian. They're here to see Renos."

"Says who?" He crossed his arms.

"Says me, bootlicker." Killian turned a bit red in the face at this. "Move or I will move you." Yom watched in shock as this man, easily a foot and a half taller than Rye, begrudgingly moved aside for her.

"So hard to find decent help these days," Rye muttered at Yom. The group shuffled into the boat house, to a small landing with a few boats moored to a covered dock behind. Dark river water sloshed against the edges.

As Yom passed, Killian watched her with disquieting attention, particularly at the way her breasts were squished uncomfortably by rope. Yom squirmed, hating the attention to her figure. In skirts and dresses, her body felt like a stranger. A cat forced into a costume.

Rye cleared her throat. "Don't even think about it. She wouldn't say yes even if you paid her." Killian swung a fist the size of Rye's face at her and she dodged it with ease, landing a single punch in the side of his ribs and causing him to double over. This was no small movement as he already took up half the doorway.

"This way," Rye turned to a set of stairs Yom hadn't noticed and began walking down.

"You're gonna regret that," Killian spat from his position. Just before Rye dipped below eye level of the stairs, she raised a two-fingered obscenity over her shoulder at him. Yom and Quia exchanged a glance before facing straight ahead, neither of them quite knowing what to make of her.

The stairs echoed with the river's current, but it lessened as they descended further. The loud swish of the river was steadily replaced by the ominous creaking of the wooden steps. Yom tried to keep track of the number of steps to figure out how far down they descended, but the dark stairs were disorienting. She figured they had climbed down at least three stories before the foot of the stairs came into view. A similar wooden door with an eel carved into it stood at the bottom. Rye paused at the landing and quickly cut the length of rope on their upper halves. Yom rubbed her skin to bring the feeling back to her arms and soothe the rope burn. Hardly waiting for them, Rye reached for the door and yanked it open, walking through it without even a glance back to see if they were still following her.

Yom crossed the threshold before Quia and her eyes widened at the size of the hall in front of them. Vaulted ceilings stretched over towering stone walls. To her right, the wall was made of large chunks of glass fused together. Behind the glass, a dark shimmering blue opened up. She realized it was the murky depths of the river rushing past them, separated only by glass. Yom stood frozen, watching it in awe. Flashes of fish raced by and dark weeds meandered through the current.

A whistle broke her attention.

"Quit gawking and follow me," Rye called from a ways ahead.

Yom reluctantly turned away from the wall to continue crossing the cavernous hall. Men crowded around several long tables spanning the length of the room, sloshing their drinks with soft splatters on the stone floor. The Eels looked thicker than the Stags. Where the Stags had a lanky grace, these men had a stocky brawn. There was a noticeable absence of women in the hall aside from the ones with Rye. As they walked, the eyes of the men followed them. Faint light and shadow fluttered over the tables and the backs of the men sitting at them, dusk light passing through the river and reflecting onto the stone. It was as if the hall itself were underwater, and all the men were great fish swimming through it.

"Welcome to the Gutter." Rye held her arms out.

Yom swayed each leg like tall grass under her skirt, preparing herself to be someone else. She had never met Renos, but the stories about her indicated she was famously unkind to strangers, and especially cruel to those who crossed her. Yom had once heard of a thief chained to a rock on the river to become eel meat. Not a quick death.

A high table spanned a dais at the front of the hall. Yom counted the seats, seeing an even split on either side of an older woman at the center. A large, intricate fishing net hung behind her like a tapestry. The woman watched them approach with unnaturally bright eyes. Her hair was long and dark gray, knotted and mangled with braids and wooden beads. She looked ancient as the river beyond the glass. Of two things Yom was sure: this was Renos, and this woman was a titan. She hoped Quia was shrewd enough to realize who they were about to meet.

Rye walked around the table and whispered in Renos's ear.

"An emissary of Cernunnos, eh? He hasn't sent men through here in decades. How did he know I would take kindly?" She squinted.

Yom saw a bottomless depth in them, all compassion long ago purged. "He didn't," Yom responded with an even voice, years of schooling away emotion coming in handy. "He sent us with a fair tribute to you, as well as a commission on our cargo." Yom reached into her pack to extract Dougal's purse that she had supplemented with Damian's coin, tossing it to Renos.

Renos opened the purse and stuck her hand in to root around and count. "Cargo?" She asked with a raised eyebrow once she refastened it. Rye held out the Aetherium pouch to the titan, who grabbed it with a thick-knuckled hand weighed down by chains and rings.

"It's a new powder. Called Aetherium," Yom said carefully, not wanting to sound too familiar with it.

"What is it?" Renos shook out a palmful and inspected it.

"A mix of euphoriants and pain blockers."

Rye looked anxious to get it back into her hands. The powder was any fighter's dream substance.

"We're smuggling it into the eternal city."

Renos closed her nails around it, a green tint spreading from the root of them.

"It's strong—" Yom tried to warn but Renos flung her hand up in the air, scattering the powder in a pink cloud over them. It floated down and Renos closed her eyes, basking in it. Once it dissipated into the air and onto their skin, Renos opened her eyes again. They somehow looked even brighter, almost glowing.

"How much are you transporting?" she asked, licking her lips.

"Ten stone. We're prepared to give you a stone in exchange for safe and—" Yom glanced back at Quia for the first time, "discreet passage to Cataracta."

Renos weighed Yom for a heavy moment. "And what are the names of these two emissaries?"

"Lior and Damian," Rye cut in. "A whore and a merchant's son."

Yom flinched at Lior's name coming off Rye's lips but tried to pass it off as a blink. It was the first time she had heard someone else say the name in six years, and it sounded utterly profane to be spoken so carelessly. She swallowed a scream.

Renos smiled. "How intriguing." Her gaze danced between Yom and Quia. A terrifying thought lurched in Yom's mind. A memory of all the instances when Cernunnos mysteriously knew the goings-on in Inisfail without being told. Would Renos have that same intuition? Yom had no idea what the bounds were of this dominion.

"Very well," Renos ruled.

A soft exhale left Yom. So the titan couldn't see inside their minds. Still, something told Yom while they were on her land, they needed to be very careful where they stepped. Even if they were alone.

"We have a cargo transport heading in that direction the day after tomorrow. You will be our guests until then, and we will pack you into a cargo shipment."

Yom nodded. They would have to make up the time, but at least it was guaranteed transport. And as for the ten stone of powder, she was fairly confident she could manufacture a fake batch if she got some uninterrupted access to the kitchen stockrooms.

"And because of my generosity, you will have the privilege of attending our Fight Night tomorrow." Renos's smile looked more like she was baring her teeth. "Perhaps you will even honor us with a fight. There is no greater tribute in my province." It was not clear who of the two of them Renos envisioned fighting, but Yom balked at the prospect of either of them stepping into the notorious arena.

"Unfortunately, neither of us are fighters." Yom bit her lip thinking about the danger of staying two nights here, compared to the danger of questioning the hospitality they were being offered. "There is no shipment leaving tonight?" She was inundated with visions of their death or discovery if one of them was forced into the fighting ring.

"Do not test my generosity." Renos narrowed her eyes. Fish scales, Yom realized. Her eyes were bright like the sun reflecting off fish scales in the water.

"Of course, you are too generous." Yom bowed her head.

Renos dismissed them with a wave of her metal-choked hand. Rye walked behind the table towards the stone side of the hall, motioning for them to follow her. With each step, Yom calculated the possible endgames in this treacherous province. She knew that being forced to stay was a test, but a test of what? Quia looked similarly wary. Finally something they agreed on.

Rye led them into a narrow hallway lined with identical doors. Yom tried to memorize the path they took around corners and down stairs through several similar hallways, but she kept losing focus thinking about how far underground they had sunk. She couldn't shake the feeling they were being crushed underneath the river. A ways later, Rye seemed to pick a specific door, although without any markings it was a mystery how she could tell them apart. She gave the door a light push and it opened, no knob in sight. Or lock.

The small room had nothing other than two mats pushed together, barely the length of a person, with a threadbare blanket on top and small oil lamp to the side.

"You don't mind sharing, right?" Rye asked, almost like bait.

"Not at all." Yom threw her pack on one of the mats.

Rye leaned in the doorway, arms crossed. "So what's in the powder?"

"I don't ask those kinds of questions, I'm just the courier," Yom lied.

"I hear Cernunnos's chemist is quite talented. Do you know him?"

Yom's pride begged her to grin as wide as possible. The mysterious figure of Bluefingers took on a life of its own out in the provinces. Most people had no idea who he or she or they were, hearing only of the potency of their powders, the slickness of their grift, and the pleased state their lovers were left in.

"No, I've never met him. I only leave the Cut for out-calls and export trips." The conversation could have ended, but Yom blurted, "He's not a frequenter of the pleasure rooms. From what I hear he doesn't need to pay for it." Rye gave her a curious look. Yom clasped her hands tightly behind her back, digging her nails into her skin, maintaining a solemn face by the skin of her teeth.

"Probably for the best, sounds like that bluefingered demon has gotten himself into a spot of trouble lately." Rye glanced between them for a second longer. "You can wash up in the third door on your right," she pointed further down the hall, "and supper begins in an hour. I will send proper attire for you."

"Attire?" Yom tried to quell the panic in her voice. Her skin crawled at the idea of being dressed like a doll.

"Renos's orders. She's quite...particular." Without another word, Rye left, and Yom nudged the door closed behind her.

"Wh–" Quia began but Yom held up a hand to silence him. She pointed to her ear hoping he understood that Eels would be listening to their every word while they were in the Gutter. She motioned for Quia to give her something to write with. Confused, he fished a scrap piece of paper and an ink quill from his bag.

They will be listening to us all night, she wrote, balancing the paper against her palm.

What's your plan? We don't have cargo of any powder, Quia wrote back.

Don't worry about it. I'll make sure we make it onto that convoy. She was about to hand the paper back to him, but added, *I'm more worried I just had to give up my personal powder stock. That was supposed to last me this whole trip.*

You are unbearable, Quia was barely done writing when Yom ripped the paper out of his hand.

She scribbled, *Renos is a*

A sharp knock on the door startled them. Yom stuffed the paper and quill into her boot before pulling the door open. The hallway was empty, but a parcel was tucked into the threshold. Closing the door again, she unwrapped it and held a swath of shimmering blue green fabric with a stitched texture like the net that hung in the hall. She unfolded it and let the end tumble down to see a long, rather sheer, dress.

A small note fell out. Quia picked it up and read it, before his lip turned up in distaste. *In honor of my men having a special feast tonight*, Yom read and rolled her eyes.

He gestured for the paper and quill once again.

Tell them we are betrothed. He turned the paper for Yom to read. *So that no one bothers you*, he added. Yom found it horribly naive but also a touch endearing that he thought a betrothal would keep anyone from taking what they wanted in the Eel's den.

I'm a whore, remember? Yom wrote back, *I'll be fine. Being available might work in our favor.*

Yom renewed her beauty powders and stains and slipped on the new dress, keeping her gloves on. The dress was too sheer and hugged her body too tightly, emulating the more cosmopolitan styles in the south. Its sleeves cascaded down her arms, widening at the wrist, and the neckline dipped down to cut across the tops of her breasts. She was primped to look exactly like the whore she was pretending to be, but she felt like a Stag missing its antlers.

Quia used the time to rearrange the room and spread the sleeping mats as far apart as possible.

When she turned back to face him in their cramped dormitory, he was struck silent.

"This is exactly why I hate dresses," she whispered.

"You're right," he mocked a moment later, "it is truly a hideous thing."

He didn't understand what it was like to walk through the world and be perceived as an object available for the taking. Yom had to toughen her exterior to be taken seriously, to be respected. The dress and the beauty powders undid every measure she took to protect herself.

Rye came to fetch them exactly an hour after she had left.

They returned to a far different scene than the one they had left in the river hall. Music echoed over a din of raucous voices and the sound of laughter and occasional theatrical squeals of women who were presumably part of the evening's entertainment. The torches surrounding the hall had been lit, washing everything in the glow of fire.

Yom felt herself drawn to the glass wall once again, yearning to see it up close. The river outside was now a dark abyss.

"Nothing happens in this river that I don't know about." Renos's voice appeared behind Yom, her approach utterly silent.

Yom turned to see her standing less than a foot away, pieces of silver added to her hair and a chain with silver hooks locked around her stole. *Titan*, Yom reminded herself.

"Rivers are cruel things. They move in one direction. They are inevitable." Renos looked at the glass as she spoke, their translucent reflection projected onto the dark water. Yom squinted to see the faintest outline of weeds and debris moving with the current. In the depths, Yom spotted a dot of yellow. The dot moved towards them until its shape was revealed: elegant fins and a beautiful wisping tail.

"But my river is also beautiful."

"One of the wonders of Arcadia, no doubt," Yom replied diplomatically.

"Stories of Traiana have reached Inisfail, have they not?"

"Many stories, as varied as the creatures in this river."

"Yes, I would hope so." Renos leaned in, speaking directly in her ear. "I reserve my most creative punishments for liars and thieves."

"I can only hope we are so lucky to have a display during our visit." Yom bit her tongue. Renos laughed, and the sound sent chills through Yom.

"A whore with quite a mouth on her." She pulled Yom's hair over her nape and rested her weathered hand on Yom's bare shoulder, squeezing slightly. "Perhaps Cernunnos will let me keep you. I do adore beautiful things. You might have noticed how far whores can advance in my ranks, with the right skillset."

"My lady?" Rye's voice interrupted. "Shall we begin the feast?" Yom turned to look at her again, recalling her posse of young female underlings. *A whore who's Bound? You must be special.*

THEY SAT AT THE HEAD TABLE, RYE ON RENOS' RIGHT AND YOM AND Quia just to the right of Rye. The hall roared with laughter and loud voices, music and ale flowing freely. The heavy sound of scraping echoed as Renos pushed back her chair and stood to make a toast. The men instantly quieted.

"To our friends from Inisfail," she nodded at Yom and Quia, "whom the river's currents have brought to our table. May your direction stay true, your bed warm and your spirit whole." The rest of the hall cheered and joined in unison, "And to our enemies, may the river drag you down to its deepest depths, and the light of day turn its back on you." Yom gulped and cleared her throat at this. Crashes of glass and sloshing of ale rang through the hall over the roar of Eels. Renos raised her own silver goblet to Yom, who returned the gesture. She took the smallest sip she could to root out if there was any powder slipped into the salty plum wine.

"Now," Renos turned back to the hall, "time for the night's festivities!" The hall cheered and two Eels stood from nearby tables. Yom dreaded any festivities someone like Renos would enjoy.

A lanky boy without a torc around his neck stumbled into the space in front of the high table. And then, trembling with fear, Clementine was thrust next to him. Except Yom didn't only see Clementine. She saw Lior, placing her small body between the intruders and her mother Eden. The memory sank its claws into her, threatening to drown her. Instinctively she reached for her powderbelt, but her waist was empty. Left without an alternative, she grabbed the goblet of plum wine and downed it in one acrid gulp.

The two Eels who had positioned Clementine and the boy in the center backed away from them.

"What's happening?" Yom whispered to Rye.

"You'll see," Rye said with a devious smile.

"At the ready." Renos's voice echoed throughout the hall. The buzz of Eels grew in anticipation. Clementine and the boy slipped into fighting stances a few feet from each other. If Yom looked closely, she could see Clementine's hands, curled into fists, shaking. Yom's stomach dropped and her head swam.

"Set." Renos leaned forward slightly. *FIGHT!*

The noise of the hall faded away. Clementine got one good elbow into her opponent's upper abdomen before he rained down several more practiced and completely overmatched crosses and hooks on her. It was like watching a wolf fight a sheep.

Clementine hunched over on all fours on the ground, putting her hands up to yield. The boy didn't look happy at all that this was his lot, but Renos jutted her chin at him to continue. He reluctantly kicked Clementine in the gut and she fell over, wheezing and clutching her sides.

The boy looked hesitantly at Renos.

"Finish it, boy," she commanded.

And with an uppercut to Clementine's jaw, he did just that.

YOM PICKED AT HER PLATE OF CHARRED TROUT—head still attached—and roasted chicory. The lifeless eyes of the fish stared at Yom while a pumpkin roll was added to her plate and her tarnished silver cup was filled with more plum wine. Clementine's limp body had been hoisted over a shoulder and carried out of the hall, without anyone batting an eye. The image of Lior being similarly thrown over a shoulder and carried away was a phantom Yom could not banish, no matter how much of the plum wine she gulped down. She needed something stronger, preferably in powder form.

Rye was taking liberal doses of the Aetherium next to Yom, keeping a calloused hand planted on the powderbelt now slung across her chest. Yom ground her teeth as she waited to catch one of the kitchen knaves serving food.

The next time one of the scrawny arms reached over the table to refill her cup, Yom turned and grabbed his tunic to pull the server's face an inch from hers. "Bring me whatever powder you have." The boy stuttered before Yom set him back upright. "Now." He nodded and scurried off. Quia gave her a look of reproach, but she ignored him. He knew so little, his judgments had the weight of dried leaves.

Yom squeezed her eyes shut and rubbed her temples, but the hall around her paid no mind as it descended further into revelry. The Eels laughed and roared like buffoons, just as quick to clap each other on the back as they were to throw a punch. But any act of violence was taken as a part of the feasting. While Yom slipped further into a pit, Rye reflected the energy of the hall, becoming louder and louder, keeping up with any of the stocky Eels around her. On Yom's other side, Quia had barely touched his wine, and watched everything with the cool alertness of a predator waiting in the reeds.

The timid knave returned to Yom and held something in his hand. Yom snatched it, paranoid that others would see it and try to claim it for themselves. It was a scratched glass bottle with a square of linen sealing the top. Inside, a meager clump of a dull brown powder. It was likely Drifter's Mettle, a common powder made of nutmeg and tea leaves. If her powderbelt carried barley spirits, this was mulberry juice. But beggars couldn't be choosers. She ripped the linen lid off.

The powder was spiced and bitter in her nose, but Yom inhaled a few heaping portions of it just the same.

The boy fighter, the one who had beaten Clementine within an inch of her life, returned to the hall with his knuckles bound. Other than his ruddy cheeks, there was no other sign of what he had done. Eels clapped him on the back and cheered.

"He will be Bound within the fortnight," Rye said, slurring her words a bit. "Lucky him." She smiled darkly.

"He knows what that entails?"

"He's well aware. They all are, and still it's what they want. There's far worse fates."

Yom couldn't be sure of that. "The girl *wants* to be Bound?"

Rye nodded, poking Yom's breastbone with an overfamiliar finger. "Citrus has to prove she can fight first."

The girl had guts, sure, but she was far from ever winning a fight. "What is she getting from Renos?"

Rye shrugged. "She came here looking for work because her mother owes a sizable gambling debt in Gallia. Renos offered—" Rye paused to burp, filling the air with the acidity of digested wine, "to pay off the debt in exchange for the Bind."

Yom sat back, deflated by the hopelessness of that story. Rye followed her, leaning into her space. "Renos is willing to offer much, in exchange for a fight."

Yom stared at her, dreading where the Eel was going with this.

"Most people would assume Damian is the muscle of you two." Rye's pupils were so dilated her eyes appeared black. She was absolutely soaked. "But not me. You're an *escort*, traveling between provinces. You must know a thing or two about defending yourself."

A whore who's Bound? You must be special.

"Did you? When you were an escort?" Yom held her breath, hoping she was not guessing wrong.

Rye rolled her shoulders. "I had to. These louts," she waved a hand towards the sea of Eels in the hall, "may have learned to fight in the training rooms, and sure some might have had to fight for their dinner, but they don't know what it's like to fight for their bodies. No, that changes a person. That's why I know that you're a survivor, just like me."

Rye held her goblet up to Yom. Yom couldn't hold her gaze, knowing she didn't deserve any of this camaraderie, but she clinked her cup to Rye's.

"When they try to break us, we are reforged, stronger." Rye shifted back into her seat, her eyes glassy. "And we will show them what it means to fight."

Yom looked down at her plate, the dead eye of the fish watching her.

"Oi!" Rye whistled at a man who had brought a woman in similar silks as Yom up to dance on the table. "Cut it out. If the lady wanted to dance with you she would," Rye called to him.

"I promise she does," he said through a belch, holding her limbs like a puppet.

The table around him started laughing, then Rye began laughing, and the woman caught on the table in the middle of it all tried to laugh as well, like she was also in on the joke.

In a blink, Rye stood and whipped a throwing star from one of her weapons garters, skewering the man in the foot. Staking him to the table he danced on.

The man shrieked in pain and the woman with him screamed, climbing down over the dirty plates as soon as his hands left her. The Eels around the table laughed harder, as did Rye, until the entire room was engulfed in a drunken madness.

When Yom and Quia were led out of the river hall, nothing but the dregs of Eels were left: drunken oafs sleeping off the ale on the table and floors and dishes crusted with long congealed food. Yom had polished off the Drifter's Mettle, already devising a plan to sneak into the kitchens tomorrow to whip up whatever crude powder she could.

Yom and Quia undressed in their small dormitory facing away from each other, and settled onto their mats on opposite sides of the room, with a lamp glowing dimly between them. Neither the copious wine, nor the powder, nor the chaos of the evening had distracted Yom enough from the girl. From Lior. *There's far worse fates.* Yom wanted to throttle them, scream at them that there weren't. That they should run while they could still prove themselves free.

Yom blew out the lamp and laid her head down, pulling the thin quilt up to her neck. She realized in the quiet darkness that Quia hadn't said a word all evening. She had been too distracted by the unstable pull of Rye's orbit. Perhaps he had spent the night watching Yom take strange powders and gulp wine like it was water, regretting his choice of companion.

How do I know you're not plotting for a way to exchange me for a purse ten times larger than the bounty on our heads? He had asked just before they walked into a den of Eels that traded in men, and Yom had withheld an answer. It was a sign of how little Quia understood her, that he needed to ask. She thought of Lior being carried away, of Moss being branded and collared. Of herself, willing to trade away anything to escape her own thoughts.

"I would never have exchanged you," Yom risked whispering into the darkness, an offering. "I know what it is to be owned. I would not sentence anyone to that life, if given a choice."

VIII

A lady's touch

The clanging of metal woke Yom, even though the room remained submerged in darkness. Disorientation lingered behind her eyelids. She expected to see her dusty bedroom in the Cut but was greeted by a scarcely padded floor. *The lamp,* she remembered. She fumbled for a match, and struck it against the wood. A dim orange light glowed with the smell of phosphorus. The lamp's oil swallowed the the small fire, leaping into a flame large enough to illuminate the room. The room in which Yom was alone. Quia was gone.

A headache pounded behind Yom's eyes, worsening by the minute. She groped around her pack and clothes for several futile minutes until she remembered that her powderbelt had been taken. Her hand scraped against something metal and she remembered the small flask of spirits she'd nicked from the real Damian. It would have to do until she could find more powder, she figured as she took a hearty swig.

A single knock was the only warning before the room was flooded with the light of the hallway, outlining the lithe silhouette of a red-headed Eel.

"Good, you got the wake up call." Rye sounded like she had been awake for hours already. Yom's eyes adjusted to the light as she squinted at her. "You're coming with me today."

"Where's Damian?" Yom saw her powderbelt sitting askew on Rye's hips like some kind of trophy.

"How should I know?"

Yom found it very hard to believe Rye wouldn't be keeping tabs on both of them. But she didn't push further, wanting to keep the waters calm.

"What are we doing?"

"Paying someone a visit. We think a lady's touch will be helpful." Yom read between the lines. Rye was under the impression that Yom was a whore. And whores had one purpose in the eyes of someone like Cernunnos, or Renos.

"Why me? I'd like to stay with Damian." *Wherever he is.* The journey to Cataracta would take forever if Quia insisted on wandering off at every opportunity. He needed to get comfortable with the fact that their best odds were sticking together, as repulsive as he found Yom's company.

"Renos has personally requested you accompany me. It is an honor." Rye's face was unreadable. "Meet me in the hall in ten minutes." She tossed another parcel into Yom's lap and shut the door behind her, leaving no room for further argument. Yom debated putting up more of a fight, insisting she needed to find Quia, feigning ill. None of it would be worth the doubt it would cast on her, if this was an order directly from Renos.

Play the game, Yom assured herself. *Just keep your head above water.*

 contraption as Rye led her down a narrow cobblestone alley, the air damp and reeking of fish. It was ten times worse than the attire of last night's feast: nothing more than a set of silk panels that had to be carefully draped so that all the important bits stayed covered. They had to have imported it from Cataracta, for Yom's personal torture. The only assurance that Yom wouldn't accidentally end up naked beneath her coat on the streets of Traiana was a hooked belt that held the panels in place just under her bust. For the hundredth time since they arrived in this infernal province, Yom cursed the fact that she had to keep up a ruse as an escort. She adjusted the meager excuse for clothing as they walked, knowing by now they must be halfway across the city from the Gutter. Halfway across the city from Quia.

"Why do you wear gloves?" Rye asked. Yom was wary; they had shared some camaraderie the previous evening, but she sensed Rye played whist while others were playing commerce. And now she seemed only too pleased to bring them Okeanus knew where in a city where Yom was an utter stranger.

"One of my first clients had rather unpleasant tastes." It was an unfortunately believable lie; many disgusting stories circulated in whispers from the pleasure rooms. She hoped Rye would be inclined to believe it enough not to probe further.

Rye nodded knowingly, but did not look at Yom with pity. *We will show them what it means to fight.*

"Lior."

"What?" Yom's heart pounded before she remembered that this was her name in this province.

"It's not a common name," Rye said. Yom tried to shrug casually. "I've only ever met one other Lior."

Yom stumbled on a cobblestone in surprise. "You have?" Her heart sped up.

"Yes, a girl named Lior passed through here a long time ago. It must have been at least five or six years. I remember her being quite distinct looking. Pretty in a way that hadn't been broken yet."

Yom's heart broke into a gallop. "Where—"

"This is it." Rye paused at the foot of a wide stone staircase leading up to grand walnut doors. She took the steps casually, and just before pulling the large metal knocker, she turned to Yom.

"You're here for an out call." Rye grabbed Yom's hand and deposited something soft in it. It was a small purple pouch, which by weight and feel Yom recognized was full of powder.

Rye banged the knocker loudly and Yom slipped the pouch into a fold of her silk.

The door creaked open and a squat man in a gray tailcoat with starched gloves stood in its place.

"Doc called for services," Rye nudged her head back at Yom.

"Master is the head of the Royal Institute of Medicine, you will not address him as 'Doc.'" The suited man puffed out his chest. "It is 'Sir,' or 'Doctor.'"

"I'll call him whatever I want," Rye muttered as she breezed past the man. Yom looked between them and followed her.

"You must wait for me to announce you!" the man sputtered as he scurried after Rye.

A domed skylight bathing everything in the townhouse's foyer in a faint glow. Two curving staircases rounded each wall, and Rye was already climbing one, two steps at a time. The man gave up trying to stop them and ran to a long tasseled rope that hung near the front door, pulling it frantically. A distant bell rang.

At the top of the stairs, Rye walked up to a set of large wooden double doors at the end of the hall, and pushed them open. Clearly she had been here before. Yom slipped in behind Rye as the doors swung closed. The room was paneled in dark wood and the walls were lined with floor to ceiling shelves of heavy, leather bound books. One corner had two skeletons displayed, and another corner had a collection of jars with murky liquid and what looked like small rodents floating in them. She swallowed and turned to the front of the room where a large wood desk laden with papers faced out, an older man standing behind it. He wore a monocle, a crisp white collard shirt, and the blue robes of a royal doctor.

"Always a pleasure," the doctor nodded at Rye, as she plopped herself into a chair that faced him, kicking her feet onto his desk. "And who is this?" The doctor turned his attention to Yom and walked towards her, a gleam in his eye.

"This is Lior, newest girl we have."

"Lior," the doctor repeated to himself as he reached Yom. She fought the urge to break his nose for daring to speak that name. The doctor pushed her coat off her shoulders. She forced herself to stand still as her skin was exposed to the chilly air of the room. As he shifted, his blue robes parted slightly, revealing a fine silk neckscarf pierced with a delicately carved skull pin. Not an encouraging symbol for a doctor to sport. A shiver ran through her. The doctor's hands traveled from Yom's shoulders down her arms to her hips and then back up to gently graze her breasts. She stayed calm by imagining herself ripping out every hair on his body, one by one.

"Why don't you get started by making me a drink, sweetheart?" He motioned to the side of the study, where a collection of corked spirits and delicate crystal glasses lined a large cabinet.

Yom walked towards it, meeting Rye's eyes briefly. The Eel winked. So this was what the powder was for. To the right of the bottles, there was a smaller collection of vials filled with medicinal powders. Yom exhaled. It was quite easy to pocket a couple vials of sedative powders, recognizable by their pale blue color, as she flitted around the cabinet. Once the sedatives were tucked into her silks for later, she pulled down two crystal glasses, and unstoppered a decanter of an amber spirit to fill them with. Keeping her movements casual, she slipped the pouch out that Rye had given her and tipped it into one glass. A momentary whiff of it traveled up, and Yom's nose scrunched in its bitter wake. Hemlock, she recognized. A paralytic. One that would keep the doctor awake, but immobilized.

Yom turned back around, glass in each hand. She slugged back the undosed drink as she walked towards the doctor, placing the dosed one on his desk. Her throat burned deliciously.

"I see you have an attitude, little girl." The doctor watched her with bright eyes. "I will enjoy breaking you in," he said, tipping his own glass back. Yom watched him drink it down, the picture of innocence. He grunted as he put the glass down on the desk, and sat in his large leather wingback chair. He patted his thigh, now peaking out from his doctor's robes, watching her intently. She sauntered towards him, swaying her hips, doing her best impression of the girls from the pleasure rooms. Perched on his lap, his hand squeezing her waist, Yom had never felt less like herself.

"Give me—" his command stopped midway. Yom pretended to listen, waiting for a sign that the powder was taking effect. As expected, his face dropped suddenly. His eyes widened, but the rest of his body stiffened like a corpse.

"What did you do—" he barely managed to snarl at Yom before his face also stiffened, only his eyes able to flit around the room.

Rye had already rounded the desk to stand behind him, tying him to his own chair with rope. His body remained frozen but his eyes traveled from side to side, fearful and angry.

"Nicely done," Rye said.

"What was all this for?" Yom asked.

"You little bitch," the doctor moaned and gurgled through his lockjaw, or at least that's what it sounded like he was trying to say.

"What are you doing?" Yom looked between the doctor's stiff form and Rye.

"I wanted to bring you here to watch this. Change is afoot. People like us have a chance to make something of ourselves in the new world."

I'm just trying to make something of this, Lucan had said about his torc, under the shade of Cernunnos's oak tree. And now Rye's eyes held a similar hungry ambition. Wherever this was going, it would be no better than what she'd narrowly managed to escape in Inisfail. Yom felt like she was on the precipice of a plummet she would not survive; she tried to take a step back, but Rye put a forceful hand on her shoulder.

"When Renos bought me from the madam and Bound me in exchange, I knew that I had escaped and I could punish anyone who touched me without permission, but I still didn't feel free. They had taken something from me, and I didn't know how to get it back." Rye turned to watch the bound doctor, who barely looked lucid at this point, with a disturbing coldness in the draw of her face.

Yom's gut began to sink. Rye had been in this house before. The doctor knew her. Yom suspected that Rye had been here before under different circumstances.

"I think you've misunderstood—"

"I haven't misunderstood a thing. I know when someone is broken, because I've been broken too. I found a way to take back my power."

You're still the same little girl who came running to me all those years ago. Broken and alone. It felt like Yom's insides bled out of her each time someone saw these pieces of her she thought she disguised so well.

You've always been weak, a voice snarled from over Yom's shoulder. Her stomach dropped to her ankles; it was a voice she would recognize anywhere. But when she whipped around, expecting to see Cernunnos leering over her shoulder, nothing but the wall of spirits and jars of preserved animal parts stood behind her.

But the torc around her neck felt electric.

Rye drew a short dagger from one of the belts strapped on her leg and cut the doctor's cheek. Instantly, the pink line began to trickle blood.

"You can't," the doctor's simpering voice was barely coherent through the paralysis. "Renos promised..."

"Renos's promise is the only reason you're still alive. You've done your job beautifully, but now you're a liability."

The doctor's mouth opened but no words came out. His eyes widened.

Rye leaned in to speak inches from him. "I've been waiting a long time to finish this. I hope you didn't think you would get away with what you did." She looked up at Yom. "Renos has given me the gift of allowing me to take the life of every person who ever used me." Turning back to the doctor, she continued. "And this is the last one."

It was all wrong. Yom had been in so many fights and spars she had lost count; she knew she had just done something similar to Damian, allowing him to drug himself and then plying him for information. But she would not harm someone who couldn't defend himself. She saw Moss's barely conscious form on the floor, his head in the triarii's lethal grip. Power acquired through the murder of someone defenseless—even someone as deserving of reproach as this man—wasn't power. It was poison. There were lines one could not return from once crossed.

"Rye—"

"I think you're like me. I think you could do great things, if you heal yourself."

You think you can run from who you are? Cernunnos's voice echoed again, followed by his deep, mocking laugh. Yom turned again, and saw nothing other than the quiet, grotesque study. *Broken and alone. That's all you'll ever be.* Still, the torc sparked ever so faintly against her neck.

Yom shook her head and turned back to face Rye and the doctor. She must have been going mad, one sniff of powder too many. But there were some truths she held onto that had not been corrupted yet.

"This isn't healing."

"I wanted to give you the chance to do the honors. To see what it could be like if you joined me. The world is about to change, and we women have a chance to be at the top of the new order." *The new order.* It was almost word for word what Lucan had said in Inisfail, and it meant that Dougal's ominous words were already proving true. *When that province turns over its people and the Amaurosis legions are assembled, where will you run then?* The Queen already had her hand in multiple provinces. But Rye was living in a delusion if she thought escaping her madam by Binding herself, body and soul, to Renos was freedom. Yom wanted to laugh at the absurdity. And now, Cernunnos and Renos would use Amaurosis as another way to enslave them. Rye would never be free. No matter how many lives she claimed and wrongs she thought she was righting.

"I've never taken a life." This was one of Yom's deepest truths. One thing that couldn't be taken away from her.

"First one is the hardest." Rye shrugged and held the handle of the dagger out to her.

The doctor whimpered.

"I—can't."

Rye looked at her with disappointment before her expression neutralized once again. *We will show them what it means to fight.*

"Suit yourself."

"I am a royal official," the doctor huffed quietly, "the Queen—"

"This is Renos' land. Not the Queen's." Rye leaned in once again to the doctor's face, hands planted on either side, caging him in. "Renos can't help if a well-respected doctor got hooked on powders and put his trust in the wrong whore, can he? The death will be tragic of course, but the whore will face punishment, and the city will move on." Yom's stomach dropped again. Was she the whore who would be punished?

I will not be merciful when you return to Inisfail, Cernunnos spoke again, the torc humming against her skin. Yom didn't bother to turn and look behind her this time. She knew that the words were only in her head. Her abnormally clear head, robbed of powder. Her hand wrapped around the sedatives tucked in her silks, resolving to slip into its comforting oblivion the second Rye turned her back.

Rye stood and rounded the doctor's chair. "Renos thanks you for your service," she said, detached, as she pulled the knife across the doctor's throat in a flash. The blood spurted and splattered over Rye's hand and the doctor's own desk. Gurgling noises erupted from the doctor's throat, the light dimming in his eyes. The death was swift but cruel. Yom watched, immobilized, powerless to stop it.

"Let's get out of here," Rye said, not sounding at all like she had just murdered someone in cold blood. "I've always hated this room." She had wiped the dagger on the doctor's robes before resheathing it.

Yom took a stunned second to follow her. Rye was already walking back down the hallway by the time Yom left the study.

"Your master has had an unfortunate accident," Rye said to the suited man who had let them in. "Renos will be collecting on his debt by taking ownership of this property, and everything in it."

The man sputtered. "You can't—"

"I just did." Rye strode down the curved staircase. "If you have a problem with it, you can take it up with Renos herself."

Yom discreetly pulled the sedative out of her silks, and dumped a large dose into her palm. She focused on the back of Rye's head to ensure she didn't see what Yom was doing. But something white flashed behind a cracked door. It was a small sitting room with one window shedding light on a table and an armchair facing a fireplace. The furthest wall was covered floor to ceiling in vines of Moonflower.

It was the exact same as the wall of Moonflower she had seen in the Inisfail herb shop, grown right next to the Amaurosis.

You've done your job beautifully, but now you're a liability.

Renos will be collecting on his debt by taking ownership of this property, and everything in it.

Suddenly Yom was certain that the Queen had not just gotten her hands into Dressen Province but had planted Amaurosis in it as well. The vines of Moonflower felt as if they were winding through the air, slowly enclosing Yom in a floral tomb.

"Keep up with me," Rye called back, breaking the Moonflower's trance.

She desperately held the sedative powder up to her nose and inhaled its crushed, chalky crystals, until its oblivion welcomed her once again.

THE COBBLESTONE STREETS AND THE STENCH OF FISH HELD A NEW horror as Rye led them back to the Gutter. The stone and wood buildings, damp and creaking, loomed over Yom like giants. Men leered and women turned their noses up. *They know,* something slithered through her mind, whispering. *They know who you are.* Yom drew her coat tighter around herself.

If Yom fell behind a step, Rye reached back and cajoled her forward with a firm grip on her wrist. Like an owner leading its pet.

Something was sinking in Yom's gut, but submerged in powder, her thoughts strung together slower. In Yom's memory, or perhaps it was imagination, the doctor's study was not filled with small animal bodies but rather human body parts, cut precisely and preserved in fluid. The Moonflower was not contained to one wall in a closed off room, but rather it overran the house, affixing itself to the expensive furnishings and the walls, as if it had grown unchecked for years. And it was Yom who sat in the doctor's chair, bound by Rye's rope, while Rye stood over Yom, twirling a dagger between her fingers.

The death will be tragic of course, but the whore will face punishment and the city will move on.

Yom dragged her heels, trying to slow them, and wrest her arm from Rye's grip. "Where are we going?"

"Back to the Gutter."

"Where's Q—" Yom caught herself. "Damian?"

"He's waiting for you," Rye said cryptically. *How should I know?* She had said earlier that day when Yom asked the same question. "And look, here we are."

The rundown boat house appeared across the avenue. Standing outside it were the two sour faced sisters, with names Yom couldn't remember. And on the other side of the door, Clementine leaned against the rotted planks of the boathouse. She had a swatch of bruises forming on her cheek and chin, though she was still standing after the fight yesterday, which was impressive. And piled at Clementine's feet was a lump in a familiar ink cloak. Quia.

Yom sucked in a breath and rushed forward, but Rye held her back. Rye seemed to communicate something to Clementine, and the girl dipped her chin before hoisting Quia's limp body up so his head lolled back against the wall of the boathouse. His eyes were half open and his mouth hung slack. *He's been drugged,* Yom realized with a surprising amount of indignance.

"What did you give him?"

"Just something to take the edge off," Rye said coolly in Yom's ear.

The avenue the boathouse sat on suddenly felt more crowded. Yom looked around and noticed there were more Eels than just Rye's minions, and they were enclosing Yom in a circle.

"Lior of Inisfail," Rye said loudly, so the whole crowd could hear her. "You are hereby arrested for the murder of a royal official." Yom jerked and tried to turn, but Rye had gathered both her wrists and pinned them behind her back. "As penance for this crime, Renos will accept your participation in tonight's match."

The ground dropped from beneath Yom as she absorbed these words and felt metal manacles being locked around her wrists. The gathering of Eels around them grumbled and cheered.

"Don't worry," Rye whispered. "This is an opportunity for you. For all of us. And just to make sure you have the proper motivation, Agathon and Aurele poured a little Ruthbane into the spirits they gave Damian." Yom looked at Quia in a panic. Ruthbane was a fatal concoction of hogbean and morning glory, an old matron's powder. The compound would kill him in less than a day, and it would drive him mad along the way. "Don't worry," Yom could hear Rye smiling through her words, "We have the antidote on hand, and he'll get it just as soon as the match is done."

We will show them what it means to fight. Now Yom knew what Rye meant, and she couldn't decide if she needed to laugh or scream at the cruelty of it. This was some kind of statement Rye wanted to make, and now Yom and Quia were caught in the crosshairs.

"Citrus," Rye called.

Clementine left Quia slumped against the boathouse and walked forward to snatch something Rye tossed at her. The key to the manacles. Yom tried to see where on her person Clementine slipped the key, but it was hard to focus with the sedative powder still dulling her senses. And to make it more disorienting, Rye shoved Yom towards Clementine. The girl held Yom with one hand on the manacles, and one hand on her upper back. The sisters—Agathon and Aurele—pulled Quia to his feet and dragged him along right behind Yom, back down the stairs and into the Gutter.

RYE AND HER MINIONS HAD LOCKED THEM BACK IN THEIR CRAMPED dormitory. Yom had been uncuffed to allow her to change clothes. It was a simple muslin shirt that laced at the neck and a pair of knickerbockers held up by braces. It was low quality fighter's garb, but Yom wouldn't complain about being able to wear pants. They were left alone, Yom's hands once again bound behind her back. Quia had passed out on one of the sleeping mats and Yom kept an eye on him to make sure he didn't swallow his tongue or choke on vomit. Fortunately, he merely snored and accumulated a large puddle of drool beneath his face.

Yom had managed to rearrange herself so that her hands were in front of her, rather than pinned behind her back, to save her shoulders. Hours went by, or at least what felt like it, as she replayed what happened that day, and tried to find a solution to the quagmire they had found themselves in.

If they ran, first they would have to escape a fortress full of Eels, with Quia in nothing close to fighting shape, and then before they could go anywhere, she would have to scrounge up an antidote to the Ruthbane. Hogbean had no real antidote; she suspected Rye planned to feed him ipecac syrup to bring up the contents of his stomach.

If Yom fought, she would either cast further suspicion on herself by showing her fighting skills, or die trying to hide them. And if she managed to survive in Renos's arena, she still had to fabricate ten stone of powder out of thin air to make it onto Renos's convoy tomorrow.

It was a crossroads with two treacherous paths, but the route that would prevent them from becoming Renos's wanted fugitives—in addition to already being Cernunnos's—seemed to be the only reasonable option. Yom and Quia would not survive a manhunt in their current state.

Yom knocked her head against the wall several times, just enough to cause a dull bite of pain to distract her mind. She extracted the remaining vial of sedative powder from the doctor's study, and held it up to the dim light of the lamp. On the one hand, it was the only powder she had, and on the other, she couldn't enter a fighting ring on a sedative. She needed stimulants.

Quia groaned and his arms raised to first rub his eyes, then clutch his stomach.

"Easy." Yom put a hand on his arm to steady him. "Don't move too quickly, keep your breath even."

"What—happened—" Quia's amber eyes blinked open, some sleep still caught in the corners.

"No easy way to say this, but you've been poisoned." Yom grimaced.

"What?" Quia looked around, disoriented.

"This is all my fault, we should never have come here. I'm going to get us out." Yom raked her hands through her hair.

Quia shook his head. "We're in this together," he said, half-slurring. He propped himself up on one elbow. Then the other, until he was sitting up. He watched Yom through eyes still hooded by whatever spirits they had poured down his throat.

"What's that smell?" he asked, leaning towards her to sniff.

Yom shrugged, thinking of the doctor's study. "Preservation alcohol. Or the lime base most of my powders are made from."

Quia shook his head. "No that's not it. You've got this sweet, metallic kind of scent on you." He leaned forward even more, close enough for Yom to see day-old stubble roughening his jawline. He was more worn—more rugged—

than the Archivist apprentice who had left Inisfail. "It's a rather dark scent actually, like poison. Sweet, but poisonous."

Quia's words lingered between them. And he did not pull away.

"You want to know something?" he asked, his voice lowering.

Yom pressed herself back. "You're knackered, you don't want to say something—"

"You scare me," he said, an earnest and intent, albeit drunk, twinkle in his eye. "You don't care what anyone else thinks. You don't live for anyone but yourself."

Yom supposed he meant this as a compliment, but it felt backhanded. Her uncertainty must have shown on her face.

"I admire it," he assured her as his hand reached up to lightly brush her cheek. Yom noticed the height of his cheekbones, the swath of dark hair that cut across his forehead, the way his lips were parted slightly, as if he was on the verge of whispering a secret.

"And you're beautiful. In this way I don't fully understand. It's quite intimidating." His thumb stroked her cheek, and at this point Yom admonished herself for allowing someone this drunk to say whatever he felt like, sure to regret it later. He had all the control of a school boy drinking his first ale.

"That's enough of that, why don't we save the talking for when you're dry again. Yes?" She patted him on the knee.

"Don't worry." He dropped his hand and leaned back against the wall. "I'm betrothed." He enunciated every syllable with a touch of bitterness.

"You are?" Yom sat back as well, finding it strange that it had never come up that he had a beloved waiting for him back in Inisfail.

Quia nodded with his eyes closed.

"To who?" Yom whispered.

Quia shrugged. "I've never met her. It was arranged when I was born."

"So, she's…" Yom recalled her own warning to Quia the night before. *They will be listening to us.* "She's in your home?"

Again, Quia nodded.

"But why would you still consider yourself betrothed? She must have moved on by now, and you have no way—" Yom paused, realizing the answer to her own question. The numenborn. Dougal had said one of their abilities was being able to navigate Okeanus, to make the treacherous crossing between Arcadia and Panchaia. Of course Quia had always planned to return home, he merely lacked the tools to do it. But once they made it to Cataracta and found the numenborn, he would have what he needed. He could return home, and carry on with his life. And apparently that included a bride waiting for him.

"I was always planning to return home. I just didn't have the proper motivation until you started making my life miserable." Quia opened his eyes and smiled at her wryly.

Yom went for a soft jab to his ribs, but it didn't have any weight to it.

"Thank you," he whispered. Yom made the mistake of looking up and meeting his amber eyes. They were full of warmth, and for the first time all of it was directed at her. He shuffled to sit closer to her, pressing their shoulders and knees together. The smell of lampblack ink and wind was a heady perfume clinging to him. His eyes stayed fixed on her, and Yom had this foreign sensation that if she were to break down in that moment, he would try to put her back together.

"Wait." His face scrunched and he doubled over for a moment, holding his stomach and his throat. "Did you say I was poisoned?"

Yom couldn't stop the laugh that erupted at the absurdity of their predicament. "You missed a lot more than just that," she said through hiccuping laughs. "You were poisoned, Rye murdered a royal official, then arrested me for it, and now they're entering me into the match in Renos's arena tonight."

Quia's jaw went slack as he tried to absorb everything, but his mind was still somewhat vacant from the spirits.

"The—murdered? Match? Where—"

A sharp knock silenced Quia. "It's time," Clementine's muffled voice said from the other side of the door.

A SURLY EEL LED THEIR GROUP BACK TO THE RIVER HALL. Yom walked a half step behind Clementine, and Quia stumbled behind Yom. Clementine seemed a bit nervous, reaching back to check Yom's manacles every few minutes. The next time she reached back, Yom noticed there was something strange on her palm, like a string tied around it. But when Clementine's hand drew back, Yom saw nothing. But it wasn't nothing. Yom concentrated on her hand, until she reached back one more time. It was something thin and white, but not a string. It was a scar. The same scar Quia had shown her the day before. A scar he said every child of Panchaia bore.

Before Yom could wrap her mind around what this meant about Clementine, the doors to the river hall flew open, and they were thrust into its vibrating energy. Eels lined the tables, playing boisterous games that involved cards, coins, and cups. Tankards of ale flowed liberally, and the hall was flush with young women and men in the same red silk clothes Yom had donned earlier. A group of men clustered in one corner playing pan flutes and mandolins.

Arrangements of pale yellow primrose, white snowdrops and violet blue irises sat on each table and hung on the wall underneath the torches.

Yom had lost track of time.

These flowers meant it was the first day of the Feria, which meant Lupercalia was only eight days away. Eight days to ensure Quia made it to Cataracta, to the one place where and when they knew the numenborn would be.

On some invisible cue, Rye appeared, giving Yom a wink like they shared some passionate cause, and led them back to the high table, to the same seats they had sat in yesterday. Seats Yom was beginning to think were convenient for surveillance more than honor. Rye removed Yom's manacles; she supposed if she ran now, she would have an entire hall full of Eels to contend with.

The roar of the hall quieted when Renos clapped her hands together. "Welcome, welcome to Fight Night. We have an excellent lineup of fighters tonight, and I'm sure it will be a night full of surprises." The crowd cheered and banged tankards and fists against the wooden tables. "But before we feast, we need to welcome our new guests."

Yom looked around, confused. Hadn't they been welcomed yesterday?

"Tonight, we have the honor of hosting three triarii, visiting from the eternal city." At her words the rest of the hall melted away and Yom's blood iced. Renos spread her hands wide and the doors at the other end of the hall opened. Three black-armored triarii walked in, glistening and noiseless. The crowd was utterly silent. Their faces weren't visible beneath their armored hoods, but Yom knew the one in the center had a swath of knotted scars covering half his face. She swallowed and a balloon grew in her throat. She reached for Quia's hand, needing something to hold onto. Misho was here. And she had no illusions that this farce of being a nondescript whore would get past him.

"To honor their visit to our humble province," Renos continued as the triarii slinked through the hall. "One of our new guests has generously agreed to enter the arena. We will have not one new champion tonight, but two."

Yom didn't need any tries to guess who would be entering the ring. Any hope of escaping Renos's fortress, of getting to Cataracta, of stopping Cernunnos's war, evaporated into smoke.

The crowd erupted and Renos smiled. The kind of smile that thirsted for blood.

IX

Fight Night

YOM SCANNED FOR A WAY OUT, SLOUCHING IN HER CHAIR AND KEEPING her hair in a curtain to block her face. Luckily, Misho and the other triarii took their seat at a table in the center of the river hall, far enough away that it was plausible he hadn't seen her yet. She knew now she should have tried to run, Quia's poisoning and their lack of transportation be damned. But the hall was packed, and the only exit she had seen so far in the entire fortress was on the opposite end of it, across a sea of Eels eager to watch blood be spilt.

Yom's mind raced as she scarfed down roasted perch and wild turkey. She had a powder in her belt that she could give Quia—the same one Lucan had used on her—that would induce vomiting as well as a brief fainting spell. She kept Quia's goblet of plum wine away from him and forced him to drink as many cups of water as he could. Perhaps he could flush out the poison that way. Yom, however, gulped down several helpings of her salty wine, as well as Quia's. It was possible Quia looked concerned at the amount she was drinking, or he was feeling the worsening effects of the Ruthbane, but either way he didn't understand the position Yom was in. It would be worse to have nothing in her system for what was about to happen. It was hard enough that the only powder she had would be a death sentence before a fight.

Every plan her mind tried to formulate was paralyzed in its tracks by the thought of Misho handing her back to Cernunnos. His voice still rang in her ears: *I will not be merciful when you return to Inisfail.* Before she knew it, the feast was waning and the crowd was riling. Yom looked at Quia, whose copper skin had acquired a pale green tint and a sheen of sweat. Yom settled glumly into her seat, knowing they would be gambling with Quia's life if they ran. And as inconvenient as it was, she needed him. Her plans shifted. Quia wouldn't have long by the time the match started; Rye would need to give him the antidote right away. Rye must be bringing it to the arena. Yom just needed to survive, and avoid the scarred triarii, long enough to find it.

Perhaps sensing Yom's flight instinct, Renos commanded an entire company of Eels to escort her and Quia after dinner. Yom was hardly done sucking the salt off the perch skin before she was hoisted out of her seat.

"Wouldn't want you getting lost, now would we?" Renos said.

Yom managed to stay faced away from where Misho and the other two triarii were seated as she was shepherded out of the hall, but she couldn't help feeling like prey already caught in its predator's net. She had a desperate thought: that the ruse was up, that Renos was just playing with her. That she would be sent back to Inisfail in chains, as well as on a stretcher.

Yom and Quia walked, his arm slung over her shoulder for support, through a course of hallways she had not seen before, surrounded on all sides by Eels. They had draped a thick shroud of red velvet over her shoulders, with a heavy hood that obscured her vision. As they moved further away from the river hall, a distant chanting grew steadily louder.

"As soon as I find the antidote, we're leaving," she whispered to Quia, confident the chanting would cover their words.

"We should make a run for it now," Quia whispered back, as if Yom hadn't spent the entire feast deciding that would be impossible. "You can't go in that arena."

"If we leave, there's no guarantee I can find the ingredients for an antidote in time. You're on borrowed time as it is." Yom could hear Quia's labored breaths and feel the tremors in his limbs.

The chanting grew to a roar echoing from somewhere above them, punctuated by the pounding of drums. She had tried to keep track of the path they had taken through the Gutter but had lost all sense of direction. A rudderless fish pulled along a violently thrumming river.

Finally they reached a narrow corkscrew staircase that twisted up through a shaft in the wood and stone skeleton of the Gutter. After a winding, dizzying climb to the top, they crossed through a door which brought the chanting and drums into near perfect clarity. Despite sounding like they were in the arena, they found themselves in a small chamber with nothing but a water basin, a bench, and a vase of Feria flowers to remind Yom how close they were to Lupercalia. The Feria was eight days long, and Lupercalia fell on the final day.

"Come out when you're called." An Eel motioned to a door on the opposite side of the chamber. "And in case you get any ideas, you have a guard." He smiled nastily before shoving a small figure inside the room with them and shutting the door.

Clementine straightened up and met Yom's gaze, trying to look authoritative.

This must be some new kind of hazing for the girl. Throw her in as a warm up punching bag.

Yom rolled her eyes. "Draw the short straw, did you?"

"I don't know what you're talking about." Clementine raised her fists and split her stance, leaning into her back leg. "I'm here to stop you from escaping."

"No, those people are here to stop us from escaping." Yom pointed at the door they had come in, where they could still hear the raucous sounds of the group of Eels that had led them in. "You're here for what? Their amusement? To see what you look like after a few minutes alone with a criminal?"

Clementine's jaw set with reproach but also a flicker of fear.

Yom stepped next to the girl, and Clementine flinched before catching herself.

"These should always be covering your face." She moved the girl's small fists to cover her face and pushed her elbows towards her ribs. "Arms tight into your body."

As Yom arranged Clementine's hands, she remembered what she had seen before the feast began. Yom snatched the girl's hands abruptly and wrenched open her fists. Clementine was too surprised to stop her before Yom confirmed the hairline scar cut in a perfect diagonal over her palm.

"Look at this," Yom hissed at Quia. Clementine's eyes bulged and she tried to draw her palm away, but Yom didn't let go until Quia had a nice long look at the scar identical to his own.

"You—" Quia began, but then thought better of it. He said something low and guttural, with harsh sounds and a melodic lilt. It was another language, Yom realized. A Panchaian language.

Clementine held her hands up to her chest. "The only way you would—is if—" her eyes widened at Quia.

"Who are you?" Clementine and Quia both whisper-shouted at the same time.

They held a staring contest before Clementine relented. "I'm from here. My community does things a bit differently than most of Arcadia. They keep the old ways alive." Quia deflated a little, and it hit Yom how excited he must have been to encounter a piece of home.

Clementine raised her brow at him.

"It doesn't matter who I am." Quia waved an impatient hand. "We're on a very important mission." Quia leaned in and whispered beneath the roar of the crowd. "They're growing Amaurosis—"

"Yes, I know," Clementine said flatly. "You think you're the only ones trying to do something about it?"

That managed to strike Yom and Quia silent for a moment.

"So, you'll help us?" Yom asked.

Clementine gave them both a hard look. "I've spent a year working my way up from a kitchenmaid, and you see how they treat me. I don't have any power to help you."

With that reality, the brief flutter of hope evaporated.

Quia naturally had more questions for Clementine, but Yom felt herself withdrawing. The inevitability of entering Renos's arena to face the triarii— and Okeanus knew what other cutthroat champions—settled into her bones.

Yom sank down into a crouch against the wall, her hands beginning to shake.

"I've never taken a life," she said loud enough to halt Quia and Clementine's whispers. There was no need to share this, but it felt important for Quia to know. His words, strange and sweet, and soaked in spirits, begged to replay in her mind. *You're beautiful in this way I don't fully understand.*

"You have every right to defend yourself." Quia hobbled over, reminding her that he was actively battling hogbean poison. He sat next to her and pressed her hands together within his to still them. "The first one is the hardest."

Yom couldn't help but laugh. Of course Quia had taken a life before. He was a warrior.

"You're going to be fine. You're the toughest person I've ever met." He nudged a finger under her chin to lift her gaze, and when her eyes obeyed, she gasped.

Winding around his neck, like a noose, was a vine of Moonflower.

Starting to go a little mad, are we? Cernunnos laughed in her ear. The same spark she had felt earlier ignited in her torc.

"No!" Yom shrieked, swatting through the air all around her. *It's not real,* she repeated over and over in her head, *I just need more powder.*

"What is it?" Quia asked, sounding completely normal, not at all like a vine was poised to cut off his breathing.

Yom pulled her hair until she felt the sting biting at the root.

You must know, Cernunnos jeered, *all chemists go mad eventually.*

"Stop that." Quia pulled her hands off herself. "You'll hurt yourself."

"I can hear him," Yom rasped.

"Who?" Quia's hands rubbed up and down her arms, trying to comfort her.

Yom lifted up the ends of her torc. "Him."

Quia looked at her inquisitively for a moment.

"Am I going mad?" Yom asked in a desperate whisper.

Quia's eyes flitted all over her face, looking unsure of the answer to that question.

"No," Clementine said from across the room. "That seal binds your numen to his, which means he can sense certain things like your physical and emotional state."

Yom shuddered at the idea that Cernunnos could have a real presence in her mind. She would have preferred being declared mad.

"I need powder," Yom said hoarsely, holding her head in her hands.

"Don't fight it." Clementine knelt in front of her and tapped the Stag antlers of Yom's torc. It didn't help that every time Yom looked at her, she saw

Lior. "This connects your numen to his. It's a path that can be walked in both directions."

"She hasn't made her numen connection," Quia said.

"Doesn't matter. All you need to do is seek it."

"And how exactly would I do that?" Yom tried to look at Clementine as she spoke, but up close all she could pay attention to were her eyes. The truest blue, like cobalt, Lior's.

"By looking inward, finding its source. Running towards it."

Yom snorted, knowing what she would find if she looked inward. Someone who stood by as Eden was killed, and Lior was taken. Someone who made powders without asking who they would be sold to. Someone who couldn't even save one boy's life. In fact, she had spent the last six years running *away* from this person.

"I just need powder, and I'll be fine." Yom scanned the room again, unconsciously searching for anything she could use to dull her mind. Perhaps a mild stimulant. A euphoriant if she was lucky. Anything that could push away Cernunnos, the looming arena, the similarity between Clementine and Lior that kept pricking her like a needle.

When I find you, you will beg me to take you out of your misery, Cernunnos's voice appeared again, becoming predictable at how he liked to crawl in when she was at her lowest.

Yom groaned in pain.

"He only has the power you give him," Clementine said softly. "But he risks his for the taking, each time he manipulates your connection."

Cernunnos was laughing now, the sound clanging through her like an alarm. Laughing at Yom, at her attempt to do something good, as if helping Quia would ever be able to undo everything else she had done. Yom was losing the delicate thread of control she had over her own mind. His presence invaded her like the thoughts Yom constantly kept at bay, except harder to quiet. As if sensing Yom slipping further and further into a well, Cernunnos's laugh amplified.

"Your mind has power," Clementine whispered over the din. *"You* have power."

Yom couldn't possibly feel more powerless. Perhaps that was why it felt like there was little to lose in following Clementine's urging, and seeking the source of Cernunnos's voice.

At first, when Yom burrowed towards it, she was inundated by the thoughts she had been avoiding all this time, her mind like a still pool she could see directly through to the bottom. Thoughts of Eden. Of Lior. Of Moss. But she didn't need to acknowledge them, she reasoned as she tucked them away, back where they belonged. All she needed to do was tuck away the parts of herself that went with them. And what remained would be—

The connection emanated from the places where the torc touched her skin, a force—a power—she could grab onto if she concentrated on it, and held it. She could see its source, in the same way she had seen the Moonflower: it was there and it wasn't. A barefoot figure was seated cross-legged beneath an oak tree in a clearing bathed in amber light, his broad chest uncovered. Great stag antlers sprouted from beneath a mess of peppercorn hair, forming a velvety crown over him. Familiar gray eyes shot up to her and she was jolted out of it, her own eyes snapping open to see the same small chamber, with Clementine and Quia both huddled over her. But something had bled into her limbs. They were charged with some foreign strength, something almost animalistic.

Yom sat up and ripped off her lace gloves, flexing her fingers.

"Wait, you can't go out there without those, they will know—"

Clementine gasped and drew back when she saw Yom's hands. "You're—"

"Bluefingers, but you can call me Yom. Nice to meet you." Yom turned to Quia. "The ruse will be up as soon as the triarii sees me anyway. If I'm going to die, I'm not dying a whore. I'm a chemist. And I'm going to show them what that means." Quia was hesitant, but Yom would not be swayed on this.

"I'll be right here," he said as he pulled her into a hug that was frighteningly weak. Yom circled her arms around his ribs.

"I'm finding that antidote and I'm getting us out of here." *Even if I die trying*, she thought.

A distant horn blasted from the other side of the door.

"Champions!" Renos' voice boomed over the crowd, amplified to sound like it was raining down from the sky itself. *"Enter your arena!"*

Yom let go of Quia, gave a nod to Clementine, and turned to the door. The roaring of the crowd sounded like it was coming from all around her, but all she could see was a dusty path that sloped upwards, lined by two high wooden walls. At the end, a sliver of light. She took a deep inhale and began to walk, each step charged with a new and strange power.

Renos's amplified voice continued. *"Tonight you will witness Battles Royal. Ten champions will enter the arena, and the last champion standing wins."* Yom slowed. She looked back and even from twenty feet away the concern was evident on Quia's face, but she kept walking.

Yom reached the edge of the tunnel and stood at the mouth of the arena, but struggled to understand what she was looking at. There was a steady stream of water. It was not the depth or width of the river that lined the river hall—it must have been a small rivulet that fed into the larger river. Across the stream, rows of people stretched up at least fifty feet. But the cheering was also coming from above and behind her. Craning her neck up, she saw an identical crowd on this side of the rivulet. Then she understood. The arena was the water.

Yom swallowed her surprise. "Antlers up," she muttered to herself, taking her first step into the stream. The crowd erupted. The arena was lit somewhat by torches lining each side of the rivulet but mostly by the ghostly light of the full moon above them. She shuddered to think of what this arena felt like on a moonless night. The water came up to just under her knees, and the base of it was lined with smooth stones. Only a few small fish and weeds were carried on its gentle current.

Yom was the first fighter to enter the arena, which gave her time to survey the battlefield. Four other tunnels lined her side of the rivulet, and the mouths of five tunnels on the other side. One by one, champions emerged. Most were Eels Yom didn't recognize, but directly across from her, a gleam of bright red flashed through the shadow of the tunnel.

When Rye emerged, she leaped into the rivulet and raised her hands to stoke the fire of the crowd. They loved her. She was practically foaming at the mouth. Definitely on powders. *Probably Aetherium*, Yom thought with a pang of envy. Though it could play to Yom's favor; as invincible as the Aetherium would make Rye feel, it would dull her to real wounds. To Rye's left, the beetle-like armor of the triarii emerged, absorbing every inch of moonlight that touched it. Misho's armored hood was pulled back only enough to expose his mouth and the scars that wrapped down his chin. His mouth cracked into a smug grin, teeth gleaming like a ghost.

"*Champions,*" Renos's voice boomed. "*Select your weapon.*"

A rack sank into the riverbed to her right. Knives, swords, axes, and truncheons lined it, and further down, less familiar weapons like whips, tridents, spears and nets. She plucked two knives that were similar in size to the one she normally carried, holding one in each fist. She tried a few test swipes through the air, getting a feel for their balance and heft. The knives felt lighter in her hands, and Yom's movement more agile. She tested a few positions, leaning back on her heels and forward on the balls of her feet. The motion of her legs was slowed by the water's resistance, but her hips and upper body were steeped in a newfound strength. Yom felt more like a true stag than ever before.

Rye held out her hand to point at Yom—a warning. The crowd went wild. Rye held a net in one hand and a trident in the other. It wasn't what Yom expected given her affinity for rope, but she wasn't surprised Rye went for something more dramatic. The Eel seemed like quite the showman.

Their eyes stayed locked as Yom ignored Rye's provocation of the crowd.

"Step forward." Renos spoke again, and Yom caught sight of the titan, perched in a large carved wooden chair directly above the tunnel Rye had come out. Renos's beady eyes were trained on Yom, something in the air shifted the moment Renos noticed her blue fingers. The titan curled forward like a bird, disbelief and rage twisting her face for a moment. Feeling almost drunk on the newfound strength, Yom waved her blue fingers directly at her. Renos seethed.

All ten champions began a slow march toward the center of the rivulet. Rye took up her stance only a few arm lengths away from Yom, the powderbelt sitting mockingly on her hips. Yom concentrated her resolve on the promise of finally returning her powderbelt to her own waist.

"On my mark," Renos prompted, her voice dripping venom.

Yom crouched, her arms raised and crossed in front of her, knives out.

Rye noticed Yom's hands. Her brow furrowed in anger and she bared her teeth.

"THREE!" Renos began her countdown.

"I knew there was something off about you," Rye snarled. "You're the chemist everyone has been looking for." Her expression hardened and her eyes narrowed. "You're no whore." The last words dripped with betrayal.

"TWO!" The crowd joined in.

"I've done plenty to sell myself," Yom said. "Just not my body." She decided to knead into Rye further, to keep her talking, maybe even infuriate her enough that she would get sloppy. With a knife against a trident, Yom's best bet was to incapacitate Rye with blood loss. "You're not the only one who's been through bad things."

"ONE! FIGHT!" The crowd roared. Immediately the sound of splashing water and metal clashing rang out around them.

Yom lunged, going for a nick to the thigh, feeling quite limber. Rye blocked her with a graceful wave of the trident but not before Yom could slice into a minor artery. Yom righted herself and regained her stance on the other side of Rye, staying out of the trident's reach.

"You have no idea what I've been through," Rye spat. Every breath, every splash of water, every movement was in sharper clarity than Yom had ever experienced. Rye flung the net at Yom, but it was as if she watched it happening in slow motion. She skirted out of the way, the net only draping over Yom's left arm. The crowd cheered as Rye thrust her trident, but Yom twisted out of its path, managing to add another nick to the inside of Rye's upper arm as it pulled back. Yom twirled to free herself from the net.

"I thought I saw something in you, but I was wrong. You're weak. You're no survivor." She swung the trident in a deadly arc which Yom avoided easily, until she realized it was a diversion to get another good toss of the net. This time, the net landed straight on, and Yom was caught in its webbing as Rye cocked her trident for another thrust. Again, the crowd crescendoed as Rye went for a killing blow. Yom managed to jerk to the side just in time for the trident to slice open her arm rather than her chest. But with the reduced impact of hitting a limb rather than her torso, Rye stumbled forward a step more than she had anticipated. A window opened up for Yom to sink her knife deep into Rye's gut. A killing blow. But already, Rye's linen shirt was plastered to her arm with blood, and a trail of crimson followed her in the water from her leg. It wasn't enough blood loss on its own to kill her, but she had to start feeling its effects. Yom hesitated for an instant before slashing the knife shallowly across Rye's stomach. Rye saw Yom's hesitation and smiled as she righted herself.

"See? Weak. But we do have one thing in common." There was a slur in Rye's words, an absent glaze settling into her eyes. Rye didn't seem to notice, the powder no doubt dampening her perception. "You and I are meant to be alone. At least I know who I am—"

Yom prepared herself for another strike but Rye's face fell. *Finally*, Yom thought. Rye looked down at herself, seeing her shirt and trousers soaked with blood. She turned back to Yom and drew her arm back for another thrust but it fell short. Then she swayed on her feet for a moment before falling into the water on her knees.

"What have you—" she muttered before she sank down onto her hands.

Yom walked towards her through the resistance of the current and kicked the trident out of Rye's hand. The rivulet carried it away. Rye panted, unresponsive. Yom reached down and unbuckled her powderbelt from Rye's waist. The Eel was gaunt, but her hands tried to claw at Yom still.

"No," Rye huffed weakly.

"Tell me where the antidote is." Yom kneeled in the water, keeping an eye on the fights unfolding around them.

Rye tried to swat her away, but Yom grabbed her wrist and squeezed hard enough to bruise. "Tell me," she ground out.

"In...belt," Rye muttered.

Yom looked down at her powderbelt and realized a vial had been slipped into it that contained a syrup rather than a powder. She flung Rye's wrist back to her side and was about to walk away, when she noticed a piece of tanned leather. Quia's sheathed knife sat in one of Rye's weapons garters. Yom slipped it free while Rye broke into a wheeze, and wedged it inside her powderbelt.

Yom backed away from Rye's collapsed form, the sound of the other matches coming back, muffled during her fight with Rye. It seemed she had one more second of everyone else being occupied by their own match, so she backed towards the mouth of the tunnel she had come in through.

"HERE!" Yom shouted over her shoulder, unable to turn her back on the arena. *"Take the antidote!"* She left the syrup on the ledge of the tunnel and was about to glance back to make sure someone saw it, when one of the other champions caught her eye. He was in the process of dragging a broadsword

across someone's throat. He dropped the body unceremoniously into the water and waded towards Yom, a bone chilling smile on his face.

Yom abandoned the antidote, hoping Clementine or Quia saw it, and gripped her knives tighter to trudge towards the champion. She considered the most strategic cuts to go for: behind the knees, the shoulder joint, maybe a gouge to the eye if it came down to it. The man had madness pulsing in his eyes, likely part powder and part adrenaline. He even had thin trails of drool on his chin, like he was salivating at the very thought of a fight. Yom's mouth dried out.

"I love when they put little girls in here," the man snarled, baring his teeth like fangs. "You have the prettiest screams."

"Hate to break it to you but I'm not much of a screamer." Yom lunged at his knees. She slashed deep enough to sever some important tendons and the man grunted in anger. But something whizzed over her head, and a jet black arrow lodged in the man's throat, a crisp stream of blood flowing down from it.

Yom whipped around. Approaching her, the rest of the rivulet suddenly emptied of fighters, was Misho. Not a piece of armor—not even his hood—was out of place. The arena hadn't ravaged him at all. Her stomach knotted and her eyes darted around. From far away she saw movement in the mouth of her tunnel. She considered trying to make a run for it, but Misho had a crossbow. He could shoot her at that range. And if he followed her, Quia would be no match for the triarii. Yom planted herself, keeping an eye on Misho's amorphous black form. She gripped her knives tighter, still feeling Cernunnos's numen accumulated in her limbs. *Survive,* she commanded herself. *Just keep your head above water.*

The scarred triarii sauntered forward; the only sounds that registered now were the soft ripples from both of their steps and the cacophony of the crowd.

"Nowhere to run, Yom." Misho spoke calmly.

"How do you know that name?" She sidestepped, wanting to draw Misho away from the tunnel.

"I know everything."

Yom stepped further from the tunnel, afraid of what *everything* entailed.

"If you run, you'll get an arrow to the heart." Misho held up his crossbow. "If you stay, you'll only need to contend with my hands."

"Don't you want to take a weapon?" Yom asked shakily, though she paused her steps. "You can't be that prideful."

"I have my weapon." He smiled crookedly, the effect even more unsettling since only his mouth and chin remained uncovered. "I looked into you. Learned all about your time with Eden and her daughter. What was her name?" Misho paused, pretending to think. "Oh right, *Lior.*"

Yom lost the sensation in her legs.

"Not a very smart name to give them here," Misho clucked his tongue. "Did you know Lior was brought through here after she disappeared? I found that out too. She was sold to a madam from a southern province."

Yom went limp. The thoughts she so meticulously guarded herself from gnashed their teeth. *Your fault your fault your fault*, they hissed.

Powder. She needed powder. Yom fumbled with shaking hands for her powderbelt, barely registering which vial held what until her hand found the leather pouch of Aetherium.

"That madam is known for having particularly violent clients. The word is that girls only last a year or two in her company. And if they do make it to eighteen, they're thrown out on the street."

"You're lying," Yom whispered desperately as she yanked open the pouch and found barely a pinch of the Aetherium left. She held it up to her nose, but not before she realized that Rye had corroborated Misho's words unknowingly that same morning. Yom's gut sank knowing that whatever exaggerations Misho spun, there was some grain of truth in it. *Murderer murderer murderer,* her thoughts sneered, until nothing of her conviction was left. She inhaled the Aetherium and the world shifted into something warm and colorful, the lights and the water softening until she became vaguely aware that every drop of Cernunnos's power had vanished.

"I wish I was. But the truth is, you failed to protect your dear friend. And she's probably buried in a shallow, unmarked grave because of it." Misho cocked his head to the side. "Or maybe she was more than a friend, maybe you loved—"

"Why are you telling me this?" Yom's voice cracked. She didn't think she could break into smaller pieces, but the Aetherium could only do so much. It couldn't stop her jagged edges from giving way to deeper fractures.

Misho stepped forward until he stood an arm's length away. "Because I know what it's like to be abandoned. And I know that only the lowest of the low would leave someone to that fate."

Something between a whimper and a cry erupted from Yom at his words. Misho was right; he had his weapon, and he had wielded it fatally.

"Now," his tone changed, "how about we finally have that spar?"

Misho wasted no time with a sucker punch to the gut. Yom doubled over, wheezing. The Aetherium softened the pain, but it couldn't help the wind being knocked out of her. Misho followed with a knee to Yom's nose. Something crunched and a gush of blood streamed over her mouth.

Whatever of her own strength remained, Yom channeled into a swing of one of her knives. She managed to make contact, but the triarii armor brushed off the knife as if it was a blade of grass.

Misho chuckled and grabbed her by the collar to pull her within an inch of his face. She was so close she could see beneath his hood, the knotted scars of his face twisting in the moonlight. His hand snaked around to grip her throat. "Cernunnos is very displeased with you," he murmured before thrusting her head underwater.

She managed to close her mouth and hold her breath before she swallowed too much river water, but the feeling of being submerged under the current disoriented her so much, she could barely tell which way was up. She tried to escape his grip, break his hold on her neck, but her fight was all but gone. The air in her lungs was dwindling and she felt her body's urge to breathe again, even though she would be inhaling water. She counted the seconds, trying to distract herself as her lungs burned, but the urge was tugging at her. Just as she felt her senses weakening, she was pulled up to the surface, gasping and choking.

Even her ability to think was fading. She grasped for something to stall Misho. "I guess if you're working for Cernunnos, that makes us colleagues."

"My master has an agreement with Cernunnos. As he does with Renos." Misho smiled like death himself. "You have no idea what you've put yourself in the middle of." Yom let her head fall back to look behind her, deciding she could still make sure Quia got out of here while she had Misho occupied. But when she looked back at the tunnel, Quia now stood at its mouth, holding a dagger he must have gotten from the weapons rack. Yom must have been imagining it from lack of air, but it looked like Quia was putting the dagger in his mouth.

"Quit playing with your food, triarii, and end the fight," Renos's voice boomed.

"Don't worry, I'll make sure your boyfriend has a cushy cell in Cataracta. They do love having a Panchaian to play with."

Yom sputtered at his words, righting herself to look back at Misho. "He's not—"

"Save your breath, I already know. You should be more worried about yourself. As you've seen, accidents happen in this arena all the time."

Misho pushed her head underwater once again. It took even less time for her lungs to cry out for air, and she flailed with the last of her energy. Her eyes bulged in the river water, seeing the distorted image of Misho above her, teeth gleaming in triumph. She thought of Moss, of Eden, of Lior. For once she hoped they did still exist as spirits somewhere, so that they could hear her pleading for forgiveness. Near the end, she went still. Ready for it to be over.

Yom's eyelids were sagging closed when the hands holding her underwater loosened. Then, seemingly hit by nothing, Misho was thrown off her. Yom floated to the surface and her lungs refilled with air. But she could barely move. Strong hands pulled her up out of the water and she was hoisted over a warm, solid shoulder.

"Any involvement of an outsider in the fight is grounds for immediate forfeit," Renos's voice sounded far away and angry to Yom's waterlogged ears. She was being carried somewhere.

"Don't let them leave," Renos's amplified voice snarled.

Hands deposited Yom gently on the dry lip of the tunnel and she shivered. The velvet shroud was placed over her and she clung to it.

"You did so well out there." It was Quia's eyes who found hers. He held her face with something like reverence. And he had a lot more color in his cheeks than when Yom had left, despite his lips being lined with red. "I know you're weak right now, but we need to go. Can you walk?" Yom nodded her head, waiting for the feeling to return to her soaked limbs.

"The triarii—" She looked back at the arena, seeing Misho hunched over on all fours, on the other side of the rivulet. How had Quia thrown him that far without touching him? But worse than Misho, Eels began pouring out of the tunnel mouths. Some especially rabid ones made the fifteen foot jump from the lowest row of the stands into the rivulet. Yom still couldn't breathe properly and a weight had settled into her limbs, wrung out completely of their energy.

"Here." Yom pulled the leather wrapped knife from her belt with shaking fingers. "Quia, you have to go without me—"

"Do you trust me? Do you promise that no matter what happens, you won't look at me differently?" Quia's face held concern, every ounce of it focused on Yom.

"I—" Yom looked around, the Eels were crossing the rivulet in a stampede. "Of course."

"I'm going to need your help this time," Quia said as he raised the leather-wrapped knife. Up close she could see what its blade was made of. Bone. He drew the tip through his open mouth, down his tongue.

Yom failed to miss the dark clumps of blood already in his mouth. "What—"

But Quia made no attempt to explain as he pulled her into a tight hug. Then it started. Over the growling mob of Eels, over the splash of feet rushing through water. A faint susurrus—a whispered chant—coming from Quia. Yom could not understand it but she held onto him tightly. If this was some kind of Panchaian pre-death ritual, then the least she could do was honor it.

Quia pulled away from her and continued chanting, louder now, blood lining his lips. The words were nonsensical, guttural sounds. He stepped away from Yom and walked calmly towards the rushing onslaught of Eels. Yom scuttled back into the tunnel, feeling the air around her pick up its speed, an almost human whistle in it. Clementine stepped up next to Yom, helping her to her feet.

Quia glanced back at them as his eyes opened. His pupils had expanded so there was no white left. Just a dark, bottomless black. The same state Moss had entered before he became unrecognizable.

Yom stumbled back to get away from him. But something in Quia's expression seemed less vacant than Moss had been. He was looking at her as if he still knew her.

"He's a numenborn," Clementine whispered, and sank to her knees in deference, eyes wide.

The Eels were closing in from all sides of the rivulet. Quia took a long breath in from his blood lined lips, crouching back as if readying a slingshot. He held the breath in himself for a split second, before whipping forward. When he exhaled, a heavy gust of wind hit the wall of marauding Eels and knocked them back like they were pins toppling over. But Quia was already bounding through the water, moving fluidly as if he was wind lapping at its surface. Before the Eels could right themselves, Quia's chest puffed up with air again and he released another exhale, turning in a half moon so he reached even the Eels still in the far stands.

It could be influence over weather, wind or rain for example, Dougal had said when describing a numenborn. Quia was a numenborn. He had been one the entire time. Then who were they seeking in Cataracta?

"You both need to leave." Clementine stood again and braced Yom's arms. "They cannot capture him."

Yom nodded numbly.

"Get his attention." Clementine shook her, and it finally roused Yom.

"QUIA!" Yom shouted, still not sure if he would respond to his own name. But those ink black eyes found her immediately. She hooked a thumb back towards the tunnel they had come in and he gave a half nod.

Quia backed towards them, releasing more gusts in each direction as he went. The crowd of Eels careened in his wake. In the distance, Renos shoved the wind blown bodies of her own Eels off herself, and narrowed in on them just as Quia latched an arm around Yom's waist. They raced back through the tunnel, not waiting to see what Renos did next.

"Quia," Yom said his name, still not able to believe she was speaking to the same taciturn apprentice.

"Yes?" His voice sounded normal, if not a bit lower and a bit rougher. His face was fierce, and his grip on her crushingly protective.

"You might have mentioned that earlier!" Clementine said shrilly as she waved them through the door with an impatient hand.

"Wait," Yom returned to herself, remembering she had her powderbelt once again. Plucking a vial from it, she wound it over her head and hurled it at the tunnel behind them. The resulting cloud of powder caught fire, immediately latching onto the wood walls. Ignium, incendiary powder.

Clementine grunted and latched the door of the fighter's chamber closed behind them.

The three of them stood in a circle, Quia's eyes still engulfed in black.

"You need to get out of here, now." Clementine watched Quia carefully. Gone was the timid Eel-in-training. The girl had a fierceness when she fought for something she believed in.

Quia nodded. "You can lead us back to the river hall and then we can get above ground."

Clementine shook her head. "You'll be dead before you reach the river hall. Either by the hand of Eels, or by depleting your own strength too much and slipping from trance."

Quia stood up straighter. He was the picture of vitality, further than any antidote could have taken him. *It must be this state he's in.*

"I can make it."

"No. You need to call him."

Quia laughed in disbelief. "Absolutely not."

Clementine took a step towards him, unflinching as she looked in his black eyes. "You try to leave out that door—" she gestured to the door ahead of them, which led back to the maze of the Gutter. "You will die, or you will be captured. And I think you know which one is worse."

Quia looked at Yom, and whatever he saw made his shoulders drop. "The cost is too steep."

Clementine rolled her eyes. "So, bargain. He's an immortal. It's what they do."

Yom's ears perked up. "Who are you calling? A titan? Would one of them help us—"

"Not a titan," Quia said softly. Distant clangs came from the Gutter side door. "But I guess we don't have another choice."

Quia directed Clementine to make a fire, leaving Yom to catch her breath. She was still winded from being almost drowned. Clementine and Quia ripped off several slivers of the Gutter-side door and piled them together, tossing a crumpled piece of parchment on the top for kindling. Quia produced something from his pack that he scraped together—a harsh sound of rock scraping rock—and suddenly the small room was filled with sparks.

Once fire caught the pile, Quia held the tip of one more sliver of wood in the fire until it caught, then blew it out. Using the charred end, he drew something on the stone floor. It was some kind of rune that Yom had never seen before, like the shape of a sun and a moon and some pathway between them connected by lines and circles.

Quia finished drawing and turned back to the fire, holding something in his hand. His other hand motioned for Yom to stand with him.

"Where will you go?" Clementine asked as Quia poised himself for something. Yom was still not sure what she was witnessing.

"I'll ask for the smallest journey, for the smallest cost."

Clementine shook her head. "You can't leave it up to him. He'll deliver you to a pack of wolves, or into the jaws of another titan." She seemed to consider something for a second. "Go to the Forest of Ardennes."

Yom's eyes bulged at the suggestion. "Absolutely not." Yom turned to Quia. "People who go into the Ardennes don't come out. It's outside the bounds of Arcadia."

Clementine pressed on. "It borders Dressen. It's the closest realm, and no one will think to look for you there. Like she said, it's out of bounds."

Quia watched Yom as he weighed Clementine's suggestion. "We have to be very deliberate with where we go. Too far and the cost will be too steep. You have no idea how these creatures operate."

"My home is in the Ardennes. If your heart is true, you will pass through it unharmed," Clementine said.

Now Quia and Clementine were both looking at Yom imploringly. Every second they wasted, the room filled up more with smoke, the crackle of the fire Yom had started in the hallway growing closer.

"Fine," Yom groaned. "But I don't like this."

"You're really not going to like what comes next," Quia muttered.

"And what about you?" Yom asked Clementine. "Are you coming with us? Or just shipping us off to certain death?"

Clementine smiled like the opportunist she was, and her eyes sparkled. In that moment, Yom's heart ached for how much she reminded her of Lior. Not just in appearance, but spirit too.

"I'm staying here. I've got my own battles to fight."

"Thank you for everything." Quia nodded, and the girl nodded back. One last look at the pair of them, and Clementine slipped out the Gutter-side door.

"Ready?" Quia asked.

"For what?"

Quia laughed and flung what was in his hand into the fire. It was a small green disc, like a coin. When it collided with the heart of the fire, the flames erupted a greenish blue. The wind picked up and swirled over the fire, funneling the smoke into a pillar, practically choking them in the tiny room. The swirling smoke took form and limbs appeared in wisps, growing more solid with each revolution, until a figure whorled into view.

Yom was certain she was hallucinating from lack of air in her lungs, or perhaps a contusion to the head she had forgotten about. "What's—"

"Thoth," Quia projected his voice clearly and calmly, though he was shaking. "The Traveler."

The figure, now solid bronze flesh gleaming in the firelight, stepped out barefoot from the smoke above the fire. He had a filled-in black circle on one cheek and a black outline of a circle on the other. He wore no clothes other than a piece of white fabric tied at the hip, his muscles taut and a menagerie of small silver wings flitting from his feet up to his knees. The smell of licorice permeated the air, cutting the harshness of the smoke. Thoth took a sharp, lingering inhale.

"It's been a long time since someone has summoned me here." He closed his eyes, soaking it in.

"I call on you for travel," Quia spoke clearly.

"You know the cost, mortal?" Thoth looked amused. He circled Quia and Yom like a vulture. "And still you ask this of me?"

"I beseech you," Quia said through gritted teeth. "You are our only hope."

At this, Thoth smirked, as if he had bested Quia somehow.

Yom's lip curled at Quia's forced obsequence. Thoth sensed it, looking straight at her. His eyes, silvery gray, matched the cold inhumanity of Renos and Cernunnos.

"I beseech you," Quia repeated, taking Thoth's attention back. "Carry us to the Forest of Ardennes. To its edge that borders Dressen."

"As you wish." Thoth's mouth spread in a wide smile, and suddenly Yom felt very uneasy about the bargain they were about to enter.

"You must keep us together, and you cannot deliver us anywhere in harm's way."

Thoth assumed a look of mock innocence. "I would never, mortal."

Footsteps pounded outside the Gutter door. The Eels were coming up the staircase. Yom briefly worried about what would come of Clementine, but the girl had survived this long. She had some instincts.

Thoth once again took up his perch above the fire, holding his hand out to Quia first. "From you, I ask for your south wind." Yom looked between the two, unsure of what anything meant at this point.

Quia looked surprised. "What will you do with it?"

Thoth shook his head. "The bargain expires in—"

"No—" Quia's jaw was tense as he jerked out a hand to meet Thoth's. When their limbs touched, a burst of wind released in the room, scattering some of the smoke. It smelled of salt and olive. In the wake of this gust of wind, Quia vanished. Now, only Thoth and Yom remained in the room. From the sound of it, the Eels were closing in on the top of the staircase. Yom prayed Clementine had a plan to stall them.

Thoth's hand stretched out to Yom. "There is something strange in your memories, mortal." He sniffed the air, as if scenting blood. Yom held herself, self conscious. "I suspect it would cost you more if I give, rather than take."

Yom stared at his hand, full of doubt, wondering what that could mean. Before she could decide, the sound of wood splintering and a fire raging erupted in the room. To her shock, it came from the door that led through a tunnel engulfed in flames, stretching from the arena.

A figure covered in black armor that glistened in the firelight emerged, his hood pulled back so the mad fury in his face was on full display. Misho had walked through fire to find her again.

A dagger glinted in his hand.

Misho's arm reared back, either to plunge the dagger or throw it, and Yom didn't wait to find out. She grabbed Thoth's hand and the second her skin met his, she whorled into his smoke, colors and light exploding in her mind, spearheaded by a pair of blue eyes that threatened to drown her in fear and longing. Lior.

X

Spirits

YOM TRAVELED THROUGH SMOKE-FILLED DARKNESS UNTIL SHE WAS thrown onto uneven, damp ground. Trees leered all around her, the sounds of animals and insects a menacing thrum. Something in her side was causing a distantly sharp pain.

"You made it." Quia's smiling face entered Yom's periphery. He brushed dirt off her clothes and straightened out some of her hair. "Hopefully he didn't take anything too precious," Quia said.

Yom felt as if she was in a dream, or a nightmare. It didn't feel real, to be one second away from suffocating from smoke in the Gutter, to now be thrust into a treacherous forest that she had intended to avoid for the rest of her likely short life.

I suspect it would cost you more if I give, rather than take.

But other than the burst of sensation when she had first touched Thoth's hand, she felt no different. She had seen Lior's eyes, certainly, but that hallucination seemed to have passed.

"We need to be careful. Forests are the home of spirits and demons alike." Quia helped Yom sit up. The same second his hand touched the hilt of something metal in her side, the sharp pain Yom had felt returned. And this time it was excruciating.

"Shit, Yom, what happened?" Quia asked, horrified, as they both realized a dagger was lodged in Yom's gut.

"Oh bloody Okeanus," Yom groaned. "The triarii threw the dagger just as Thoth took me." As Quia examined where the blade sunk into her side, they could both hear the squelch of Yom's shirt, rapidly becoming soaked with blood.

It may have been the sound of all the blood, the pain that was finally hitting her, or the adrenaline and Aetherium of the arena wearing off, but suddenly she was woozy and disoriented. Her eyelids were drifting closed, coating the whole world in a blur.

Quia was flitting around Yom, emptying both their packs, searching for anything that could help her.

Her entire body was feeling limper by the second, as if she could melt into the forest, should she please. The pain in her gut was sharply demanding, although after a few minutes it too was swallowed by numbness. Almost like she was on powder. The thought of powder awakened a craving, but she was able to set it aside. The numbness could only mean one thing. Death was closing in. Yom smiled.

"Stay awake, Yom." Quia gripped her jaw and tilted her head to meet his rabid eyes. "You're not dying here." Quia's voice sounded as if it was projecting through a tunnel. The gray light of dawn was bleeding into the sky. Everything felt light, like she was made of air, only tethered to the ground by Quia's hand. Or perhaps made of earth, ready to return to it.

A twig snapped, and something red swished behind a tree.

"Eden?" Yom cried out, leaning towards the sound. It had to be her, there to lead her into Death's arms. *Or it's nothing more than a hallucination, like the Moonflower vines*, another thought countered. She shoved the dissenter aside, wanting it to be real with every thread of her unraveling mind.

Something in her side ached. A thorn that needed to be removed.

"There's nothing there, Yom." Quia's voice was soft behind her. But Yom saw it again, more clearly: the edge of a red apron disappearing around the trunk of a tree. The echo of Eden's voice, round and musical.

The thorn was pulsing now, and Yom groped for it. When her hand found the edge sticking out of her, she gripped it tightly and prepared herself.

"No!" Quia tried to grab her, but Yom ripped out the thorn before he could stop it. She pushed herself up and warm blood gushed from where the thorn had been. She managed to stumble away before Quia could get to her. "You're losing too much blood!" he yelled.

Yom ran towards Eden's voice, bracing her hands on the roots and trunks she passed, desperate to see Eden's face again. As she chased after it, the sound of laughter grew, and another laugh joined it, one that belonged to the most beautiful person Yom had ever known. One that she only heard in dreams and the deepest recesses of her memory. Images of Lior invaded her: clear blue eyes, dark hair and rosy cheeks, twirling in a dance.

Yom was moving so fast, she almost missed it. A hand jutted out between two roots, as if it had been buried alive underneath them. It hung lifeless, the skin dirtied and turning a sallow gray. She skidded back, startled, then changed direction and continued.

You'll never catch me! Lior said with a melodic giggle. Her voice sounded lower, older than Yom recalled, but she couldn't be sure. All Yom could see were the edges: a lock of dark hair blowing in the breeze, a sliver of her hip swishing behind a moss-covered tree, a hand and a slender forearm wrapping around a branch. Yom chased her, each crumb making her hungrier for more.

"Wait!" Yom shouted after her. "Don't go on your own, it's not safe!" she begged. Lior was fearless, willing to take on death itself if it were to tempt her. Fearless and foolish. Yom had seen death too many times before she came to Inisfail not to fear it. Each visit had withered a piece of herself. But Eden had found her, taken her in. Started to nourish the parts of her that felt like dead branches, weighing her down, whispering to Yom before bed that one day these dark pieces of ourselves could be shed and regrown anew. Never what they were, but something new. But then death had returned once more to claim Eden, as if sensing that Yom had grown too comfortable in its absence.

Her mind was caught straddling the past and the present. When she looked around the forest again, all she saw was a sea of green, endless. Turning in circles over uneven root-covered ground, she searched for any sign of Eden or Lior. There was a flash of something pale; a slender leg escaping from inside another tree trunk. Its toes were bright white and the calf attached to it was blueing around the edges, a color that no blood could beat beneath.

"*EDEN!*" Yom bellowed desperately. "*LIOR!*" She blazed ahead, unsure if she went forwards or backwards. "There's a monster in these woods, it's not safe!"

Tell me the recipe for a sleeping draught. Eden's instructions echoed all around her, taunting her.

"It's belladonna, extract of poppy, and—" Yom mumbled to herself, "and oil of lavender..." The ground beneath her was dirt and gnarled roots and fragments of stone. Quia called her name still from far behind, but the thick trees had already swallowed her whole.

Very good, my little chemist. Yom preened under Eden's praise.

Yom stumbled on unsteady legs until she collapsed to the ground, catching her breath. She tried to remember why she was so weak, why holding onto her thoughts felt like catching water with bare hands. She braced herself on the roots of a tree, preparing to stand. She had to keep looking for Eden and Lior.

Tucked into a large knot in the bark of the tree in front of her, there was a torso. Yellowed with bruises and drained of life. Yom startled and scrambled backwards, but something glinted from the torso. A bronze torc wrapped around its neck with a raw, knotted wound beneath it.

"Moss," she whispered.

I'm always just out of reach, Lior taunted.

"Please, please, come back," Yom cried. "Come back! There's a monster in these woods!" *And I'm afraid it's me.*

The plant's spirit will teach you its power, teach you how to live, a gentle voice whispered in her ear. *In the plant's spirit we discover the hidden truths of life. The mysteries, the miracles.*

Lior skirted around Eden's workbench, grabbing Yom's wrist with her soft hands to drag Yom outside, but Eden caught her. "Ah ah." She tapped her cheek, and Lior leaned in to peck her. Yom stepped up to peck Eden's other cheek before Lior yanked her away, out of the laboratory, and onto the street. Yom wished Lior could appreciate what a miracle it was to have someone to say goodbye to.

Yom tripped over a root and fell forward, catching herself painfully with her hands in front of her. Her face was wet and her breathing slow. She pushed herself to continue crawling forward. Small hazy lights floated into her vision from behind the trees, lighting the path as she tried to continue following the voices.

Yom's hands were swollen as she wrapped herself around a tree, half kneeling. The lights gathered around her, crowding her vision until the forest was barely visible. She was illuminated like a beacon through the trees.

Yom was thrust into the days following Eden's death. The world was drained of color as she wandered the streets, unable to return to the laboratory or the small apartment above it, unable to look at the space without thinking of the two people she had lost. She had spent two days hiding between stalls of the freeman's market, pocketing food when she could. Until she had been cornered by three men with hooked noses and snaggleteeth. She had escaped and sprinted, concentrating on looking behind her to see if the men followed, until she ran right into a newly Bound Stag, blond and lanky. He had promised there was someone who could protect her, fill the painful void that had been ripped open in her. All she had to do was give this creature everything.

The ground pushed up and slammed into Yom's cheek, turning the world sideways. The earth shook and the lights scattered into a thinner cloud around her, still dotting her vision. The shaking grew to a deeper rumble. It was a massive boar, galloping over a ridge in the distance. A reddish brown coat matted with dirt, great sharp tusks jutting up from its lips, and the eyes of a beast. Eyes that bore into Yom even from a hundred feet away. And something astride it. *Someone.* A woman, with auburn hair and ribbons of green whipping gently in the breeze.

Death, Yom thought with some comfort. The forest faded, and her eyelids slipped closed.

A familiar voice shouted her name in the distance.

SOMEONE WAS SLAPPING YOM. Repeatedly.

"Wake up, Yom, wake up, damnit." Hands shook her shoulders. "Stay awake." The hands gripped her face. "Please," the voice cracked. Quia's amber eyes took over her vision. The color of earth, of burnt sugar, of the fairest doe's hyde.

"He gave too much," Yom mumbled. "Take it back." Quia's brow furrowed.

"She needs medicine." Another voice was far away, but faint footsteps were getting closer. Yom knew she had heard it before but could not place it. Her eyes rolled looking for it, but her head was being gripped and elevated, held still.

Twigs cracked under footsteps, closer now. Two fingers pressed in around the point where her pain was searing.

"She's lost too much blood, the wound needs to be treated and sealed before she can be moved." The fingers left and Yom's vision blurred again. Time crawled and rushed by, dilating and contracting senselessly. Something wet and slimy was placed at the nexus of the pain, soothing it. Something was put in her mouth and she bit down on it instinctively, a sweet reediness released on her tongue. Yom knew it but could not draw the name out in her haze. The world was gyrating now, folding in on itself until nothing but colors remained.

YOM SAW WOOD WHEN SHE OPENED HER EYES. Wood slats above her, wood ahead of her. For a moment she thought the forest had swallowed her whole and this was what its belly looked like. As soon as she came back into her body, she became aware of the cold sweat covering it. Tremors wracked her arms and legs. She tried to settle her aching limbs, but every time one calmed, another shook in its stead. Through the sludge of the ache and tremors, a sharper edge of pain hit her, emanating from a point in her gut's side.

Her fingers shakily walked up to the source of the pain, and she felt something wet. She finally dared to look down at the strips of fabric draped over her body. Because beneath them she was bare—someone had removed her clothes. The wound was covered by a clump of something dark green, leaking a blue fluid. Leaves. She knew the smell but couldn't name it, her mind blanketed in a fog.

Yom lifted the clump gingerly and saw a seam beneath, small precise sutures lining it. She rubbed her eyes, trying to summon the memories of who cared for the wound, where they took her—any inkling of what happened. Each movement sent chills and heat through her. She tried to pull the fabric over herself, but it was too flimsy to soothe the chill. Yom knew these symptoms, had seen them first hand on patrons who came to the Powder Parlor, trembling and sweaty. She was powdersick.

"I could heal the wound, but that I am not able to help with, unfortunately." A woman stood in the doorway, light gray apron tied around a dark gray shift. Her brown hair was peppered with silver and her tan face etched with soft lines. "Good to see you awake," she said, smiling slightly. Yom searched her muddled memories for the voice. The forest. The voice before the colors, saying that the wound needed to be sealed before she could be moved.

"Who are you?" Yom's voice was raspy from lack of use. "Where am I?"

"Yom," Quia's voice was filled with relief. Before she knew it he was next to her, pulling her into a tight hug, making her wince. His warmth and his hands, steady and sure, felt better than Yom would ever admit to him.

"Careful, young man," the woman interrupted. "The yarrow can only heal so quickly. And she has her own demons to expel." Quia pulled away and gently lowered her onto a surprisingly soft bed.

"Where are my powders?" Yom looked at Quia. She held up her hands and saw them shaking, unable to hold still.

"Your body is withdrawing from whatever you've been taking," the woman said.

Yom counted in her head. The last powder she had taken was the Aetherium in the arena, so it had been at least a full day since her last dose. And that was assuming she had been out for one night. The fighting clothes from Renos's arena were neatly folded on a table across the room. Balanced on top of the pile of clothes sat her powderbelt, every single loop emptied of its vial.

"What happened to my powders?"

"I got rid of them," the woman said sternly.

"You *what*?" Yom's voice raised, indignant. What gave this woman the right? The moment of outrage cost her a sharp pain in the abdomen. She doubled over, coughing and bracing her wound.

"You use a single one of those powders in these woods and you won't last the night. I did you a favor."

Yom looked at Quia, hoping he saw the madness in this. To her dismay, he looked contrite. He was taking the woman's side.

"You don't understand, I need powder." Yom grabbed onto Quia desperately.

"You'll find none of that kind of powder here," the woman chided.

Yom caught Quia's eye and widened hers. He still had yet to introduce who this frustrating and presumptuous woman was.

"This is Sophia," Quia explained. "She found you—us—" He swallowed. "We weren't sure you would make it. You were—" he paused and looked momentarily like he was still recovering from something painful, "in bad shape."

Yom closed her eyes and rested her head. Without warning the image of the boar surfaced. Its rider. Red hair. Green ribbons.

"Did you see the woman?" Yom asked Quia. He slid his gaze purposefully to Sophia. *The woman standing right here?* He seemed to say. "No," Yom shook her head, "another woman. She was riding a giant boar." Quia looked even more confused, about to say something, to tell Yom she was crazy, if she had to guess.

"The Lady of the Ardennes." Sophia cut in, watching her curiously. "Her name is Arduinna. She has not revealed herself to a mortal in decades." She tilted her head slightly, looking for something in Yom. "Who are you?"

"We're just travelers passing through. Headed for Cataracta," Quia said cagily.

"And you just happened to stumble into our forest?" Sophia looked at them with a touch of suspicion.

"Someone sent us here. A girl named Clementine. She said this was her home and we would be able to pass through unharmed." Quia gripped Yom's shoulder, perhaps preparing to fight if necessary.

Sophia's eyes lit with recognition. "Clementine sent you?"

"We met her in Traiana."

"Always been a firecracker, that one." Sophia looked away. "Her mother will be happy to hear any news you can share about her."

Yom cleared her throat. "The lady? The boar?"

Sophia hummed. "Arduinna is the keeper of our realm. Our protector."

"A titan," Quia said, and Sophia nodded. Yom sat up, trying to recall more of what she had seen of this supposed titan.

"And she came to you?" Quia asked, concerned. "What does it mean?"

Sophia took Yom's chin in her hand and tilted her head side to side, inspecting her, and then put the back of her hand up against Yom's forehead.

"You still need to rest. You can't get too excited." She pushed Yom's shoulders back down with a gentle force and adjusted the strips of fabric covering her. "This can wait." Yom couldn't disagree more, but when her head hit the pillow, her eyes involuntarily drifted closed.

"Give her some space," Sophia said to Quia. "Her body needs time to heal itself, even with the help of the plants." The questions flowed off Yom's tongue, all blurring together, until she realized that she hadn't spoken them out loud and had drifted into a heavy sleep.

THROUGH THE MIST OF DREAM YOM SAW THE BOAR AND THE WOMAN in green riding it. A huge black wolf walked next to it, padding on paws the size of Yom's head. They were weaving through the trees, the branches and the forest floor bowing to them ever so slightly as they passed.

YOM WAS IN AND OUT OF CONSCIOUSNESS, ALWAYS WAKING UP TO A chill or intense heat. Sometimes she woke with only the flimsy strips of fabric, sometimes with a thick blanket. No matter what, it felt wrong for her body. Fruits and nuts were left in a bowl by her bed and she ate them, sometimes managing to keep them down, sometimes hurling them back up into the bowl before passing out once again. She knew this sickness could be soothed by powder, but with the wound in her side she was too weak to even try to look for it. Quia's presence could be felt but not seen in these small acts of care; Yom supposed she was too pitiful a sight to stay around for too long. She sensed days passing right under her as she waited in misery for the sickness to lessen or consume her completely.

Then, finally, Yom roused from another strange dream of the forest and realized her body had—for the first time—broken the cold heat. She opened her eyes, finding herself engulfed in a dark stillness. She took inventory of her state: the sharp pain in her side had lessened, and she was able to hold her hand up, without tremors. She tried moving her limbs and they followed her commands more easily, allowing her to roll to her side.

Quia sat hunched at the lone table across the room, working by candlelight. His copper skin glowed in the dim light, and his spectacles reflected the candle's flicker hypnotically. Yom felt a wave of relief that he was here, safe and by her side.

It was a strange feeling, one she didn't want to pay too close attention to, so she cleared her throat to shake herself out of it. "Quia," Yom rasped.

He sat up immediately and turned. "How are you feeling?" he asked.

"A little better." She rotated her head around, feeling each movement with a clarity she hadn't experienced in years. "What happened?"

"Your body is withdrawing from the powders."

Alongside the clarity in her body, her mind was cleared like a room that was dusted for the first time in years. Distorted, ugly thoughts stretched awake, sinking their teeth deep into her without anything to dull them. *Your fault your fault your fault.*

"I need the powder back." Yom pushed herself to sit up, trying to ignore the stiff ache in her body. Quia jumped up and crossed the room to hold the strips of fabric up and cover her. Yom forgot they had removed her clothes. Once Quia had ensured she was somewhat covered, he avoided looking at her and placed her neatly folded pile of clothes on the bed. Yom was beginning to think Quia was rather scandalized by a naked body.

Quia shook his head and spoke as he remained turned away, "The powders slow you down. If that's what you're capable of doing on them, imagine what you can do with a clear head?" Yom dressed herself back in the scratchy muslin and knickerbockers, carefully avoiding the wound in her gut that was bandaged in cloth. The garments had been cleaned, the only sign of what had happened was a frayed rip that now hovered over her bandage.

"I don't want a clear head," Yom snapped. "I want powder."

"We can find you some. As soon as you're healed." Quia turned around and brought his hand up to her face to wipe something crusted from the edge of her mouth. Yom realized her skin and hair was matted with dried sweat and shuddered to think of what else stuck to her skin after two days of vomiting.

"There's no powder here," Quia added gently.

"Where exactly is 'here'?" Yom pushed herself up and walked on stiff legs towards the table. A detailed map of Arcadia lay on it.

"I've been trying to figure that out myself," Quia said sheepishly. "We are here," he pointed to the mountainous region of the Ardennes that stretched to the east of Traiana, one of the two territories remaining on the continent that were unincorporated to the network of provinces. "But there are no records of any settlements here. According to every map I have ever seen in the Archives, this place does not exist."

"What place?" Yom looked along the wall for the seam of the door and found the notch to open it.

"Careful—" Quia was cut off by Yom's gasp.

Outside the door sat a narrow ledge lined with a thin railing. Yom looked down what must have been over a hundred feet. Her stomach dropped and all the blood rushed from her head. Unbalanced, she felt like one wrong slip could send her tumbling over the edge.

"Careful," Quia repeated. He gripped her waist and guided her hand to the railing. "Look out, not down." She closed her eyes and took a few deep breaths until the dizziness subsided. When she reopened them, she looked out.

They were suspended against a massive tree trunk. The tree above them must have stretched another hundred feet up.

"What is this?"

"We're close to where Sophia found us. Apparently it's some sort of outpost tower. She left us here and said she would return when you're well enough to make the journey to her village."

"We should go. I don't like this. There's a reason people who enter the Ardennes don't come out again."

"I trust Sophia."

Yom gave him a skeptical glare.

"She did save your life."

"Maybe she wants me to be nice and healthy for when she decides to eat us," Yom said darkly.

"No, if she was going to eat us, it would have been when she found us. You looked very appetizing passed out on the ground," Quia grinned, sarcasm dripping from his words. Yom rolled her eyes but didn't argue more.

The forest was lit only by slivers of moonlight, but there was a faint glow illuminating the trees and the forest floor. It came from small floating lights. One of the lights floated closer, and Yom scrutinized it, expecting to see a firefly or a tiny lantern. As it danced inches from her eyes she realized it was just a hazy ball of light. A few more found her and circled her arms. Almost like they were playing with her.

"Those things are the only reason I was able to find you after you ran off," Quia whispered. "I think they like you." Yom moved her arms and the lights followed. She laughed and turned in a circle, watching the lights turn with her. The wave of dizziness returned but this time it was exhaustion as well. She grabbed onto the railing again for support.

"You still need to rest." Quia pulled her arm over his shoulder and walked her back inside. He deposited her onto the bed and gently arranged her under a blanket. The lure of sleep pulled at her once she was laying down again but she resisted it.

"Yom," Quia hesitated. Yom waited to hear what he was about to say, wondering when they would have the conversation about everything she had witnessed in Traiana. "Who is Lior?"

Yom didn't speak, so Quia continued, "I thought it was just a random name when you gave it to Rye, but you were saying the name over and over the day Sophia found us."

"She—" Yom picked each word carefully, avoiding Quia's eyes, "was a friend. Her mother, Eden, took me in when I was young and—on my own. We–we grew up together."

"Where is she now?" Quia's voice was furtive, perhaps sensing he approached a painful subject.

"I don't know." Yom's voice cracked. Everything Misho had told her was a specter hanging over her, haunting her. "She was taken six years ago, when we were thirteen." Yom dug her nails into her skin. "And the people who took her—" she gulped, the words felt like they were ballooning in her throat, thrashing around to avoid being spoken, "They killed Eden."

"Shit," Quia murmured. "Were you hurt?"

"No." Yom laughed bitterly. "I just hid." She turned on her side to face Quia. "I did nothing," she confessed quietly, waiting for him to recoil from her.

"You didn't do nothing." He reached to stroke the apple of her cheek. "You survived." Yom shook off his hand and turned back to face the ceiling.

"I'm a coward."

"You were only a child." He brushed her forehead, trying to keep touching her.

"What would you have done?" She turned to him, lip quivering, bitter tears welling.

"I–I have no idea how I would have reacted, I wasn't there. I probably would have done what you did."

"You would have helped them. You would have done something." Yom pressed the heel of her palm into her eye to stop the cursed tears. "You're a good person."

"No," Quia said quietly, withdrawing his hand, "I'm not."

"Of course you are, you saved us in Traiana. You're the reason we have a chance at stopping this entire bloody war."

"The only reason we were even in that mess was because I pulled us off the train. Every time I try to do something good, something worse takes its place."

"I think you could do a lot of good if you were more accepting of who you are." Yom eyed him shrewdly. "Don't think I've forgotten what I saw just because I almost died."

Quia laughed. "I would be concerned if you had."

"You lied to me."

"I didn't lie," Quia said as he began fussing with the blanket. "I just didn't tell you the whole truth."

"You've been lying to me since the beginning." Yom shrugged the blanket off to free her hands.

"I'm sorry," he said, regret clear in his voice. "Arcadia is a dangerous place for someone like me."

"A numenborn," Yom supplied, the word feeling out of place on her tongue when using it to describe Quia. He nodded. "Why didn't you tell me?" He remained silent and fiddled with a loose thread on the blanket, ignoring her question.

"Why didn't you tell me?" Yom repeated softly. She curled her arm under her head as a pillow and waited for his answer.

"I—" he faltered. Emotion clogged his throat. Yom reached over to hold onto his wrist. "I was ashamed. I *am* ashamed." A tear escaped from his eye but he wiped it away.

"I know about shame," Yom offered, stroking the inside of his wrist with her thumb. "You can tell me. I won't judge you." He glanced at her with a sad smile and sat silently for a few moments. Just when Yom thought he would stand and leave, he spoke.

"I've known I was a numenborn since I was seven. There aren't many of us these days, and almost all numenborn children are born with the numen of the less powerful gods. Before I was born, our augurs divined that the numen of two of the four Immortal Rulers would be reborn in this generation. They didn't know why the World Tree had made it so, only that these would be two of the most powerful numenborn the world had ever seen. My people waited for a numenborn of exceptional ability to be discovered, and then I went through my Trials. I found out I was born with the numen of Quetzal, one of the oldest and most powerful immortals.

"You can't imagine the pressure it put me under, to be named the heir of such power. From the second my family found out, they spoke of nothing else. I trained with the finest warriors and the highest ranking priests to learn how to control the power. All that attention does something to a kid. I was so cocky." Quia shook his head bitterly.

"Years passed after my Trials and there was no sign of the other numenborn. They surmised from the original augury that the other numenborn couldn't have been born much earlier or later than me. So the augurs cast the stones again, and read the stars. And they saw the other numenborn, but they were on the other side of Okeanus." Quia laughed. "As soon as I heard, I knew what it meant. We were meant to reunite the two halves. What else could the World Tree have planned?

"They began devising how to extract the numenborn. They figured in this godless land the numenborn would have no knowledge of their power. And if the titans discovered them, they could be used against us.

"I volunteered to go. I knew with my training, even though I was young, I was one of the most skilled warriors we had. But they forbade it. They decided they would send a company of warriors with a less powerful numenborn to navigate the crossing. They claimed it was too dangerous to risk sending me.

"You have to understand," Quia looked directly at her, imploring, "ever since my Trials, everyone told me I was so special, that I would save the world. And then they forbid me from doing the thing it felt like I was meant to do. Who else but me could seek out the twin to my power? I could feel something pulling me from across Okeanus."

Yom sat up, wide awake as she listened.

"I snuck away, in the middle of the night. I convinced four warriors to go with me, tempting them with the glory we would bring home with our victory. To steal a numenborn right from under the nose of the titans? It was easy. And," Quia swallowed, "I asked a servant who worked for my father to come with me." He scrubbed his face. "He had become a close friend, assigned to me when I began my numenborn training. We grew up together, like brothers if not for our different castes. He didn't even need convincing, he said that he would go wherever I went. Even if it meant crossing Okeanus. We didn't need any more people, I should have never asked him to come." Quia's voice cracked. He moved his hands to brace either side of his head as he hunched forward, leaning on his elbows.

"I led us to the Touching Rocks. We walked down the cliff sides to the water's edge with a small but fast boat hoisted between us. From where we pushed off, it shouldn't have taken long, but it felt like we were trapped between those two points for days."

Yom held her breath. There were a myriad of fantastical stories of what happened to sailors who ventured into the waters of Okeanus, and even more from the seaside cities where fishermen spent all their time tending to their nets at Okeanus's edge, but Yom had never heard a story from someone who actually sailed across it and survived. Some said Okeanus was full of great scaled creatures, monsters with fins and fangs who could gnaw you in half with a single bite. Others said it was where souls with unfinished business wandered after death, doomed to haunt its waters until its justice was reaped.

"Mist descends as soon as you leave the shore, obscures any view of where you came from and where you're going. The mist whispers to you of your faults, of your mistakes, tries to lead you off course. And the waves—" Quia shook his head. "Some of them topped thirty feet. I entered trance to navigate us—it's the only way to see through the mist. And the only reason we made it to Cape Tindra upright was my wind. A couple of the warriors had been so riled by the voyage that they were ready to rip each other's throats out. And one of them had withdrawn completely after what he had heard in the mist. He never spoke again. Only my brother and I seemed to emerge unscathed. I kept us going, tried to reignite our fire as we ascended the shores of Arcadia. I had studied all the accounts of the land from the few Panchaian exploration companies who had ventured here and knew that we were in the territory known as Ibernia. We found a farmer who lived on the outskirts of the closest village and stole clothes from him."

"How were you planning to find the numenborn?" Yom asked with genuine curiosity.

Quia smiled slyly. "I stole an augur's casting stones before we left. I figured all would be forgiven when we returned with the numenborn, that I would prove everyone who had doubted me wrong. I only knew how to repeat what I saw them do, but I observed enough to divine simple questions. I was able to navigate us in the direction the stones told me.

"It was strange, as we traveled inland from the waters, the stones seemed to change their answer, as if the numenborn was moving. They led us into Inisfail. Then, everything fell apart." Yom had, without realizing, interlocked her hand with Quia's as he spoke. She squeezed it, encouraging him to keep going.

"We were walking through a market when I heard someone scream. A girl. I told the men to keep their heads down, and asked my brother to watch them while I looked into it. I was only going to be gone for a few moments, but I had this weird feeling as I left. I followed the sound of the scream, even though no one else around us seemed concerned by it. I found her in an alley off the market. She was cornered by three grown men, and she couldn't have been any older than me." Yom froze, the story sounding eerily familiar.

"When I saw what was going on I shouted at them to leave her alone. They dropped her and turned on me. It was easy to incapacitate them, like fighting uncoordinated children. I had a fighter's high, this rush of feeling that I was following the path Wacachan had laid out for me. I turned around, looking for the girl to make sure she was alright, but she was gone. Then I walked back towards where I had left the men, but across the market, I saw triarii standing where my men had been. I didn't know what the triarii were at that point, but something told me to stay away. I stayed on the other side of the market to wait until they had gone." Quia's shoulders hunched. "When they finally left, I went back to where I had left the men and saw nothing. I searched the whole market until I found an area where the vendors piled their trash, and I found their bodies. All four of them. The triarii had killed them and thrown them there like they were garbage. I still don't fully know why. Did the triarii figure out that they were Panchaian? Or did the men fail to recognize the triarii and pay their proper respects? Was it a meaningless death, for the sake of pride? It haunts me, not knowing. I brought them to this strange place and abandoned them. And they were killed. Because of me."

Yom took in the full weight of Quia's story and was silent for a moment. The triarii practically had free rein to do whatever they wanted outside of the queen's command, and unlimited weaponry hidden within their armor. If they had run into four strangers who were not aware of their status and felt slighted by their lack of recognition, she could see it ending how Quia described.

"What about—"

"My brother was gone. I stayed in that area of the city for days, waiting for him to resurface. When he didn't, I considered that he might have been captured. I decided I would go looking for him. I used the stones to guide me through the city, until they led me towards what I later found out was the Cut. You can imagine what happened after I crossed into that area." Yom nodded.

"I was surrounded by five Stags before I knew it, and I could tell by looking at them they weren't bumbling street rats like the ones I had taken on before. These were trained fighters. A few of them attacked me at once, and the others wrestled my pack away from me. The pack had the casting stones in it, and I was about to do something reckless to get them back. That's when Dougal found me; he was leaving from a meeting with Cernunnos. I think he knew what I was just from watching me fight, even though I was trying not to show anything that would give me away. He told the Stags I was his new apprentice, and they let me go by the skin of my teeth. They kept the pack. I was livid at Dougal for interrupting the fight, but if he hadn't, I think I would have resorted to using my power, and then who knows where I would have ended up."

"Probably locked deep underneath the House of Flowing Waters," Yom offered solemnly.

Quia nodded. "After I cooled off, I came to terms with how ill-equipped I was to navigate this place, how little I actually knew about this world. I made a deal with myself: I would stay with Dougal, allow him to hide me, until I was able to go out on my own and finish what I came here to do, and find my brother. But weeks stretched out into months and then years. I got so comfortable, and when I immersed myself in Dougal's work at the Archives, I could forget everything that had happened and pretend I wasn't a massive failure. I didn't even notice how comfortable I had gotten in my cocoon until you came in and burst it." Quia poked her playfully in the ribs. Yom laughed.

"Bursting cocoons is one of my specialties. Along with being unbearable." Yom leaned in and pulled him into a tight hug. His hands wrapped around her, warm and sturdy and safe. "Quia, the triarii are the most dangerous fighters in Arcadia. They would have killed you too if you had been there."

"Sometimes I think about that, about whether I would have been better off if they had."

"You did the same thing anyone would have done in your position. You're a survivor."

"You're a survivor," he countered. "*I* am a coward who got lucky."

Yom shook her head, but his expression was resolute. "You haven't been a coward since I've known you," she said, her hand drifting up to cup his jaw, rough with stubble. "Do you know how many people would dare cross Cernunnos to do what we're doing? Or unleash the wind itself on Renos and her Eels?" Quia smiled. "And you were right about me. I'm just a powderhead thug. I'm not a good person."

"I was completely wrong about you, Yom," he said earnestly. "Anything I said to you was just an echo of what I have been telling myself for years." Quia's eyes lifted to hers and something connected between them. A bridge they could see each other across, with understanding.

"You're this powerful numenborn, and you have this amazing destiny ahead of you." For some reason, thinking about Quia's future of wielding immense power and saving the world made Yom sad, and she did not entirely understand why. "What you did in Traiana was...awe inspiring."

Quia laughed, humorless.

"What happened in Traiana was a fraction of what I *was* able to do. I haven't been able to access the majority of my numen since I lost my brother and those men. Yet another reason I am a failure."

"It will come back. No matter what you say, I know you haven't lost who you are."

"If I haven't, then you haven't either," he said softly.

Yom looked away, knowing better than to believe that.

"We should go to bed." She laid back and turned to her side, pulling the blanket up to her chin. Quia leaned down to kiss her forehead.

"Thank you for listening," he whispered as he pulled back.

Quia moved to the floor where a mat spread out next to the bed. Yom laid there for a long time, unable to sleep, a soft heat blossoming where Quia had kissed her.

MISHO WAS INCENSED AS HE WATCHED A FIGURE, CLEARLY NOT HUMAN, whisk the chemist into a plume of smoke, and out of his reach. His knife had glinted in the firelight before it disappeared along with her, but the wound he hoped it inflicted was barely a consolation for them slipping through his fingers. The task had been simple: figure out what they knew, and stop them in their tracks. But now, it was personal. Now that he knew what kind of person the infamous chemist truly was, and who she traveled with, he knew exactly where they were going.

The room was filling with smoke, too fast for Misho to examine anything carefully, but he caught sight of a mark written in char that confirmed his suspicions. In a fit, he picked up a crumbling stone vase and hurled it against the wall with a thunderous crack.

Misho wrenched open the Gutter-side door to see a group of Eels readying themselves to ram the door open.

"They're gone," Misho growled before shoving the Eels aside and shouldering his way back to the center of the Gutter.

"Misho," the deep voice of one of the other triarii yelled to catch his attention as he stepped back into the river hall. Misho hated this place. He needed to get back above ground as soon as possible.

"Where were you?" Misho asked as the other black figure joined him in stride.

"We got caught behind Renos's men. There was a whole blockade of their bodies in that arena." The triarii shook his head, trying to rid himself of the image. "I don't know what it was that did that to them."

"I know exactly what it was," Misho hissed. "Where is the other one?"

The triarii gulped and looked backwards. "He was right behind me—"

"Leave him," Misho said coldly. "He'll find his own way home. We're not wasting another minute."

After ascending the steps out of the Gutter two at a time, Misho took several deep gulps of the musty fish and kelp-ridden air. "Map?" He thrust his hand out to the triarii, who deposited a tightly folded square of parchment in it. Misho unfolded the map and surveyed where the chemist and her companion could have gone.

The one who summoned the Traveler with those marks would have taken the smallest journey possible, knowing the steepness of its cost. Misho circled his gloved finger in a small radius around Traiana, seeing it barely overlap with the next province further south, Gallia, but also cross over the mountainous forested region that lay beyond Arcadia's boundary. It was marked Unincorporated on the map, but it was known as the Ardennes, and it was the fodder of Arcadian children's ghost stories.

The Ardennes would allow them to side step Gallia, and escape from Renos as quickly as possible. If Misho were chasing something, he would take the fastest route there, which would mean taking their chances, and crossing into Gallia. But if he were being chased, he would escape as quickly as possible. And go somewhere it would be difficult to be followed.

"They're in the Ardennes." Misho walked towards the triarii, who looked at him like he might explode. He thrust the map at the triarii, shoving him back a step. "And we're going to follow them," Misho said with an eerie calm.

"But that's outside of the Queen's jurisdiction—"

"Now," Misho snarled, boarding his single seat transport and cranking the powder fuel pedal without another word.

XI

The Village in the Trees

Yom woke to see a strange woman, who she identified as Sophia after a dazed moment of panic, pressing into her abdomen.

"This is healing quite nicely," Sophia said. Yom's knee jerk reaction was to push the woman away, but the sharp twist of her body right at her wound sent a lance of pain through her. "You're going to want to take it easy," Sophia told Yom as she stood and walked to the other side of the room.

"Why are you here?" Yom asked groggily.

"Just checking on our little morning glory." It took Yom a moment to understand that she was the morning glory and that it was, in fact, sarcastic. "How are you feeling? Are you up for a day's walk?"

Yom groaned and rolled to sit up. She peeled her shirt up to see the gash with a fresh bandage on it.

"I'm not sure," Yom mumbled.

"I'm concerned that Arduinna won't allow you to stay another day this far from the village." Sophia spoke to Quia, who was wide awake and fully dressed. "We've already tested her patience by allowing you to stay this long."

A current of panic swept through Yom. "How long was I out?"

"Two days," Sophia said, unaware of what a catastrophe losing two days was. Yom did the math in her head, recalling Fight Night marked eight days until Lupercalia. They had five days to get to Cataracta, and intercept the numenborn at Lupercalia.

"We need to go—"

"You need to rest. You'll barely make it to the village in this state." As if on cue, the wound in her side throbbed.

"She'll make it," Quia said. "I'll help you—carry you if I have to."

"Please," Yom snorted, "I won't be carried like some helpless daisy. You can take your help and shove it up your—"

"Glad to see you're feeling like your normal self." Quia smiled.

TO LEAVE THE TREEDWELLING, YOM HAD TO DESCEND A RICKETY SET of stairs that curved steeply around the trunk. She put on a brave face, but every time she saw a sliver of the ground between slats of the steps, she had to squeeze onto the small hand ridge carved into the trunk. That, combined with the constant turning, had her heaving by the time they reached the bottom.

"How did I get up there?" she asked, hunched over with her head braced between her legs. "Quia?" She balanced her elbows on her knees, still breathing heavily. He just winked at her. She reached over to shove him and he laughed. She wasn't sure when exactly this unspoken truce had developed, and she was even less sure how to feel about it. Keeping people at a distance was a necessity for survival in the Stags, if not for sanity in a world that seemed to destroy anything Yom found that was good.

"Let's go. We can't get too comfortable on the forest floor." Sophia had hitched up the skirt of her shift and started walking. Once she turned away, Yom saw a large basket strapped to her back. "Step gently," Sophia added. She took purposeful steps, preferring to use the roots of trees rather than step on the green foliage that covered the earth.

"What's in the basket?" Yom asked under her breath as they began to follow her.

"She took the yarrow out of it, and the other plants she used to treat you. I think she was foraging when she found us," Quia replied.

Yom stored this information as they continued walking. Perhaps she would be able to replenish her powder supply with some of the plants in that basket.

The energy that Yom had left the treedwelling with dwindled quickly. Her wound ached with each movement, and her breath left her quicker than usual. She found herself having to pause more and more frequently to regain it. Quia waited with her each time, and after a particularly grueling stretch, he pulled Yom's arm over his shoulder to keep her going. Even with this support, Yom's steps slowed. She refused to ask for more help, but Quia stopped them of his own accord and knelt down in front of her. Full of resentment, but also a tiny bit of gratitude, Yom slung her arms around his shoulders and hooked her legs into his waiting arms. He stood with her hoisted on his back, and they continued walking.

"If you speak a word of this to anyone," she whispered right next to his ear, "I know about a dozen ways to kill someone with just my hands." His chuckle exasperated her greatly.

"I'd like to see you try." Quia patted her shin. "I'm still one of the greatest warriors Panchaia ever had." Unfortunately, Yom had not seen any evidence to the contrary. She settled for being carried in glum silence.

The sun rose to its peak above the forest canopy and had made it halfway through its descent before Sophia told them they were getting close. Yom was only half lucid by then, in a near constant state of hunger and lightheaded delirium. Her eyes drifted closed and her cheek rested on Quia's shoulder, and she was lulled to sleep by the rhythm of his steps.

"We're here." Quia's voice woke her, accompanied by a gentle shaking of her legs. Yom rubbed her eyes and found herself dropped back down onto the ground, her legs numb.

"Welcome to Sylveaux, the Village in the Trees," Sophia said. Yom looked around and saw nothing but the same forest they had been walking in all day. Then she noticed Quia looking above them.

She craned her neck to follow his gaze. There was a network of ropes and slats of wood strung between trees. Treedwellings dotted the trees all around them at various heights, all of them at least as high as the dwelling they had just left. The floating lights flitted all around.

"Over here," Sophia called, and Yom spun around to see she stood at the base of a massive tree, starting to climb a set of steps similar to the ones they had descended at the beginning of the day.

"Why couldn't it be the Village on the Ground?" Yom muttered as she begrudgingly followed Sophia up the stairs.

They arrived on a ledge that stretched and snaked between trees in both directions. Dwellings dotted it, and rope bridges connected it to a similar network of dwellings across from it. Sophia walked along the ledge and then up a short rope ladder. People in similar gray clothes as Sophia watched them from inside dwellings as they passed, their expressions a mixture of surprise and distrust.

Quia must have noticed the same, making a point to follow Yom closely. They climbed up the ladder Sophia had taken and arrived at a large dwelling. Yom hesitated at the threshold, but Sophia called them in. Yom crossed through the doorway, taking it in cautiously.

The room was much larger than the outpost they had left, with an iron lined hearth emanating light and heat in the middle. A young girl kneeled by it, tending to the contents of a large pot, something with onion and garlic based on the intoxicating smell filling the room. In the back corner, an older woman worked at a loom, her hands moving gracefully in front of her.

"Mother?" The girl stood up in surprise.

"Come in, come in." Sophia waved an impatient hand at Yom.

"Who are these people?" the girl asked, holding a wooden spoon as if it was a weapon.

"They are travelers, and they will be staying with us until they are ready to continue on their journey." Sophia turned back to Yom and Quia and smiled warmly. "This is my daughter, Moira." She motioned to the girl. "And my mother, Aisa." She nodded to the woman sitting in the back.

Moira angrily stepped up to her mother. "How could you bring outsiders here?" she hissed, as if Yom could not hear her.

"They are friends of Clementine," Sophia said sternly.

"Clementine would never send strangers—"

"Lady Arduinna has allowed them to pass unharmed," Aisa interrupted in a raspy voice.

"Yes, mother. And we will welcome them as our guests, as well as Lady Arduinna's." Sophia directed these words to Moira.

Moira stepped up to Yom and scrutinized her. She gasped when she saw Yom's torc.

"She bears the seal of the Horned One!" she screeched and backed away.

"We don't need help. Let's go," Yom said to Quia before turning to leave.

"Please stay. You need to rest." Sophia grabbed her forearm. "Whatever the reason, the forest led me to you. I will not question the path set out for us by Wacachan." She turned to Moira. "None of us will."

"What is this place?" Yom asked, unsure if she should be suspicious or relieved to hear the World Tree's ancient name.

"I'll tell you about it, if you stay." Sophia smiled and the lines around her eyes crinkled.

Moira pursed her lips. "She'll get us killed," she said under her breath.

DESPITE THE COLD WELCOME, YOM SCARFED DOWN THE ONION STEW Moira served them like it was her last meal. They passed around a loaf of bread to rip off chunks and this too Yom swallowed almost whole. Moira helped Aisa eat, and Sophia kept the group entertained by telling stories of Yom in her withdrawal delirium. Quia happily joined in, and Yom resigned to take whatever mockery they had as long as her bowl was full of stew.

"Tezcat knows it was the last thing you needed," Sophia laughed and wiped the corner of her eyes.

"Tezcat?" Yom asked through a mouthful of bread.

The group quieted.

"Tezcat. The Sorcerer," Sophia said, eyes bright with knowledge. "One of the four Immortal Rulers. He and his brother Quetzal, the Teacher, created the first humans." Yom glanced at Quia.

"Why do you know of the gods? And Wacachan?" Yom asked the question they had yet to be answered.

"We are something of a relic of the way things used to be, before the Separation. We've kept the old ways alive." Sophia held out her hand and showed the hairline scar on it.

Quia set down his bowl, and held his hand up next to Sophia's, bearing a twin scar.

"I didn't think I would live to meet a child of Panchaia," Sophia said, voice swelling with emotion. "Are there more of you? Have you come to relinquish

Arcadia from the House of Flowing Waters?" All of a sudden Moira and Aisa were watching Quia intently as well.

"It's only me. We're just trying to get to Cataracta." Quia withdrew his hand.

It was impossible to miss the disappointment that flashed across their faces.

"How has this place remained free of the Queen's governance?" Quia asked.

"Arduinna does not share the same views as her siblings. She has prevented interference of outsiders in the Ardennes, and we have found a way to live in peace with her realm"

"She didn't look too peaceful to me," Yom muttered, thinking of the massive boar the titan rode like a one woman army. Again, the group quieted.

"You saw her?" Moira whispered.

"She was far away. And I might have hallucinated it."

"You did not hallucinate," Aisa said definitively in her throaty rasp of a voice. "The Lady has allowed you to pass through her realm unharmed, and revealed herself to you during your lowest moment."

Yom stuttered, caught off guard by how much this old crone seemed to understand. "How do you know—"

"The forest is the home of spirits. The spirits reflect back the best and worst of ourselves. Through their light, sometimes those they permit can see the past and the future. They take away the illusion that we can be whole without each part of ourselves."

"That's enough, mother. They've only just gotten here," Sophia chastised. "Who wants honey pudding?"

Yom shook her head as she stared down at the remains of her bowl, her appetite suddenly gone.

THE STONE ROAD OUT OF TRAIANA SLOWLY FELL INTO DISREPAIR, UNTIL eventually it was replaced by a dirt path that cut through hills and bluffs and fields of wildflowers. Misho kept his pedal flush with the footboard, the engine growling between his legs, powder fuel on a continuous drip. The tinted steam belched by the engine smelled of false sweetness; he shook his head into the wind to clear it from his nose.

It was incredible, once they crossed the boundary into the Ardennes, how quickly any sense of the path disappeared. Misho slowed to observe the trees as he passed, looking for signs of human tracks. A freshly broken branch, a recently overturned stone or leaf, a shoeprint, if he was lucky. But there was nothing. A thought tugged on the back of his mind: that he had guessed wrong, and they hadn't traveled to the Ardennes. That they were halfway through Gallia by now. And Misho had just wasted precious fuel chasing no one.

Misho's transport stuttered to a stop and he dismounted, flicking off the engine so he could listen properly. He took his first steps onto the forest floor, the ground redolent of dew and moss. Misho scanned in a careful perimeter around the transport for tracks, sniffing for the smell of smoke, the scent of blood. The other triarii flicked off his transport as well, sitting back in his seat to watch Misho.

"Hey what's—" The triarii stuttered.

Misho turned back to where he had parked the transport to see patches of moss already forming on it, and vines snaking around its body like fingers. Misho sprinted back towards it, racing to rip away the vines that had already covered it, but more grew in their place.

The entire transport was sinking. Roots were snaking up from the earth to pull it down into the dirt. Misho tried to hold onto it, but the surface had no purchase with the growths of moss all over it. The metallic body slipped through his fingers and the transport was swallowed by the tongues of roots into the earth's mouth.

Misho stepped back in shock.

"So it's true, the forest is haunted," the other triarii spoke just next to him. Which meant—

"You idiot!" The same thing was happening to the other transport, now dismounted as well. They both rushed towards it, but Misho watched in horror as the inevitable vines claimed it, their only remaining vehicle dragged into the earth.

He stepped back, the reality of where they found themselves sinking in: a forest that people did not exit after entering. He looked in all directions, hoping to see some indication of a path or route, but there was nothing but endless green. Except, there was a patch of something dark a few feet away. He pounced on it, seeing a circle of dried brown with a sheen, and ran a gloved finger through it. Some of the brown lifted, still drying. It was blood. And it was a lot of it, judging by the size of the pool here. Misho squinted at the area around it. *It has to be the chemist*, Misho hoped desperately.

"We need to go back to the Queen's jurisdiction," the other triarii said, wary. "Nothing good will come of this place."

"They're here," Misho pointed at the blood, hoping the triarii wouldn't ask for further proof.

"You're sure?" The triarii looked at him as if he had gone mad.

"Of course I'm sure," Misho snapped.

Lights floated into Misho's vision. He batted them away, but they just latched onto his movement, following his flailing arms. He stepped back from where the transport had just sunk to escape them, but the lights followed him.

They illuminated the glisten of his armor, clouded his vision until all he could see was light. But the light was shifting, and through cracks in it he could no longer see speckled tree cover and earth blanketed in roots. He saw dark, wet stone. And he heard the incessant drip of water.

"What's going on?" The voice of the other triarii was far away, behind a stone wall.

"No—" Misho thrashed, but the lights clung to him, *"No!"* he shouted louder. He would not be taken back there. He was outside, in the sun and the air. He had made a deal.

"I'll make this easy," the faceless voice spoke from all sides around Misho. "Tell us what you were doing, and we'll let you go." Misho was chained to the floor.

"No, you won't," Misho cried, "I know nothing!" he insisted. He pulled on the chains, but their wet links did not budge. He only succeeded in cutting into his own wrists. "I am no one." He repeated these words until they morphed into something strange and unfamiliar.

Misho saw a hint of the forest and wrenched himself back. He searched desperately for the sunlight filtering through the canopy. But it was only a momentary flash; he was still in a stone cage.

"You're making this difficult on yourself," the faceless voice tsked. "All you have to do is talk to us." The voice had a false sense of comfort.

"I know nothing," Misho whispered.

"That's too bad," the voice lamented. Then the stone walls and the face were illuminated in the crackle of fire. But there was no face. It was a glistening beetle of a man, hood covering his eyes. The fire was brought closer and its heat on Misho's skin was becoming unbearable.

"Please," Misho begged, "I am no one." The fire licked his skin into something blistered and angry, and it kept coming closer.

"No," Misho growled, sinking to the ground, feeling dirt and rocks and roots beneath him, even though he saw nothing beyond the fire and the beetle man in his cell. He dug his hands into the earth, attempting to ground himself, but only falling deeper into the pit of memory.

Misho had not seen the sun in months. Insanity had ossified into a shell around him, protecting the delicate sun that stayed burning deep in his chest. His poet, his warrior, the one he had followed to the edge of the world, would come for him. The sun was tested, doused with water, suffocated, but it endured. Misho understood that finding him would be an undertaking, not something that his poet could do in a few measly weeks. He held onto the memory of his poet warrior in the late evening sun: the heat on his golden lit skin, the calls of jewel feathered birds a ubiquitous din, the black tips of their spears cracking and glinting together as they sparred. Months passed, and Misho only saw his poet in the distorted mirror of dreams. The sun dimmed. When Misho returned to his vision, it started to show early signs of rot. The lush fields dried, withered. The jewel feathered birds mutated from a call to a shriek. The sound of their black tipped spears became more aggressive, their dance became more violent, skin nicked and blood shedding.

Misho tried to regain warmth, some feeling he could hold onto. Left on his own in his cell, he pushed his body to its breaking point. He gifted his body with physical pain, but no matter how hard he pushed himself, nothing stoked the sun in his breast.

Then, the creature visited Misho.

"Do you know me?" the creature asked, silken voice floating through the musty air, face obscured in shadow. Misho crouched on the ground and reared back on his haunches.

"Why would I?"

"Look again."

Misho squinted up and saw two yellow eyes cutting through the shadow. He stiffened and pushed back, returning his gaze to the ground.

"How?" He asked through chattering teeth.

"The question is not how, but why. But I don't think you'll be privy to either of those answers."

This was the first time since his capture Misho felt true fear. He stayed silent. He knew these creatures fed off fear, off of weakness.

The silken voice inhaled deeply. "I've missed that."

Misho inched ever so slightly backwards.

"I want to know what your emperor seeks, what he dreams."

"I am no one," Misho said, a chant.

The silken voice clicked its tongue. "My servants have told me this, but I do not believe them. Your will is strong, that of a warrior. You are not no one."

Misho tilted his head up to meet the yellow eyes. "I am no one," he repeated so softly he couldn't be sure he had spoken at all.

"We shall see."

The visits continued, always with the same question, just in different forms. Does your Emperor seek the numenborn?

The silken voice never entered the cell. The beetle men would beat Misho or drag him to a sluice of water to hold his head under it for hours at a time. Misho was starved, force fed, held over fire, but still he repeated his truth, I am no one. *Beneath the words, in his chest, the sun was nothing but an ember. He could not recall the moment when it was snuffed out completely, but one day he noticed his soul had been plunged into the same darkness that surrounded his body. He did not even feel grief for this loss; he felt nothing. He repeated his same chant, reminding himself:* I am no one.

"No," Misho growled, digging his hands further into the earth to hold fistfuls of dirt. He would not allow himself to be dragged back to that prison.

"Keep moving." He pushed himself up and began to walk, only able to see brief flashes of the forest but holding onto them as tightly as his sanity.

THE FIRST MORNING IN SYLVEAUX, YOM WOKE WITH ALARMING CLARITY. She had dreamt of myriad colors, of blue eyes, of a red apron. Of Moss's body fused into the tree, a memorial and a warning. *Your fault your fault your fault.* It was the absence of powder, Yom reassured herself. *Just find some powder.* She groped through her bag in search of Damian's flask and quickly turned it upside down over her tongue. Nothing but a drop of the spirit remained.

"I emptied it," Quia spoke and Yom jerked up.

"Why would you do that?" her voice barely concealed its irritation.

"I didn't want you to have any temptation once everything was out of your system."

Yom's mouth was dry, as if simulating the effect of powder—crying out for it. "You shouldn't have done that." She pulled back the covers and reached for the clothes piled next to the bed. Even the small movement raised a shooting pain in her abdomen. She clutched her side, hissing out a ragged breath. Quia's mat on the floor was perfectly made with the blanket and pillow arranged neatly. Something fluttered in her chest knowing he continued sleeping on the floor so that she could have the bed.

"I think this will be good for you." Quia's face was hopeful as he rested a hand on her upper back. "It's a chance for a fresh start. A place to heal before we can keep moving."

Yom grunted in lieu of correcting him. If everything he had seen so far hadn't robbed him of his hopeless optimism, she would not waste her breath. His clinging to hope would only make it more painful when he learned the inevitable truth that there was no fresh start for her. This was all she would ever be.

Quia had mentioned Sophia's basket of foraged plants. It wouldn't be the same, but she could put together something rudimentary like Drifter's Mettle. She would chew on leaves if she had to.

Yom fixated on the foraged plants sitting somewhere in Sophia's dwelling like a hound. She found the door, similar to the one in the outpost, and pulled its notched handle. The first step onto the suspended ledge brought a familiar lightheadedness, but Yom shoved it away and grabbed onto the railing for balance. To her left, there was a gap in the planks of the ledge that she recalled climbing through after supper the night before. A short climb down a rope ladder and she found herself back in front of the large room where they had eaten. Where it looked like Sophia, Moira and Aisa had all slept, if the sleeping mats stacked in one corner were any indication.

The three women were already bustling around the room: Moira tending to the hearth, Aisa's fingers moving nimbly over her loom, and Sophia flitting about a cluster of work tables.

"Good morning," Quia said from behind Yom, far too cheery.

"Good morning!" All three women chorused back. Moira gave Quia a smile that lasted a beat beyond friendly, and Yom rolled her eyes. Moira's gaze shifted to her, and her smile instantly cooled.

Yom scanned the room in daylight. Much of the walls were covered in tapestries, with images that looked like they came straight from Eden's stories. One depicted a great tree surrounded by water and sky. Another showed majestic forested hills dotted with stags, with a figure sitting cross-legged in the dead center. The figure had horns of a stag, though Yom still recognized him. *Cernunnos.* But there was no sign of Inisfail, or any of the villages that covered Ibernia. No, this was Cernunnos as she had seen him in her mind, when she had searched for his numen in Renos's arena. For the first time since the arena, she tentatively reached out for that tether once again. She half expected to have imagined it, for the whole thing to have been an adrenaline induced hallucination. But it was there, even clearer than it had been on Fight Night. Like a rope she could grab hold of if she wanted, and pull.

"He traded the soul of his realm for the pursuit of revenge," Sophia's voice interrupted. "Many of the titans have been corrupted, and forgotten themselves." Yom turned to see Sophia looking at the tapestry wistfully. "They see humans as a weapon to wield against the gods." Yom sensed there was much gravity behind Sophia's words, much that had been lost between the image on the tapestry and the city that surrounded Cernunnos now. Yom recoiled from the weight of it and stepped to the next tapestry.

This visage was of four people, balanced out on the four points of a star. It was the same four-pointed star that was inset into the marble floor of the Inisfail Archives branch, Yom realized. To the left stood a woman engulfed in flames, as if she were the sun, with a hummingbird kissing her lips. To the right, a woman covered under a cloud of rain with a whisper of lightning behind her, a lithe doe standing at her side. At the top, a man with scrolls in hand, surrounded by gusts of wind, a snake winding up his leg and wings at his back. At the bottom, a man cloaked in night and its purpled shadows, a fox curled at his feet next to a crop of something green, smoke unfurling from his hands.

"Quetzal," Yom said the name Quia had mentioned, staring at the man who sat at the top of the star.

"And Tezcat." Sophia motioned at the shadowed man at the other end of the axis. "Huitzil," she pointed to the woman of the sun, "and Tlaloc," the woman of the rain.

"The Immortal Rulers." Quia had moved to stand behind Yom's other shoulder.

Yom looked back at the tapestry of Cernunnos and recalled pieces of Eden's story, faded over time like a sun bleached book. "The gods and titans are both immortal creatures made of the World Tree. What makes them different?"

Sophia reached out to stroke her hand over the tapestry's delicate threads. "All the World Tree's children have their limitations. The titans draw power from the realms and creatures they created, but they are in turn bound to them, unable to leave their realms."

Yom had never seen Cernunnos leave Ibernia. It had never occurred to her as strange, but anytime trade or other business needed to be conducted outside of the province, he sent an emissary.

"The titans have many forms. Their true shape is that of giant half-beasts, but they can morph into many animal and human shapes. They have brute strength, and dominion over their realm. And they can amplify this power by drawing from the creatures Bound to them." Sophia looked pointedly at Yom's torc. "Before the Separation, the thought of Bound humans would have been an abomination to the titans, an alliance with the very faction they sought to eradicate. But like I said, much has been sacrificed in the quest for revenge."

Yom touched her bronze torc. *An abomination.* "And do they have rulers, like the gods?"

"No," Quia said sharply. "The realms are all equal. But the power of the gods is inherently hierarchical. It has always been a sore spot for the immortals. The gods believe, because they are born of Wacachan's branches, of the celestial heavens, that they are destined to rule this world. From the heavens come much farther reaching powers: influence over the skies, storms, the sun, the minds and hearts of their humans. And the more powerful gods have always held themselves above their lesser siblings. But the gods rely on worship—on fear and reverence—to fuel their power. The titans have severed the connection of Arcadian humans to the gods, taking away almost all their power here."

Yom's hand returned to her torc, recalling the way Cernunnos's power slipped from her fingers after she took the Aetherium, as if it relied on some kind of presence or will.

"Do the gods Bind humans, in the same way as titans?"

"Occasionally, a particularly ardent priest will offer themselves up to a god," Quia said. "But it is rare. A human must be willing to sacrifice their very soul to the mercy of the god—either in worship, or desperation. It provides a bastardized form of power, less reliable than ordinary worship but more potent. Gods trade in insidious exchanges, rarely what they seem."

Yom recalled the bargains they each made with Thoth, that the god had taken some of Quia's *wind*. The memory of meeting Thoth spurred on a new question. "Have you met them?"

Quia chuckled. "The Rulers prefer to be felt more than truly experienced. The lesser gods do their bidding most of the time. But a god will always reveal itself to its own numenborn during the Trials, though not always in the way one would expect."

Yom kept hearing about this mysterious ritual known as the Trials. All she had seen of it so far were the hairline scars across three people's palms. Yet it somehow led to power like what Quia had wielded in the Gutter.

Sophia watched the gears turn in Yom's mind. "As I'm sure is the case in Panchaia, every child here goes through their Trials when they reach seven years, and almost none reveal any excess numen intrinsic to themselves. But the immortals are not the only ones who can harness numen outside of oneself." Sophia turned to look at the far wall.

The wall was lined with shelves, on which sat rows and rows of jars of different ingredients, various glass vessels for mixing, and journals stacked with pieces of paper sticking out of them. She walked closer to examine the jars, recognizing their contents. The midnight plum of black hellebore blooms, the eerily doll-like mandragora root, the rotted green and orange skin of oak galls. They were in the form that Eden had taught her to use—their raw, whole state. Once Yom had gotten her foothold in the chemist laboratory among the Stags, she had stopped using the ingredients in this state, opting instead for the extracted and purified compounds.

"You're a chemist," Yom said.

"The plant spirits choose who they reveal their secrets to. We call the pursuit of their knowledge the Path of Night. Those who walk it are all students of the great master, Tezcat. He was the first being the plants chose to gift their numen to. In this land, some call themselves chemists, true students or not." Sophia smiled. *Plant spirits.* It was the third voice she had heard in the woods among Eden's and Lior's, the one she did not recognize. *The plant spirit will teach you its power, teach you how to live.*

"I think I heard your voice," Yom said quietly so that only Sophia could hear, "in the forest. Before you found me. How is that possible?"

"Like my mother said, sometimes the light of the spirits allows those it chooses to see in all directions through time, not just where we find ourselves in the current moment." She considered Yom. "Perception is a rare and precious gift." The way her eyes bored into Yom made her think she spoke of more than the visions in the forest. It was like she knew of Yom's hallucinations of Moonflower in the Gutter.

"I think," Yom spoke slowly, working through the thought as it left her mouth, "I'm meant to learn from you."

"That might be the case." Sophia's eyes turned stern. "I know what it is you seek. But powder will do you no good here. The forest has a way of turning the things we protect ourselves with against us."

"I don't know what you're talking about." Yom took a step back.

"I can take you on as my student, but only on the condition that you do not misuse any of the plants while you're here." Sophia held out her hand. Yom reached to shake it, but Sophia withdrew it at the last minute. "If you break this rule, I won't be there the next time the forest passes judgment on you." She reextended her hand, and Yom stood for a moment, considering.

A part of Yom wanted to respect these rules, wanted to be a good enough person to earn this tutelage. But another part of her knew the thoughts that crouched in waiting for her, without the comfort of powder. Misho's words were a requiem playing over and over in her head, reminding her again and again of the horror of Lior's fate. *Your fault your fault your fault.* Yom knew it would be easy to sneak something without Sophia realizing. Something small, just to take the edge off, if she needed it.

Yom grasped Sophia's forearm, and they shook on it.

MISHO HAD LOST ALL SENSE OF TIME AND PLACE AS HE STUMBLED OVER gnarled tree roots, half engulfed in the shadow of his cell, half holding onto the dying light of the forest. The other triarii was speaking somewhere nearby, though he sounded unaffected by whatever was causing Misho's hallucinations. Misho continued to remind himself they were nothing more than ghosts of a memory. But irrespective of what was real or imagined, the memory would not stop clawing tooth and nail for control over him.

The silken voice came to visit once more, but this time something was different. The cell door opened.

Misho kept completely still as the yellow-eyed one crossed the threshold into his cage.

"You are my favorite to visit." He ran a cold hand up Misho's arm. "There is something intoxicating in your numen." He inhaled deeply, leaning in. Misho held his breath, frozen like an animal caught in a trap.

The other hand stroked up his arm until both began to descend down his chest, leaving a wave of chills in their wake. The cold hands brushed further down, over his abdomen—

"What do you want?" Misho choked out.

"I want to give you a chance to earn your freedom." He smiled widely and something stirred in Misho's chest.

"Why?" Misho tried to ignore the delicate warmth those words sparked.

"I think we can help each other." The cold hands dropped from Misho's waist. "I need someone who can be a ghost. There are more Panchaians here. In Arcadia." Something desperate clanged inside Misho, immediately thinking of his poet. "They will keep coming. I know they are looking for her. You will hunt them down, and deliver them to me. In this you may obtain your freedom, the exchange of one life for another."

Misho was wary. He knew how quickly bargains could be twisted out of their original forms. "How many lives?"

"As many as it takes." Anger flashed in the yellow eyes. "They will not take what is mine. I will not lose her," the silken voice snarled louder, losing its control. The creature inhaled and his face relaxed, his yellow eyes the only thing betraying his desperation. "Do you agree to the terms?" The creature's hands found their way to clasp each of Misho's forearms. Fear and hope quaked inside him.

"Why not send your own men?" Misho needed to know what he walked into, even if he was escaping something worse.

"My men know nothing of how a Panchaian mind works. They know not how Panchaians navigate, how they fight. We cannot afford for a single one to slip through our fingers." The creature scrutinized him. Misho knew the words this creature sought.

"I agree," Misho whispered. He had seen this position painted in the codices, carved into the walls of the temples. He knew what came next but was not prepared for the pain. His skin beneath the creature's hands felt as if it was being

ripped off, as if a hundred needles pricked his forearms so deeply they hit bone. Misho's face screwed up in agony. Within the dark shroud of pain, he knew the creature was smiling, power pulsing greedily in his eyes. Misho could not tell if it was seconds or minutes or hours that passed, but his forearms were eventually released. He could barely feel below his elbows, but what he could sense felt like a scarred wound being ripped open over and over again.

"What have you done?" Misho refused to look down at his arms.

"Merely inked our agreement." The creature circled him. Misho concentrated all his energy on remaining standing.

"I knew it," the creature said softly. "You have a warrior's heart. You will do quite nicely." Misho closed his eyes, tried to keep a grip on who he was beneath the pain.

In another world, on the forest floor, Misho's markings itched with the reminder of their origin, his skin long ago healed over the ink that had been carved into it.

The creature waved a slender hand, and two of the beetle men entered Misho's cell, carrying with them a set of the same glistening armor they wore.

"You are a triarii now." The creature said. "You leave at dawn." The mention of dawn, of light, cut through Misho's haze. Whatever shape this agreement took, he would see the sun again. The creature crossed the threshold but turned back. "If you speak of me, of our agreement, it is violated." With that, the creature disappeared back into the shadows.

The beetle men stripped off Misho's clothes—stiff with dirt and rancid to smell—without ceremony. They fastened interlocking plates of glistening armor over Misho's limbs. The armor was cold at first but warmed quickly, as if it was a second skin engulfing his body. He ran hands over his torso to feel the outside of it, a cool oiliness beneath his fingertips. His hands were pulled away too and fitted with gloves, the hairline white scar across his palm covered as if it never existed. When the beetle men got to his shoulders, Misho steeled himself to finally look at his forearms, before those too were obscured from view. The pain of the creature's grip had diminished, but still throbbed. On the left, characters were inked up and down his forearm in a dark red pigment. On the right, a deep gash stretched from his wrist to the crook of his arm. Already the skin was a bulging pink, knotting itself back together. Misho turned his attention back to his left arm, getting one final look at the characters before the armor was locked into place. He recognized them as Ancient Panchaian, though he had no way to translate them. Until the last one. This was a character any child of Panchaia knew, one of the oldest characters ever written down. Its meaning was simple. Death.

XII

The Lovers

Two days and nights passed frighteningly quick in the Village in the Trees. Yom was still weak, but each night she spent in the treedwelling—lulled to sleep by birdcalls and rustling leaves—she felt her strength returning. Each daybreak, Sophia woke Yom to take her out foraging while the dew was still wet. After the sun had dried out the forest floor, they returned to Sophia's worktable. Sophia insisted that Yom begin with the basics of the Path of Night, identifying each plant's abilities, before Sophia would show her how to massage the numen from them. Quia spent his days around the hearth of the treedwelling with Moira, or sitting on the ledge outside listening to the symphony of the forest while tending to his scrolls. The nights, however, they all spent together, sitting around the hearth and listening to Sophia enchant them with stories.

Moira's eyes shined when she made her request on the third night. "Mother, will you tell us a romantic story?" Yom hardly noticed how the precocious girl's gaze flitted to Quia, but was instead struck by an overwhelming sense that she had experienced this whole scene before. Except she was back in Inisfail, crowded around the smaller fire in Eden's laboratory, and the hungry eyes were not Moira's brown ones but Lior's blue ones. *Can you tell us a story?* Lior's voice rang through Yom.

Sophia hummed. "I have a story for you. But I must warn you, most love stories do not end happily. Love is, by nature, finite." Moira waved a hand in dismissal of Sophia's warning.

"Very well." Sophia smiled and closed her eyes. She took a handful of leaves and threw them into the fire, the flames changing to a deep pink, and the smoke rising in a glittering blush column. "Tonight, I will tell you about the Lovers." Everyone leaned in to watch closer.

"Of the World Tree's children, one god was a single being born into two bodies. Some thought of them as twins, some as lovers. Some as both." In the enchanted smoke, the shadow of the World Tree appeared. One of its branches shed and split in two, and those halves morphed and shaped themselves into two figures, both not quite man and not quite woman, walking hand in hand. "They presided over sexuality and fertility, but they indulged art, poetry, dance, any act of creation. Anything that fed the soul. They were the pulsing heart of the gods.

"The squabbles between titans and gods never concerned them. But among their siblings, they had a special relationship with the titans. They often snuck away to be alone in the titan's lush gardens. They explored grottos, meadows, and shimmering pools of water untouched by a single other hand. It's said that they molded each other's eyes to match the color of the daffodils they laid in. The titans did not mind their presence, for they never disturbed the lands they visited. They were followed by a trail of butterflies, and they filled the valleys of their cousins with music.

"When war broke out, the Lovers insisted on remaining uninvolved. They made a deal with the titans, that as long as they maintained neutrality, they could continue to occupy their lands. This worked for a time.

"But the gods were losing ground. The fight was uneven with two of their own on the sidelines. Tezcat, sorcerer trickster that he is, saw an opportunity. If he could convince the Lovers to turn on their titan allies, it would give the gods one shot of unfettered access to them.

"Tezcat visited his siblings many times, trying to convince them to forsake their neutrality. He promised them wealth and power, but nothing could sway them. 'We have all we need, right here,' they would tell him. So finally, the Sorcerer decided to sow fear and doubt. He told them that the titans planned to ambush them the next time they visited their lands, intending to separate them. That it was a desperate act of war concocted by a losing side. This, finally, got their attention.

"Faced with the prospect of losing each other, they agreed they would do whatever they had to in order to evade that fate. Tezcat told them that all they needed to do was reveal the secret pathways that lead to the titan lands, and that Tezcat and his brother, Quetzal, would take care of the rest. He said that once they were in the titan lands they would use the advantage to put an end to the war, peacefully. The Lovers conferred between themselves and felt this was not so hard a task.

"The Lovers showed Tezcat and Quetzal the hidden path they took to enter the titan lands, and the two brothers set off, a far darker mission in mind than what they had shared with their siblings. The two brothers killed one of the titans, and it was only made possible by the Lovers' betrayal of their titan allies. The Lovers of course had no idea that this was their goal, and the titans had never concocted a plan to separate the two. But their naivete could not negate the fact that the two brothers, Tezcat and Quetzal, killed a titan. It sent shockwaves throughout the world.

"Wacachan gathered all the immortals once again under its shade. The war had carried on for far too long and needed to be put to an end. But the titans, newly mourning and enraged with grief, only had one thought when they came to this meeting. Retribution. They wanted a life for a life. The life of one of the gods for the life of their fallen brother. It was Tezcat who stepped forward.

"He suggested a different trade. Since it was the Lovers who had committed the betrayal, it was them who should be separated, the rending of one soul into two unmendable halves being tantamount to a life lost.

"The titans agreed. Tezcat dragged his two younger siblings to the fore, the very ones he had convinced to enact the betrayal. The Lovers kicked and screamed, insisting that Tezcat and Quetzal should be the ones punished, not them. But it was not a trial; judgment had already been passed. Using his sorcery, he reached between them and severed the tether between the two halves of their numen. A bright light that glowed between them died. They could still touch each other, but never again be joined as they were. The siblings sobbed and ached for their lost half, trying to hold each other but feeling a chasm of distance.

"It was not enough for the titans. They wanted more. 'The life of our brother was worth more than this!' They cried amongst themselves. The two sides became more agitated as the gods insisted the price had been paid.

"Wacachan would only accept a single outcome of the meeting. The war would end, one way or another. As the titans and gods began readying themselves for an immortal battle in the shade of their own creator, they felt a tremor in the earth beneath them. The tremor grew into a quake until the very ground beneath them split and separated. The waters of Okeanus that ringed the world flooded to fill the chasm between the two halves."

"What happened to the Lovers?" Moira asked.

"When it was clear that nothing could restore their tether to each other, the Lovers withdrew from their siblings. Together but not able to be one again, they drifted through the centuries that followed the Separation, until finally, they disappeared altogether."

"But that can't be the end of the story!" Moira whined.

Sophia winked at her. "My dove, you must know by now that no story is ever truly over."

Yom gasped quietly. Another vivid fragment of that night in Eden's laboratory returned. *And you, dove?* Yom's fingers itched for her powderbelt, but it sat in their room upstairs, emptied of anything that could help her.

"That was sad. And not very romantic, either." Moira sighed.

Yom spared a glance at Quia and saw that instead of watching the enchanted smoke exhale its final puffs, or the exchange between Moira and her mother, he was watching her.

YOM TOOK STOCK OF THE TOOLS SPREAD OUT ON SOPHIA'S WORKBENCH in front of her. It was almost every piece of equipment she had back in Inisfail, albeit about a century out of date. A mortar and pestle in lieu of a crank grinder, a balance and weights instead of a scale, a blowpipe, a brass funnel, an oil burner and a kettle. Yom ran a hand over it all, the set and the bench kept meticulously clean. Just as Eden had always drilled into her. Yom's blue fingertips buzzed with promise.

Perhaps out of habit, Yom's gaze wandered to find Quia. He perched on a thick branch to the side of the dwelling, large tome cracked in his lap, quill poised in his hand. It seemed the rigid rule follower had loosened up when it came to defacing Archive property. Sunlight mottled by leaves covered his cheeks, practically making him glow. His shirtsleeves were rolled up in the warmth, the muscles in his forearms flexing subtly as he turned a large, cracked page.

I was completely wrong about you, Yom. Quia's soft voice repeated in her ears, the memory of his words warming her cheeks and fluttering in her belly.

Yom admonished herself. For what, she couldn't quite say. But now was not the time to be whisked away by daydreams. She turned back to the workbench in front of her and thought of the one thing that was easy to conjure, facing this workbench, to cool her overexcited mind: Eden.

Yom would never allow something like that to happen again to someone she cared about. And whatever she could learn from Sophia would be another tool to arm herself with. This fortified her, and staved off the distracting thoughts about Quia. Tools. Weapons. Protecting herself. It was all she had.

"Start by showing me your process." Sophia looked over Yom's shoulder with her hands clasped behind her back. "Make a remedy for, let's say..." Sophia tapped her chin once, twice. "Madness."

Yom nodded, her mind taking off to its catalog. She rounded the bench to stand at Sophia's wall, spotting the black hellebore blooms once again. Grabbing it, and a couple other plants that struck her, Yom returned to the bench and lit the burner. She scanned the shelves for soda ash, her usual starting point for distilling a consumable powder, but didn't see any. In fact, she didn't see any bases for any kind of powders. No lye, lime, or magnesia milk at all. Yom cracked her knuckles. It appeared that she would be doing this the old fashioned way. She set the water kettle on the burner to boil. Looking around the rest of the room, she found a dish of salt sitting by the hearth. Dropping a palmful of salt into the mortar, she extracted the hellebore stalk from its jar with a pair of tongs and prepared to dump it in over the salt.

"What are you doing?"

Yom looked up at Sophia, suddenly feeling self conscious. "Purifying the—"

Sophia shook her head. "Slow down, it's not a race."

Yom stopped what she was doing.

"You're too worried about the plant's physical properties." Sophia took the tongs out of Yom's hands. "The plants also have metaphysical properties. Physical properties address the physical state, and metaphysical properties address the spiritual state. The numen. And the way you're going about accessing them is tantamount to beating a stone and expecting water to come out." Sophia dropped the wilted hellebore from the tongs into her palm and held it between them. Yom's shoulders curled in, a bit deflated. She had been questioned about many things but never her skills as a chemist.

"You picked the right ingredients, you just need to treat them differently," Sophia added.

This is all the chemical arts are, accessing these hidden truths of every living thing. Eden's voice returned, clear as if she stood next to her. Yom couldn't help the tear that welled and made its escape; since the withdrawal, it felt like her chest had opened and been left ajar, any emotion that wanted to was able to make its escape. "Hidden truths," Yom said softly.

"Exactly," Sophia smiled now. "Hellebore, for madness." She picked up the other jars that Yom had been drawn to. "Mugwort, a healer of trauma. And Agrimony—"

"A forger of boundaries." The words came out of Yom unexpectedly, drawn from some deeply buried memory, or intuition. While Eden had never stated these metaphysical properties during her lessons, Yom had always sensed them, like a coin with two sides, waiting to be flipped over.

"Excellent." The edges of Sophia's eyes crinkled as she smiled. Yom had received plenty of praise for her work in the Cut's laboratory, and eventually in her leadership of the Powdery, but none of it had recreated the warm glow of Eden's praise. None until now. "You have the intuition, you just need to listen."

Sophia enclosed the Hellebore in Yom's hand, and guided her fist over the kettle, whose water was now boiling. "Harnessing numen is an act of discovery, not a battle of will. You will not impress your bidding upon the plant. The plant is your teacher, and it will give you the respect that you give it." Sophia pulled her hand away. "Similar to communing with an immortal, you must give an offering to the plant. And if the plant deems you worthy, it will share its secrets."

"That's it? 'Give an offering'? How exactly am I supposed to do that?"

"That is the part of this that can't be taught." Sophia's words were contrite, but her eyes were full of mischief. She was enjoying this. "You can start by closing your eyes."

Yom watched her in disbelief for another minute before returning her attention to the stalk of hellebore still clasped in her hand, and closed her eyes. At first, there was nothing but the creaking groan of the treedwelling around them. Within seconds of silence, Yom's thoughts began to crowd her, both the ugly and the mundane. Her knee jerk reaction was to try to rein some control over them by making her voice the loudest. *I am seeking—* She felt rather silly trying to speak to plants, but blazed on. *I am seeking hellebore, a remedy for madness. I can offer you three coins and one of Lucan's wands that he left smushed in the bottom of my pack.* Yom shook her head.

"This is ridiculous," she muttered, her eyes opening.

"It's not," Sophia said firmly. "I think perhaps you are trying too hard. Use your instincts, don't overthink it."

Yom shifted on her feet and screwed her eyes shut once again. It would help if it wasn't so quiet. In the silence, she had little to no control over her thoughts. But she recalled in the fighter's chamber of Renos's arena, it was when she was left alone with her mind that she finally found the tether to Cernunnos. Simply by looking for it. Realizing her shoulders were tensed in concentration, she relaxed them. And decided that instead of fighting her thoughts, she would allow them to flow around and through her, until she found what she sought.

Yom loosened the tight reins on her mind, and thoughts and memories crashed over her in a barrage, like a burst dam. At first, she flinched, girding herself, her fears and suspicions playing in a loop: Quia jumping out from behind, telling her these days they had spent together—where it felt like they had actually gotten closer, and perhaps seen something in each other—were all just a ruse to expose her for the horrible person she was; Sophia turning away from Yom, realizing that she wasn't worth her time; Eden watching Yom sign her life away to Cernunnos, disgust curling Eden's lip. But Yom tried ignoring these thoughts that couldn't be faced, turning them over like stones so they remained hidden from everyone, even herself.

There was a quiet that resulted, strange and tenuous. And Yom heard something. A low thrum, a hushed whisper. She moved towards it, and it became clearer. *Madness is naught but the heart and mind at odds, the heart wanting something the mind knows it can never have. It is a way to protect oneself from the contradiction of being.* Yom approached the thrum as it continued, its words repeating and winding in a lazy meander, until she found its source. A soft light emanated from Yom's palm, from the places she touched the hellebore stalk.

"Steady, now," Sophia's voice cut in softly. "Keep hold of it." Her hand wrapped under Yom's and guided it closer to the kettle. The light almost felt like a heartbeat trapped in Yom's hand. "And then, let go." Sophia's fingers unpried Yom's from the hellebore, and it slipped into the kettle with a hiss and a bubble.

The treedwelling came back into focus as Yom's eyes blinked open. Colors felt deeper and truer, and shadows contrasted more starkly, like Yom was looking at a painting. Her mind felt a bit raw, like it had held itself in an uncomfortable position for too long and now shook out stiff limbs. Yom's hands pressed in on either temple, kneading. The chemistry she was familiar with wasn't quite as mentally…taxing.

"Well done." Sophia squeezed her shoulder. "Now, again." Sophia gestured at the jars of mugwort and agrimony sitting unopened on the bench. The kettle's water continued to simmer, taking on the dark plum hue of the flower swirling in it.

Yom groaned. "I have to do that again?"

"This is nothing, a simple decoction. You need to get used to paying the toll before you can do anything more grandiose."

Yom's hands dropped and she glanced at Sophia from the corner of her eye. "Toll?"

"The more you ask of the plant, the more of yourself you must give. Even Tezcat himself must pay a toll each time he uses their power."

"That's all he can do? Harness plants?" Yom couldn't help but compare that to the winds Quia had summoned in Renos's keep. And he had said that was a fraction of his full power.

Sophia tittered. "Tezcat's power lies in his cleverness. He is the eternal trickster. Master illusionist. Freer of slaves, bringer of change." Yom looked to the far side of the treedwelling, at the tapestry with the four-pointed star where she could barely make out the figure at the bottom, cloaked in night. "He is also an artist of seduction. The tale goes that he seduced the plant spirit to convince her to share her secrets."

"So the plant is a she?"

"All plant spirits are feminine."

"How do you know?"

"Do you think a man could keep a secret like this?"

Sophia and Yom shared a wry laugh.

MISHO COULD NOT BE CERTAIN WHERE, OR WHEN, HE WAS. Vaguely, he knew his body had been scratched and pummeled, but all he saw were the rolling golden hills and sparkling turquoise lakes of his home. He saw a young boy with an indentured caste brand on his forearm, skin as dark as the witching hour, running over the hills like a tiny god.

Imagination was a powerful thing for this little boy. He saw himself growing up into a fierce warrior, so fierce they would have no choice but to accept him into the most noble caste of all. The warrior caste. The caste his master's son had been born into. A boy who was the fiercest warrior of their generation, or so the sages said. Who was honest and true, and treated Misho as if he was more than an indentured boy. Treated him like an equal, or as equal as two boys from such different castes could be. His master's son didn't understand the dynamics of power at play in their relationship, but Misho didn't begrudge him. Because the boy warrior had a secret, a love he kept hidden from all eyes but Misho. A talent with words: an ability to take and string them together like beads into the most sublime necklace. A poet.

Wherever Misho was, he was smiling. When he proved his worth and was accepted into the warrior caste, he could finally confess to his boy warrior everything he had been holding inside. He held it so tightly, it threatened to suffocate him. He would tell his poet that his scent was that of the wind the eagle rides. That sometimes, Misho wanted his poets hands to be the only thing that ever touched him again. That his poet's eyes carried their own divine lightning, a spark shared between them each time their gazes met. Misho wondered if everyone at this age knew something so deeply it was like it was written on their bones. He couldn't imagine anyone had ever felt feelings this grand before, for surely they would have burst.

Misho couldn't understand why he had decided to wait until they accepted him to the warrior caste to tell his poet all these things. He feared not having the chance to share the part of his soul that beat ardently for his poet; it was the greatest loss the young Misho could imagine. So on those grassy hills, he ran to his poet. He saw him in the distance, sitting in the shade of a banyan tree, fig tree bark and charred stylus in hand, writing. Misho smiled, almost in tears. He was within shouting distance of his poet, his heart about to beat out of his chest. He would not consider the possibility that the poet did not share his affections, for even in his youth, he knew that the smallest glimmer of a chance that his poet felt the same way could banish the shadow of fear that he did not.

"Brother!" he called out. This was how he and his poet referred to each other, despite their different castes. His poet looked up from his writing, wide smile opening his face.

But something flitted in front of Misho's eyes. A light. He was distracted and tried to swat it away. It did not leave. Instead, it was joined by another light. They were floating into Misho's vision, crowding him. As soon as he saw one light, there were dozens. Cracks began to show in the golden hills, in the turquoise lakes. Misho ignored them. He tried wading through the sea of lights, intending to get back to his poet. But soon the golden hills were the thing showing in the cracks, and Misho was surrounded by green moss, tree bark and the foreign hum of insects. This was not his home.

The forest bled back into his consciousness. He looked down at his armor, scratched and some of the seams torn, but still glistening like a beetle. The glow of golden hills and turquoise lakes drifted away, like a fleeting memory of a dream.

Someone grunted to his side. The triarii he had come to the Ardennes with walked on his right, crossbow drawn from the concealed compartment on his back. His armor was untouched.

"What happened?" Misho asked warily.

"You've been out of your mind for two days. We've been walking but I don't think we've gotten anywhere. I think the forest is taking us in circles."

Misho sobered at his words. Two days had passed? As he remembered himself with each passing second, he would have guessed it had only been an hour since they had entered the forest.

"We need water and food. I haven't seen a single animal we can eat yet." The triarii sounded quite irritated. "If you didn't come to within the next day I was going to start eating you." He laughed. Misho did not laugh. He knew that he had never been fully accepted into the triarii; it had been a reluctant admittance because of the knowledge he possessed. It had not gone unnoticed that Misho was never forced to endure the Trials that initiated warriors into their order. They could not know that Misho had already endured the Trials, many years before, on the other side of the world.

Misho understood the full scope of where he was. He had chased the fugitives outside of the Queen's jurisdiction, which also made it outside the jurisdiction of the triarii's rules. He could take any triarii on in a fight—they were mere toddlers wading in the pool of their numen —but his chances were drastically worse if he fell into another hallucination.

"Do you hear that?" Misho heard the faintest sound of running water. He followed it.

"If you go into another episode, I'm leaving you behind," the triarii said, colder now than his joke about eating him.

"I'm not imagining this," Misho snarled, his anger trickling back into him, giving him purpose. He pushed through low hanging branches and moved over the uneven terrain until he found a tiny stream at the bottom of a small slope, nothing more than a sluice of rainwater. He was so thirsty, it felt like his body was drying out from the inside.

Misho half-walked, half-slid down to the stream and yanked off his gloves to submerge his hands in it. He lapped up the water greedily, uncaring that it dribbled down his chin. A flash of black and the triarii was next to him, drinking the water with equal fervor. Misho splashed it onto his forehead and the back of his neck, the skin of his armor feeling oppressive.

"Finally," the triarii growled. Misho followed his gaze. Further down the stream, a doe was lapping up its own fill of water. But this was no ordinary doe. It had a coat as white as snow, so light it almost glowed in the shaded forest. Misho instantly felt the draw, the intoxication with its beauty. His mouth salivated and he could almost taste it, butchered and quartered and roasted over a hearty fire. Somehow his own crossbow was drawn. He sensed movement and saw the triarii was already walking closer, low and silent. Stalking it. The ultimate prize.

But this was not the first time Misho had seen something misleading in this forest. He shook his head, trying to clear the foreign influence in his mind. The other triarii was already halfway to the doe.

"Wait," Misho hissed. He sensed something treacherous lurking beyond the slaughter of a creature so beautiful. The triarii looked back at him with murder in his eyes. He held a single finger to his lips to silence Misho.

"No—" Misho ran to catch up with him and landed his hand on the triarii's shoulder. The triarii snapped to look at him, but they both heard the rustle of the doe move. It was looking up at them now, not a lick of fear in its eyes.

The triarii snickered. He stalked closer under the gaze of the deer, but it did not move.

"Leave!" Misho shouted at the doe. "Go, now!" But the triarii was cocking his bow. He would not miss. Before Misho could utter another plea, the snap of the bow releasing its arrow sliced through the air.

When the arrow hit its target between the doe's eyes, the animal burst into a cloud of light, com the smaller lights that had surrounded him in his vision.

"What was—" The triarii backed away, the doe's spell broken the second the arrow had landed. The clearing they were in suddenly filled with the snapping of twigs and low growls. Misho whipped around, but the growls were coming from all sides. The rustling became clear as large paws padded into the clearing. Paws attached to massive wolves.

"The doe is fine," the triarii managed to stammer in the face of the wolves, "No one was hurt." Misho knew better than to reason with these creatures. Their fate was sealed the second the arrow was released. Judgment had been passed. All he could do was attempt to separate himself from the other triarii.

Misho backed away from the triarii as the wolves descended on him. He was begging now, swinging his crossbow around in a desperate threat. The wolves did not hesitate. They pounced on him with teeth as thick as sabers, gnashing at his limbs and his innards. His armor cracked and crumpled like paper. The triarii's whimper was quickly drowned and then muted altogether.

Misho remained untouched. He tried to keep backing away, without calling any attention to himself. He took in the scene, senses heightened, preparing for a battle. Every snarl of the wolves, the constant trickle of the stream, the sound of bones cracking and wet sloshing of blood. The bodies of the wolves seemed even larger when he took them in next to the ancient trees. They had coats of every color: russet red, amber, white, silvery gray, and even one that was midnight black. And around each of their necks was a collar of spun twigs.

A presence entered Misho's mind. It did not speak with words, but its message was communicated. *This is your only warning. Leave these woods and you may keep your life.* Misho looked back at the circle of wolves to see the black one standing up straight, gray blue eyes boring into him even from a distance.

"Where are we going?" Yom laughed as Quia led her through the woods, her hand grasped in his. It was midafternoon, and the heat of the sun was heady on the forest floor.

Sophia had let Yom take the rest of the afternoon off, after finishing their decoction. The act of sitting in silence with her mind, in order to hear the plants properly, became easier each time she did it. It almost made Yom think she didn't need powder, if she was able to separate her thoughts in that way without a drop of it in her system. Not to mention, connecting with the plants provided its own intoxication. It reminded her of how she felt working in Eden's laboratory, with her head clear and a wealth of ingredients at her fingertips. Like she could do anything.

"It's a surprise." Quia squeezed her hand as he led her through brambles and over tree roots. "I found this place yesterday, and I asked Sophia if I could borrow you for the afternoon to show you."

Yom hummed. "So that was why she gave me the afternoon off. And here I thought I was just the best student she's ever had."

"She definitely mentioned that as well." Quia paused to look back at her and wink. Yom didn't know what had happened to the snarky, disdainful apprentice she had met in Inisfail, but she was certain this was not him.

"So this is what you're like when you're trying to charm someone?"

"Who says I'm trying to charm you?" Quia asked.

Yom yanked his hand back. "If that's not the case, I should really get back, I have a lot to catch—"

"No you don't, you're staying with me. We're almost there." Quia wrapped his arm around her waist and pulled her even closer to his step.

Yom's stomach twirled with excitement and nerves. Wherever they were delving was uncharted waters. She had not felt this kind of draw to a person, both in body and heart, since Lior. Even the comparison brought dark clouds into her mind. The glow of Quia's attention and his touch prodded the blurred edges of guilt. *It's my fault Lior and I don't have moments like this.* The thought hit Yom sharply, but she turned it over, tucking away the ugly face of it.

"Time to close your eyes." Quia covered her eyes with one of his broad hands, and he led Yom up what felt like a slight ridge, still holding her waist in case she tripped.

"Ready?" he whispered in her ear, his voice skittering over her skin. Yom nodded, flushing. Quia's hand fell away.

They were at the edge of a basin lined with evergreen trees and a bright cerulean pool whose surface was dappled with shards of sunlight. The air smelled of pine and minerals, filled with the music of songbirds and the rhythm of woodpeckers.

"Quia." Yom spoke without taking her eyes off the pool, already walking down the slope. "This is so beautiful." She made it halfway down before looking back, Quia still standing at the rim of the basin.

"Yes," he said, his eyes locked unmistakably with hers. "So beautiful."

Yom couldn't stop a blush heating her cheeks under his intense gaze. She tried to shake herself out of it, to remind herself of the hard walls she had constructed to avoid this very vulnerability. But logic would not stop the blush from deepening, and spreading to her chest, so she turned back to the pool and walked to its edge. The rim was lined with bright algae, the center a clear and bottomless blue.

Quia stepped up behind Yom once again, so close she could feel his breath on her neck.

"Should we swim?" she asked, more breathless than she liked.

"Well, I didn't bring us here to watch." Yom elbowed him but could not bring herself to turn around and meet his eyes again. There was too much at stake.

Quia finally stepped back and stood a few feet away on the bank of the pool. Yom snuck a glance as he pulled his shirt over his head. His luminous copper skin continued over the planes of his chest, svelte lines of muscle curving over his arms and onto his abdomen. He unlaced his boots and yanked them off along with his woolen socks, leaving only his trousers. Her tongue ran over her bottom lip, hungry.

Confident and graceful, Quia dove headfirst into the water. The splash cut through the forest's silence, breaking Yom's spell. His head bobbed up almost instantly, his black hair plastered to him as if carved from stone.

"Come on," he sent a splash of water in her direction. "Get in here."

Yom forced herself to exhale and nodded. She peeled off the linen knickerbockers, and then made quick work of her boots and socks. With nothing but her shirt grazing her thighs, she stepped onto a boulder at the precipice of the pool, staring at its intimidating depth.

"What are you waiting for?" Quia asked, sending another splash in her direction.

"I've never swum before," Yom admitted. She hadn't come across many opportunities in the stone jungle of Inisfail. And her last experience with water in Renos's arena had been rather treacherous, she recalled with a shiver.

"I'll help you," Quia insisted. "I promise I won't let anything happen to you."

Yom nodded but felt her stomach about to take flight. The longer she stood atop the boulder, the more lightheaded she felt. She scolded herself for her hesitation and resolved to take the leap. As soon as she counted to five. Well, maybe ten. But then the lightheadedness gave way to an off balance feeling and she worried that she would slip before she was ready and crack her head on the boulder.

Hush, she scolded herself. *You're a Stag. You can jump in a pool of water. You have done far more dangerous things before and come out completely unscathed.* Puffed up sufficiently, she closed her eyes and held her nose as she jumped into the water without an ounce of the grace Quia had shown. Within seconds of breaking the surface, Quia's sturdy arms pulled her up and held her afloat. His face was inches from hers and his arms caged around her, warm and safe and protective. *Completely unscathed*, indeed. She had gotten herself to take the plunge, but with words that were the truest lie she'd ever told.

"Let's swim to the center." Quia pulled her with him. "I'll show you how to float."

Yom choked and sputtered in the cold shock of the water. She flailed like a bumbling pup, trying to find her rhythm in the foreign weightlessness, not helped by her shirt ballooning as it filled with water. Quia took sure, broad strokes, though still keeping watch of her. By a miracle, Yom made it to the center of the pool.

"Your body will float on its own," Quia said as he arranged her body to be splayed on the surface of the water. He treaded next to her with ease. "You just have to trust it." Yom couldn't help but squirm, not yet feeling the buoyancy Quia mentioned.

"Stop moving," he laughed, holding her from underneath, warmth radiating from the places his hands touched. Yom took a deep breath and tried to still her limbs, tried to imagine she was somewhere safe and relaxing. Eventually she found some stillness and started to float as Quia's hands slipped away.

Above her, the tall jagged edges of the trees gave way to a clear blue sky. The water muffled the noise of the forest and Yom was cocooned in quiet.

"Not so hard once you relax and let your body take over, right?" Quia's voice sounded distant and waterlogged.

"Why are you so good at everything you do?" The cradle of the water seemed to chip away at her filter. She hadn't intended that to sound so flattering.

"I grew up around lakes. Not quite like this, but I did a lot of swimming when I was young." Yom felt the tips of Quia's fingers find her arm and trail down to her hand.

"That's it?"

"And I might seem a little more graceful than I am because I have a little bit of wind on my side."

"I knew it!" Yom's outburst disturbed her precarious balance and she found herself quickly back to flailing.

"Whoa, careful," Quia laughed and caught her, steadying her back to a standing tread. Only this time they faced each other, foreheads almost touching. Quia's hands gripped her ribs, and his gaze was flitting between her eyes and her lips.

"I'm not good at diving headfirst," Yom blurted. She didn't know exactly what she meant by that—it certainly wasn't something literal—but it seemed important to share.

"I can do it for the both of us," Quia whispered just before his lips brushed hers.

The gentle touch of his lips distracted her for a second and she lost her balance. She slipped beneath the surface of the water before Quia's hands raised her back up.

"Can we do this on solid ground?" Yom sputtered.

QUIA DELICATELY DABBED AT YOM'S DRIPPING WET FACE WITH HIS DRY shirt. It was a surprisingly intimate gesture and a strange thought occurred to her, that this was what it felt like to be cherished.

Quia leaned in to kiss her dry cheek. Then he shifted to the other cheek, his lips soft and still wet from the pool, but their touch firm. Like he knew where this was headed, and he would be the one to take them there. Yom barely breathed as his lips moved to her forehead, then to each eyelid, treating her with reverence. This was not what her encounters in Inisfail had been. This had the same precious glow that Lior's kiss on her cheek had, so many years ago. That simple kiss had survived in her memory longer than any of the kisses she had received since. Until these. These, Yom could already tell, would make their way onto that same pedestal.

Finally his lips hovered over her lips. Her eyes were still closed and she held her breath, the whole world coming to a standstill as his lips approached hers, as if time itself was stopping to witness this moment. His lips brushed hers in waves, gaining confidence each second she did not pull away. His hands shifted to cradle her face, his thumbs stroking along her jaw. His fingertips ran over her neck and down her shoulders, leaving a trail of sparks in their wake.

Yom's own hands found their way into his hair, thick and coarse like the pelt of a wolf. She laced her fingers through his strands and squeezed before mounting her own exploration down his neck, over his arms. Finally able to feel the taut cording of muscles she had tried to stop herself from admiring, she soaked in the feel of his skin through her fingertips. What a wondrous thing, she marveled, the magic that is passed between two people by touch.

They continued to delve further into each other's lips, and Yom's hands became more brave. They ran back from his arms down the planes of his chest, over his ribs and around his abdomen. Instinct nudged her further down. Desire condensed on her skin, a honeyed dew. The heady euphoria of a connection between bodies called out to her. Her fingers found the edge of his trousers and she fumbled to unbutton them.

Quia pulled back abruptly. "What are you doing?" His pupils were dilated, his own breathing labored.

"What two people do when they're having fun," she whispered as she leaned in to plant soft kisses from the top of his breastbone up the side of his neck. His hands found her shoulders and ran over her upper arms. He relaxed into Yom, and she moved her hands back to their task at the buttons of his trousers.

"Stop." Quia moved back so they were no longer melting into each other. "Is that all this is?" His hands held onto her wrists, restraining them from going any further. "Fun?"

"Isn't this why you brought us here?"

Quia looked puzzled. "I didn't bring you here for that. I just wanted to spend time with you." He dropped her wrists and ran his hands over his neck. "I care about you. I don't know what it means yet, but I do. This isn't just 'having fun' for me." His eyes searched for something in Yom, perhaps some matching declaration.

"But you're betrothed," she said flatly.

"I didn't say I was happy that this happened!" Quia snapped.

Yom flinched, her whole body pulling away from him. "Sorry to inconvenience you."

"That's not what I meant—" He moved to grab any part of her still within reach. All he found were her hands. "I haven't let myself get close to anyone here, knowing I would be leaving eventually. All I'm saying is that I didn't see this coming. But I don't want to ignore it."

The mention of leaving broke the spell Yom had slipped into. "Maybe you should." She tried to pull her hands out of Quia's, but he would not let them go. "It's not like anything is going to happen after we find the numenborn. You two will go to Panchaia and I'll stay here." Yom's eyes drifted down to look at her hands clasped in Quia's.

"Come with us." It was a whisper, barely audible. "Come with us," he repeated, more confidently.

"To Panchaia?" Yom's eyebrows furrowed. The thought of actually seeing the mysterious land on the other side of Okeanus was a mirage glimmering far away, not a future that truly existed. And what would that mean for her and Quia? Would she have to watch him marry someone else, and have this moment hang between them like deadweight? Or would the betrothal be renegotiated somehow? It hurt, imagining him marrying someone else, and Yom resented herself for it. He was always planning to return home; nothing that happened on this journey had the power to change that. He *belonged* there, and Yom belonged nowhere. In theory, she *could* go anywhere. And if he was suggesting she come with, he couldn't possibly still plan to go through with marrying someone else. Perhaps in Panchaia, there was a future for them, together.

Quia nodded. His hand gripped hers tighter. "You would love it there. Look at what you've learned from Sophia in a few days, imagine what you could learn training under Tezcat's high priest. What you could do if you went through the Trials and connected to your numen."

Yom watched Quia carefully, scrutinizing him for signs that he was toying with her.

He barreled forward. "You should see Tezcat's temples: libraries of plants and minerals with walls that stretch up to the height of these trees." The trees around them seemed to bristle at the mention of a rival to their greatness. "You've only had a taste of what someone with your affinities can do."

Yom turned his words over in her head, tasting each one tentatively. The rush she had felt massaging numen from those plants, and even the power she had accessed from the small piece of Cernunnos's numen in the arena, had left its imprint on her. It had felt like a beginning, a hidden door that she had discovered and nudged open. Her senses crackled with the promise of more, the promise of what she could discover if she wrenched that door open all the way.

The trees that bordered the pool and crept down into the basin, morphed into towering walls of endless flora in Yom's imagination. She looked at her hands and blue stained fingers, something that had always represented how she made her own way in the world, carved her own path. The reality was that after the cobalt accident, the blue had eventually begun fading. But she had restained her fingers each time it began to fade, to remind herself that no matter what collar she wore, the only person who decided her fate was herself.

Finally, she shifted Quia's hands, so that they sat on top of her palms, tracing the hairline scar on his palm forwards and backwards. *You've only had a taste of what someone with your affinities can do.* The tether of Cernunnos's numen she had clung to was only a fraction, according to Quia. The plants whose whispers she had heard, whose numinous light she had accessed, had scarcely scratched the surface. There was something out there to be discovered, a well of numen with depths unknown, and Quia had dangled it in front of her.

"Show me what I'm missing." Yom's finger stopped in the center of his scar.

"How?" He smiled, clearly surprised she was considering his offer.

"Show me the Trials."

Instantly, Quia's smile fell.

XIII

May darkness give you sight

"No." Quia's voice did not contain a single ounce of discussion. "It's too intense, it needs to be performed by a priest. It can be dangerous, especially for someone our age."

"If I'm going to follow you to the other side of the world, I need to see for myself what these promises you're making are made of."

"You could hurt yourself, or do worse," Quia insisted.

"Is this how it would be if I came with you? Hold me back because something is dangerous?"

Quia's eyes closed in exasperation.

"In case you haven't noticed, I'm not afraid of a little danger."

"That's exactly what I'm afraid of," he huffed. "You're actually considering it?" His eyes flashed with a moment of unbridled hope.

Yom's resolve solidified. "Not if you don't show me this." She had spent enough time in her life following someone blindly.

Quia sighed in defeat. "It wouldn't be the same without Amaurosis. It might not even w—"

Yom stood up from the rock before Quia could finish. The stalk she had cut in Cernunnos's growing room, the one she had pressed between the pages of her journal to ignore after seeing what it did to Moss, still sat at the very bottom of her pack.

The wilted and dried Amaurosis stalk was in her hand in a matter of seconds, and as soon as it touched her skin, its scratching whisper reached Yom's ears. She tried to ignore the chill it sent through her body as she sat back down.

Quia gaped at the Amaurosis in shock. "You've had that this whole time?"

"I didn't exactly trust you when I took it. And it turns out I had a good reason for that." Yom tilted an eyebrow and Quia conceded with a slump of his shoulders.

He reached for it but Yom held it away. "Tell me how it works." The memory of Moss's bottomless black eyes haunted her.

"Amaurosis is sacred. It is one of the four instruments that open the path between the conscious self and the numen that sits at the center of being."

"It enslaves you," Yom said hoarsely as she felt the ghosts of Moss's hands clawing at her face. "It takes away your will."

Quia's expression shifted. "Have you seen it used before?"

"Moss," she whispered.

His eyes glazed as he imagined what she was implying. "Before he…?"

Yom nodded.

Quia's expression was weighed down with a deep remorse. "It's a potent substance. It leaves the taker in a vulnerable state, which is why it is only used in sacred ceremonies, for specific purposes. To use it to force your will on another is despicable." He sighed heavily. "The priest guides the child through the Trials in front of the community. The child uses every instrument to access numen, and by the end, the god of their numen will have revealed him or herself. But much else can be revealed in the process." Quia's tone shifted to a warning. "Things that are found during the Trials cannot be lost again easily."

Yom held out the stalk to him, but he did not take it right away.

"Please don't ask this of me," Quia whispered. His hand raised not to take the Amaurosis, but to trace Yom's bottom lip. "I don't want this to change anything between us."

Yom leaned in, knowing she was manipulating this delicate spark between them, but unable to resist. "It won't." She brushed her lips against his. "All you have to do is show me. Everything will be fine." Yom lingered for a longer kiss, her hands slipping back into his hair and his stroking down her waist, towards her hips. Just as he seemed to lean in to continue, Yom pulled away and watched him expectantly.

Quia gave one last look of longing and apprehension before yielding and retrieving his own pack. He slowly laid out a handful of items between them, as if questioning this plan with each move. A flat shard of shiny black rock, two milky black stones, and his own bone knife. He put the dried stalk of young Amaurosis on the other side of the shiny rock.

"Poison, mirrors, smoke, and blood." He pointed to each of the four items while he spoke, his words reticent. He repeated it, this time in the guttural words Yom recognized as Panchaian. "You're sure this is what you want?"

Yom thought about how she had felt, held underwater by Misho, haunted by his words. Utterly powerless. "Couldn't be more."

Quia closed his eyes, pursed his lips. "Then, we start with poison."

He pushed the items to the side and arranged a small pile of sticks and brush. He took up the two black rocks and scraped them together. Yom watched in confusion as sparks erupted from the scrape of the rocks and caught onto the brush. Soon he had a tiny but crackling fire going between them.

"The Amaurosis," Quia instructed. Yom handed him the leaf, instantly feeling its absence once it left her palm. He held it over the fire until it caught and then rested it on the smooth surface of rock. They both watched it burn violet until nothing but ash remained, its sweet stench already clogging Yom's nose. Quia picked up a fingerful of ash.

"Close your eyes."

Yom hesitated. "You're not going to let anything happen to me?" The question made her sound childish, but she needed to hear him say it before she fully surrendered her trust to him.

"I won't let anything out here happen to you." Quia reached up with his empty hand to touch her forehead. "But in here, I won't be able to help you."

Yom steeled herself and dipped her chin in assent before she closed her eyes. Quia's fingertip, light as a feather, smudged ash over both her eyelids.

"May darkness give you sight," he said softly before his lips grazed hers for one lingering moment.

Then, a cloud of dark, sweet powder coated everything.

"Focus your energy inward." Quia spoke quietly. "Numen is constant, but accessing it is the challenge. It comes most intuitively to children, which is why this is normally done on a child's seventh annual of birth. The Amaurosis is a teacher to guide you, not an enemy to battle. Don't fight it."

As Quia spoke, he faded away. Yom sensed the ground beneath her but also slid down through it, as if it were sludge. Slowly, the Cut came into focus. Lucan lunged at her like a vulture, but she batted him away. She was in the Powder Parlor, seeing the hazy delirium of its patrons, all soaring on powders of her own creation. Except she saw them as the shells of who they had been before powders, abandoning everything in search of the high. She heard the sounds coming from the pleasure rooms on the other side of the floor, falsely exaggerated moans mixed with shrieks of pain. And worse, the rooms where she heard no noises at all. The rooms where the patrons had opted to sedate their servicers with one of Yom's powders. She recoiled from these scenes; this couldn't be who she was. There had to be more. No sooner had she decided this, than she felt something tugging her further. *The Amaurosis is a teacher to guide you, not an enemy to battle.* Yom followed it, and found herself plummeting.

She landed in the room beneath Cernunnos's garden. Eternally dark save for the glow of the fire, she watched boys and the occasional girl be branded and collared, while she stood separated behind a wall of Stags. Until a would-be thief with sandy hair struck a deal with Cernunnos. *No!* Yom shoved through the Stags until she was in the middle of the room. *Don't do it!* Moss looked at her like she was a complete stranger. *Perhaps you would like to do the honors, Bluefingers.* Cernunnos's cold smile turned to her. She didn't know how she hadn't seen the truth of the titan before, cruel and inhuman as he was. *Or maybe you can just save us all time and end the boy's life now?* There was a knife in her hand and she couldn't control it. She grabbed onto Moss's trembling shoulder to steady him while the knife plunged into his chest. The last emotion on his face before it slackened was betrayal, intimate and scalding. She stumbled and fell back, leaving the knife lodged in his chest. Yom clawed at the walls, refusing to stay in this vile room. *There has to be more!* she demanded, and another tug led her further down.

Yom dropped again until she caught her footing directly in front of the door to Eden's laboratory. It was cleared of cobwebs and its red lacquer polished, the golden chemist's symbol gleaming. Without opening the door she found herself inside the laboratory, everything bathed in golden light, all the bottles lined up on the shelves, each drawer of herbs righted and pushed in perfectly. Two young girls chased each other around the skirts of an older woman with a red apron and a smile anyone could find a home in. The day shifted to night in a blink, and the three of them huddled around the small hearth in the center, the woman gesturing broadly with her hands as she whispered, *the chemical arts are nothing more than accessing the hidden truths of every living thing.* Yom finally understood Eden's words, and an illusion faded. An illusion that life could be made of separate compartments; that a weed on the side of the road was any less knowledgeable or crucial than the traveler who passed by it without a second glance.

But the pale girl with blue eyes wasn't paying a speck of attention to her mother's words. She was watching the girl next to her, whose olive skin glowed bronze in the firelight, whose curls fell in a heap over her shoulders. In her blue eyes, there was a fluttering pulse of adoration. An answer to a question that had never been asked. Yom's breath caught in her throat. *Lior—* she reached out for the blue eyed girl and Lior began to turn, looking for the source of Yom's voice, but the laboratory once again shifted with a crack and a splinter. Two cloaks inched towards Eden from the shadows.

Yom backed away, knowing what came next, understanding where the Amaurosis had chosen to lead her. If reliving this moment was what it demanded, then its price was too high.

Racing out of the laboratory, Yom found the cobblestone street outside submerged in an ink black witching hour. She whipped around, searching for a way back to Cernunnos's chamber, or the Powder Parlor. Anywhere else, knowing the events that would unfold if she stayed in the laboratory. *Help!* she cried.

I thought you were ready. A voice prowled from below. Yom scanned the street around her desperately for its source. A small black fox emerged from the shadows into the moonlight.

What is this? she asked, taking a step away from it. She hoped it was some manifestation of the Amaurosis's guidance, but she would have also believed it was her mind truly losing its grip on the real and the imaginary. On memory and truth, and the chasm in between.

The creature did not answer her question. *You wanted to understand the power that awaits you.* For every step Yom took away from it, it mirrored her with a step closer. *Go back inside,* it commanded.

No. Yom shook her head.

You have no idea what's at stake, the fox snarled. Lior's howls erupted and Yom knew what had happened. She was too late.

I can't, Yom pleaded, tears erupting. *I'm sorry.* She turned away from the fox and ran. The tears would not stop. *Please,* she begged anyone listening. *Please let me out!* Yom thrashed as she ran, trying to claw her way out. She felt hands on her shoulders, shaking her, and a distant voice calling something. The sound and the feeling gave her something to grasp onto. She followed it, propelling herself up, past the layers she was buried in. The voice became clearer. *Yom,* it called, *wake up.* The sludge began to feel like water, the pressure releasing as she swam back to the surface. Finally, her eyes wrenched open and she heaved, unable to get enough air with each inhale. Quia held her up by the shoulders and her head swiveled around, taking in his face inches from hers and the same forest basin she had left, now in the softer, paler light of the late afternoon.

But Yom was not the same. The weight of everything she saw piled onto her like rocks, heavy and blunt, making it difficult to breathe. Quia looked at her with care she did not deserve. In fact, the whole time she had spent in the forest had been a delusion that it was time to wake up from. Yom was not someone who things could work out for. Not after everything she had done. She destroyed anything she touched. It had been blissful ignorance to think she could become anyone other than Bluefingers. A powderhead and a thug. A coward. No power in the world could change who she was. And now that Quia's wide eyes were watching her, she knew she could not drag him down with her.

Yom wrenched herself out of his grip and staggered back, almost slipping off the boulder before she found her feet.

"Yom!" Quia called but she was already scrambling off of the boulder and climbing the uneven slope of the basin. "Wait!" his voice sounded breathy. He must have been trying to follow her.

"Just stay away from me!" Yom shouted as she ran, practically falling over herself in her desperate escape. Once she made it to the lip of the basin, she took off, sprinting over the tree roots, knowing the forest would do the work of separating the two of them for her.

YOM RAN UNTIL HER LUNGS BURNED. Her feet were cut up and aching; she hadn't taken her boots with her. And now, after all that exertion, her stomach growled angrily. It had become too accustomed to the hearty meals Sophia provided. Yom slowed to a walk, and her legs began to shake. Eventually, she had to stop altogether, wrapping her arms around a tree for support, sinking onto her haunches at its base.

As she neared the ground, white buds caught her attention. Vines of Moonflower slithered over the ground and snaked up the trunk of the tree, its white petals waiting for night to fall before unfurling. Yom rubbed her eyes, waiting for the hallucination to disappear, but it was still there when she opened her eyes. She reached out to touch it, and sure enough the leaf was waxy and solid in her hand. Either it was very much real, or Yom had truly lost her grip on reality. Perhaps sensing the presence of an escape, her head began to pound. Sophia's warning rattled in her ears. *The forest has a way of turning the things we protect ourselves with against us.* But no one would know, Yom assured herself. She would take the smallest amount she needed to relieve this ache. Could it really be considered misusing the plants if their gift was escape?

Yom snapped a leaf off its vine.

The leaves released a bitter juice when ground between two stones, and she sucked on the pulpy residue greedily. She slipped into a soft and buoyant euphoria, her cheek pressed against the bark of the tree as the insects began their twilight march. It took her far from the Amaurosis and its dark visions, to a place bright as a rising moon.

Yom heard a voice. Muffled by the sounds of the forest, but a voice nonetheless. She waited a moment, giving it the chance to reveal itself as a mirage. But the voice remained steady. In fact, it was coming closer, and as it did, Yom realized there was more than one.

"They tell me that you almost killed her in Renos's arena," a silky voice snarled.

"It was a tactic. I wouldn't have killed her." Yom knew this voice well. She also knew that its source would be noiseless as he moved, and had a face mottled by scars. "Renos's servant was the one who went for the killing blow first."

"She would not have permitted her champion to kill the chemist. Anything you think you saw was carefully orchestrated. She knows it is forbidden to kill the servant of another." The silky voice sent chills down Yom's spine as it came into clarity. Something about it was familiar. "Something you seem to have forgotten," the voice added coldly. "These laws are as old as they are. Breaking them has *consequences*."

"I got carried away," Misho ground out. "It won't happen again." Yom spotted the black smudge of the triarii armor through the trees.

"It won't. You're to return immediately until I determine your episode has passed."

Yom crouched down further as they got closer, listening intently.

"You can't—"

"Your incompetence has already cost me one of my men. You're lucky I don't collect on our contract."

Misho was only a few yards from Yom now, holding a small fire in his gloved palm, with a plume of smoke floating from it.

"Yes, master," Misho said through gritted teeth. Master? Suddenly Misho's words from their fight returned: *My master has an agreement with Cernunnos. As he does with Renos.* Misho's master was male. Her understanding of the triarii was that they were the Queen's elite warrior unit, but now it seemed like they had a different commander. It made Yom wonder what else in the House of Flowing Waters was not as it seemed.

"Do not disobey me again." Up close, it seemed like the voice was coming *from* the smoke. But the fire died and the smoke dissipated into the air before Yom could hear anything else.

Misho growled and ripped off his gloves to throw them on the ground. Underneath, the sleeves of his armor stopped halfway down his forearm. One of his forearms had dark markings on it, like writing. She squinted but she couldn't make it out; it wasn't any recognizable writing system. Everything was off. What she just saw belonged to the world she was slowly discovering, not the numenless world the titans had created in Arcadia.

But Quia had hinted at this, that the triarii's abilities were enhanced by a connection to numen. Perhaps someone in the House of Flowing Waters was secretly helping them use their numen, while the rest of Arcadia remained in the dark.

Yom barely thought through her plan as she stepped around the tree into Misho's sight. In the Moonflower's glow she felt braver, and Misho clearly knew more than she had realized.

"Who was that?" Yom asked. Misho's head shot up and he drew his crossbow in the blink of an eye. "Doesn't sound like you can kill me," Yom said flippantly, though beneath the bravado she was imagining how that crossbow could rip an arrow straight through her.

"Even if I wanted to, I couldn't tell you." Misho walked towards her, arrow cocked. Yom's heart pumped faster, and her eyes flitted to the markings on his forearm. On his other arm, a thick scar snaked up the inside.

"What's that on your arm?" she asked, barely a whisper as the arrow settled inches from her throat.

"You have your shackles, and I have mine." He tapped the metal tipped arrow on her torc with a clink. "He's barely told you anything, has he?"

Yom couldn't control her face fast enough to hide her surprise. He couldn't mean Quia, could he?

"How much do you really know about him?" Misho leaned in so close Yom could see the sweat beading over the ridges of his scars. She held her tongue, so he continued, "Your illustrious...travel companion."

"What do *you* know about him?" Yom couldn't stop the tremor in her voice.

"I know he's a long way from home," Misho said cryptically. "And that he will do anything for his cause."

Yom faltered. The way he described Quia sounded...personal. "And you're better than him?"

"At least I'll admit what I'm doing."

"Is that what you tell yourself to be able to kill boys like Moss?"

Anger and regret flashed over Misho's face. "It was a mercy killing. I took his life quickly and he passed peacefully. Cernunnos would have done worse tenfold." The crossbow dropped limp at his side.

"And if you had killed me in that arena? Was that a mercy killing too?"

"Like I said, I got carried away. I wouldn't have killed you." Something in the glint of his eye made Yom think even he didn't fully believe what he was saying.

Regardless, it was now or never to seek out answers. "Where are they keeping the numenborn?"

"Of course she's what he's after." Misho shook his head, amused. "He doesn't care at all that they grow Amaurosis here, just as long as she can't lead them to Panchaia with it."

"That's not true. He does care. He cares about boys like Moss."

"He would sacrifice a hundred boys like Moss if it meant helping Panchaia." He said this soberly, like it had already started coming true.

Yom couldn't help but think of Quia's story, of the men who had already become collateral damage in search of this numenborn. But Yom didn't believe Misho; she had seen how these deaths had torn Quia up. She shook her head and backed away.

"I'm supposed to return you to Cernunnos, and bring him to my master. But I'm willing to let you disappear if you tell me where he is."

"I won't do that."

"Don't be foolish. He would give you up in a heartbeat if it helped him find his numenborn." *His numenborn.* There was something possessive about it.

"You're wrong, and I'm not running away from this," Yom breathed, taking slow steps backwards.

The crossbow released with a snap, and an arrow whizzed within a few inches of Yom's head, splintering into a tree behind her. The forest roused and rustled at the sound.

Misho's face shifted, his eyes narrowed and his lips pursed. He looked more like a predator. "I can make it look like an accident, you know. I can end your life faster than you could blink." Yom's heart sped up. "We're outside of the Queen's jurisdiction, you wandered into a dangerous forest, ran into some of the locals. They decided to kill first and ask questions later."

"You might be a killer, but I don't think you're a murderer." Yom tried to inject belief into the words.

"You don't know anything about me," Misho said coldly as his finger twitched. The crossbow snapped, releasing an arrow. Before she could see where it landed, a huge black body leapt over her head and charged Misho.

The creature's steps thudded on the forest floor and wet snarls escaped its maw. Gnashing teeth and metal ripping filled the tranquil forest air as the creature pounced on Misho. The triarii cried out.

Yom ran forward to see around the towering black mass of fur.

"I wasn't going to kill her," Misho garbled, wrestling with what appeared to be a giant black wolf. "It was a warning shot!" The wolf had Misho's shooting arm in its mouth, the armor mangled beneath its fangs.

"Wait!" Yom rushed forward, not sure why she thought this creature would be able to understand her or listen to her if it did. To her shock, the wolf stopped, Misho's arm still deep in its mouth. Misho's unswallowed arm braced the wolf's muzzle. Yom looked at the scarred half of the triarii's face and imagined what enduring that kind of pain could do to a person.

"Let him go," Yom breathed. The wolf growled but did not release the arm. "Please." The wolf had a collar of twisted twigs around its neck, almost like a torc. Something passed between them, and the wolf slowly released Misho's arm. It wasted no time picking up the emptied crossbow with its teeth and hurling it against the trunk of a tree to crack into pieces.

Misho crawled away from the wolf, not letting his eyes stray from it.

"I ran into her while I was leaving!" Misho raised his voice despite no one having said anything. The way Misho directed his words to the wolf made her think it wasn't the first time they had met.

For whatever reason, this wolf seemed to be on her side. Yom took up a stance just in front of its shoulder and felt its warm, wet breaths on the back of her neck. It was snarling.

"You were saying?" She challenged Misho without an ounce of sympathy. It had all been used up when she asked the wolf to spare him.

Misho opened his mouth to retort but nothing came out. Then, the breathing behind her became heavier. The snarling was giving way to a pant, and the wolf fell back on its heels, then onto its side.

Yom whipped around at the sound of the wolf's faint whimpering. She gave it a wide berth, walking towards its head. She sought the creature's eyes, a depthless bluish gray, like the sky before a storm. They had a look she recognized. Pain.

"I wasn't going to kill you," Misho muttered to himself from behind her.

Returning to kneel by the wolf's head, it whimpered more plaintively now, eyes wide. Yom slowly reached her hands to the wolf's head to stroke down its neck. She roved its fur cautiously, feeling its breast.

As soon as Yom's fingers found damp fur and the wooden body of an arrow, the wolf yelped.

"You hit him," Yom accused and turned to make sure Misho was watching what he had done.

He stepped back. "I wasn't going to kill you," he whispered. "The animal should not have interfered."

Yom felt gently for the length of the arrow still outside the creature, and tried to recall the size of the arrows loaded in Misho's crossbow. Her gut sank. The depth and location it hit was far too close to important organs.

"What have you done?" she snarled, feeling almost rabid.

"I wasn't going to kill you," Misho repeated, to anyone listening.

Death swam in Yom's vision as the wolf's whimpering became more desperate.

Misho's hand lightly touched her shoulder. "I can—"

"Go," Yom said without any of the venom she wished she had.

"I can help the creature. Take it out of its misery."

Yom recoiled at the idea that he would give up so easily in the face of death. "You've done enough," she spat. "Leave us." The hand retreated but his presence remained behind her. "I said, *LEAVE!*"

Misho stumbled in surprise. After another second of their gazes warring, he turned and ran.

Once he was gone, Yom's last battlement crumpled.

"It should have been me," Yom whispered, over and over, as she looked desperately through the trees, hoping something would reveal itself. As she repeated this chant, she felt the lights of the forest return, and the ghosts they illuminated. Moss raging with eyes that were swallowed in black, and his lifeless body laying on the floor at Cernunnos's feet. Eden's body crumpled on the floor in a heap in the laboratory. Lior drugged and taken away like chattel. All accompanied by the refrain of the wolf's whimpering. Yom heaved for air.

But this animal wore a collar. Just like her. And Yom knew what it meant: there was someone here who could help the creature, and was choosing not to.

"*HELP US!*" Yom cried out. "*The wolf needs you!*" This animal had taken an arrow defending her, and she didn't even know its name.

Even without understanding the intricacies of the forest, she knew what she was about to do was a flagrant transgression. But she did it anyway.

"*ARDUINNA! I know you can hear us!*" Yom bellowed, looking in all directions for the gleaming white of the boar tusk, the red of the titan's hair. "*You will not leave your servant here to die!*" But she saw nothing, and the buzz of the forest receded, as if it too was waiting for its keeper to reveal itself.

Yom brimmed with fury. The animal had sworn itself to Arduinna and was laying here, abandoned. It had probably signed itself over as a pup, before it could really understand the weight of the choice. In fact, it probably didn't have much of a choice to begin with. And now, in the one moment where its master could exhibit gratitude, or show any lick of care for the creature, it was left utterly, crushingly alone.

But the wolf wasn't alone; Yom was here. And if she had to battle death itself for the right, she would not watch another life be snuffed out.

The wolf curled to look at Yom, and she met its gray eyes. They seemed to be urging her to do something, as if the creature knew she was learning to harness plant numen. But Yom's first attempt had been for a minor decoction, not healing a mortal wound. Yom petted the wolf's neck as she scrambled for an idea. *Use your instincts*, Sophia's voice repeated in her head. *Don't overthink it.* Yarrow, Yom thought on an impulse. It was the herb Sophia had used on her when the enchanter had discovered her in the forest, bleeding out. But it couldn't be enough for a wound of this magnitude, a creature of this size—

Not by itself, the voice of the fox that she had first heard in the Amaurosis vision hissed in her head. Yom startled, and figured it must have been some lingering effect of the Amaurosis. A part of her shuddered at the thought of going anywhere near that voice again, after where it had led her. But the wolf's whimpering was becoming more insistent, and the voice's interjection had given her an idea. Physical and metaphysical properties. Two halves of the same coin, just like her torc.

"It's worth a try, right?" Yom asked the wolf. It didn't answer with words, but its eyes agreed with her. "I'll be right back."

Yom shot to her feet before the wolf could react. The days she had spent foraging with Sophia had to be good for something. Yarrow would not take her too long to find, of that she was confident. And she loathed to admit it, but the Amaurosis fox's voice was right. She needed something with it, perhaps an offering, something that would amplify the plea for healing. As if the forest had heard her plan, she found a thicket containing the snow white starbursts of myrtle within minutes. She ripped a few of the stems off and clutched them in her sweating palm.

"If you care at all about your servant, you'll help me find yarrow," she muttered to herself. It was hard to tell if it was her imagination, but a breeze wafted over her, carrying the scent of pine. Figuring there was little to lose, she walked towards it and stood on a knobby tree root to get a higher vantage. Scanning in every direction through squinting eyes, she saw it. A flash of white. Without hesitation she darted towards it, finding her stride over the gnarled tree roots, leaving the flora on the ground largely undisturbed.

There was a whole pocket of yarrow growing in the shade of a sapling ash tree. Kneeling down, Yom snapped off a few of the feathery-leafed stalks at the root, and took off back to the wolf. Her direction never wavered, in complete contrast to her first stumbling voyage into the belly of the forest. By the time she returned to the wolf, its breaths had slowed and it was no longer able to hold its head up.

"Hold on," Yom begged. "I'm trying." She made quick work of grinding the two plants down into a pulp between two stones. "Please help me," she said out loud to the plants without thinking. Holding the wet pulp in her hands, she turned back to the wolf and searched through its fur for the wound. A sharp mewl confirmed when she found it.

Yom's instinct took over. A steady hand drew out the arrow mercifully quick, and the other compressed the plants as a poultice onto the wound. She closed her eyes and searched for their whisper, for their light. It had been easier before, when there weren't any stakes, experimenting with plants at Sophia's workbench. Now, knowing the life that balanced precariously in her hands, her limbs shook and her chest ballooned with pressure. It was a bad idea to try facing her thoughts in this state, but she had no choice.

When she gingerly opened the gates in her mind, everything came in a violent torrent. Thoughts and memories, truths and lies. Yom was submerged, disoriented, the tumult like an out of tune symphony played at full volume for her ears alone. Her strategy of tucking the thoughts away, of turning them over like stones, couldn't work when she was at war with her own mind. One memory crashed over her, of Moss eating a steak as he walked through the Cut, goofy and unflinching. Tied to it, inseparable, was an illusion masquerading as another memory, that it was Yom's hands around Moss's neck when it snapped.

No! Yom pulled away, but there was no escaping it. The illusion played over and over, hounding Yom, forcing her to watch. *Stop fighting it*, the Amaurosis fox's voice returned, sensing Yom was close to losing everything. *You give it too much power, the voice intoned*, calm as night. *It is not your fault. You did not kill the boy.*

"It is my fault!" Yom howled, the thoughts ripping through her. Ripping her apart. "It's always my fault, people get hurt because of me." She squeezed the plants tighter, but the very position she was in now was further proof of this. Everything blurred, became unbearably heavy. "It should have been me. They were looking for me."

Your mind does not control you, you control it. The Amaurosis fox was growing more impatient.

"I can't." Yom's voice cracked. She was weak, or mad, or some combination of the two.

Allow yourself to feel it, the fox growled. *Allow it to pass through you.*

But Yom was done. She curled into a ball, blocking out everything, the torrent around her freezing mid-crest. Eden, Lior, and Moss. Dougal, Clementine, and Sophia. Even Quia. Until she couldn't feel a single thing.

Don't turn away from me! The fox's voice quaked. Yom tried to freeze it as well, eject it—

I said FEEL, the voice snarled as something cracked, and then shattered.

In the split second of surprise, Yom was overwhelmed and unarmed. The thoughts wrecked into her like waves, demanding to be felt—to be witnessed—carrying with them anger, misery, fear and loneliness. It all wrestled for her attention—truths and lies alike—until the boundary between them disappeared. Yom thrashed but she was unable to escape it, unable to put her guard up before being thrust into an endless loop of all her faults, all her mistakes, all her fears.

But something strange began to happen.

The illusions were fading. Thinning out and, then, dissolving. And what was left was real. It was painful, still, but real. A memory of Moss riding the streetcar, looking out at the city like he had discovered an entirely new world. A memory of Lior twirling around glass beaker sets, the edges of her skirt coming much too close to the equipment. A memory of Eden handing her a vine of Moonflower, passing it on like some kind of inheritance. And woven through these were delicate threads of something Yom had not felt in a long time. Joy. The weight of it all crushed and lifted her, as if it was demonstrating the burden and gift it is to be alive, to be able to feel. It was so much she couldn't physically hold it in. Tears erupted with abandon. She didn't even have time to feel foolish before the light emanated and pulsed from the plants in her palm. A light that offered itself to her.

Before Yom could second guess it, she pushed the pulsing light towards the wound, her breathing ragged. The wolf's light was dimming, weakening by the second. Just by holding the plant's numen in her palm, she knew that it could heal this wound. The mewling yelps of the wolf faded away as she set in to concentrate, wind cooling the sweat on her brow.

You cannot run from yourself forever, the Amaurosis fox prowled through her mind once more but seemed to be retreating, making it all the more easy for Yom to ignore it. Though its voice had helped her this time, it was becoming far too familiar for comfort.

Yom used the plant's light to bolster the wolf's own, and coaxed the breast that had been ripped apart by the arrow to knit together once again, to become whole. It was incredible what the plants were capable of when their metaphysics were understood. As she worked steadily, moving between tissue and organ, she considered what these metaphysics could do for medicine, for weaponry—even for the powder operation—if all of Arcadia were to have access to it. The clump remaining in her palm seemed to reach out and sting her, as if communicating that it was not a commodity to be bought and sold, even in a daydream. Yom's cheeks burned at the notion that the plants could hear her thoughts.

The wolf's breath spiked in pain, but evened out as the plants continued to do their work with Yom's direction. After a time that seemed to rush or crawl depending on the second, she drew her hands away. Nothing remained but a dry, shriveled clump, and a knotted scar lacing through the wolf's dark fur. Yom smiled wide, the salt of her tears crusting her cheeks.

The wolf rolled onto its front slowly, squirming until it stood back to its impossible height, shaking out its limbs. It walked in a circle, sniffing around Yom until it made a full lap. Satisfied with whatever it found, it bounded to Yom, gently knocking her over with an oversized paw and licking her backwards and forwards with a great pink tongue. Yom couldn't help but laugh as the scratchy wet surface tickled her whole front.

Yom stayed laying on the ground, admiring the faint sounds of birds, the glowing buzz of the lights still lingering around them, the twilight sky peeking through slivers in the canopy. The wolf eventually laid down next to her, its head resting on her stomach. A feeling of peace washed over Yom. She told herself it was the glow of accomplishment, but if she was truthful, some of it was the catharsis of feeling so much for the first time in so long. A beautiful lightness, as if her tears had washed away some of the weight she had been carrying.

The ground began to vibrate softly, radiating from behind Yom. She tipped her head back and watched upside down as the faint shaking grew more thunderous. Something moved between the trees. A giant boar in the distance, galloping straight for them.

Yom scrambled to her feet and the wolf stood in a flash. It snarled in the direction of the boar, leaning back onto its haunches, fur raised. Yom could feel the tremor of the earth in her bones as the boar came to them impossibly fast. The boar was closer now than the first day she had seen it, and it was massive. Larger than the wolf. And its rider was staring at Yom, ire bubbling in the titan's eyes.

But Yom was done bowing. She readied herself behind the wolf.

The boar skidded to a halt ten feet away, spraying dirt and rocks beneath its hooves. The wolf growled.

"Hush, Sassa." Arduinna said in a commanding voice that was rich as the whistle of wind in the trees. Her hair was a coarse auburn, her alabaster skin clothed in strips of green, her limbs graceful and lean. She looked like a painting, with sharp cheekbones and stained lips, stoic and cold and cruel. The wolf's growl silenced, but its lips remained in a snarl.

"I ought to slit your throat and hang you from a tree for leading those men into my forest."

Yom paled but used every ounce of will not to flinch.

Arduinna, graceful as a falling leaf, bounded down from the boar's back, bare feet landing on the ground. The titan seemed to grow in size as she stalked towards them. By the time Arduinna stood in front of Yom, she was easily twelve feet tall. Yom had perhaps held out hope that the vision she had of a larger than life Cernunnos, holding court in a forest clearing, was nothing more than that. A vision, an apparition. But this was no mind game. No, this titan was standing in front of her, plain as the remains of daylight slicing through the forest's canopy. Yom understood the moniker of *titan* better now.

The wolf prowled to insert itself between them.

Arduinna towered above Yom, the forest around them seeming to bow, or cower, in her presence. "Perhaps I should maim you just to send a message to my siblings, to remind them what happens when they interfere in my realm."

Arduinna laughed, loud and high. The sound had nearby birds taking to the skies. "Cernunnos has always had a soft spot for the damaged ones." She skirted to the right and circled Yom, the wolf circling to follow, remaining in between them. "Why he would ever admit a weakling human into his House is beyond me."

Before Yom could respond, the wolf let out a great bark at Arduinna, as if it was speaking to her.

"I would have you killed," Arduinna spat at the wolf, "for protecting a human like her," disgust dripping from her words. "Do not forget who your master is."

The wolf barked another two times. The sound rang in Yom's ears.

"Sassa has seen fit to remind me," Arduinna reluctantly returned her attention to Yom, "that I owe you a debt, for saving the life of one of my servants." The wolf's shoulders relaxed slightly. "You may ask one favor of me." Yom was getting the sense that there were laws and social intricacies at play of which she had no knowledge. She couldn't help but think of what Misho said. Of how little Quia had actually told her since they had embarked on this journey.

"Well?" The titan prodded.

Yom's voice caught in her throat. A favor? For the first time since Arduinna arrived, the wolf turned back to Yom, waiting for her to speak.

"I—" Yom swallowed, "I need—" She considered the wild goose they were chasing; Quia would not hesitate to ask a favor related to the numenborn. But Yom had always been a visitor in that story, a passerby. Everything that had happened today had made her realize how little she would have at the end of this, once Quia had thwarted the titans and the Queen. Where would it leave her? Following him to Panchaia did not have the same gleam in the sobering twilight as it did in the drunk light of the afternoon. But there was one story that was her own, one story she had been turning over and over in her head, once she learned there was a slim chance its ending had not been written yet. When faced with asking a favor of a powerful immortal, all she could think of was one thing.

"I need to know if Lior is still out there."

Arduinna smiled. "Typical mortal pride, not choosing to use a favor to preserve your own life." She clicked her tongue.

"But you have to tell me, if I choose this as my favor."

"Yes, but," Arduinna examined her hand, which from Yom's vantage point didn't have a single blemish on it. "Know that my granting of a favor today will not keep you safe tomorrow."

Yom had spent her whole life eluding threats. Immortal or not, everyone had a weakness.

"If I am an agent of your sibling, would it not be prudent to see what Cernunnos has planned, before harming me?"

Anger flashed on Arduinna's face. "What would you know of the affairs of Immortals, human?"

"I know enough to be sure that even your precious realm won't remain untouched if another war breaks out."

Arduinna scoffed. "I care not of the wars between my siblings. They may have their alliances, even their human Queen, but they will never intercede in my realm."

Yom smiled, confirming what she had hoped. "You know nothing of the larger forces at work. Your siblings have plans that extend beyond Arcadia's borders."

Arduinna's nostrils flared. Clearly Yom had struck a nerve with this piece of information.

"You can never stand against him," the titan fumed. "The seal you wear ensures that."

Yom tried not to show any emotion even as the ground seemed to tilt. It was yet another piece of the puzzle of what she had gotten herself into by allowing the torc to circle her neck, and she hated that she was always the last to know. That she had blindly walked into something so riddled with rules and power.

"Maybe," Yom admitted, bluffing confidence, "but he does not own my mind. That remains under my control."

"And why should I not string you up this very moment, until you tell me what he plans?"

The wolf let out a low warning growl.

"Because you would lose the one person who can inform you of his actions in the future."

"Trust a mortal?" Arduinna laughed. "I have never taken a mortal into my House." Arduinna began pacing in the opposite direction. Her footfalls were eerily silent on the forest floor. "But..."

Yom raised her eyebrows, rotating to remain facing Arduinna as the titan paced.

"I need not take you into my House to get what it is you offer," Arduinna continued. "Were one of my servants to follow you, they would fulfill the promise you have laid out."

Yom held her breath as Arduinna seemed to appraise this. "But I warn you, it is an immutable transgression to take the life of another's servant."

"I don't take lives." This truth warmed Yom's breast.

Arduinna scoffed. "All humans do is destroy." Yom held her tongue, waiting for Arduinna to weigh the deal being offered. Finally, her cold voice broke the silence. "The one you seek still lives."

A weight lifted in Yom's chest, and her breath returned feverishly. *Lior is alive.* Relief and adrenaline flooded her.

"She is in Cataracta," Arduinna said drolly, like it bored her.

"Where in Cataracta?"

Arduinna smiled. "I have fulfilled the favor. Need I remind you that you are lucky you're permitted to leave my forest with this knowledge?"

Yom moved to step towards her and demand more information, but the wolf bowed its head to rest against Yom's chest, preventing her. Yom took a disgruntled step back.

Arduinna began walking to where her boar rested, calling out over her shoulder, "I expect you to be out of my realm by daybreak or I will make good on my promise to string you up over my forest floor."

By the time Yom found her way back to Sylveaux, it was well past nightfall. The floating lights gathered around her, leading her back to the village. The wolf had stayed with her, no doubt slowing its steps to match her pace. Sassa was the name Arduinna had called it. Gratitude emanated from the wolf, but also concern. Yom spoke out loud to her, unsure of what Sassa could understand. "This is nothing," she assured her. "I've been through worse."

Yom left Sassa at the base of the tree to climb the winding steps up to Sylveaux. Only dim lights glowed from the dwellings, everyone squirreled away and readying for bed. She skipped right past the main room of Sophia's dwelling, straight to the small chamber she and Quia slept in, on light feet.

It was empty when she burst through the door. Quia must have still been eating dinner. At the thought of this, Yom's stomach growled, but she ignored it to begin packing up all her spread out belongings. Over the days they had spent here, she had built up a collection of plants distilled into ashes, tinctures, and decoctions. She refilled the loops of her powderbelt with these vials. The stock was quite different from the sparkling powders she had left Inisfail with, but no less useful with her budding knowledge of plant numen.

"Yom?"

Before she could even turn around, she was enveloped in Quia's arms. "I was so worried about you," his voice held the same tenderness it had on the bank of the forest pool, but that moment was so far away. He pulled back to look her over. "I only just came back to eat something before I continued looking for you."

"I'm alright," Yom said awkwardly as she tried to extract herself from his grip.

"I'm so sorry I agreed to do that," Quia's hands would not drop from Yom no matter how she tried to pull away. They shifted to hold her face. "I knew it would be too intense. When you come to Panchaia it will be much safer to do it in a controlled environment with a priest."

"I'm not going with you to Panchaia."

At this, Quia's hands finally fell. "What? I thought you said—"

"I got carried away." Yom tried to ignore the hurt on his face. "But I found Misho in the woods and then saved a wolf's life, and then talked with Arduinna—"

"You did what?" Quia hissed. "That triarii is here?" He looked angry but also worried as he moved her limbs around to check for signs of harm.

"I'm alright," Yom repeated. "Misho is gone, and Arduinna and I made a deal."

"Have you learned nothing about bargaining with Immortals?" Quia fumed.

"I can handle myself fine," Yom said flatly. "But that's not important. What matters is that Arduinna told me that Lior is still alive, and she's in Cataracta!" Yom allowed the excitement to leak into her voice. Quia gave her a heavy look. "It's a win-win. We still go to Cataracta, and then you find the numenborn and I find Lior."

"You mean go our separate ways?"

"That was always the plan. At least this way, we both get what we want."

"What if separating isn't what I want?"

"Quia, the idea of me going to Panchaia was ridiculous from the start. I have a chance here to fix what happened all those years ago. If anything, this past week has made me realize I won't be any kind of free before I do something about what happened." Yom searched his face. "You must understand that," she said more softly, "don't you?"

"I think I understand this is about more than guilt." His voice was strangely cold.

"What are you talking about?"

"It's about Lior. You love her." The way he said it sounded like an accusation. "It was obvious when you told me about her. I just didn't realize you still felt that way."

"I haven't seen her in six years, I don't know how I feel." Yom looked at him, confused where this was coming from. "But no matter what I feel, it's not actually your business, is it?"

Quia laughed in disbelief. "Oh, you've made sure of that."

"Look, I'm sorry if you've confused what's been happening between us, but this was always going to be temporary. A week ago you wanted absolutely nothing to do with me." Yom took a breath to refocus on the point of what she was trying to say. "I need to find her. It's important to me. The same way it's important to you to find your numenborn." Quia flinched. Something in his reaction confirmed the possessiveness Misho had implied. *His numenborn.*

"Why don't you just stay with me until we find the numenborn, and then you can decide whether you want to seek out Lior. You haven't exactly thought this through. After everything that's happened, she might not even want to see you."

Yom nodded solemnly. As always, Quia had the privilege of voicing her private fears. "I'd like to find out for myself. Maybe if she does hate me, that will give me some kind of closure too."

"Closure is an illusion."

Yom hardened her expression. "Well, maybe all I have are illusions." She turned to continue packing. "I'm leaving for Cataracta, tonight, with or without you. You only have two days before Lupercalia, so I suggest you start packing."

XIV

The House of Flowing Waters

YOM TOOK ONE LAST LOOK AT THEIR ROOM IN THE TREEDWELLING before notching the door closed behind her. Quia had packed sullenly, and by the time he was ready to leave, the stars had long risen to their glittering throne in the sky. Sophia, perhaps sensing something had shifted, had not come to visit their room that night. A nagging thought whispered to Yom that Sophia somehow knew about the Moonflower, knew that Yom had gone back on her word. But Yom dispelled it. Sophia, Moira, and Aisa were likely already asleep by the embers of the hearth, and Sophia had left them alone because Yom and Quia were clearly, and audibly, quarreling.

The treedwelling had started feeling like a home, and every home she had ever lost had almost destroyed her. She wasn't about to give this one the same power. It was better to leave now, without lingering.

The night outside was coated in a humid chill, the moon and stars blocked by a thick layer of clouds. Quia stood on the ledge outside the door, looking up at the sky. Yom brushed past him to start descending the stairs.

"I've always felt best during the day," Quia said, seemingly to himself. "Quetzal is the light of truth we find during the day. But Tezcat is the dark, sublime mystery we encounter at night." Their eyes met. Yom could almost see the war raging in Quia's head, could hear it in his cryptic words.

"Sounds like you and your numenborn will make a great team." Yom put it to bed. They were going down separate paths, and fighting it would only make it hurt more.

Yom slipped inside the silent room where Sophia, Moira, and Aisa slept. It smelled faintly of the okra stew they had eaten and the smoke of the hearth. She headed straight for Sophia's wall of supplies and began pocketing important ingredients as quickly and quietly as she could. Small jars of mugwort, wormwood, verbena. Tinctures of dittany, hemlock, agrimony. She spotted a jar of starlike Moonflower blooms and their prickly leaves and only hesitated for a second before taking that as well. A current of energy emanated from it, a connection that had grown in strength without her realizing it, ever since that day she first encountered the Moonflower ash in the Powdery.

"What are you doing?" Quia hissed when she walked back out.

"I need supplies in case we need medicine or weapons." Yom said this as if it was obvious. She walked towards the staircase that wound down the towering height of the tree trunk. It was treacherous to descend in the dark, but Yom wasn't going to wait and see if Arduinna would make good on her threat at daybreak.

"You mean for powder." Quia shook his head in disbelief.

Yom didn't dignify this with a response.

"What about Sophia?" He grabbed her arm from behind.

"What about her?" Yom shrugged his hand off.

"You're not saying goodbye?"

"She will be glad to be rid of us," Yom told him, and herself. "This is easier for everyone."

"How can you do that after everything she's done for us?" Quia asked, appalled.

"She won't want to see me anyways," Yom muttered to herself. "I broke a promise."

YOM DESCENDED THE FINAL DOZEN STEPS AROUND THE TREE, ONE wrong sway from tipping over the edge and one breath from heaving the contents of her stomach. Quia's hand grabbed her waist to steady her. When she looked back at him, anger was the only emotion on his face. As if it was Yom's fault that he cared whether she made it down the stairs in one piece. Shrugging off the gesture, she hopped to the ground from several steps up. She reached back to extend her hand as a peace offering, but he jumped down next to her, pointedly ignoring her hand. He started walking straight ahead without even a glance in her direction.

Yom followed him, her eyes drawn back up to Sophia's dwelling, swearing there was a light on where there hadn't been several minutes ago. She also could have sworn she saw someone standing on the balcony, through the branches. She squinted up at it until she ran into a shoulder blade.

"What are you—" Yom muttered as she walked around Quia, who stood stock still, eyes wide and hands lifted. Sassa towered in front of him, ready to lunge with her teeth bared.

"I see you've met Sassa." Yom strode to the wolf and reached out to stroke behind its ears. Sassa let out a satisfied growl.

"You know this creature?"

"Oh yes." Yom walked around to the side of the wolf, running her hand along its fur. "She's coming with us." Quia looked incredulous. "I talked Arduinna out of killing me by suggesting she send a spy to follow us. And, I like her."

"You truly cannot be left alone, can you?" Quia asked, both exasperation and admiration in his voice. He approached the wolf, crouching low and stretching out his open palm, face up. Sassa watched him carefully and sniffed him from wrist to shoulder before giving his palm a long, wet lick with her oversized tongue.

"I knew you two would get along." Yom walked ahead and Sassa loped to her side, so tall she ruffled the low branches of the trees. "Now, what's the fastest way to get out of here?"

Quia caught up to her. "I'm not sure."

"I wasn't asking you."

Yom waited for Sassa to reply. The wolf laid down so her back came up to Yom's waist.

"She...wants us to ride her," Yom said.

"So it seems." Quia eyed the wolf warily.

"Here goes nothing," Yom muttered, taking two fistfuls of Sassa's inky fur and hoisting herself over the wolf's broad back. She shifted and squirmed to get comfortable, the hard lumps of Sassa's spine jutting into her seat.

"What are you waiting for?" Yom turned to Quia and jerked a thumb behind her. Of course he was able to gracefully mount the wolf and hardly squirmed at all. She rolled her eyes as his hands settled on the juncture of her hips to steady himself. But she kept her remarks to herself.

"What now?" Quia asked.

"Not sure, I thought she would just st—" Sassa rose to her full height, almost sending them sliding over her backside, but Yom kept a miraculous hold on her fur, and Quia kept a hold on Yom. Without so much as a second's wait, Sassa took off in a blur.

Despite having situated herself in front to maintain some control, Yom hunched forward to cling to Sassa's wide torso, eyes firmly shut. Quia meanwhile sat upright behind her, yelping and hollering in delight as they catapulted through the roar and swish of the forest. *Show off*, Yom thought bitterly. An hour passed like this, and while Quia had quieted down, his hands had not left Yom.

"You should try looking up." One hand squeezed her side. "It's not as scary as you think." Perhaps it was because Quia was using the gentle voice that had tempted her to ridiculous ideas by the bank of that pool, but Yom squinted one eye open. The foliage and roots melted into one green and brown blur, stitched with brief flashes of color here and there of night blooming flowers.

"I'm not scared." Yom opened both eyes and looked ahead, seeing the trees passing them faster than she had ever moved before.

"No, you're never scared," Quia said dryly.

Yom was too busy tensing every part of her body to stay astride Sassa to reply to him.

"Yom," he whispered her name like a prayer, and it almost undid her. "What happened during the Trials? What did you see?" His thumbs stroked along her ribs. "Whatever it was, we can get through it. Together."

Quia's words contained an unspoken plea. For them to stay together, to not separate when they arrived in Cataracta, to make the journey back to Panchaia with the numenborn. He still believed there could be something between them. This week together had blinded him to the truth of who Yom was, but for her, it had reinforced it. There could be no happy ending for her, no redemption. She didn't deserve it. And the sooner Quia let go of it, the better.

"I saw Lior. And she will always come first." Yom hesitantly looked back. Quia's jaw was clenched tight. She worried her lower lip, knowing what she said to him was nowhere near the full truth, but she couldn't drag him down with her. She had to push him away.

"Got it." Quia's hands finally let go of her.

MISHO'S RETURN TO CATARACTA WAS MUCH QUICKER ONCE HE MADE it to the edge of the Ardennes. He stumbled through the trees, trying to follow the sun west, back to the edge of Arcadia. His triarii armor was in tatters where the wolf had shredded it, and he had puncture wounds along his arm where it had been in the wolf's jaws.

The debt Misho owed Yom for asking the wolf to spare his life weighed him down. It was a debt he would not have consented to, if given the choice. If it came down to it, he would have to live with defaulting on it, if it meant upholding his agreement. He could live with guilt—it had become almost a comfort at this point—but he would not live at all if his agreement was violated.

Misho sent out a message from the signal tower in the first town he could find. "Bring the nearest transport to me, *now*," Misho hissed at the legionary who responded to it. Misho supposed he looked like some sort of ghost or demon at that point, something the forest had chewed up and spat back out. The legionary looked like he was going to wet himself.

Misho found himself on an old, rattling transport that seemed to belch out double the steam it should have, hurtling towards Cataracta. The air warmed and became tinged with salt as he rode further south. Ash and pine sprawling over rolling hills and granite mountains gave way to spindly bundled olive trees and pockmarked dolomite rock forms.

After a full two days of riding with hardly any stops, the tall white marble walls of Cataracta came into view in the distance. Misho skidded down a dirt path that followed the cliff-edged sea, where the water of Okeanus kissed the rock face with turquoise waves and white foam. Even from this distance, he could see the towering columns of the House of Flowing Waters at the highest point within the city walls. The grand structure of the palace gleamed under the sun like an open jaw.

Misho's first stop once he returned to the royal grounds was the triarii quarters to dispose of his ruined armor. Each piece was custom made for each triarii, so he was forced to don laughably inadequate brass plate armor until his could be replaced. It was heavy and clinked with every movement, like he was a common provincial legionary. He scowled. His second stop was to the kitchens to find the leftovers of whatever the last meal served was. Most of the servants were busy prepping lavish roast boar and honey milk pudding for Lupercalia, so no one bothered to stop Misho from scavenging scraps of wild game and stewed pears, long cold. Ravenous, he scarfed down as much as he could get his hands on, sitting on a wooden stool in the kitchen as the servants flitted around him like flies, dreading his third and final stop.

Unable to avoid it any longer, Misho wiped away the juices of his meal and weaved through the harried servants to pass from the dull service quarters to the decadent royal halls.

His master was sprawled out over a velvet lounge on the hanging garden balcony off of the Great Hall. Young male servants, bare other than a piece of linen wrapped around their hips, doted on him, feeding him figs and massaging his hands. Misho fought to keep the disgust out of his expression as he noticed the predatory way his master watched them. He kneeled in silence.

"So you haven't completely lost your mind," his master remarked as his hand stroked over one of the servants arms.

"I am at your service," Misho grumbled.

"Don't sound so excited." His master chuckled. "Remember, there are always ways to be at my service that you would enjoy less."

Misho couldn't help but shudder at the thought of it.

"You will remain in Cataracta until Lupercalia."

"But—"

"Do not question me." The creature's voice took on its chilling, heightened quality that sometimes slipped through when he lost patience. Misho silenced instantly. "You are to remain in Cataracta. You will take on the post of the Queen's personal watchman."

"Master," Misho searched for the right words to question the order. "Would my specific skills not be better served out—"

"The Panchaian is coming for her. If you stay with her, he will come to you. Since you failed at stopping him when you had the chance."

"Yes, master." Misho dipped his head in resignation.

"Now, leave us."

Misho barely looked up as he heard the stomach curdling sound of soft kisses on skin, turning on his heels and marching back through the grand hall, any noise drowned out by the clang of his armor.

A FULL DAY AND NIGHT HAD PASSED, AND STILL YOM AND QUIA RODE on Sassa's back. As the Moonflower steadily wore off Yom's senses, something prodded at her. Like a forgotten memory that begged to be found. Every time she tried to sort through her thoughts enough to triangulate it, her numb lower half took her attention away. She had tried to steal a few hours of sleep here and there on the rhythm of Sassa's steps, thinking that perhaps the respite of dreams would bring her clarity. But the sparse sleep she had been lulled into was restless and dreamless. Quia had tried the same, his cheek slipping to rest on Yom's shoulder. She wanted to stop him, knowing his waking self had pulled away from her, but another part of her knew this would be one of their last days together. And it was selfish, but she wanted to soak it in. They knew so little of what Quia was walking into once they arrived in Cataracta; she suspected, based on Misho's words, that there was more waiting for him than he realized. And even if all went smoothly, his path still led him back to Panchaia, where the treacherous expanse of Okeanus would separate them for good.

Misho's words, Yom thought with a start. She had been too consumed with his accusations of Quia, then the peril of the Sassa's injury, and then the revelation of Lior, to consider the brief snippets he had let slip about his master. The thought gave her a thin rope to hold onto.

You have your shackles, and I have mine.

He's barely told you anything, has he?

Yom shook off the doubt Misho sowed, and looked for more. It was shimmering just out of reach, she merely had to follow the path the memory led her through.

My master has an agreement with Cernunnos.

Cernunnos's cryptic words, *Will your master's end of the bargain be kept?*

The Queen plans to demonstrate at Lupercalia.

Of course she's what he's after.

She, Yom realized with a start. The numenborn was a woman.

He doesn't care at all that they grow Amaurosis here, just as long as she can't lead them to Panchaia with it.

Lead them, Yom heard over and over again.

Damian, that infernal lordling, spewing words during his powder haze: *This year is the Queen. She has never done it before, always someone in her place. But not this year.*

It couldn't be. What were the chances? It was improbable. Absurd.

"Quia?" Yom broke their long spell of silence. He was resting on her shoulder, but at the sound of his name, he jolted awake and grumbled something unintelligible. "I have an idea, but you need to promise not to laugh."

"What is it?" he murmured, his voice still riddled with sleep. "I would never laugh at you." Despite the fact that he had laughed at her many times already, Yom believed him.

"What if it's the Queen?" She rushed to explain her improbable, absurd idea. "Cernunnos and Misho's master have a deal. Misho's master will be fulfilling his part of it at Lupercalia. The Queen is demonstrating at Lupercalia. But whatever is happening at Lupercalia, Damian said it is the Queen doing it, no one else. He said someone has always done it in her place before. What if whatever happens at Lupercalia, will also be the demonstration that Misho mentioned? Some display of numen, like the Trials. And if it's only the Queen, she must be the one who's undergoing the Trials." The words cascaded out in a waterfall, piling on top of each other, but Yom took a deep breath before she spoke the conclusion out loud.

"What if the Queen is the numenborn?"

Quia was silent. Yom didn't want to care about what he thought of her, but she hoped he did not think her ridiculous.

"It's possible," Quia said slowly.

"What are the chances?" Yom countered. "Out of every child born in Arcadia, the future Queen is born with this power?"

"Wacachan does not work in the ways we expect." He mulled this over in silence for a few minutes. "I've always wondered how the titans have allowed a human Queen to have this much apparent power."

"You think they bred her for this? Is that even possible?"

"I think they might have been waiting for her."

It was almost nightfall when the trees Sassa raced past began to thin. Yom and Quia had returned to silence, both sitting with this new theory. As much as she turned it over in her mind, she could not understand it. What it meant about the Queen, what it meant about Cernunnos's plan, what it meant about Misho's master. Her head ached.

The trees eventually spread out so they were further apart than one of Sassa's massive strides. Through the thicket of branches peeked the edge of a golden field. Even the air was warmer, the sun heating it more than where they had come from. Sassa slowed her pace to a gallop and then to a prowling walk. She was panting, but considering she had run more than a full day at breakneck speed, she seemed surprisingly energized.

Sassa paused at the final rim of trees and kneeled for them to dismount. Quia moved first, sliding off and shaking out his limbs. If Quia looked stiff, Yom shuddered to think of what was in store for her. As if reading her mind, Quia braced her middle and pulled her down off the wolf's back. He set her on the ground, and Yom intended to stand, but her legs were numb. She wobbled before catching herself on Sassa's back, shaking out one leg at a time, until the sharp pinpricks of feeling returned.

"Where to?" Yom asked hoarsely, taking her first steps without the support of Sassa.

Quia reached into his pack and pulled out the map. "I think we're here." He pointed to a spot at the very southern tip of the Ardennes, at the edge of Helvetia, which bordered Cataracta on its southeastern edge. Sassa circled around and towered over their shoulders. Yom would think she was actually reading the map if she didn't know better.

In response to Yom's skepticism, or in response to Quia's assertion, Sassa chuffed. Yom once again was pelted with a feeling that seemed to be pushed into her mind from outside herself. It appeared Sassa was communicating that

Quia was correct. Yom made a note to stop assuming what the wolf could and could not do.

"If I'm not mistaken, there should be an interprovincial road we can intercept a couple hours walk from here that will take us the rest of the way to Cataracta."

"And if you are mistaken?"

"That was a formality, I'm sure that I'm not."

"Let me guess, Quetzal is the modest one of his siblings."

Quia winked. Yom smiled before she could stop it. She turned away from him quickly, reminding herself not to give him the wrong idea.

"What are we going to do about you?" Yom turned to Sassa, the wolf's stormy eyes watching her intently, and stroked her snout. Sassa purred. "Oversized wolves aren't exactly common in Arcadia. I'm not sure how Arduinna expected you to follow us without calling attention to yourself," Yom muttered.

Sassa darted out her large pink tongue and gave Yom a scratchy lick before retreating and beginning to spin around herself as if she was chasing her own tail.

"What's this?" Yom began to ask but Quia held up a finger to shush her. He looked enraptured by what they were seeing. Sassa circled herself tighter and tighter, which Yom realized was possible due to the fact that her body was shrinking, smaller and smaller in comparison to the trees, until instead of a massive wolf, there was a small black fox spinning in its place. The fox exited its spin and bounded to Yom, leaping up Yom's body until it was perched on her shoulder.

Yom was speechless as she turned to face it, meeting its recognizable gray blue eyes.

"You—you were—wolf—" Yom stuttered dumbly.

"I never thought I would meet one," Quia marveled, petting the fox now situated on Yom's shoulder.

"Meet one what?" Yom's gaze bounced between Quia and the fox.

"She's a numenborn." The fox purred as Quia scratched between her ears.

"How is that—what?"

"She's born of titan numen. Their abilities differ from human numenborn," Quia explained. "Titans are able to take on various animal forms, and the myths are that the animals born of their numen are able to as well. We haven't seen an animal numenborn in Panchaia in centuries." Quia finished speaking mostly to himself.

The fox—Sassa, Yom supposed its name remained the same—yapped, telling her they needed to keep moving. For a second she had been worried that the fox would speak out loud, the same as in the Amaurosis vision. But she shook her head to clear it; that hadn't been real. This was Sassa, the wolf who had saved her life more than once. Her shapeshifting was just another improbable thing to add to Yom's running list. She could process the shock of it later.

"She wants us to get going. Which way to the road?"

"Due west." Quia nodded in the direction.

The three of them took off into the golden grass, the tips coming up to brush Yom's knees. As they walked, Sassa kept them entertained by leaping between their two shoulders and sometimes taking the plunge into the grass to lead the way with her lithe, black bundle of fur.

"How safe is this province?" Quia asked.

Yom shrugged. "No province is truly safe, but the ones around Cataracta are milder. They trade in textiles and fruits. The governance here is less hawkish with hoarding wealth since they have more favorable relationships with the Queen." At the mention of Queen Andromeda, Yom faltered. "Or I suppose, with the House of Flowing Waters."

"And what is Cataracta known for?"

"Officially? I'm sure I don't need to tell you it's full of artisans and craftspeople and academics. The cultural center of all of Arcadia," Yom said, imagining the way a snob like Damian would describe it.

"But unofficially?" Quia prompted.

Yom avoided his eyes. "Pleasure."

MISHO CURSED THE LEGIONARY ARMOR AS HE WALKED OUT TO THE hanging gardens attached to the Queen's chambers, a floor above where his master had been. The brass plates rattled, interrupting the rhythm of cicadas. He waded through the leaves and flowers hanging from all heights in the garden until he saw the Queen, still powdered in gold and piled with the delicate chains of the evening before, sleeping among a bed of poppies. Her dark hair cascaded over the poppy petals, and she was wrapped in the flimsy silks they decorated her in every night. She looked like a statue toppled over, tragic and beautiful.

Misho ignored the Queen's companion. She accompanied the Queen as a lady-in-waiting, but she watched Misho's movements with far beadier eyes than any lady-in-waiting would. Leah was the name she went by now. She shared the yellow eyes of Misho's master and even though she lacked the predatory sharpness of his features, their resemblance was disquieting.

Before he could disturb the Queen, he pulled off his armor and set it down on a soft patch of plants, until he only had a strip of blue linen stretching from his shoulder down to his waist and then wrapping his hips. Once again able to move quietly, Misho reached down to pick up the Queen with one hand under her knees and another holding her shoulders. He carried her back through the garden, towards her bed, her body cold despite the warmth outside. Judging by the bones that protruded from her wrist and collar, perhaps it was because she did not eat enough, wasting away on the powder they kept diligently stocked at her bedside. Without any attempt to remove the chains from her wrists and neck, she rolled over on the bed, wrapping herself up in a silk sheet.

Misho was the only triarii who had successfully avoided being assigned directly to the Queen. His talents were better served in the wilds of the provinces, hunting down Panchaians that dared to cross Okeanus. The thought had stayed alive that perhaps one day he would find the boy he had lost, see that he had a perfectly reasonable excuse for being unable to find Misho and rescue him. It was not so alive that Misho would consider it a hope, but a thought nonetheless.

Now he knew better. There was no reason that his poet had abandoned him other than the fact that it was no longer convenient to care for him. On the Morningstar it had been clear Cernunnos's chemist had teamed up with a Panchaian, but Misho hadn't been certain of who it was until he was blown back by a swift gust of wind, coming directly from the chemist's companion. He would admit he had been a bit harsh on the chemist, using her as a target for his rage. But the more he thought about it, the more he knew his master was right. The boy he had known, now a man he barely recognized, was coming for the Queen. And his best chance to stop him was to stay by her side.

"Who knew she would be so beautiful." His master's silken voice appeared from just over his shoulder, also watching the sleeping Queen.

"You allow her to use too much of the Amaurosis. The mind can only take so much before it begins to lose itself."

His master clicked his tongue. "She hardly responds to it anymore." His master paused, seemingly deciding whether to share more. "I thought it would be easy to awaken her power, but she has been taking it for years without a single hint of Tezcat coming to claim her."

"Have you ever considered that this is not without cause?" Misho felt emboldened by his master's candor.

"I'm done waiting for the precious tools of the mortal Trials to stir something in her," he said with venom. "I can feel something inside her. Come Lupercalia, I will use my own methods to draw it out."

"Perhaps the problem is her lack of knowl—"

"That's enough." His master's deep, echoing voice peeked out. "I will reveal her power to every immortal in our two worlds. And afterwards, she will beg on her knees for me to do it over again."

XV

Essential Laws

THE GOLDEN GRASS FELT ENDLESS FOR THE HOURS YOM WADED through it. It was jarring after the forest, where the sky was almost entirely blocked by the canopy of trees, to be in the open expanse of intense sun that warmed the southern provinces. Without shade, the heat suffocated Yom, and sweat soaked her clothes. Her torc was so hot it singed the pieces of skin it touched that weren't numbed by scars. She knotted her hair on top of her head and tried fanning herself to cool down, but nothing could break the heat.

"How much longer until we find the road?" Yom breathed heavily and adjusted the pack on her shoulders, unable to find a comfortable position for it. Sassa had slowed to walk in between them, the constant leaping and bounding leaving her exerted in the heat.

"Should be ahead soon." Quia looked perfectly at ease.

"How are you barely sweating?" Yom wiped a hand through the streams of sweat pouring down her forehead.

"I've missed this. Inisfail was always too cold." Yom shook her head to herself. Inisfail's weather was one of the few things she couldn't complain about.

"What if we missed it? Are we even going in the right direction?"

"We've been walking in a straight line," Quia answered flatly.

"I think I'm going to pass out. Is that possible? From heat?"

Quia looked like he was debating the merits of her claim before he paused, pulled out a skein of rainwater, and shoved it towards Yom. "Drink some water."

Yom gulped it down as she plopped into the grass. Sassa stuck her small, cold nose against Yom's hand, and she turned the skein to pour some in the fox's waiting mouth.

"It can't be far now," Quia muttered to himself, still standing and looking out.

"If it's much further I'm not sure I'll make it." Yom laid back in the ticklish grass and draped an arm over her eyes.

The first thing they heard was the hiss of steam. Then the rattle of a wheel on stone. Then giggling laughter and playful squeals.

Yom yanked Quia below the grass just before the first caravan appeared. It was a rickety yellow thing with red swirls painted on it. A conductor sat on a tall bench at the back, tending to the steam engine, and the area in front of him had its fabric awning drawn open with benches full of young women, strips of silks and linens rippling in the wind as they rode. A grubby man in a threadbare top hat sat on one edge, watching the gaggle of girls around him disdainfully.

Behind that caravan, another followed. And another. All full of young women.

"Come on." Yom pulled Quia to run hunched in the grass, towards the parade of caravans ambling over the uneven stone road. Several more passed, until the last caravan trundled at the end. It had a solid wood roof and pipe smoke seeping out the sides. It was emptier, but had a smattering of unsavory men in it. Yom picked up her pace to run up to the back of the last caravan, blocked from their view by the compartment of luggage. She grabbed onto the latch and pulled it open, Quia and Sassa keeping stride behind her. The compartment had several steam trunks and leather cases piled into it. Yom wasted no time tugging them to topple out onto the road, until there was enough room for two bodies to huddle inside. She held onto the edge to hoist herself into the compartment, helped by a lurch of the caravan over a sharp crack in the road. As she settled herself to sit facing the opening, Sassa had already lept in to join her, settling herself on a trunk.

"Now you," Yom held out a hand for Quia to do the same.

"Why do you always choose the hardest ways to get places?" he panted as he grabbed her hand and the lip of the compartment. One decisive jump and he landed half on top of Yom, safely inside.

"Just working with what we have. You're welcome by the way."

They both adjusted to make room for each other, and Quia reached out to pull the latch closed again. Yom stopped him from shutting them in completely, leaving a sliver of road and sky visible.

Yom settled, trying to keep herself from touching Quia but finding the task difficult in such a cramped space.

"So, do you travel this way often?" Quia asked, holding in a laugh.

"I usually prefer stowing away with murderers."

Quia snorted.

Their laughter petered out, and Yom's mind wandered. "How exactly are you going to get a private audience with the Queen?"

"I have a plan. It involves using my dazzling wit and good looks."

Yom elbowed him.

"What about you? How are you going to find Lior?" It sounded like he was trying to keep his voice light, but Yom could hear the strain.

"I suppose I'll start looking through the pleasure houses."

"And when you find her?"

Yom picked at dirt that had gathered underneath her nails. "I'm not sure. If she wants to talk to me? Get her out of whatever situation she's in and make sure she's set up somewhere safe."

"And if she doesn't want to talk to you?"

"Probably do the same, but it will be considerably more difficult."

"She will forgive you." Quia's eyes were too sincere for Yom to hold their gaze. She shook her head.

"I don't expect her to forgive me. I just hope she lets me help her."

"Forgiveness is something you give yourself. It's like closure."

"I thought you said closure was an illusion?"

"It's an illusion to think it's something someone else can give you."

Yom nodded. She understood what he was saying, but it didn't mean she had to accept it. "You should save your infinite godly wisdom for the Queen."

"I've got plenty," Quia joked as he crossed his arms and leaned against the hard edge of a trunk. "Besides, the gods aren't necessarily wise. Quetzal is supposed to be smart, but it's not the same. A lot of the time, they do very unwise things." Yom waited for Quia to continue. "Like falling in love with mortals, breaking laws, picking fights with each other."

Yom had heard something of laws in Misho's mysterious conversation.

She knows it is forbidden to kill the servant of another. These laws are as old as they are, there are consequences if broken.

"Laws?" she probed, keeping her voice casual. She still hadn't shared the details of her encounter with Misho. His goal had been to sow doubt, and he had succeeded to some degree.

Quia nodded. "The immortals are bound by their own laws, but only a few are truly important. When a titan takes a servant," he cleared his throat, "that servant receives some measure of protection. They cannot be killed by another immortal or the agent of an immortal. They must always be returned to their master."

"Wouldn't that have been nice to know in the arena?" Yom stared at him in disbelief.

"Just because the laws exist doesn't mean they're never broken. They just deal with consequences. I didn't want you to let your guard down." Yom felt the puddle of doubt creep just a little bit further. *He's barely told you anything, has he?* She looked up at the leather and wood of the compartment ceiling to clear her head.

"What else?" Yom ground out.

"The power of the gods is controlled by a mortal's belief in them, by their worship. They cannot enter a mortal's mind and force them to believe, and they cannot outright kill a mortal."

"And if they do? What are the consequences?" Yom felt foolish for not having learned this before, for never having the foresight to ask.

"They are banished from their celestial home, the thirteen heavens."

"Forever?" That sounded quite extreme. Even for a mortal, murdering a fellow mortal could not outlast one's own lifetime. Or at least, Yom supposed not.

"It depends."

She raised an eyebrow.

"On the caprice of Wacachan. Though I think it's safe to say that nothing lasts forever."

Yom fell silent, and his words settled in the air like a coating of dust.

MISHO PACED THE ROOM AS THE QUEEN SLEPT. She looked peaceful, less like the statue she appeared when awake and swimming in clouds of Amaurosis ash, more like a young woman. With hopes and dreams and follies. Her breathing was quiet, the only evidence of its presence the gentle rise and fall of her chest.

"This will be the last step of your official initiation to the house of Lords," a deep voice boomed from the other side of the Queen's door. Misho only had time to draw the crossbow on his back before the door opened and an older man waltzed in with a younger man—father and son if their aquiline noses were any indication—both in stately Lord's robes. His master followed them with bright eyes.

The young lord licked his lips as his sights set on the Queen's bed. "May I have some privacy?"

Misho moved to block their path. "What's the meaning of this?" He sought out his master for an answer.

"Step aside, boy." The older lord waved his hand.

"I apologize, this is Misho's first time being assigned to the Queen. He does not know yet of her agreement with the House of Lords."

"Agreement?" Adrenaline pumped through Misho. Whatever was happening, it was setting off every alarm bell in his mind.

"Her agreement. She is the Queen of Arcadia. She serves Arcadia body and soul. Just as the Queens before her." His master almost looked bored as he droned this out.

"I won't ask you again. Out of our way, boy." The older man stepped up to look down his curved nose at Misho, despite Misho having several inches on him. Misho took one last look at his master to see no sign in his angular face that he would stop this.

Misho took an almost imperceptible step aside, and the two Lords blazed past him. He watched in disbelief as they approached the raised platform of the

Queen's bed as if they owned it. As soon as one of them pulled back the sheer gauze canopy that shaded the bed, the other reached out a hand to touch her. Misho flinched and turned away.

"This is wrong," he hissed at his master, whose eyes were brightening even more as he stayed facing the bed.

"Her body serves Arcadia," his master said coldly. While Misho refused to look, his master seemed to relent a hair. "Nothing will happen until after Lupercalia. She remains unused, for now." Misho's lip curled at the repulsive words.

"Don't be so sanctimonious. Before I got here, my cousins were warlords of a lawless land. You think they would have banded together long enough to accomplish any of this? You think the humans would have ever experienced peace without my intervention? I tamed *wilderness*. I created unity from chaos. As soon as my cousins saw how easy it was to influence the human mind, how weak it became in the face of a little temptation, they understood what I understood. That humans are the greatest weapon we have. All we needed was a common goal. You think my cousins would have had the foresight— the wherewithal—to consult the stars, year after year, looking for flesh of our flesh?" his master asked derisively.

"All this," he waved his long, manicured fingers around them, "is to give the humans the order they so desperately crave. And out there," he waved his hand in the direction of the provinces, "any places where I can't touch, my cousins keep their own form of order. Every piece is delicately placed."

Misho reeled at this unexpected flood of information. "But why keep the Lords?"

"The Queen by herself is not enough to preside over a population this size. Representatives are required, agents of her will. In return for their service, the Queen gifts them with riches. And in return for their loyalty, I gift them with the Queen."

Misho swallowed, understanding the words, thinking of the generations of Queens cast in stone, standing in stoic silence in Queen's Squares in each province. Considering what the service of their reign entailed.

"And the Lords are willing to wait for this particular Queen?" Misho steeled himself to turn back around. Wincing, he made out that indeed his master had not lied. The two Lords merely prodded at Andromeda's limbs, leaving the majority of her untouched. Still, the act of allowing them access to her in this vulnerable state made Misho's stomach churn.

"They have their stand-ins for the agreement until the time comes," his master said absently as he turned his bright eyes to the left. There, Misho saw the ink-haired lady-in-waiting, Leah, watching the room from a slivered shadow. Even from far away, her haunted yellow eyes returned his master's gaze without a single blink.

Yom woke from a fitful sleep on the bumpy path of the caravan. The sliver of road showed that it was no longer surrounded by golden grass, but rather by stone and brush, rich with the smell of olives. The air in the compartment was stale and warm, and now had the faint taste of salt. They had reached the warm southern waters of Okeanus.

Looking around, she saw Quia's amber eyes fixed on her. "You're awake," she said groggily.

"Couldn't sleep."

"We're almost there." Yom rubbed her eyes and leaned toward the slice of sunlight. The terrain was unlike anything she had seen in the northern half of Arcadia, all pockmarked rock forms and scraggly trees with bitter looking leaves. Nothing of the fecund greenery of the Ardennes, or the hills of Inisfail that sparkled like oversized jewels in the sun.

Quia seemed to be too preoccupied to take in the scenery. "What would you do, if you could do anything? Be anyone?" He squirmed to look her straight in the eyes.

"Is that what you've been up all night thinking about?"

Quia stayed quiet.

Yom considered for a moment, accepting that there was little else to do while they waited for the caravan to crawl to the gates of the eternal city.

"I would open up my own chemist's laboratory. Like the one Eden ran. And I would help people." She was briefly thrust into the fuzzy, golden light of her memories of Eden's laboratory. Lior and her running around the legs of the workbenches and stools. Eden's hands creating the closest thing to magic Yom would ever see. For even true magic could not compare to the enchantment of childhood memory.

Quia hummed, breaking the spell.

"And you?" Yom turned to him.

"I wouldn't fight ever again. I would write every day." Despite all that he had shared with her, this seemed like the thing he had held onto the tightest. As if he had doubted he would ever speak it out loud again.

"What would you write?"

"Verse," he said. The longing in his voice edged close to regret. "I used to compose it all the time, before I left Panchaia." He cleared his throat. "I haven't felt I could since what happened. But, maybe I could. Sometimes, when I'm with you, I feel like I can again."

"Quia, we can't—"

"I didn't ask to be born with this burden," he muttered bitterly. "If I could, I would give it back. I would be anyone else. I would be no one."

"There's no world where you could ever be no one." This was the only hint Yom could offer at her feelings without losing her nerve. Quia's face warmed and eyes crinkled for a moment before he caught himself. They each had their paths, and they were going to follow them. Any further rumination on this would only make it harder for both of them. "You're going to find the numenborn, and you're going to return home. I know it."

The caravan began to slow.

Quia's eyes bulged. "Why are they stopping?" he whispered.

"I think we're at the gates." Just as Yom answered him, more caravans and transports neared behind them. "They must be stopping every transport to search." *For us*, Yom finished in her head. "We need to find a better hiding spot."

YOM AND QUIA CLUNG TO THE UNDERSIDE OF THE CARAVAN. Yom sputtered as quietly as she could, trying to keep from swallowing the dust and dirty steam that surrounded them. They'd had to move before the caravans behind them had gotten too close, and Yom had rushed to cajole Sassa into climbing out with them. But the fox had circled defiantly in the luggage compartment, insisting on staying there. Eventually Yom had run out of time and had climbed down to the undercarriage, hoisting herself up from the wood beams.

She thought she had decent strength, but suspending her own body weight was tiring her much faster than it should have. She huffed with effort.

"Will you make it?" Quia whispered.

"I'm working on it," she gritted out in a coarse whisper. She thought of the irony that this whole voyage could be nullified by a weak upper body. She hissed breaths in and out and concentrated all her willpower on the thought of finding Lior. For once, her life felt important to preserve, if only for that purpose.

The caravan moved at an excruciating crawl, but eventually, they saw the brass footcovers of legionaries walking along the side of the caravan.

"Everyone stay put while we search," the legionary instructed gruffly.

Yom held her breath, her arms now shaking uncontrollably. Legionaries boarded the caravan, their metal footsteps pacing the aisle above them. Then, another set of footsteps rounded the back, to where the luggage compartment was. Yom waited for the sound of surprise at the discovery of a wild animal, but she heard nothing following the click of the latch opening. Just a low grunt. *Clear*, the legionary acknowledged.

Yom did not have time to consider what happened to Sassa as even this inkling of a distraction was enough to lose the grip of one of her hands. Barely able to yelp, she braced herself for a sharp impact with the road, but a firm hand was there, pushing her up between her shoulder blades. Quia was turning red at the effort of supporting her and himself, but the second of assistance was all she needed. She regained her grip.

"Next," one of the legionaries called.

Yom released a deep breath as the caravan chugged back to life, lurching forward. The only sign of the famous marble walls of the eternal city were their shadow on the stone road as the caravan passed through them.

As soon as they were over the threshold, the city thrummed to life. Yom couldn't see anything besides the ground, but there were more caravans, colorful tents, and hoards of people. Vendors shouted, peddling wares and bartering. This road must pass through a market just inside the gates.

Now Yom needed to figure out how to get down, though the ache in her arms made it difficult. Then, a vibrating thump came from the back of the caravan.

"Do you hear that?" A muffled voice spoke above them. The thumping continued.

"What is that?" Another voice cut in.

"Oi, pull over there," the first one raised his voice. The caravan pulled to the left down an offshoot of the road and jolted to a stop.

A couple sets of footsteps jumped down from the topside of the caravan and circled around to the luggage compartment. Yom met Quia's eyes before she twisted her body to fall onto the gravel path. She crawled to the edge so she could see the surroundings better. They were only a couple feet from a purple-tented booth where a toothless man sold fruit.

They needed a distraction to pull the eyes of the market away from them long enough to slip into the skirts of the booth. Before Yom had much time to think, more shouting came from behind the caravan.

"Bloody Okeanus—"

"Where are the trunks—"

Then there was the unmistakable aggressive growl of a fox and the sound of scratching skin.

"Look at that," voices around the market whispered. Yom didn't hesitate before crawling out from beneath the caravan and under the shade of the fruit booth. Quia's sturdy presence pulled into a crouch beside her.

"I'll kill you, you scrawny little cat!" The grimy caravan riders were wrestling with Sassa, but her lithe body jumped away from them, having inflicted a fair number of scratches, and disappeared into the booths.

"Let's keep moving." Yom gestured to Quia to follow her behind the booth, to the narrow aisle between the row of stalls and the walled edge. She barely had time to take in the sunbleached buildings around them, concentrating on slipping away unnoticed.

"What about—" Quia began, and by his voice Yom could tell he was looking back.

"Don't look back. She will find us." This had been Sassa's plan when the fox insisted on remaining in the trunk. And Yom knew Sassa would come back.

Once they rounded the corner back to the main road, where the crowd and the vendors were twice as dense, Yom felt their words could fade into the background easily. She turned to face Quia, alternating her focus between him and the path behind him, where she hoped to see a clever black fox prowling.

"Is this it?" Quia asked heavily, eyes locked on her.

"Think so," she replied, keeping the emotion from her voice.

Quia cupped her cheek in his warm palm. "It's been an honor traveling with you, Yom." The way he said her name almost broke her resolve, made her want to abandon her plan and stay with him, come what may.

"Even though I'm unbearable?"

Quia laughed, rueful. "You are utterly, madly, ingeniously unbearable."

Yom couldn't help but be engulfed by the sincerity she saw in his eyes, by the tingling electricity of his touch. "You are too," she whispered.

If Yom were to recount the story, she would say that Quia pulled her into a fierce hug. But the reality was, Yom was the one who threw her arms around him. Since they had become acquainted, every truth of her world had been rocked, again and again, but no matter what doubt was planted, no matter what distrust remained, she cared about him. More than she thought she was capable of. He held her tight enough that they could be convinced for a moment that they never needed to let go.

Yom pulled back an inch, and her attention fell to his lips. She figured it couldn't do any damage now, to steal one last kiss. The embers heating in his eyes told her he felt the same.

With a harsh, shared breath, their lips came together like two magnets that couldn't help but find each other. His scent filled her nose until she was swimming in him, buoyed in his wind, painted from his lampblack ink. Her hands tangled into his hair, memorizing how it felt in her hands. She put all her unsaid words into that kiss, hoping it would be enough to last.

Yom pulled away slowly, reluctantly. An iridescent black butterfly fluttered in between them, before landing on Yom's shoulder. Quia marveled at it for a moment before holding a finger up for it.

"You are quite skilled," he said to the butterfly form of Sassa. "Thank you." He lowered his hand, and Sassa's delicate feet landed, wings tucked, on Yom's shoulder.

Quia studied Yom like he was cataloging and storing her face somewhere he would never forget it. Some speck of debris must have floated into Yom's eye, because she felt her vision blurring.

"It seems almost too simple, after everything we went through, for our story to end here." Quia's amber eyes searched Yom's.

"You said it yourself, nothing lasts forever. Right?"

"Right." He nodded solemnly. And took one step back. Then another, before turning. Yom stayed where she was and watched him as he continued taking deliberate steps away from her. He did not look back, and already he was several booths away, something tugging impossibly taut between them as he left.

XVI

Lupercalia

CATARACTA WAS AN OLD MYSTERY, AND A YOUNG ROMANCE, ALL AT once. Yom had known that it was littered with ruins—some dating back as far as the ancients—but the city was alive with all instances of itself, stretching in all directions through time. It made sense now why they called it the eternal city. Yom and Sassa padded through the narrow stone streets, Sassa taking her fox form to walk by Yom's side. They encountered secluded waterways full of lovers whispering sweetnesses into each other's ears. They found market stalls whose layered curios looked like they had been accumulating long before their shopkeeper took on the mantle of selling them. They saw entire shops and dwellings built into old ruins, generations of history etched on the face of the stone. Inisfail was never so precious with its structures. Buildings were torn down and constructed at will, any semblance of history forsaken.

Despite her own curiosity, Yom did not allow them much time to marvel as she searched for a pleasure house. She did, however, permit a brief fantasy of locating Lior and finding a small corner of the city they could tuck themselves into once everything was over. It would be a small life of color and art and knowledge. She tried not to put too much stock in the hope that Lior would be glad to see her, but being this close to finding her once again made it difficult to control her emotions. Yom felt as though they had walked half the city by the time she glimpsed the tell-tale red door of a pleasure house. She hardly let herself doubt her plan before asking Sassa to find a shaded spot to wait, and marching up to the red door to wrench it open.

Inside, the familiar aroma of powder and scented oils wafted through the air. Yom scanned the room as her eyes adjusted and saw an older woman in a corset seated behind a table, writing in a ledger.

"Well, hello, darling," the madam purred in a voice that soured Yom's stomach. "What can I do for you?"

Yom steeled herself. "I'm looking for a girl."

"We have plenty of those." The madam's eyes twinkled.

"Not like that." Yom clenched her jaw, imagining how many people came to a place like this with those intentions before being led straight to Lior. "She's from Inisfail. Dark hair, blue eyes. Very beautiful."

The woman's eyes narrowed. "Does this beautiful girl have a name?"

Suspicion curled inside Yom. "No—I never caught her name. Have you ever met a girl in Cataracta like that?"

"I haven't," the madam said coolly as she stood from her table and set down her pen. "But you should be careful, girl, ours is not a city that takes kindly to people looking to disrupt the peace."

"I'm not looking to disrupt anything." Yom took a step back, towards the door. "I'll just be going then..." she trailed off as she fumbled behind herself for the door handle.

"Yes, I think that's for the best." The madam narrowed her eyes.

Yom stepped outside the pleasure house, not turning her back on it until the door was firmly shut once again. She took a couple hesitating steps back, looking around to make sure Sassa had not wandered off too far. Something about that encounter unsettled her. It was almost as if the madam had known who she was looking for.

"Hey," a voice whispered just as Yom felt the brush of Sassa's body against her leg. Yom spun in a circle to find it. "Hey!" the voice repeated, more urgently. A streak of white hair glinted from a shadow next to the pleasure house.

"Yes?" Yom whispered back, walking towards the source. It was a girl, younger than her, with cornsilk hair. A purple bruise bloomed around one of the girl's eyes.

"You're looking for someone?" the girl whispered.

"I am," Yom said, unsure if she was wandering into a trap.

"You said she's very beautiful." The girl swallowed and her eyes darted to the wall of the pleasure house. "If that's the case, she's probably already inside the House of Flowing Waters. All the finest girls in the city are brought there for Lupercalia."

Yom's eyes narrowed. "Why are you telling me this?"

"If someone was looking for me, I would want them to find me." Her words, genuine and plain, were a dull jab through the air between them.

Yom nodded. "Thank you." She took a step back but hesitated, looking once more at the girl's blotchy bruise. Reaching into her pack, she quickly found the jar of belladonna.

"Grind up a leaf of this and slip a pinch into the drink of anyone who comes to see you. They won't be able to do that again." Yom held the small jar out to the girl, who looked at Yom with wide eyes and reached a hand slowly to it.

"I hope you find her," the girl said, now clutching the belladonna to her chest like a life raft.

"Me too," Yom muttered as she left the shadows and turned towards the House of Flowing Waters.

THE PALACE SAT AT THE TOP OF THE TALLEST HILL WITHIN THE GATES of Cataracta. The House's grounds had their own gates, with more blackcoat guards, which meant Yom needed another disguise. Unfortunately, the easiest thing to get ahold of were silks from an atelier that was clearly accustomed to discreet work done for pleasure houses. Though Yom conceded it would make it easier to blend in with the escorts that were coming to the House for the ceremony.

The pathway that trotted up the hill to the gates of the House of Flowing Waters was lined with a procession of nobles, courtiers, and wealthy merchants, all esteemed guests of the Queen. Throughout the crowd people carried lanterns suspended on tall poles, creating a river of light that carved up the hillside. Yom's heartbeat ratcheted up at the thought of seeing Quia again, of having to say goodbye, again. She assured herself that she would be in and out, long gone by the time he did what he needed to do.

Yom adjusted her silks—she had insisted on green this time, refusing to wear red like she had in Traiana—and smoothed down her hair. The panels of silk cut from her shoulders down her chest, meeting below her breasts and leaving very little to the imagination. At least her powderbelt was still buckled around her waist—a comforting weight—beneath an extra sash of silk, and her hands were obscured by lace gloves once again. Sassa had shifted into her butterfly form, flitting in and around Yom's pack. All she had to do now was find someone willing to vouch for her as their escort. One of the shop girls in the atelier had shown her how to straighten out her curls with hot irons. The girl had smudged kohl powder all around her eyes, and coated her lashes in a dark mud she spread with a fine comb. It made it heavier to keep her eyes open, but she was confident no one would recognize her. She barely recognized herself.

Absent-minded, Yom tugged her lace gloves tighter as she walked. She was surrounded by nobles in elegant garb of sable black, midnight blue and sumptuous green, all bathed in lantern light. Some wore the heavier robes of the north while others wore the skin bearing wraps of the south. Yom wasn't sure what it said about them that no one batted an eye at her presence. She felt the eyes of someone on her backside and she turned to see an old man with wisps of white framing his face and age spotted all over his cheeks. He leered at her.

Yom twisted her face into a demure smile. "Why hello there," she drawled at the old codger.

His milky eyes lit up. "Pretty," he rasped.

Yom twirled to take his arm gently in hers, feeling his paper thin skin even under his robes. "How would you like to arrive together?" she cooed.

"Yes, pet," he said, patting the arm interlocked with his with a bony hand. "I've been looking forward to this for the past year," he sighed.

"What could be more exciting?" Yom muttered. While she had always been curious about what happened at Lupercalia, seeing it for herself felt like opening a box that would be difficult to close again.

Her pace had slowed to keep up with the old man, and her gaze settled on the procession ahead of them. The heads and lanterns bobbed rhythmically, punctuated by the harried breaths of her elderly companion. It took several minutes for her to realize she was watching a particularly tall blond head bobbing with each step a ways ahead of them.

Yom cursed under her breath and hunched over so she wouldn't be visible at all beneath the crowd. She hadn't considered that Lucan would be attending tonight, though she recalled in the same conversation where Misho had mentioned Lupercalia, that Cernunnos had insisted one of his emissaries observe the ceremony. Cernunnos may not be the only titan who had made these arrangements. Her stomach dropped at the thought of seeing an Eel again, after the stunt they had pulled in the arena. Luckily, she was unrecognizable.

"Hello, pretty, who are you?" The old man's voice sounded like a child discovering a small creature. Yom filed away memory loss with the list of things she was learning about this lecher. Though, this she could use to her advantage.

"I'm your date," she told him.

"How marvelous!" His eyes lit up again.

They crested the hill, reaching the gates of the House of Flowing Waters. The blackcoats—the name a bit of a misnomer when they wore their coatless southern uniform—seemed to be waving people through based on nothing but how they looked. She held her breath as they approached the blackcoats.

They were just about to cross the threshold when she heard a low, "Wait right there," come from one of them. She bit the inside of her cheek as she paused, keeping the old man with her.

"What's all this about, son?" The old man asked the blackcoat.

"Just a routine check, sir. Need to search everyone coming inside tonight." For a moment Yom blanched that they would search inside her pack, but as soon as the blackcoat was there, his hands were pawing at her body through the thin silks. *Of course,* she thought to herself. *Still blackcoats.* The blackcoat groped her under the guise of a search for several minutes before they were waved through.

"You haven't been misbehaving, young lady, have you?" the old man asked as she continued to walk him the way one would walk a hobbling, elderly dog.

Yom almost laughed out loud. *You have no idea.* "No, sir, never."

"Good girl," he said absently.

The grounds of the House were perfectly manicured with all manner of flora that Yom had rarely seen in Inisfail. Pomegranate trees, curved junipers, aromatic olives. Explosions of purple and fuschia and coral from irises, dianthuses, and lilies. Straight ahead, Yom's attention was stolen once again by the gleaming marble walls of the House of Flowing Waters. The entrance was open, the halls inside lit by evenly spaced lanterns, with blackcoats and servants lining it to greet guests.

Every child in Inisfail knew of the House of Flowing Waters, but only the select few of the wealthy class would ever see its legendary walls of water in person. Yom tried to look nonchalant as they crossed the threshold into the House, but it was a sight to behold. The walls stretched up towards the sky, water sluicing down them in an eternal flow, reflecting and refracting the light of the lanterns around them. The wall of water showed an imperfect, distorted mirror of the procession. Yom caught her own eye, not seeing herself but rather a seductive, beautiful escort. She looked down to avoid becoming too entranced by it.

The hallway they walked did not have any rooms for a distance. Finally, Yom saw an offshoot she could slip into. She loosened her grip on her companion's arm until only the tips of her fingers held him. As they passed the hallway opening, she let go and veered away from the procession.

Queen Andromeda sat idly as she was prepared for Lupercalia. On top of her usual silk, hands were layering panels of chiffon and piling strings of gold and glass beads. Her face was powdered with its usual coating of gold, but instead of a rigid statue, they made her look the part of the seductress: glossy red lips, dark kohl around her eyes, and a rosy blush. They made her look as if she was not of this world, rather a fleeting view into the next. The chains on her wrist that stretched up her forearms made a delicate chorus each time she moved. She kept them on always, like a crown. No one around her knew what her forearms looked like underneath. It appeared to the outside world that they were the same flawless porcelain as the rest of her skin. But Andromeda knew they covered something else, something Hector had told her the attackers had left behind that day they invaded the House of Flowing Waters and killed her mother. A thick seam of a scar stretching up one, and strange markings on the other. *Panchaian savages*, Hector had condemned them. *Marking you as if you were some animal. You're lucky I got there when I did*, he would always repeat.

Time seemed to float by, and before Andromeda realized it, she was walking the marble and water halls, approaching the Great Hall. There was a hand at her back, and she sensed Hector's bright eyes burning next to her.

Ready, your majesty? His hand moved to cup the back of her head.

Yes, she blinked, eyelids heavy with tinted powder.

The Great Hall was adorned with flowing banners of blue, garlands and arrangements lining every surface. The crowd glittered with gold and their finest garb. A woven crown of poppy was placed on her head. Time continued to drift, control over its pace just out of her reach.

Your majesty, a melodic voice spoke behind Andromeda. She turned to see a woman with bright red hair and a smattering of freckles. Standing behind her, like a servant, was a younger girl with strikingly blue eyes. You look beautiful this evening, the red-haired woman added.

Andromeda stood still without responding.

The House of Flowing Waters is as beautiful as they say, this stranger offered, looking around.

I sometimes forget how beautiful it can be, Andromeda found the words to reply slowly.

Forgive me, I have not introduced myself. My name is Rye. She extended her palm and Andromeda dutifully placed her hand in it. The skin was soft but had rough edges. The woman brought Andromeda's hand to her lips to place a chaste kiss on it.

It's a pleasure, Andromeda found herself saying. The woman smiled.

The pleasure is all mine. The woman stepped closer. I wanted to tell you personally how excited I am for the changes you plan to make.

What changes? Andromeda found herself responding, trying to remain stoic. Though beneath it, confusion bled into her already wisping mind.

The new order you plan to instill, the fact that we will finally have the chance to be in charge, under your leadership.

What are you ta—

Your majesty? Another voice came close, and Andromeda turned to see dark, knotted skin. She knew this face, but she could not place from where.

We were in the middle of a conversation, triarii, the woman bristled. Rye, Andromeda remembered her name vaguely.

Her majesty has much to attend to this evening, the scarred man said tersely. And then he stepped into her vision, right in front of where the woman stood. She recognized the face, but she had seen it before surrounded by glistening black armor.

You're the triarii, she said softly.

Misho. He nodded. I'm here to attend to you this evening, your majesty.

Andromeda had never seen one of the black-armored guards in plain clothes.

Your armor... she trailed off.

It was damaged, I will have a replacement within the fortnight. He waved a hand as he spoke, and Andromeda caught a peek at the inside of his forearm. She saw markings.

What is this? Her hand shot out to grab his arm and turn it squarely towards her. A shock registered when their skin touched. The markings were darker but their strange forms were familiar. She brushed her hand against it. Again, the faintest shock at the touch.

It is my mark of service, he said slowly, watching her. A symbol of my devotion to the House of Flowing Waters. Sealed with Moonflower and my own blood.

Andromeda was yanked away from her body while the triarii and the Great Hall twinkled in the distance. She sank inward.

Moonflower. It had a white bloom. It was connected to something familiar and just out of reach. Something that skirted the edges of her memory. A bundle of vines—of Moonflower vines—hanging—no, being held—against a red apron.

Yom didn't make it far before a blackcoat spotted her.

"Oi, where are you going?"

Yom swallowed. "I was—"

"All the girls have to wait over there—no coming out early," he said sharply as he pointed behind him.

Yom held her breath and nodded, trying not to look too relieved as she hurried towards the door he had pointed to. It was an antechamber of sorts, wall-to-wall filled with beautiful young women, and a few young men. Yom darted through the room, searching the face of every young woman. While all beautiful, none of them were the singular beauty for which she was looking. She tried to get her bearings within the chamber, but the air was thick with perfume and powder. The powders were child's play compared to the ones she normally indulged in, but the smell in the crowded space was testing her limits of restraint. She needed to keep her focus sharp tonight.

"Is this everyone?" Yom asked a girl sitting alone next to her.

"No." The girl's voice was almost too faint to hear. She cleared her throat before continuing, "Some of them are already in the hall, they have them serve food and provide entertainment." The girl looked at the far end of the chamber. Blackcoats lined the entrances to the room, watching the girls predatorily. "The rest of us won't be brought into the Great Hall until after the ceremony." Yom gathered the entrance the girl had glanced at was the one that led to the Great Hall. Two blackcoats stood guard in front of it.

"Thank you." Yom nodded and gave her a bracing smile.

Yom strode up to them and pointed at the door. "I'm supposed to be in there."

One of the blackcoats snorted. "Everyone who's supposed to be in there is already. You'll have to wait until they're done."

The other one cut in. "If you're bored in the meantime, we're happy to keep you busy." His mouth widened into a toothy smile.

"Sure," Yom said flatly. The blackcoats looked at her, a bit dumbstruck that she was actually taking them up on the offer.

"I knew we lucked out on this post tonight," one of them said eagerly.

Yom held up a bottle of mandragora ash she had readied in her hand. "But do you mind if I take something first? It helps get me in the mood." Yom poured it into her palm and made to inhale but one of the blackcoats stopped her.

"Don't forget to share." He grabbed her wrist and brought her palm up to his nose to inhale.

"How is it?" the other one asked. "They always give whores the best powders." The blackcoat who had taken the mandragora could do nothing but smile dreamily.

"Give me that." His partner took what was left in Yom's hand and inhaled it himself. She counted the few seconds it would take for the compound to set in. Right on cue, the blackcoats swayed and then collapsed against the wall. Their hands twitched before they succumbed to a deep sleep.

"Have fun." Yom winked at them before stepping over their bodies and opening the door to the Great Hall.

YOUR MAJESTY, A SILKEN VOICE TUGGED ANDROMEDA OUT OF HERSELF. Returning slowly to the Great Hall, she met the eyes of Hector. Hector, who had told her for years that the strange markings on her forearm that had been covered up with chains were the work of the mysterious intruders. Hector, who was the only one who was personally there when these intruders attacked her. Andromeda didn't even remember the attack herself—the royal physicians always assumed it was due to the shock. She searched Hector's eyes for some sign that this was all a misunderstanding. They were the same amber irises, but now there were specks of yellow she didn't recall noticing before. The triarii's scarred face floated in her periphery, but when Andromeda turned to take in the room, he had disappeared.

Yes? Andromeda turned back to face Hector, waiting for something to surface that would halt the freefall. Some scrap of information that would validate everything he had told her, something that hadn't come from his lips.

Are you well? Did you take your powder this morning? he asked.

The thought of the darkly sweet stench of the powder made her stomach turn. Why did that powder have such power over her? In that moment she couldn't remember why she had started taking it in the first place.

Y-yes, she mumbled, I'm just—warm, I think I'll take a turn in the gardens.

Allow me to accompany you. A soft hand snaked around her.

No, she said quickly. She found a familiar dark head of hair in the crowd. My lady will escort me, she said, trying to keep the panic from her voice.

She crossed the hall, reaching for her lady-in-waiting, Leah, as she went, pulling her out the doors and into the hanging gardens.

THE CROWD MILLING AROUND THE GREAT HALL WORE THE TUNICS, pallae, and skin-baring silks that were the style in the eternal city, piled with more gold than Yom had ever seen in one place. She slinked around the edge of the crowd, meeting the eyes of each servant girl she saw, never finding the familiar blue that lived in her memory.

Once she checked the edges, she wove through the crowd, keeping a careful eye out for Lucan. Girls in jewel-toned silks stood out against the crowd, and Yom's lip curled up at their forced entertainment. But Yom couldn't let herself be distracted. She only sought one girl tonight.

The crowd thinned for an instant, and Yom caught sight of Queen Andromeda in the center. She had seen carvings done in stone and prints in ink, but she saw now in the flickering firelight of the hall that they did not do her justice. Her eyes were rimmed in a black, glittering kohl, and her skin shimmered with gold, as if she was gilded in the metal. She was hauntingly beautiful, and regal. *Someone whom Quia would be proud to have by his side,* Yom thought bitterly.

The Queen stood with a beautiful man with white hair and bright yellow eyes set into pale as snow skin. The Queen turned to face Yom's direction and pulled a woman with ink black hair to walk next to her. The woman had equally pale skin and the same yellow eyes as the man. There was clearly a resemblance between the two.

Something in the Queen's walk bothered Yom, something that tugged at her. There was a certain swish in her hips. It was the walk of a dancer, Yom realized. Suddenly she saw a different person walking towards her: a young girl with dark hair and blue eyes, graceful yet ready to pounce. As the Queen walked directly towards Yom she could not stop seeing it. The deep blue of the Queen's eyes became more and more luminous, until it was all Yom could see, until she was drowning in it. Yom stood dumbfounded as the Queen came an arms length away from her before passing without a second glance.

A name rang out over and over in Yom's head, a siren. *Lior Lior Lior.*

Andromeda kneaded her fingertips into her temples as she blazed into the hanging gardens. She paced, holding onto the scrap of the image she had found, the red apron and the hand holding a parcel of Moonflower. There was more that begged to bleed into the memory: golden light, shelves lined with jars of more plants, a hearth that radiated love and comfort. And there were green eyes. Eyes that for some reason she knew did not belong to the wearer of the red apron; eyes that drew her in hypnotically.

Are you alright, your majesty?

How do you know Hector? Andromeda was blunt, pleading.

She took in the sight of the lady. Her hair seemed darker somehow. A midnight black, a color that absorbed light. Darker than Andromeda remembered. She stepped closer and saw flecks of yellow within the golden brown eyes she had become familiar with. The same flecks of yellow she had seen in Hector's eyes.

Did you forget to take your powder this morning? Perhaps you did not take enough. Leah stepped closer but Andromeda heard it. The silk in her voice, the familiar arch in her eyes. It was the same as Hector.

No—no, Andromeda stammered as she backed away from her, I don't need any more.

She looked behind her to see if anyone in the hall was watching, if any triarii had followed them out to the gardens. No one paid her a drop of attention.

I'm sorry. Andromeda whipped back around as the lady's voice was suddenly within a few inches of her. I have to insist.

The lady's remorseful eyes, now as yellow as a daffodil, were the last thing Andromeda saw before a cloud of purple dust coated her vision.

XVII

Daughter of Eden

As soon as Quia parted from Yom, he knew it was a mistake. The pull he had felt towards her since that day in the Powder Parlor had magnified itself in response, as if to reinforce the notion that he was an idiot for agreeing to separate. But he had worked through these thoughts as he walked away, and when he had finally drummed up the courage to turn around, to see if she had waited for him, all he saw was an empty patch of wall where she had been standing.

"It's for the best," he muttered to himself. "You can go home after this." Home—not the one in the overcast city of Inisfail, but the one on the other side of Okeanus, where the sun ruled all from its throne in the sky—was distant and intoxicating at the same time.

The House of Flowing Waters was easy to spot on the tallest hill of the city, though it felt like the whole city was conspiring to keep Quia from reaching it. Aggressive vendors inundated him with wares: bolts of silks, bushels of pears, and entire crates of lush plums. The girls who stood outside the pleasure houses seemed to take a special interest in him, with two or three of them crowding his path, running their hands up and down his chest and over his arms. Each time, he removed their hands as he tried to continue and eventually made it far enough that they had to cease walking with him to return to their posts. He was even caught behind a few herds of animals, goats and donkeys being led over the stone and gravel streets of the city by urban farmers, plodding slowly as they grazed on greenery sprouting at the edges of roads.

When he finally caught sight of the walls of the royal grounds, a thick procession of people marched towards it. Whatever was happening tonight, Quia wanted to get to the Queen before it started. His best chance to smuggle her out would be before she was surrounded by guards and the entire royal court and assembly of Lords.

Cutting away from the crowded procession, he walked along the base of the hill, looking for a servant entrance. A small path further down that cut up the hill in a delicate ribbon caught his eye. As he walked, he tried to create a plan, but Yom had been quite good at making plans. His thoughts meandered to memories of the very endearing way her eyebrows pushed together and her lips tilted to one side as she was concocting one. In fact, he had become so distracted thinking about this that he missed a small company of triarii prowling behind him on silent feet.

"What do we have here?" was all he heard before his arms were twisted behind his back, and the tip of a crossbow suddenly poked his throat. He was barely able to register the black triarii armor before a closed fist uppercut his jaw and the lights winked out.

Yom followed the queen and the raven-haired, yellow-eyed woman out to the gardens, pushing aside the lush foliage to watch. All she could see was Lior.

"Are you alright, your majesty?" the voice of the woman carried from the center of the garden, stopping Yom's heart. It was a voice she couldn't forget even if she wanted to, scratching on the panes of her memory like a feral cat. A similarly calm voice replayed over the buzz of the garden. *We heard you have a very special girl.*

Lior stepped towards the woman, and Yom couldn't make out what she said, but then Lior started to back away. The woman traveled inhumanly fast, and a cloud of purple powder erupted between them that turned Lior deathly still.

The yellow-eyed woman led Lior back inside as if she was a pet on a leash. Trailing them cautiously, Yom stepped into the clearing. Dread and adrenaline gathered in her limbs. She strained to remember all the history she had learned of Queen Andromeda. The young princess had appeared, seemingly out of nowhere, upon the untimely death of her mother. The story had always been that the future heir was heavily sheltered within the House of Flowing Waters and only entered society to take up her role as Queen out of necessity. But it turns out, she had appeared out of nowhere because she hadn't *existed* until they stole Lior. Yom stood frozen for several moments, seeing the cloud of purple powder over and over. Purple powder enveloping the Queen, purple powder blowing into Moss's face, purple powder surrounding Lior before she was picked up and carried out of the laboratory. A weight crushed Yom's chest, begging her to run, or curl into a ball, or simply sink into the earth and grow roots.

Snap out of it, Yom shook herself. *You crossed all of Arcadia to find her, you will finish what started that night. You're a chemist,* she reminded herself. *And this is all the chemical arts are, accessing the hidden truths of every living thing.*

Yom took a deep breath and ripped off her gloves, turning her attention to her pack with new eyes. Sophia's jars clinked as she rummaged through them. She already knew what she would use. Black hellebore, a remedy for madness. Mugwort, a healer of trauma. And agrimony, a forger of boundaries. Yom combined pinches from the three into a spare vial and tucked it into the first loop of her belt. It could have been her imagination, but it seemed to pulse with energy, like a talisman.

Sassa seemed to sense a change in the winds too, shifting back into her fox form and rubbing herself against Yom's leg.

"Stay by my side," Yom told Sassa before she started walking back towards the Great Hall, each step steeped in purpose.

The atmosphere was becoming downright hedonistic as the court imbibed heather wine and anise spirits. Powders were being passed around as well, the sweet dust permeating the air. Yom dodged multiple drunk lords stumbling on their feet, as well as some young women who tried to grab for Yom's silks as she walked. The ceremony hadn't even started yet; Yom shuddered to think about what the atmosphere would be afterwards.

As Yom waded through the crowd, she saw a raised platform in the center of the room that had been constructed since the start of the feast. It looked like there were pillows and silks strewn about it. Yom clenched her fist as Lior was led to it, eyes almost completely black and jaw slack. The little food Yom had eaten threatened to come back up as she realized what it was. A bed.

The white-haired, yellow-eyed man stepped forward, but something didn't look right. There was a shimmer in his skin, an unnatural brightness in his eyes. Something whispered across the stone floor, a thin strip of leather in his hand that snaked behind him as he walked.

He shook off his robe with nothing but a cloth stretched across his hips, and the shimmer permeated every stitch of skin. Yom looked around, to see if anyone else was noticing this, but the crowd was too blissed out on spirits and powders to tell up from down.

Servants guided Lior to lay down on the bed, with her back facing up. Yom stood in shock, unable to do anything but watch as the pale shimmering man raised the whip. It curled in a silent arc before it snapped against Lior's back with a sickening crack, leaving a pink welt in its wake.

"ONE," the crowd erupted in semi unison around Yom, startling her out of her daze. She started to push past the people, her limbs leaden. Two more cracks sounded, followed by the roaring count of the crowd. The faces around Yom were full of amusement. So this was the mysterious and guarded ceremony of Lupercalia? Yom had expected something excessive, but the court whipping its own Queen? She couldn't make sense of it as she tore through the crowd, watching another two welts rise from strokes of the whip.

"Lior," Yom tried to speak now that she was only steps away from the platform, but her voice came out small and broken. She swallowed, and as the whip rose for the fourth time, she shouted, "Lior!"

The man turned to face her, and she saw the shimmer head on. His snowy skin glowed and large yellow eyes pulsed. The shimmer dimmed for a moment and the man looked to the other side of the platform. Following his gaze, Yom saw Misho, in robes like the rest of the crowd and without his armor, looking at Yom as if she was impossible.

Lior's eyes had drifted closed. Heavy clouds of guilt loomed at the edges of Yom's vision as she stroked a thumb over the face she had met countless times in her dreams. Lior's thick beauty powders smeared beneath Yom's finger.

Hands seized Yom's arms and held them behind her back.

"You'll pay for this," Yom snarled at the man holding the whip as she thrashed in the grip, her rage consuming her.

"This must be Cernunnos's talented chemist I've heard so much about." The yellow-eyed man spoke calmly as he regarded Yom. "Whose heart is as stained as her fingers."

"Yes, master," Misho said from behind her.

"What did you give her?" Yom raised her voice, already knowing the answer but trying to buy herself more time.

"Nothing," he said silkily, "just her favorite powder. One she's grown very fond of over the years. Who could you possibly be to her?" he asked, amusement twinkling in his eyes.

Yom looked around the crowd wildly, searching for any face that registered even a hint of what was happening here. She couldn't find Sassa's small black ball of fur; she must have been lost somewhere in the crowd in Yom's haste to cross it.

A small smile curled up the pale man's lips. "Don't worry, they're on such heavy powders, they'll barely remember any of this."

Where is Quia? His search for the Queen should lead him here, too. *Shouldn't he be here by now?* her mind raced.

"Your friend isn't coming," Misho answered as if reading her thoughts. "He's got a nice cozy spot underneath our feet."

Yom's last hope of someone else intervening withered and died. Even though she didn't trust a word out of Misho's mouth, something had to have happened to delay Quia from getting here.

"Why did you come back?" Misho hissed, only loud enough for her to hear.

"Now, where were we?" The yellow-eyed man cooed as he turned back to Lior's unconscious form. Yom scanned the area around the bed desperately, seeing toppled silver cups with wine spilling out, pouches and vials of all sorts of sunset-colored powders.

Another crack sounded. *"FIVE!"* the crowd bellowed gleefully.

Towards the opposite edge of the bed, Yom spotted a cluster of vials arranged with more purpose than the others, and they all had an identical purple-gray powder in them. Amaurosis. Yom turned away from the vials, refusing to entertain the idea of using it. She searched instead for weapons, testing the limits of Misho's grip.

Another crack. *"SIX!"*

There was nothing but endless supplies of wine and powder. The mood in the room was swelling with desire, the crowd becoming more rabid, thirsting for pleasure and pain without any care for the difference.

Another crack. *"SEVEN!"*

"How can you let this happen?" Yom turned to force Misho to meet her eyes.

Another crack. *"EIGHT!"*

"There's nothing I can do," he said stoically, though Yom could swear his eyes were tinged with anguish as he watched Lior.

The whipping ceased, and a new sound took its place. The almost inaudible sound of the leather strip being dropped onto the floor, and the delicate swish of cloth being unknotted. Yom's neck craned to watch in horror as the yellow-eyed man's cloth fell from his hips, and the shimmering she had seen before turned to a pulsing shine as his naked form climbed onto the bed. The crowd was cheering in a rage, practically foaming at the mouth.

"Give me something, help me, do anything!" Yom pleaded with Misho.

"You don't understand," he gritted, "I cannot disobey him."

"Then do something through inaction. If you help me now, the debt of the Ardennes will be repaid."

Misho widened his eyes just as his grip slackened a bit. Then, his voice reduced to the faintest whisper, "If he asks it of me, I will kill you."

The weight of a knife's handle was pushed into her palm. Yom dipped her chin before twisting out of Misho's grip and shoving him away.

The yellow-eyed man was already laying on top of Lior. There was something in the air, heady and insistent, that threatened to drag Yom down into a cloud of lust. But she could fight it; she had plenty of experience fighting her own mind. Adjusting her grip on the knife, she leapt onto the raised platform, landing the blade on the snow-white neck of the shimmering man, her knee touching Lior's cold skin.

"Get off her," Yom said coolly.

"This isn't the time for games, girl." The man batted at Yom with shocking strength and she flew off of the bed, crashing into the crowd. Hands immediately reached for her, grabbing onto anything of hers they could find. But the hands weren't fighting, it was as if they wanted her to join them.

Yom shoved them off, using the knife to break skin as needed to extract herself from their grip. Deciding to continue trying what she knew would take his attention away from Lior, she climbed back onto the raised platform and jumped, latching her arms and legs around the yellow-eyed man, holding the knife at his throat. She tried to press the blade into his skin, but it was as if it was made of stone, or diamond.

"What is this?" she huffed. The yellow-eyed man jerked his limbs with inhuman force, but Yom clung to him for dear life.

"Take your powders like a good little girl and join the rest of the court!" he snarled.

"I'm cutting back," Yom ground out. "Why are you doing this?" she asked more desperately, hoping to learn anything she could arm herself with.

The yellow-eyed man laughed, even as he continued wrestling within her hold. Her grip was slipping.

"This is my renewal. Just as the land renews itself each spring, so must I."

Yom was seconds from being wrenched off. So she angled herself and aimed to land forward.

"But what does that have to do with Li—the Queen?" As Yom bit out her question she lost her grip, falling forward to land between him and Lior. She oriented herself to face the yellow-eyed man and saw him from Lior's perspective. Every inch of skin was flawless, like a statue. It reminded her of Thoth.

"The Queen," he sneered at the title, "has a power inside her that can also be awoken with this ritual. By receiving me."

Just her favorite powder. One she's grown very fond of over the years.

Your master has had six years with nothing to show for it. What's changed now?

"You've been trying all this time," Yom thought out loud. "But you haven't accessed her numen."

The yellow-eyed man fumed. "That's enough—"

"Use me," Yom breathed. "I can help."

"How could a disgraced chemist help me?"

"You're trying to wake the numen of Tezcat," Yom improvised as she spoke, "I'm one of Tezcat's students. I've walked the Path of Night."

This name seemed to pierce some barrier; the yellow-eyed man sat back on his heels. "You're lying. Only a handful in Arcadia maintain the old ways."

"Yes, I know." The truth stared Yom in the face. "I was raised by one."

The yellow-eyed man seemed to mull this over. "If you seek the girl who left Inisfail, you will be disappointed. Any trace of her is gone."

In her marrow, Yom knew this was not true. Her own feelings had withstood years of guilt and shame, and she was not half as strong as Lior had been. "Why don't you let me try, and we can find out who's right?"

"I've shattered her. Reforged her into what the world needed." The yellow-eyed man pounced to shove his face an inch from hers. His yellow eyes were so bright up close that Yom almost got lost in them. Like she was in a field of daffodils. "You have one chance," he whispered.

Well aware, Yom thought bitterly. She could hear the vial of Sophia's plants already murmuring, and this time she had no trouble understanding them. *Use us*, they whispered. *We will show you the way.*

Without breaking eye contact with the yellow-eyed man, she reached inside her silks for the vial. The makeshift mixture tittered and buzzed with excitement. Yom turned her attention to Lior and rotated her so that she faced up. She lay like the dead, her mouth and eyes closed. As Yom brushed over her neck, a faint pulse beating. Rushing, she unsealed the vial and emptied the mixture into her palm. She had barely scratched the surface of Sophia's teaching, and that mysterious fox had guided her through much of it. Yom did not expect any such help this time. But if the key to harnessing numen was to feel, nothing made her feel more than being this close to Lior once again, after all this time. Though the beauty powders were thick, Yom could see the girl she knew underneath.

As Yom allowed the floodgates to crack open, the guilt and shame came easily. She searched for the light to balance out the dark. Lior's laugh, her antics around the laboratory, her braveness even in the face of death. *I'm sorry*, Yom repeated in a chant, as the feelings washed over her like water. The plants pulsed in her hand, and she could feel the access to their light. She blew the ash into Lior's face, using her other hand to keep her mouth parted. Under Yom's stained fingers, Lior's light fluttered with the beat and size of a butterfly, choked by dark tendrils of purple-black shadow. The two bright lights of the plant numen and Lior's numen reached out for each other. Tenuous strings between them bonded as the ash settled into Lior's skin. The two lights finally merged. The plant numen wrapped around Lior's numen and banished the tendrils of the shadowy intruder, mending and strengthening as it worked.

Yom let out a breath of relief. But it was short-lived, as this had only been a momentary distraction. Because she knew the girl these intruders had taken that night so many years ago as well as she knew herself. And that girl was no numenborn of Tezcat. Lior had steadfastly despised their time in Eden's laboratory, which Yom now recognized as Eden's introduction to the Path of Night. If she had no interest in that birthright, how could she contain the essence of its progenitor?

"Fascinating," the yellow-eyed man breathed, a new rabidity in his face. "We're so close, sister. Do you see how the Sorcerer's numen already attracts his students?" His voice seemed to have lost its artifice and crawled through the hall with inhuman volume. "Tell me, what is the name of this enchanter?"

Yom leaned to shield Lior's shallowly breathing form. "Yom."

"Brother, the ritual has been set in motion," the woman with ink black hair and similarly yellow eyes sauntered from behind him. "A coupling must occur before you lose control."

"Yom the enchanter." The yellow-eyed man licked his lips as if he tasted Yom's name while she spoke it.

The yellow-eyed woman stood next to the man, her hand resting intimately on his chest. Their angular faces were almost identical, and Yom finally saw it clearly.

The faces of the first Queen and her procurator, Lucretia and Tarquin.

One face that had been cracked in half and given to two bodies.

Their eyes were yellow as daffodils. *Some thought of them as twins, some as lovers. Some as both.* These were the gods of Sophia's story, the ones whose numen Tezcat had cruelly severed under the shade of the World Tree. The Lovers.

QUIA WOKE UP IN DARKNESS, CHAINED TO A DAMP STONE WALL. His wrist was enclosed in an iron shackle, nothing but a small seam of light a few feet away from him.

The seam grew and expanded until there was a flood of light from torches, and the doorway was filled with a glistening black form. "Good morning," a brusque voice cut from the silhouetted triarii.

Disorientation clogged Quia's senses. Morning? But then that would mean he missed the entire Lupercalia ceremony. It didn't feel like an entire night had passed. And there was no window to see outside.

"Found you right where he said we would. I'm sure he'll come to see you himself soon, but for now I'm keeping you company." The triarii came closer until he wound back a fist to land square in Quia's gut. He doubled over, the air knocked out of him.

"He?" Quia coughed.

The figure nodded. "He's quite anxious to meet you."

"Tell him to get in line," Quia spat. "I have business to take care of first." It was a calculated risk, hoping that this triarii would take the bait. The triarii seemed to hesitate a moment before taking a swing directly at Quia's cheek. Just as Quia had hoped, the impact forced his teeth to cut into his tongue.

Quia laughed, blood lining lips. "You shouldn't have done that." Then, he began chanting. Even if he could only draw a fraction of his power, it would be enough to take out this triarii.

"What are you doing?" The triarii sounded on edge. "Cut it out!" He shook Quia and tried covering his mouth to muffle the words, but nothing he did mattered. The ability to speak the words out loud was irrelevant, it was just the way that Quia focused his mind. Power accumulated in his limbs and his senses heightened. As soon as he had enough to get one good blow to the triarii, he sucked in a deep breath and blew out as strong a gust of wind as he could muster. The triarii hit the stone wall with a crack, his head unprotected. His body slumped on the ground.

Quia's shoulders relaxed and he twisted around to address the chains. Now with less distractions, he could shape the wind more deliberately. The most precise bursts came from his hands, but he hadn't accumulated that much power yet. And he couldn't wait, lest another triarii join them. *You're going home*, he told himself. *You're going home. This is not where this ends.*

Holding up his first two fingers like a weapon, Quia formed the shape of the wind, sharp as any blade. He brought his two fingers down in a slice through the air, a ripple of wind emanating from its wake. The first half of a chain link cracked, but it didn't cut all the way through. A faint rhythm sounded from outside the door, like something scraping along a stone wall. *You're going home,* Quia repeated. He balanced a foot against the stone wall for leverage and used it to push himself away, pulling the chain with all his strength. He resituated himself and held wind between his fingers like a whip. With a prayer to anyone listening, he tried one more slice. The chain link snapped in half, and he fell back onto the stone floor with a harsh thud.

Quia groaned and rubbed at his aching limbs and sore wrist. The shackle still closed around it, but the chain hung from it limply. He stumbled towards the door before hesitating. *Yom would be smart about this*, he thought.

Turning back to the unconscious triarii, Quia yanked the panels of his armor off. The armor was a strange texture, so cold it felt wet but when his fingers remained dry. The triarii was almost the same build as Quia. He thanked the stars as he locked the panels of armor around himself until he was covered in the black shell. The armor seemed to breathe as it settled over Quia's skin, giving him chills. It was unsettling, looking like the very thing that had pursued him all the way from Inisfail, across Arcadia.

Quia left his hands ungloved and crossed the threshold into a narrow hallway that slanted up. The scratching noise he had heard thankfully came from further down the tunnel, perhaps a sentry patrolling. He walked up the incline, hugging the wall, trying to stay in the shadows of the torches that lined it. The passageway turned in a shallow spiral up, and Quia followed it, seeing similar doors to the one he had left along the way. The armor was eerily noiseless as he moved, allowing him to make quick work of reaching the top. The door he approached was larger and had a brighter seam of light beneath it.

The seam grew as the door was opened from the outside. Quia stepped back into the shadows, hoping the stolen armor would blend into the darkness.

It appeared to be someone in plainclothes, from the outline Quia could see against the bright light of whatever lay beyond this dungeon. He allowed a single exhale of relief before straightening his spine and continuing to walk.

"Where are you going in such a rush?" the figure asked casually.

Quia responded with a grunt as he moved closer to the door, hoping to pass as a stoically silent soldier.

The figure stepped forward. "I asked you a question, Quia."

The shock of hearing his name from this stranger caused Quia to take a step back.

"Who are you?" Quia searched for anything he recognized in this stranger, but it was impossible in the relative darkness. If only Quia could get to the other side of the door—

"Let me illuminate it for you," the figure said as he hoisted one of the small torches off the wall and held it next to his face.

In the firelight, Quia saw the vague outlines of scars he knew to belong to the triarii that had followed them across Arcadia, the one he had first seen through the narrow slits in the crate they had hidden behind in Inisfail. But something else emerged now that he was seeing this triarii without his hood: a broadset nose and high cheekbones, wide eyes so dark they appeared black, and large lips. Lips that Quia normally saw set with a wide grin, laughing about some inane prank. The voice that came from these lips suddenly became familiar as well, if Quia imagined it to be higher pitched, just on the cusp of dropping in adulthood. His skin was lighter than the boy Quia thought of, the boy who used to glow black against the golden hills, a film of sweat making him shine in the sun. That boy was his own sun, radiating light on the few fortunate enough to be allowed past his prickly shell.

"I don't have all night," the stranger growled.

With each word, Quia could see the twisted evolution of that boy in front of him. The boy who had followed Quia to the other side of the world. The boy who had been so close, they had called each other brothers.

"No—it's impossible—" Quia, normally in complete control of his words, stuttered.

"I've been through enough to know that *everything* is possible, brother."

Yom. Andromeda heard a strange name rattling through her as the world returned. *Yom, Yom, Yom.* It had a familiarity—a warmth—attached to it.

"Yom?" She spoke it out loud. The name on her lips rang out clearer than anything she had heard in a long time. The figure in front of her turned. A girl with green eyes, olive skin, and chestnut hair curling with sweat around her brow. "Who are you?" Andromeda asked the girl. Again the words felt too clear, too solid. The materials beneath her suddenly caught her attention, the distant sound of running water, the silence, the noise. Andromeda ran her hands over her skin and silks, feeling every fiber, every hair. A tidal wave of panic rose in her.

"What—what have you done?"

"Nothing," the girl said dumbly as she watched Andromeda, "I just reversed the effects of the powders you were on, brought you back to equilibrium."

Andromeda flexed her fingers into the soft surface beneath her. Anger rippled through her.

"Bring it back," Andromeda commanded.

"Lior, do you remember me?" the strange girl half whispered.

Yom, Andromeda thought.

"Do you remember Eden?" The girl's eyes were pleading.

Andromeda looked at her as a stranger. She saw a momentary flash of a young girl who spent too much time reading by firelight.

"Of course I don't recognize you," she said coldly. She looked around to find anything familiar. Hector and her lady-in-waiting stood so close that their shoulders touched. Why were they standing so close? And had she ever noticed the similarities between their features before?

"Hector? Who is this?" Andromeda called out.

"You need to begin, or it will be out of our hands." Leah turned to Hector. The lady's voice was strange.

"What are you talking about?" Andromeda called out again. "Remove this person," she waved a hand at the strange girl with green eyes. "I want her out."

Hector walked towards them, but his eyes were utterly detached. And they were bright yellow. Like no color Andromeda had ever seen.

The girl turned back to her with frantic eyes. "Lior, you can't trust them, they're the ones who—who took you." The girl placed a hand on her shoulder as she spoke to Andromeda, and the Queen felt electricity in her touch. But it was the use of that false name that unleashed a flash of anger. Her name was Andromeda.

"Answer me!" Andromeda raised her voice, still waiting for Hector to acknowledge her, shaking the stranger's hand off her shoulder.

"No—" the stranger turned to Hector, "You said that I could do it, that you wouldn't need to continue what you were doing—"

"I never said that." Hector smiled but it did not contain any warmth. He looked at Andromeda, but not in the way you look at someone you're listening to. He looked at her as if she was an animal he was observing. "But I believe you were right about one thing. This will be much more effective now that she is fully lucid for it."

The stranger turned back to Andromeda. "Lior—"

"*STOP CALLING ME THAT!*" Andromeda shrieked and turned the full force of her rage on this girl whose name she vaguely recalled as Yom. "Do you have any idea who you're speaking to? Your Queen?"

"I do know you." Yom swallowed, watching Andromeda as if she held the full weight of this girl's heart in her hands. Andromeda wanted to erase that look; it was unsettling to see in a stranger's eyes. A familiar stranger, albeit.

"You are Lior, daughter of Eden—"

"Enough!" Andromeda closed her eyes, shut out the longing in Yom's eyes.

"Lior, daughter of Eden, of Inisfail."

The mention of Inisfail was the last straw. What could the Queen of Arcadia, born and raised in luxury in the House of Flowing Waters, have anything to do with the distant, dirty province of Inisfail?

"*ENOUGH!*" Andromeda squeezed her eyes tighter and covered her ears, but Yom continued, her voice desperate.

"Lior, daughter of Eden, fierce, loyal, brave—" The red apron swayed behind Andromeda's eyelids, taunting her.

Finally, the Queen could hear no more. She cut Yom off by lunging at her. Yom's eyes bulged as Andromeda wrapped her fingers around her neck and squeezed. Fear bled into Yom eyes, but also hurt. Andromeda squeezed harder, feeling the rush of blood and air being crushed under her hands.

"You—" Andromeda huffed as she spoke, "are—" pulsing her grip with each word, "mistaken."

All Andromeda heard was a gasp from this stranger as Yom refused to fight back, her eyelids slowly drifting closed.

XVIII

Illusions

Misho watched Quia shake his head, refusing to allow the recognition to take hold. "My brother is gone."

"Gone? I was abandoned." Misho spat. "By you."

Quia stepped back. "Mixcoat?"

The name had not been spoken in years. "Took you long enough."

"I tried to look for you, but it was dangerous, the triarii killed—"

"I know what the triarii did," Misho snarled. "The only reason I wasn't killed as well was because they needed to interrogate one of us, and I was the smallest. I looked the weakest."

"How could you become one?"

"I ran out of time to wait for you to save me. I had to save myself."

"You've lost yourself." Quia looked at him with repulsion.

"No, I was lost." Misho's lip twitched with the effort to keep his face emotionless.

"It's not too late, you can still help me get the numenborn, and we can both go home."

Misho smiled up at the ceiling in disbelief. "After all this time, that's still all you care about."

"I'm doing this for the—"

"The sake of the world. I've heard that before." Misho drew his crossbow, the one weapon he had kept after leaving behind the tattered armor. "I made a deal to get myself out. The tiniest part of me thought that maybe you were stuck in your own cage somewhere, and that's why you never came to help me. I thought if I got out into the provinces, I would find you myself. But then, I come to find out that you've not been in a cage at all. You were living the cushioned life of a Royal Archives apprentice, blending into this land as if you were born here." He threw the crossbow away, sent it rattling down the slope of the endless black hall. If this was the moment for Misho to face everything that had happened, he would not hide behind weapons.

"I had a plan, I never forgot about you—"

"The world has always been so important to you, you've forgotten that it's nothing more than the sum of people in it. Am I not the world? Is the world not me, as well?" Despite Misho's best efforts, he couldn't keep the bitterness, the hurt from leaking into his words.

"One person cannot be my whole world. I always thought you understood, I've had no choice. You know where my duties lie."

"I understand perfectly. And I expect that you understand that I cannot allow you to finish what you've started." Misho lunged at his poet.

The world had faded completely before Yom became aware that air was once again allowed to enter her body. She was on the ground on all fours, heaving for it.

Lior was being hauled away from her by two triarii. "What are you doing? Get off me!" The Queen flailed in their grip.

Sassa's wet nose touched Yom's face as she sniffed all over her, the fox sitting right in front of her. Yom reached out for her in relief.

"I'll continue with her awake." The yellow-eyed god still stood on the raised platform. "Make sure the chemist does not interfere again," he said, sounding almost bored as he nudged his chin out at a small company of triarii near him. The triarii turned their attention to Yom like dogs following their master's orders. She struggled to her feet, still short on breath, with Sassa scooped up in one arm. Lior wouldn't even look at her as she was arranged back on the platform, restrained on either side by triarii.

"What is happening, Hector?" Lior demanded. The yellow-eyed god did not bother to answer her, merely climbing back onto the platform with her. "What are you doing?" Lior asked more shrilly. Yom's neck ached from Lior's hands, but her heart was far more damaged by the violent rejection. And now, between Yom and what was happening to Lior on that platform, a wall of triarii were closing in.

Yom pushed Sassa up onto her shoulder, scanning the room desperately for a tool or weapon. There was only the crowd behind her and the powder stockpile in front of her. She needed more time; her mind was reeling and her body was still trying to recover air. Even if by some miracle she was able to latch onto some piece of Cernunnos's strength, her own was so depleted it wouldn't be enough to face the triarii and their impenetrable armor. She mumbled a hoarse curse before grabbing the vials of Amaurosis and stumbling backwards, narrowly escaping the reach of the triarii before being swallowed up by the fray of the powder-dosed court.

The crowd swayed like its own turbid ocean as Yom rushed through it. Everyone seemed to have crowded in further, all on the verge of their own coupling or fighting. Clothes were being torn off and body parts grabbed every which way. Every couple she saw reminded her that Lior was on that platform, helpless. But a glance backwards showed flashes of triarii armor between the madness of the crowd, still chasing her. Yom barreled forward, allowing her thoughts to coalesce. It all made sense now that she knew it was gods she was dealing with, not just political animals currying favor with the titans. But whatever this was, these gods seemed a far cry from the Lovers of Sophia's story. *They presided over sexuality and fertility, but they indulged art, poetry, dance, any act of creation. Anything that fed the soul.* It was like their domain had been twisted and distorted, until it was practically unrecognizable as an act of love or desire. Nothing but an exercise of power.

Yom's thoughts were interrupted as she was jostled by a courtier taking a swing at a middle-aged, squat looking lord right next to her. The two were on the verge of a full on brawl, and no one around them seemed to oppose it. The crowd might be able to do her work for her. She twisted and shoved two courtiers into the path of the triarii. They all knocked into each other like marbles. The triarii tried to shove them out of their way, but each new person who was knocked by the scuffle immediately turned their attention to it.

Yom spotted a tall blond head further into the crowd. As the triarii were distracted trying to fend off more and more of the court, she raced towards it. Lucan's head was dipping up and down, and when she finally reached it, she realized why.

Lucan was tangled with a mess of freckled limbs and a swath of bright red hair. Yom's stomach dropped as she realized who he had managed to pick out in this crowd, coincidence or not. Lucan and Rye were attacking each other like feral animals, their hands running through each other's hair and down their necks and arms, their tongues mashing together. Yom was minutely relieved to see that Rye had survived the arena, but this was swallowed with sobering memories of the Eel's penchant for murder. Despite everything Lucan had done, he didn't deserve to *die*.

The plan formed without much time for doubt. Yom reached into her pocket and pulled out two of the Amaurosis vials. She gently shook Lucan's and Rye's shoulders and they paused their mauling of each other. As they both turned to her, Lucan being the first to reach his hands out as if to bring her into their thrall—clearly in a deep powderhole—Yom slipped the top off each vial and emptied them into her palms. *If they can do this to people like Moss, it can be done to them.* Letting the vials fall to the stone floor, she held both palms up to her mouth and blew a cloud of Amaurosis ash into each of their faces.

The effect was instantaneous. Their pupils widened, and they both stilled. She reached out and ran a blue-stained finger from their forehead, down their noses, over their lips, just as Misho had done to Moss. They both looked at Yom as if she was the source of the air they breathed and the water they drank. Yom's skin crawled but she pushed away the feeling.

"Defend me," she commanded, just as two triarii broke through the crowd into their clearing. Lucan and Rye turned their attention to the triarii and walked forward with limber grace. Yom knew she had made the right choice in champions as she watched them take on the triarii with ease, their natural fighting skill bolstered by the Amaurosis. It was awe-inspiring and frightening all at once, seeing two fiercely independent and skilled warriors brought under her yoke with nothing more than a handful of powder.

Yom remained shielded long enough to look up at the raised platform. She couldn't hear what was happening, but the female god held down Lior as the male god loomed over her. As soon as it had become clear that it was a bed in the center of the room, Yom had feared this was what it was for. And she was powerless to stop it. Any illusion of power she had gained on the road from

Inisfail—Cernunnos's tether, Sophia's teachings—was just that. An illusion. In the one moment she needed it, it would never be enough.

Without warning, Sassa leapt from Yom's shoulder and bolted towards the edge of the room. Yom lost sight of the fox. And she didn't begrudge Sassa a single inch. Yom had failed. Lior wanted nothing to do with her, and even so, Yom could do nothing to save her. Rye and Lucan would only be able to hold off the triarii for so long. Her puppet defenders would crumple, and Yom would have to face a host of triarii and two gods on her own. Quia wasn't coming.

Yom stumbled back and considered her options. She could run, escape the House of Flowing Waters, go into hiding somewhere and continue on with her life. She could stay and fight to her last breath, probably making it no further than the wall of triarii. It would be a fitting end, giving herself over to the warriors who had chased her all the way across the continent. She supposed running would be a fitting end as well. That was how this had all started, wasn't it? If Yom had been braver, perhaps she would have stopped Lior from throwing herself in the path of the intruders to begin with, that night so impossibly long ago.

Flashbacks to the Amaurosis vision, the last time Yom had been forced to revisit that night, pelted her. *Imagine what you could do if you made your numen connection*, Quia had urged. *You wanted to understand the power that awaits you.*

Go back inside, the Amaurosis fox had commanded her. Everything always led back to that night. Her hand fiddled with the third and final vial of Amaurosis in her pocket. She supposed there was little to lose, now that she was already waist deep in a mire of failure. She could run straight towards it. Perhaps sacrificing herself on the altar of that memory was the most honorable path she could take.

Yom held the vial of purple ash in her hand. *It's just another powder*, she told herself. *It can't hurt you.* The Amaurosis's scratching seemed to increase in response to this, as if contesting it. *I can hurt you*, it whispered. *Or I can help you.* Yom dug her nails into her skin, not sure if she was losing it.

Rye's battle cry erupted, and Yom looked up to see her in a deadlock with a triarii, with two others trying to break through.

You will find that which you seek, the Amaurosis whispered.

But a sibilance was growing from somewhere else, somewhere behind Yom. She pulled her pack off in a rush, and the sound became clearer. Unlatching it, the hissing became clearer still. And when Yom's hand found the jar of Moonflower she had taken from Sophia, the sound transformed into a message.

Only in darkness is the moon able to shine, it murmured, over and over in a refrain.

At that moment, one of the triarii broke through Rye and Lucan's hold. Yom was out of time. She opened the jar and ripped off a handful of the Moonflower's leaves, just as she had in the forest. She crushed them in her palm and put them under her tongue, instantly feeling the warm colors released with their juices. She uncorked the Amaurosis vial, spreading the ash over her eyelids and pouring the rest into her palm. Instead of holding it directly up to her nose, she threw the fistful into the air and allowed it to shower down over her face, as Quia had done in the forest.

May it give me sight, Yom thought desperately, hoping to recreate Quia's ritual as best she could. Just as the edges of her vision were fading, a great growl pierced the din and Sassa's massive wolf form bounded from deep outside the crowd, shoving the soaked lords and courtiers aside like they were rag dolls. The wolf grabbed the triarii closing in on Yom in its great jaws and flung him halfway across the crowd. The last thing Yom saw before everything went dark was Sassa's shining furred body wrapping around her in a protective coil.

MISHO GOT IN SEVERAL GOOD HITS BEFORE QUIA COULD GET HIS bearings. He had the advantage now, with Quia still reeling from the revelation, but it would not last long. He was under no delusions that just because Quia had been hiding in the Archives he wasn't still as fierce a fighter. They had always taken their similarly matched fighting skills as a sign that they were meant to find each other, meant to train together. But now it seemed cruel. When they were actually turned against each other in a fight, they threatened to destroy each other.

Misho's other advantage was that he had spent a year in the darkness here. He was acquainted with the stale air, the damp stone, the incessant trickle of water. While Quia struggled to fight in the unfamiliar and disorienting terrain, Misho attacked the weak points in the oversized triarii armor Quia had donned. His jabs were swift and precise, controlled hits to weaken Quia slowly. As they tangled, he drew the hidden weapons out of the armor and threw them out of reach, to the same sunken depths as the crossbow. The suit was a trove of hidden compartments stocked with knives, bundles of rope, slender clubs. He had to be extremely careful not to allow Quia to draw blood, or this fight would go from evenly matched to a wipeout. Although, it had given him some satisfaction to see in Traiana that despite Quia entering trance, he didn't have nearly the same power that he had left Panchaia with.

"It's not too late, brother," Quia pleaded as he dodged and rolled to avoid another hit. He was trying to avoid fighting Misho, and it enraged the triarii. "You can still come home with us."

"Us?" Misho laughed. "And if the numenborn doesn't want to go with you? Will you take her by force?"

"She will see reason. The Queen might have apparent power here, but she will not fully realize her potential until she comes to Panchaia."

"Are we talking about the Queen? Or your little chemist?"

Quia's eyes widened and he shoved Misho off more forcefully. "Stay away from her," he said through heavy breaths.

"Sensitive," Misho teased. Of course he had no interest in the chemist. He had no interest in any woman, but if Quia was too thick to understand that after all this time, he did not want to explain it to him now.

"I think she and I will be great friends after all this. We had a rather... illuminating chat in the forest."

Quia's face screwed up in confusion. "She said you attacked her."

Misho weighed his hands in front of him. "Attacked, talked, bonded, I don't know." He forced his grin to turn wolfish, just to taunt Quia. Misho wanted a real fight; he wanted pain. "A lot happened in the woods between us, it's hard to remember."

Quia swung at him wildly. Misho dodged it and Quia's force collided with the hard stone wall.

Misho clicked his tongue. "A fight happens just as much in the mind as in the body, right, brother?" He quoted one of Quia's own instructors. "Careful, or I'll start to think you care about this chemist more than your precious numenborn."

"I wish you cared about something more than your own skin," Quia huffed back, shaking out his hand.

Misho hardened into something furious and bitter at the insinuation that saving his own life was a selfish act. It was time to end this fight; he had given Quia long enough to think he still had a chance of winning.

"You shouldn't wear triarii armor," he muttered the words with measured calm as he changed his attack to begin ripping off the panels of armor at their release points. "It doesn't suit you."

Once again Quia went on the defensive, trying to hold onto the armor and land decisive jabs at Misho's own weak points. But what Quia failed to realize was that Misho had done away with his own weakness. His mind had been immunized against physical pain, after the torture he received in this very dungeon. While Quia's mind was mired with pain, Misho's was clear. Sometimes pain was all he felt, and he reveled in it.

Misho made quick work of the armor, until Quia was reduced to nothing but the shirt and trousers he had entered the city with. Quia's swings became more desperate, like an animal backed into a corner. Weakened by every precise hit, it was easy for Misho to pull Quia's head into a tight grip and squeeze away his connection to consciousness. Quia struggled and tried to yank himself out of Misho's grasp, taking wild swings at his groin and his shins. But he held onto Quia with monastic calm. Slowly, Quia's own movements dulled until he hung limp in Misho's arms.

Misho wasted little time retrieving the shackles from the triarii armor Quia had taken, clasping them around his wrists and ankles. Once Quia was restrained again, and still unconscious, Misho allowed himself one moment to look at him.

Quia was even more beautiful than Misho remembered. His boyish features had sharpened into those of a young man who felt no need to prove himself, who was confident in his own beauty. His skin was lighter than Misho remembered, no doubt because of his time under the overcast skies in Inisfail. It had faded from a deep russet to a lighter copper. His hair was just as thick, though he had cut it. When they left Panchaia it had reached down his back, but now it hovered at his shoulders.

Misho permitted a single act of tenderness, smoothing the hair ruffled by their fight over Quia's forehead and out of his eyes, before he hoisted him over his shoulder and carried him from the dark dungeon of the House of Flowing

Waters into the light above. It was time Quia and his chemist saw each other for who they truly were.

THE COBBLESTONES WERE THE FIRST THING YOM PERCEIVED. *You wanted to understand the power that awaits you. Go back inside.* The fox's voice echoed again in the air as if it had just spoken, as if Yom had never left this realm. The street came into focus, the bare storefronts of the artisan district glowing in the moonlight. Everything was as she had left it, but something glowed in her. Some warmth. It must have been the Moonflower. Still, she could hear its whisper. *Only in darkness is the moon able to shine.*

The lacquered door of the laboratory appeared blood red. Yom waited outside it, hearing the splintering and the crack she knew all too well.

She took a step back.

If you leave, you will not be given another chance. The fox's voice sounded closer now, and Yom felt its furred body prowling over her feet. Even in this realm of nightmarish dreams, she remembered what awaited her beyond it. Triarii warriors, a court rabid with powder, and two vengeful gods. *Only in darkness is the moon able to shine,* the Moonflower's words repeated over and over, an incantation, warming her from the inside. She steeled herself and opened the laboratory door, the gold paint of the sign flashing as it moved.

At the foot of the stairs, a younger version of herself in thin nightclothes crouched at the entrance of the laboratory.

"Go back upstairs!" she hissed at herself, trying to pull the girl away from the laboratory, but her touch turned to smoke. Yom would not be able to alter the course of this night, even in a dream. Her curse was to watch.

"Who are you?" Eden's voice sounded brave, but Yom could hear the tremor it masked. Yom stood in the door of the laboratory, watching the scene with a clear vantage this time.

Eden backed up towards the workbench, groping for something behind herself. Her hand found a stone pestle and clutched it behind her back.

The edge of the two cloaks came into view, and Yom took her first steps inside the laboratory. Lior crouched behind a table, and Yom took up a stance just in front of her, futilely trying to block her from view of the intruders.

"You don't recognize us?" One of the cloaked voices spoke, and from this position, Yom could see its yellow eyes glowing in the dark. Even in a memory, the voice made her flinch and raised pebbles on her skin.

The two cloaks inched towards Eden.

"Run!" Yom yelled at her, even though she knew no one would hear her.

"What do you want?" Eden's face was guarded.

"We heard you have a very special girl." The second cloaked voice spoke, the woman who Yom had recognized in the garden. Her voice had the same chilling effect on Yom, and her yellow eyes glowed equally brightly.

"There's no one else here," Eden said evenly. Yom held her hands over her ears, trying to block out their words.

"We know she's here," the male snarled. "The one gifted with the numen of Tezcat. The one whom the plants already whisper their secrets to." Yom collapsed into a ball on the floor as the words that she had buried beneath powder and bodies floated to the surface.

"Did you think you could hide your little prodigy from the world? A great destiny awaits her. She will not stay shut in here with you, playing with a child's chemical arts," the male said with cool authority.

It was at this moment Lior blazed through Yom like she was a ghost. Yom shot after her, trying to stop her, but it was too late. The cloaked gods had seen Lior, and the precocious, courageous girl took up a stance next to her mother.

Eden cursed and pushed Lior to stand behind her.

"Is it you, little cub?" The yellow-eyed male's voice turned sticky sweet as he addressed Lior. But Lior was not the one they had come for. Lior did not stay in the laboratory long past Eden's chemist lessons, tinkering with what they learned each day until she mastered it. She did not seek out Eden's extensive library of books on the chemical arts during her free time, soaking in the stories of the secrets and magic contained within the natural world. She did not sometimes get carried away when she thought no one watched, hearing the plants whisper to her. Lior was not the one who, on these occasions, attempted to whisper back.

"Tell them it's me!" Yom cried. "They're looking for me!" But no one changed their course.

"You can't take her," Eden said.

"It was supposed to be me!" Tears streamed down Yom's cheeks as she threw herself between the two cloaked gods and Eden.

"We can do whatever we want." The god crossed the room impossibly fast and passed through Yom again like she was nothing more than a mirage. Crimson blood dripped from the knife onto the floor in sickening plops.

It was supposed to be me, Yom repeated over and over. It made no difference. The yellow-eyed goddess blow a cloud of purple powder into Lior's face. The goddess hoisted Lior's limp body over her shoulder and walked out the door, leaving Eden's cooling form on the floor.

It could have been seconds, or hours, that passed as Yom stood there among the ruins. A crushing pressure bloomed in her chest. A static ring of noise clouded her mind. Her thoughts were potent, dangerous things, the weapon and its wielder. *My fault my fault my fault. They were looking for me.* It had been too much for any child to endure, and it was still too much for Yom, weak as she was. She had buried it. Lashed out at the world with a sharp, white hot anger. Nothing could take credit for destroying her if she destroyed herself first.

Things that are found during the Trials cannot be lost again easily, Quia had warned. But this was not all Quia had shared with her. He had shared his own pain, and sadness, and shame, and Yom had seen it without the harsh criticism she had always turned on herself. *That has to mean something*, she insisted. The Moonflower's warmth magnified in response. Enveloped her.

Yom walked out of the laboratory to see the little girl with unruly curls and eyes as green as the emerald hills of her home curled in a ball, rocking herself on the floor. Yom reached out a hand to the girl, and this time she met solid skin. The girl startled and looked up at her. Yom saw a child, someone young and scared. Someone who shouldn't have been put in this position in the first place.

"It's me." The girl's green eyes widened at Yom. "They were looking for me."

"Yes," Yom told her, voice cracking. "They were."

"I'm scared." Tears streaked the girl's cheeks as she wrapped her arms around Yom's middle, clinging to her.

"I know," Yom breathed out, her own tears threatening to spill again. "You're only a child." She stroked the girl's curls, trying to soothe her.

"I'm sorry," the girl sobbed softly into Yom. "I'm sorry," she repeated over and over.

Only in darkness is the moon able to shine, the Moonflower whispered its refrain. *Only in our darkest moments, can we see how brightly we glow*, Yom realized it was trying to say.

"It's okay." Yom felt the gates open and tears stream down her own cheeks. "It's not your fault, it was an impossible choice for a child." She held her as tight as she could. "I forgive you." *I forgive you*, Yom repeated, more forcefully, no longer sure if she spoke out loud or in her mind. *I FORGIVE YOU*, she screamed with abandon and a mad, teary laughter.

The realm shifted before her eyes in the revelatory light of this embrace. The little girl in Yom's arms seemed to melt back into her, to rejoin with her own spirit. Pieces cleaving together into some mottled, wholly new thing inside her. Jagged edges mending.

She was once again alone with the fox, blanketed in a breathtakingly clear night.

Except the fox was splitting and shifting, unfurling with purple smoke into another figure. The figure before her glowed with the light of the morningstar, the bringer of dawn, the illusion of a boundary between day and night. His purple cloak shimmered in the starlight and black marks lined his chin. Tezcat. The Sorcerer.

"The world has been waiting long enough," Tezcat said stonily. In an instant, he was an inch from her, his dark gold skin inhumanly perfect. "Do not run from who you are again."

Before Yom could respond, Tezcat clapped two black-tipped hands together in front of her face, and she was jolted out of the dream realm, back to the cocoon of Sassa's fur.

Every inch of her skin felt different, like it was flooded with something heady. I *am the numenborn*, Yom whispered to herself. All the friends she had collected over the journey joined in, a thunderous chorus that lifted Yom up.

The Bind is a double-sided coin, Dougal murmured.

Your mind has power, you have power, Clementine whispered.

Tezcat's power lies in his cleverness. He is the eternal trickster. Master illusionist. Freer of slaves. Bringer of change, Sophia said.

Sensing her return, Sassa uncurled herself from around Yom. Her gaze focused on the Great Hall again. Twenty or so triarii were closing in on them in a circle, with the raised platform just outside of their glistening black ring.

"Antlers up." Yom smiled, ready to show them who she was.

QUIA'S EYES DRIFTED OPEN TO SEE A LOFTY STONE HALLWAY SWAYING upside down. This had to be an illusion. The last place he remembered was underground. As his mind returned to his body, he realized he was hanging over something hard. Legs and feet stepped steadily below him, and he remembered to whom they belonged. He tried to adjust his hands, but they were bound tightly with metal shackles. A light jerk of his feet revealed the same.

"Welcome back," Mixcoat said gruffly. "Hope you don't mind, didn't want you to hurt yourself by fighting any more." Quia tried to move and squirm himself off Mixcoat's shoulder, but an iron arm banded his body. Delicate streams of water ran down the walls, and flowers and flags of royal blue lined the hall.

"Where are you taking me?" he asked cautiously.

"Is it not obvious? I remember you being quite sharp back in the day."

Faraway, a crowd chattered. Through an opening at the end of the hallway, the sky was the deep blue of dusk. Relief shimmered in front of him as he realized it was still the night of Lupercalia. Despite being captured and bound, he could still figure out a way to find the Queen.

They were walking towards the chatter, and they passed through several hallways before Mixcoat paused. A curtain of water parted to let them pass, then closed behind them.

The chatter turned into a loud cacophony as the edges of the room swayed in Quia's vision. They were in a large feasting hall, full of people dressed in the finest clothes. But a wildness crackled through them, all on the verge of fighting or rutting into each other. Their eyes were vacant and their faces had evident tracks of powder on them.

Mixcoat was shoving through them as if they were a herd of animals. Quia was still trying to get his bearings in the room when he was released from Mixcoat's shoulder and fell onto hard ground. He struggled to right himself with hands and feet bound. He had been set down at the foot of a raised platform.

"And who is this?" A silky voice slithered towards them. A figure, skin pale and completely bare of clothes, with white hair and yellow eyes, laid on a bed at the top of a platform. A woman with similarly pale skin and yellow eyes, though with hair a soulless black, approached him. She was a female analogue to the first figure. Quia stiffened and tried to scuttle backwards, away from this creature, but he ran right into Mixcoat's legs.

"A Panchaian. And someone the chemist cares about." Mixcoat did not give anything away when he spoke.

"Yes, I can feel it," the woman spoke as she inhaled deeply, treacherous as a snake and beautiful as a butterfly. Her eyes beat down on Quia like wings.

"Can you be quick, brother?" the woman called behind her. This brother had returned his attention to something that lay beneath him on the raised platform. And he was not alone on the bed. Quia could see the edges of dark hair, limbs wrapped in elegant silks, and scores of gold chains.

"You know this mustn't be rushed, sister," the creature grunted as he continued his movement.

Suddenly Quia understood who he was laid out in front of like an offering. He understood what this mysterious ceremony of Lupercalia was as well. They had not been heard from in centuries, their temples in Panchaia had gone into disrepair with neglect. Two halves of the same whole. The Lovers. Xopilli and Xochi, their names in Panchaia.

Of course the Lovers still needed their ritual; it was as old as they were. The act of coupling on the day of their greatest power—the day whose two halves were perfect equals—sustained them for the entire year ahead. The moment when every creature shared the same need to procreate. But the other half of this ritual stood in front of him, not in the bed with her twin.

Quia looked up at Mixcoat. "Who is that up there? This rite is to be performed between the gods."

"My brother gifts his body to another this year," Xochi cut in. "The transfer of his essence into the numenborn, on this the night of our greatest power, will reveal her own numen."

Quia blanched. "Or it will kill her," he growled. He struggled in his shackles to crawl closer to her, to begin summiting the steps leading to the bed.

"Please, stop," he begged Xopilli, whose movements had become even more aggressive. "She won't survive this, no human would—"

Finally nearing the Queen's arm that hung limply off the bed, he looked around wildly, searching for anything sharp he could draw blood with. Then, something green flashed from the corner of his eye.

ALL OF YOM'S SENSES WERE HEIGHTENED. She could hear every drop of water cascading down the walls, see every delicate fiber of the expensive silks and wools that clothed the room, smell every individual powder that left its mark in the air. But more than that, she could feel the light at the center of every being in the hall. It was their numen, and in it, truths clearly written. The emotions, fears, and longings of a being shone through their light. And it was so easily manipulated. How simply an illusion could be suggested to this vulnerable, flickering light.

Yom searched over the heads of the triarii for a glimpse of the raised platform and Lior, seeking out her numen. When she found it, Lior's numen was dim, like the faintest heartbeat. There were tendrils of another light choking it. The other numen felt different, a twisted and intoxicating light. It was the yellow-eyed god. He had paused, caught between watching Lior beneath him and what was happening within the circle of the triarii. From the state of Lior's light, Yom knew she was too late to prevent the god from touching her. But there was always some part of oneself that could be saved, and she hoped to do it before the yellow-eyed god consumed Lior completely.

First, there was the small matter of the wall of Arcadia's fiercest warriors standing in between them. But they had the same light as the rest of the room. The excess powders shimmered in the air. She could call to the essence of their being, draw them towards her, dull the sharpness of the triarii's light. *Eternal trickster. Master illusionist. Freer of slaves, bringer of change.* Yom repeated these words over and over to herself as she beckoned the powder swirling throughout the room to cloud around the triarii, pushing them into a euphoric haze, pulling them closer to the center of the circle where she stood with Sassa.

"You might want to shift back," Yom said to Sassa and received a growl of acknowledgement. The circle of triarii began to close in, but their eyes were hazy with powder. Sassa curled back into her fox form and leapt up Yom's body to perch again on her shoulder. The glistening black triarii arms reached out to grab at Yom, but just before they found her, she bounded over their heads, agile as a fox herself, with Sassa following suit. The triarii collapsed in on themselves and—as Yom had intended—did not perceive it was their fellow triarii they attacked across the closing aperture of the circle.

Yom landed, more graceful than she had ever felt in her life, with Sassa at her feet. The torc bounced against her collarbone, and she felt a ripple of the tether to Cernunnos, starkly clear now. She held her breath as she reached out for the string in her mind that led her to the twilight grove. Cernunnos sat in the same spot, limned in shadow, his antlers the size of small trees. The titan's lip curled in a snarl when their eyes met, but Yom merely winked at him before returning to the House of Flowing Waters, holding in one hand the power of

Tezcat, and in the other the might of Cernunnos. Strength accumulated in her limbs, and her mind. She sensed how easy it was to bend the firelight flickering around the room into the shapes that she wanted everyone to see, how simple it was to create illusions so real you could reach out and touch them. She reared back on her heels before barrelling forward on a warpath, the twin gods at the center of her wrath.

QUIA COULDN'T CATCH HOLD OF THE FLASH OF GREEN, BUT HE heard a loud scuffle behind him as a tall blond man and a red-headed woman burst from the crowd into the clearing at the center. They looked half-rabid as they lunged for the triarii, clawing with their bare hands and using goblets and servant trays as weapons. Quia's stomach dropped doubly when he realized who they were, and registered their abnormally wide pupils. Then the green flashed again, landing behind the two Amaurosis warriors.

Quia crawled back to stay out of their way. He was distracted watching the green figure flitting from place to place. It moved like a doe or a vixen, agile and strong. Quia noticed familiar olive skin and curly hair. If that had not been enough to recognize her, the small black fox that leapt in harmony with her movements was. Between movements, she returned to Rye and Lucan, to whisper in their ears, as if she was the puppetmaster controlling them. She moved with more grace than he had seen in the brief time he had known her, and only when she paused to clap her hands over head was Quia able to see her eyes, her pupils expanded to swallow up every stitch of white.

As Yom's hands met above her with a crack, the light of the room shifted and morphed, reforming above them into a heavy shroud of stars that coated everyone and everything in a glorious night. In this fantastical illusion, the greatest illusion of all lifted like a veil from Quia's eyes: the person he'd had in his company this entire time, was the numenborn for whom he had been searching.

XIX

Truths

THE BLANKET OF CONSTELLATIONS PULSED ABOVE YOM, ITS ILLUSION radiating from her fingertips. Power coursed through her hands, all the light—the numen—in the room open to her touch. But it was more than the access to Tezcat's numen. Yom felt like herself, or something closer to that truth. The act of facing her darkest thoughts, her most deeply buried truths, had taken away their power over her. Those thoughts were nothing more than thoughts; they did not define or limit her. She wrote her own definition. Knowing this, feeling it down the quick of her nails, gave her calm. Gave her control. Made her feel like she could wrestle gods and emerge victorious.

"Get away from her," Yom commanded the two yellow-eyed gods. Lior's limp form sagged on the bed.

"What is this?" The yellow-eyed god growled as he leapt off the platform, leaving Lior behind, and stalked towards Yom. Unabashed in his own nudity.

"There were two," the yellow-eyed goddess cut in, loping towards Yom from the other side of the platform. "Weren't there? That night in Inisfail."

Yom remained silent.

"I always felt something was off after that night." She turned to her brother. "We took the wrong one."

"It's you I wanted," the god said angrily, as if it was Yom's fault she had not allowed them to take her that night. "But now I have you. I knew this night would reveal your power." He smiled. He tied a cloth around his hips once again, lazily, as if he had come from a luxurious bath, but Yom would never forget the sight of him leaving Lior behind on that bed.

"You don't have me," she said, brow twitching with barely lidded rage.

With inhuman speed, the yellow-eyed god slinked whisper-close to Yom, smelling of pomegranate. His influence rubbed against her mind seductively. His eyes were glowing yellow orbs and his skin stone-like. The god's numen burned, not as a delicate light but a raging star in his chest. She could *feel* his anger, his desire, his regret. But Yom would not be intimidated. She had battled far worse things than an exiled god.

"Yom, numenborn of Tezcat. I can see my brother in you," he said, rancorous. That was it, Yom realized. According to Sophia's story, Tezcat had been the one to sever the two Lovers. The god must have thought Yom could fix it somehow, or be punished as revenge.

"*Yom!*" a voice called out. Her eyes widened; it sounded like Quia.

"You're mine," the god snarled as he latched onto her arms with an iron grip. The god's touch increased his influence tenfold, lust and desire and freedom a heady cocktail that soaked her mind.

"*Yom—*" The sound of her name cut through the fog enough to keep her alert. This second time she was certain it was Quia, but she had to distract the god long enough to find him. She attempted to cut off the parts of her mind infected with the god's desirous influence, and focus what remained on recalling any scrap of information she could. She sifted through useless details about the laws Quia had shared with her, and the rules tied to her torc, until she remembered something of note.

The gods rely on worship, on fear and reverence, to fuel their power.

That was it. He fed off of fear, off of any measure of belief in him. She had to make him small in her mind, to refuse him a single drop of fear. This god had killed Eden as a man would, and now he held her as a man would, intending to inflict his will on her. But Yom was a Stag. Bound by a titan with the numen of a god coursing through her. It was this god who should be afraid.

Yom gripped hard onto that tether that led back to Cernunnos's grove and channeled the strength into her palm. "You shouldn't have touched her," she ground out as she thrust her palm, endowed with the might of a stag's hoof, at the center of the god's chest. His eyes widened with a second of surprise before he and Yom were each thrown back several feet.

Yom didn't waste any more time watching him and rushed in the direction she had heard Quia's voice. But her pace was immediately slowed and her sight obscured by the dense crowd of nobles.

"GET HER." The god's inhuman voice crawled through the hall like a shattering swarm of butterfly wings.

As if controlled by his words, the triarii cropped up in her path.

Yom batted at them, aiming for any swatch of skin she could, and imbuing her touch with lies. Some she drowned in daffodils, some she placed on a cliff edge of Okeanus, one perilous step from its abyss. Yom was familiar with the tricks a mind could play on itself, and with Tezcat's numen, it was easy to project this onto another. The triarii crumpled one by one, the illusions robbing them of any assurance of power. Yom's path was clear long enough to see a figure whose wrists and ankles were shackled. This bound figure, with copper skin and coarse black hair, watched Yom with awe and distrust. Quia.

"I have to admit," a familiar voice interrupted the reunion. "Even I didn't see this coming." Misho stood next to Quia, but his armor was gone. He wore a plain linen tunic and similar linen sash across his hips. Misho looked between Yom and Quia, seeing Quia's hurt and Yom's hesitance. Without his armor, he was more vulnerable, yet more dangerous, like he had already lost everything.

Yom needed time. The triarii she had plowed through would slip out of their illusions, and the twin gods would close in any second. The first time she had bent the firelight in the room, she had shown them stars. Now, she needed darkness.

Driven by instinct, she held her palms out on either side, the torchlight of the hall accumulating in it, as if it were moths, and she the flame. The light was heavy, like a star burning in her hands. It was like she held her combat powders, Luminix and Tenebrax, but this time they were limitless. First light, to blind, and then darkness, to engulf. In seconds, the torches of the room appeared to hold only a gray and lightless flame. Everything rested in Yom's palm, her hands aching under the weight of it.

Misho registered an inkling of her plan. "Don't you—"

But Yom was quicker. She hoped Quia recalled that night in the Archives that felt so long ago now, as she shouted at him, "Quia, look away!" The light that she had gathered burst out in a symphony, an explosion of unbearably white brightness for the entire hall. As soon as it flashed, it was gone, leaving the room submerged in darkness.

The nobility in the hall shrieked and flailed, temporarily blinded, and Yom felt for Quia's form. She found a leg, with a metal cuff around the ankle. "It's me," Yom whispered beneath the wails that filled the hall. "Crawl this way." She pulled him away from where Misho stood.

"Yom," he whispered back, her name a prayer on his lips, as he allowed her to pull him.

Once they were a safe distance from Misho, Yom reached her blue-stained fingers into her belt and extracted her hooked tongs. It may have been Tezcat's numen, or just her adrenaline, but she picked the locks on his shackles in seconds.

"Interesting skill," Quia whispered, and with these words—the same ones he had said dryly as she picked the lock that first led them to the Amaurosis and began this insane quest—she knew he would forgive the secrets she had kept. He had to understand, she hadn't meant to deceive him. She had kept those very same secrets from herself, as well, all these years.

"Bluefingers!" Misho's voice rose over the bluster of the hall. "You think a little darkness can scare me?" The armorless triarii sounded unhinged, like the delicate threads that had held together his sanity had snapped.

Quia took over removing his shackles, working quietly. Yom stood and groped for the edge of the platform bed, considering the best route to get all three of them out of this marble prison once she found Lior. The god's voice was a distant screech; she could hear him knocking nobles out of the way and trying to order triarii around futilely. They still had a cover of blindness for several more minutes.

"I don't need sight to find you," Misho said raggedly. It was like he wasn't talking to Yom; he was speaking to someone who he was far more intimate with.

The sharp edge of the platform found Yom's fingertips. She snaked her hand over the silks that lined it until she felt Lior's form, even colder than the last time she had touched her skin. Up close, Lior's numen was frighteningly dim. It bubbled irregularly, like something in it had broken.

"Lior," Yom hazarded a whisper, but the form barely stirred. Yom tried to stoke Lior's numen, to ensure it did not extinguish completely. Though perhaps it was a good thing Lior was weak, Yom thought bleakly. The feel of Lior's hands strangling her was still fresh.

Quia stood, a hand on Yom's waist, tethering them in the darkness. "We need to go," he whispered.

"Help me carry her." Yom lifted her knee onto the bed to get enough leverage to pull Lior to the edge.

"Why do we need the Queen? She's obviously not the numenborn." A hint of Quia's displeasure with Yom's secret bled into his voice. Yom was a bit surprised that even after seeing what the god did to the Queen—to Lior—Quia would feel no inclination to help her. His hand tightened, trying to pull her away from the platform.

"This is Lior." Yom managed to hoist Lior's body over the edge and loop Lior's arm over her shoulder. Lior's head lolled into Yom's chest.

Yom turned to meet Quia's eyes, so he would know how serious she was about her next words. "I'm not leaving without her." *Even if she wants nothing to do with me,* Yom added a bit hopelessly in her head.

Quia's face was stone but he didn't argue. He stepped to Lior's other side and draped her other arm over his shoulder. Over the expanse of Lior's back, their hands touched, a spark emitting with each brush.

"This way." Yom took a step towards the exit.

"You could have left Inisfail with the chemist and returned to Panchaia within a day," Misho spat, his words placing him a mere few feet in front of them.

Yom changed direction. The garden. They would leave through the garden balcony.

"But you crossed the entire continent, chasing the wrong person!" Misho's words were getting closer. He was following them. "Even if the chemist didn't know what she was, I'm sure she began to suspect the truth."

"That's not true," Yom whispered breathily to Quia. Yom led them around the platform, towards the balcony, hoping Misho's words would fade away. But Misho managed to follow them, led by invisible reins.

"I should have figured it out, but my master covered his tracks well. In all records, the daughter of the chemist was brought by human traders through Traiana, and sold to a madam in a southern province. But she wasn't. Her name was changed, and a lowly chemist's daughter was placed on the throne."

When Misho laid it all out, it made perfect sense. The gods had been waiting for the numenborn, and when they thought they found it in Lior, they put her on the throne. *She belonged to the people of Arcadia, body and soul.* Tezcat's numen, and the one who supposedly wielded it, was placed in all of Arcadia's thrall. The Grieving Queen Andromeda was a more apt moniker than Yom ever realized; Lior grieved her mother and her freedom, stolen on the same night. The reminder of what happened that night threatened to cloud Yom's mind, but she kept steady. She had forgiven herself. Was actively forgiving herself, by dulling each canine-sharp thought that managed to slip through, until it lost its edge. Until it was just a thought, a piece of driftwood floating by. And perhaps one day, Lior would forgive her too.

Yom pushed through the crowd, the throng losing its might in darkness. But the illusion was fading, and Yom could already sense dim light returning to its home in the hall's torches.

"Even as Yom began to suspect the truth, she couldn't say anything before she saved her precious friend. Two numenborns have a better chance of defeating a god than one, right?" Misho continued needling into them with his words.

"Don't listen to him," Yom spurred them on. They just had to get to the garden, and escape this hall.

Finally, over the heads of the crowd, through the balcony door, Yom saw the moon. It had waned to a sliver since the Fight Night in Traiana, but still it glowed like a beacon.

"Although knowing Quia, he probably would have done the same thing in your shoes. You two really are perfect for each other." The doubt that Misho had sowed in the forest turned over in Yom's mind like a slumbering animal yawning awake. It was a ridiculous notion, that this fearsome triarii could be the companion Quia lost all those years ago—

"Do you ever stop talking?" Quia hissed over his shoulder, and Yom wanted to smack him. If Misho wasn't sure he had picked up their trail through the crowd, now he could be certain.

"That's not what Yom asked in the forest." Yom could hear the smile in Misho's words. "She was quite curious, weren't you?"

"So he was telling the truth? You knew who he was?" Quia was no longer whispering, his eyes bright with indignance.

"I—he, we—" Yom tried to protest that it was only a far-fetched idea she suspected, but she was too focused on crossing the threshold into the garden.

"I all but told her." Misho's voice was smug, as if he had won something by Yom not mentioning their interaction. She supposed he had.

They finally crossed into the garden, the humid air perfumed with flowers and herbs.

But Quia was slipping away. "How could you keep something like that from me?" He looked at her with new wounds in his eyes. Yom heard the rest of his words loud and clear. *After everything we went through together? After what we shared?*

Misho crossed the threshold as well and kicked away the jamb that held the heavy wood doors open. The doors closed with a clap, and the four of them were left alone on the balcony. The action confused Yom. Was it not his intention to deliver them to his master?

"Have you considered that she wanted to keep you focused, to make it easier to find the girl? This girl who is, perhaps, more than a friend." Misho's mouth widened in a toothy smile; in this state he was even more unpredictable than the last time they had fought. "On the up side, this entire thing will be a great story for the wedding."

"Mixcoat," Quia growled a strange version of Misho's name, like a warning.

"What is he talking about?" Yom looked between Quia to her side, and Misho to her front, something warring between them.

"She doesn't know?" Misho laughed. "That's the kind of thing you should tell a person."

"Know what?"

"It's all here." Misho pulled something out of his waist. It took a second before Yom realized it was Quia's bone knife, with leather wrapped around the handle. Misho unwrapped, and below the hilt, symbols were carved on the handle. "It was given to the numenborn after his Trials, engraved with the tale of his *destiny*." Misho spat out the last word, as if Quia's destiny was a cursed thing. "It's all in ancient Panchaian, but it goes something like, 'Greatest numenborn of our age, fated to unite with his only equal on this plane.'"

"Mixcoat, that's enough," Quia said forcefully.

Yom felt something looming, just on the cusp of her understanding.

"Quia is promised."

"You said you were betrothed." Yom began piecing it together. "You said she was in Panchaia."

"Can we talk about this later? You haven't been honest with me either," Quia pleaded. But it was too late, everything was coming into harsh focus. Quia said he was betrothed. *Fated to unite with his only equal on this plane.* Fated to unite with the numenborn. With Yom.

"You were looking for your *bride* this whole time, and you had the nerve to suggest I return to Panchaia with you both? Like some kind of mistress?" Yom seethed. She had imagined Quia's betrothed was some homely girl whose father intended to marry her off to Quia, and that Quia's behest of Yom coming with them meant that the betrothal would be...renegotiated. But this was so much worse. This was more than a betrothal, it had been something as fated as

Quia's own numen. Written in the stars. And Yom knew, without a shadow of a doubt, that he never intended to dissolve the betrothal.

"I was going to make it right," Quia insisted, though Yom saw through the words. He hadn't the faintest idea of how he would have done that, had the numenborn been someone else. "But now it makes sense why I was so drawn to you. There was never anyone else for me."

Misho let out a maddened laugh.

It was one secret too many. An irreparable rupture cleaved the space between Quia and Yom. Quia *knew* she had spent the last six years Bound to Cernunnos; he knew what it had cost her. And yet, now, he had every intention of tying her down in a different way. He had unknowingly planned not only to bring her back to Panchaia—regardless of her wishes—but to marry her when they got there. Yom couldn't help but hear Cernunnos and Rye's words, echoing in her ears, telling her they could see right through her, to the broken girl beneath. But Yom was *mending*. She was done being yanked this way and that by the chains of others. Even if that person was Quia.

"Let me make one thing perfectly clear." Yom narrowed her eyes at Quia from the other side of Lior. "I am promised to no one. *If* I marry, I decide whom I marry. And if I have to confront that bloody World Tree itself to make that clear, I will."

"Can't you see he's trying to drive a wedge between us?" Quia implored her.

"Yeah, well—"

The doors to the garden burst open, and the yellow-eyed god was there, his twin one step behind him and an entire company of beetle-armored triarii flanking them both.

"Get the spares," the god growled, and the triarii leapt into action. "The numenborn is mine."

Yom's trance was fading. She didn't know if it was the distraction of the last several minutes, or the diminishing effects of Amaurosis, but either way the powers this state had given her access to were slipping away. Her strength was weakening in its absence, all the exertion of her actions catching up to her.

Quia shrugged away Lior's arm to fend off the triarii. Yom was left supporting her weight, and trying to dodge any triarii that got close before Quia intervened.

Misho had skulked to the side, not coming after them but not helping them either.

Two triarii dodged Quia and came straight for Yom and Lior. Yom kicked at them and dodged their hands, but it only worked for a few blows. One triarii got his hands on Lior, and the other got leverage on Yom.

Yom screeched as they were wrenched apart. The triarii who held Lior had a compact dagger drawn and poised at her throat, pressing the tip enough to draw a drop of blood. Yom froze.

"Yom!" Quia shouted and held out his hand, blood smeared across his teeth. His lips were moving in a chant and his eyes sought her out desperately. Yom took one look back at Lior, already being towed away behind a wall of triarii. Quia was the only hope of getting her back. Yom grabbed onto Quia's hand and he pulled her to collide with him, his arms wrapping around her like he would never let go. It was warm and familiar, but bitter after everything Yom had just learned. It was tainted.

Before she could ruminate further, Quia took a gulp of air and breathed out gales of wind in a fan around them, holding Yom safely at its center. His wind threw the triarii back like dolls. Misho had managed to shield himself behind a tree trunk but still had to cling to it to stay planted. Only the two gods stood firmly in the wind's path, a bit ruffled but hardly shaken.

Quia's arms loosened from Yom and he shifted to stand next to her, their hands still clasped.

"So you know a magic trick." The god clapped mockingly. "The power of my brothers, reunited at last." His mouth looked amused but his eyes were full of wrath. "Misho, did you know we had two numenborn guests tonight? I wish you had told me, I could have been a better host."

"I did not," Misho said, still half-obscured by the tree. Yom knew he was lying, and the god did as well.

"I'll deal with you later." The god flicked his wrist, and Misho crumpled to the ground, writhing in pain.

Yom looked between them, waiting for it to end. "What are you doing?"

"Teaching a lesson."

Misho's garbled scream pierced the air.

"Enough, you've made your point." Yom's voice rose.

"I decide when it's enough," the god growled. His voice had changed again, echoing and multiplying.

Even though it was Misho, Yom couldn't stay silent seeing someone tortured like that.

"Tezcat doesn't care at all about me. You're wasting your time if you're trying to seek revenge through me."

With another casual flick of the god's wrist, Misho stilled. "Tezcat is the quivering hand of the sick body. He is the symptom, not the cause," the god said, his pale fingers clasping together in front of his bare, flawless chest.

Yom hesitated. "Then what exactly is your endgame? Invade Panchaia, take it away from the gods? Create a new world order with you and the titans at the top?"

"You mistake retribution for ambition." The god paced calmly. "Do you yet know that they need the humans as much as the humans need their precious gods? My siblings live off of the fear and worship of their humans. It is the nectar that sustains them. My twin and I were different. We needed nothing but the other. We did not care for the power that the belief of humans brought us. But our siblings were always jealous of our indifference. They searched for a way to drag us down, make us as dependent as they were. So when Tezcat saw his chance, he pounced. He used his twisted witchcraft to sever the tie between my twin and I, and our siblings watched on in silence. The only thing even close to love my siblings experience is their connection to the humans. *That* is what I plan to take away."

The garden had fallen utterly silent.

"I will kill all of their Panchaians, and the Arcadians will turn their backs on them. They will wither away in their drought of power."

Misho spoke from behind the god. "That's not what you—"

"Silence," the god hissed. Misho's mouth closed as if it was forced.

Quia took a step forward, Yom's hand clasped in his. "I won't let you kill my people."

But the god's attention, with the weight of a cloud pregnant with rain, had returned to Yom. Something in her understood something in him, despite being two creatures of completely different paths.

"Punishing your siblings won't put you two back together."

"What has passed can never be undone!" the god snarled.

"No, it can't." Eden's words bubbled to the surface, clear as the day she had whispered them in Yom's ear. "But sometimes the dark pieces of ourselves can be shed and grow something new. Never what they were, but something new." Yom straightened her spine. "Eden taught me that."

"Someone must pay the price for what has been committed." The god looked almost like a child, hurt and angry, beholden to the same emotions and weaknesses as the creatures he and his siblings had created.

"It is you who will pay for the atrocities you have committed." Quia let go of Yom's hand to step in front of her. The wind picked up, warm and smoky from the fires of Lupercalia. It swirled around them, laced with particles that bit at Yom's skin. "Are you done hiding behind children you call warriors?"

The god's nostrils flared. "I have never hid."

"Is that not what you've been doing in Arcadia all these centuries?" Quia was baiting him. "Allowing your temples to fall into disrepair, your priests to be neglected? Only a handful remain, and some say they only worship the god of fertility for self-serving reasons."

"Enough!" The god silenced Quia. "If it is a fight you want, a fight you shall have." The god's body moved subtly, shifting himself into a limber stance. "Sister?"

The yellow-eyed goddess took several steps back from her brother. Yom briefly wondered what her involvement was in this scheme. Was it a cause she believed in just as fiercely? Or did she do it to make her brother happy?

"Quia," Yom whispered, "My trance is gone."

"We don't need it." Quia's jaw ticked. Yom hoped he wasn't faking his confidence. "This ends here. You may have lived a thousand of my lifetimes, but in this one, I am more powerful than you." The wind became harsher, the debris it carried even sharper.

"Power is a funny thing. It can hurt as easily as it can help." The god smiled. "My sister has always had a connection to plant numen. Did you know this?"

Quia hesitated, minutely. But Yom noticed.

"Where do you think Tezcat learned it all? You think he figured it out on his own? He learned from my sister, under the guise of altruism of course. He claimed its benefits would be shared with the world. But for the master illusionist, the plant magick presented another vehicle of power. That is all my siblings care for. Power."

Yom realized the raven-haired goddess had slipped away. "Quia—"

"And so he learned from my sister the language of the plants, and then he seduced them into sharing their secrets. And when the stories were told, and passed down through the ages, it was Tezcat who first learned the plant's secrets. Tezcat who first walked the Path of Night. My sister's gift was lost over the generations."

Yom's skin pebbled despite the warm air around them. The goddess had disappeared, and they were in a garden lush with flora.

"Quia, she's—"

"What are you waiting for?" Quia sounded wilder, more on edge. "Let us fight!"

"The world may have forgotten, but my sister was the first enchanter." The god had no sooner spoken than his yellow-eyed sister appeared behind Quia, holding one hand over his mouth and one hand over his heart. Yom could hear the plants the goddess held in her hands singing as their numen seeped into Quia. Quia thrashed for a second, taken completely by surprise, before his black eyes drifted closed and an expression of bliss took over his face.

Misho was still hobbled by the god's torture, and Lior was half-lucid in the hold of the triarii. Desperately Yom scanned the garden around them, a brief flash of hope that if the goddess was an enchanter, perhaps a patch of Amaurosis grew somewhere.

"You won't find any Victor's Root here," the god said haughtily. He stepped towards Yom, looking at her as if her skin was transparent and her insides were spread open for him. "I can see your desires like jewels of a necklace hung around your throat. Even the ones you try to hide from yourself. You want to settle down. Perhaps, one day, have a family." The god smiled softly.

"You made sure I would never have a family." Her voice broke as she thought of the knife being pulled from Eden's gut, dripping with blood.

But she blinked and the god stood in front of her, his cold hands wrapping around her forearms. Yom sucked in a breath and the god's yellow eyes bored into her, his face curled over hers. His hands tightened, his touch carrying a foreign sacredness.

"I can give you what you want. Freedom, power, even love." The god spoke to Yom. His thumbs stroked the skin of her forearms and the touch was hypnotic. He looked to Lior and under his gaze, she took a large gulp of air, and her eyes opened. "She can be yours. Or he can be." The god turned to look at Quia, still entranced in the goddess's hold. "Or you may keep them both. All I ask is your service. We could accomplish great things together." The garden faded away, and Yom saw herself robed in armor, leading a fleet of great ships on Okeanus, tethered together as she navigated the treacherous crossing. When they arrived on the shores of Panchaia, the Panchaians rejoiced. Greedy and power-hungry gods held them prisoner, and Yom offered them a simple path out. *If you go, you take their power with you*, she said to them. The Panchaians nodded fervently and fell on their swords, into a serene rest. It was peaceful, and Yom was a hero.

One voice raised over the cheers of victory. It was quiet, a boy's voice, and Yom had to ask everyone to hush so she could hear it.

"This is wrong, Yom." The words were simple but it was their source that quaked the earth Yom stood on. It was Moss who stood among the strewn bodies, in the center of the vision, looking at Yom as if she had failed.

"No, I wouldn't do this," Yom protested as she looked around at the carnage and destruction. "I've never taken a life—"

"No—" a cold voice snarled before a pale hand backhanded Moss to the ground.

The vision faded enough for Yom to sense the two hands holding her in place. The god's influence was harder to resist when she wasn't in trance, but she could still feel it, like a blanket muffling her own thoughts. This god didn't deal in physical blows. He couldn't be baited into fighting. His warfare occurred in the mind. But Yom had fought her own thoughts for years, and because of this her mind had built its own resilience. Its own invincibility.

Sever the connection, Yom realized. *He needs touch to exert this kind of control.* Yom summoned every drop of strength she had left, and imagined this god to be a small, broken man.

"This isn't me," Yom said as she jerked her arms inward, bringing him close enough that she could land a knee to a place she knew any man would be sensitive, even a god.

He huffed when her knee made sharp contact with his groin, the only indication that she had caused any pain. But his hands momentarily lost their grip on her. The vision lifted just as Yom darted backwards, towards the edge of the dense garden.

"Perhaps you need a different kind of motivation," the god shouted, making no effort to chase her. Yom leapt into the thicket of leaves and blooms, but no one was coming after her. The god knew perfectly well that he held all the cards.

"Bring them in," the god's distant voice rumbled.

Yom peered through the cracks between leaves. Triarii led Lucan and Rye, scuffed up and a bit peaky, to stand next to Lior. And then one more figure, small and hunched, with dark hair. Clementine. Yom's throat closed, her breath escaping her. She hadn't seen Clementine in the hall, but she must have traveled from Traiana with Rye. *I've got my own battles to fight,* Clementine had said. Rye and Lucan had committed their own atrocities, but Clementine was not a soul who could become tangled in Yom's web. It was Moss all over again.

"You say you've never taken a life, Yom, numenborn of Tezcat. But you have been responsible for several lives." Even from her obscured view in the garden, she could see the god smiling. "And we shall add several more to the tally, until you yield."

Yom sat back on her heels, her vision threatening to tunnel. The lush garden extended over her head, and above the tips of the tallest leaves, another layer of foliage hung down, breaking up the night sky with draping vines and curling blooms. The perfume of flowers in the air was intoxicating, almost intoxicating enough to convince herself that the last week had been nothing more than a dream, and soon she would wake in the Cut's Powder Parlor.

But this was real. Lior was alive, and Quia remained unhurt—for the moment—and now, three more lives hung in the balance. And Yom risked losing them all if she couldn't come up with a plan. She had seen what the god's influence looked like in Misho. *You have your shackles, and I have mine,* he had said in the forest. It was different from the bridge created by the Bind between her and Cernunnos. To Bind herself to the god seemed to mean pure obedience. And now that she knew his plan was to wipe Panchaia from the map entirely, she couldn't pledge herself and the numen that came with it to him.

"Shall I begin with Renos's whelp?" the god's voice boomed. Yom swallowed and as he stepped up behind Rye's dazed form. *"Or start off somewhere more interesting, with our grieving Queen?"* The god ran a pale finger down Lior's face. Yom instinctively leapt forward, her heart crying out for the girl she had lost. But the god withdrew his hand from Lior's cheek.

"So that we do not misunderstand each other," the god snarled and flicked two fingers at Rye. A legionary appeared behind her, and Rye barely had time to sputter before the blood soaked tip of a sword pushed through the center of her chest. Rye's eyes vacated and her head lolled back an inch before dropping down onto her chest, lifeless. Yom gasped, her limbs filling with lead. She had to do something, but she was frozen. Robbed of everything.

Something iridescent caught her eye. Yom thought she imagined it until she saw it again. An iridescent black wing. Of a butterfly.

"Sassa," Yom said out loud, tears gathering, either from the relief of seeing her or the sting of smoky wind in her eyes. Delicate feet landed on Yom's forehead and her iridescent wings flapped soft bursts of air onto her face.

The second of relief was swallowed by reality. *"I'll take the girl next,"* the god continued on, emotionless about the life he had taken. Yom watched in a panic as he moved to stand behind Clementine.

You can do this, Sassa's intangible words came to Yom. *You have all the tools.*

"I have nothing," Yom whispered under her breath. "None of my powders, no Amaurosis, no chance."

"On the count of three," the god snarled. Yom's vision split from watching Clementine from afar, to seeing Moss in Misho's arms. And Cernunnos's emotionless sentencing: *and now, Bluefingers, it's time for your demonstration.*

You have this, Sassa's wings flapped more insistently on Yom's forehead. *You are more than your birthright, than your abilities. More than your chains.*

My abilities and my chains, Yom repeated to herself, a delicate idea sparking, the spirit of the trickster still flickering inside her. The god wanted her, for whatever reason, even though he already acknowledged he had two numenborn in his presence tonight. He wanted Tezcat's numen. But Yom did not only hold Tezcat's power; she belonged to Cernunnos in some twisted way too. What was it Quia had said? *A servant cannot be killed by another immortal or the agent of an immortal. They must always be returned to their master.* Something else had followed. *A god cannot enter a mortal's mind and force them to believe, and they cannot outright kill a mortal.* But she had witnessed this with her own eyes. A pale hand plunging a knife into Eden, then pulling it out and allowing her to bleed out on the ground. *They are banished from their celestial home, the thirteen heavens.*

The idea was fanned into a plan beneath the gentle flap of Sassa's wings.

"One," the god began his countdown.

Yom's hand hastily came up to the torc around her neck, to the antlers carved into its ends. No sooner had she sought it than she returned to the clearing, where Cernunnos sat. At her entrance, he stood. His antlers reached well over fourteen feet, and his steps were silent as he padded towards her, despite walking over dried leaves and mossy brush.

"I knew you were of value," Cernunnos growled. Every syllable was as clear as if they spoke in person, and not in some crevice of her mind. "The numenborn of Tezcat, under my snout the whole time."

"I belong to you," Yom said, staying her hands from shaking in the presence of his giant form.

"A fact you have conveniently forgotten." Birds circled above them as Cernunnos appraised her. "But it seems your little deviation has revealed far more valuable power."

"If I accept your will without question, will you claim me?" Yom held her breath.

"Who would I need to claim my own servant from?" Cernunnos's voice turned hostile.

"The Lover wishes to enter into an agreement with me." Yom's mind flashed to the puppet-like control the god had over Misho.

Cernunnos smiled, his eyes going somewhere distant. "I hold his most valuable piece."

"He will sever your Bind if you do not intercede."

Cernunnos tipped one finger, thrice the size of Yom's own, under her chin to tilt her face towards him. "I will claim you. But I will not be made a fool. If you are not returned to my realm in seven days, I will sever the Bind. Permanently. And then no one will have you."

"Two," the god's countdown reached her faintly.

Yom swallowed. It was a lifetime ago when she had told Moss the two ways one could be Unbound from Cernunnos. She had never told the boy the third way. She was not foolish enough to think that Cernunnos wouldn't find a way to exercise this third method of Unbinding, even from afar.

"Will you keep watch for the moment you need to intercede?"

"I am always watching." Already his presence faded as Yom backed away from that grove, but she knew better than to feel relieved. She grunted as she pushed herself back to standing. The night sky was open above her, a blanket of lights punctured by the moon. She let herself lean into its comfort as she waded back towards the clearing, ready to finish this.

"Three!" the god said, clearly angry this had not drawn her out yet.

"Wait!" Yom stepped from the edge of the thicket, finding the god's yellow eyes even from several dozen feet away. "I yield," she announced.

The god bared his teeth in a grim smile.

Once she left the brush of the garden, the god circled her. "I knew you would come to your senses. I can give you anything you want."

"The only thing I want is for Quia and Lior to be freed." Yom made it a point to avoid looking at Rye's body, a halo of blood creeping in all directions from it. If she could free Quia and Lior, she was confident she could keep Clementine with her—in one piece—and make sure the girl landed somewhere safe, as far from this cursed palace as possible.

"You wish to make a bargain, after all."

"Prove you'll do it. Release them both now."

The god's jaw ticked, but he dipped his chin. "Bring our Queen and the boy here," he turned to command.

The goddess released Quia from her grip, and his eyes reopened. He looked around in a panic until he found Yom and hastened towards her.

"Ah ah." The god held up a hand when Quia was still several feet away. "No closer." He had grabbed one of Yom's forearms, and Quia watched his grip carefully.

The ring of triarii closed in, Lior now squirming like a frightened animal. Lucan and Clementine were pushed forward as well, and Lucan looked at Yom with glazed eyes.

"They will be released outside of the city gates, you have my word." The god waved his hand.

"What's going on, Hector?" Lior asked sheepishly.

"Not good enough." Yom squared up to the god.

"Watch your tone—"

"Quia will summon Thoth. The Traveler will take them to Panchaia."

The only noise in the garden was the rustle of leaves in the breeze.

"What? I—" Lior sucked in a breath but she was silenced with a flick of the god's wrist.

"You wish to stake their lives on the caprice of my brother?" The god clicked his tongue. "I would think you smarter than this."

Yom smiled back at him. "*You* will pay Thoth's toll."

The god laughed. "This is hardly the time for humor, mortal."

"I was there the night you took Lior. I know what you did." Yom steadied her voice as she spoke. The god studied her, his mouth turning down in a frown.

"How dare you attempt to blackmail me."

"I am not the only one." Yom readied her bluff. "A contact in Inisfail will release the information if Quia does not send word from Panchaia, safe." The god pursed his lips but remained silent. Yom had no clue how the affairs of the immortals were arbitrated, but she banked on there being some sort of system, if Quia's words on their laws were to be believed.

"You can't bargain with him—" Quia spoke but the goddess covered his mouth.

"And you will enter my agreement?" The god flexed his fingers around Yom's forearm impatiently.

"Once they have been freed, I will." Yom knew by the look in his eye that she had him.

"Do not try anything," the god hissed.

"Quia," Yom turned away. "Now, please?"

YOM REMAINED IN THE GOD'S GRIP, ONLY A COUPLE FEET FROM QUIA as he built a fire. The restraint was unnecessary; she had no plans to escape. She had one final trick up her sleeve, once Quia and Lior were safe.

Quia ripped a branch away from a nearby tree and held the jagged edge into the fire. Moving with purposeful slowness, he blew out the flame and allowed the smoke to wisp away from the charred edge, caught somewhere between liquid and air.

"You can't stay here," Quia whispered. "You heard what he plans to do to my people."

"I know what I'm doing," Yom whispered back. "Just trust me."

Quia began tracing the charred end over the stone path. "You don't have anything to prove by martyring yourself," he muttered under his breath. For all his resistance, at least he was following Yom's directions.

Shrill grunts escaped from Lior, whose lips were sealed by the god's order. Yom looked at her, willing her to one day understand everything that had happened here.

The wind began to pick up around the shape that Quia was delicately tracing. Yom held her breath, a part of her fearing that Quia would go off script, and try to pull something that would get Lior killed.

The wind swirled over the fire. Yom watched the god's face carefully as his brother took shape from the smoke.

Thoth's form solidified as if carved of gleaming bronze, the scent of licorice bleeding into the wind around them. The Traveler stepped down from the fire into the circle of triarii, radiant with power. Side by side, Yom saw the difference in vitality between Thoth and his twin siblings, the cost the Lovers paid for remaining in this land where no one believed in them enough to fear them.

"Twice in a fortnight, mortal?" Thoth spoke to Quia. "If you wish to see me, I have many temples you may visit instead."

"I beseech you," Quia ground out.

Thoth looked delighted. Then, he caught sight of the yellow-eyed god. "Xopilli?"

"Hello, brother," the god said without emotion.

Thoth scanned the garden, looking for something. "Xochi?" He found the goddess standing to the side of Quia.

"This is not a reunion," Xopilli said coldly.

"We have been looking for you for—"

"You are here for the mortals. Take them and leave."

"You are always welcome home," Thoth said with some longing in his voice. "We have missed you."

"We have no home." The yellow-eyed god dismissed him, though his coolness was betrayed by his refusal to meet his sibling's eye.

"Allow her to say goodbye," Quia asked Xopilli.

Yom had been so caught up in the weaving of her plan she had forgotten this would likely be her last chance to say goodbye to either of them.

"Please." Yom turned to Xopilli as well.

The god was clearly distracted by the presence of his brother, enough that he relinquished her forearm for a second and waved his assent.

Quia wasted no time pulling Yom into a tight hug. "You have nothing to prove," he whispered in her ear.

Yom leaned back to give him a forlorn smile. Something had changed between them, but the night was so muddled that Yom still saw the royal apprentice she had left Inisfail with: haughty, frustratingly charming when he wanted to be, and fearless. The boy who had kept secrets, but also shared pieces of himself that made Yom understand her own self better. For that, she would always be grateful to him.

"It's not about proving anything. I want her to be safe." Yom cleared her throat. "I want you both to be safe." Yom hoped he understood that even if she wanted to stay with him, righting what happened to Lior all those years ago was still the most important thing. It was the final act needed to close the chapter of what happened that night in Eden's laboratory.

"I'm sorry, Yom." Quia's voice came out in a broken whisper as he rested his forehead on her shoulder.

"There's nothing to be sorry about." Yom's tears leaked onto his shirt. "This is the first good deed I've been able to do."

The hushed murmurs of Thoth and Xopilli quieted.

"That's enough. Return to my side, mortal. The toll has been paid." The yellow-eyed god beckoned Yom with an insistent hand.

Yom pulled back from Quia, but he kept a tight hold on her. She tried to tell him with her eyes that she would not let the god use her for his twisted revenge. She had a plan.

"Now," Xopilli growled, more impatient.

A breeze rustled as Thoth returned to his mantle over the fire.

She turned to Lior, but Lior's blue eyes were closed off to the world, most especially Yom.

"Forgive me," Quia whispered, drawing her attention away. "This is my duty." His eyes implored her for something. She was about to remind him there was nothing to forgive when Quia's hand locked around her arm in an iron grip. And started to pull her.

Yom inhaled sharply as she realized that his other hand was inches from reaching Thoth's outstretched palm.

He hadn't tried to resist Yom's plan, because he intended to hijack it. Xopilli had paid the toll for two, and Quia intended to take Yom with him instead of Lior, even if it was against her will.

"No!" Xopilli's inhuman voice rang out at the same instant as Yom's, and time itself seemed to slow down as the entire ring of people lunged towards them, trying to stop Quia.

Yom was frozen as Quia pulled her. Forming any thought was like trying to shape mud in those charged seconds. Lior was right next to them, if Yom could just reach her, she could—

The second Quia's other hand touched Thoth's it sent an electric current through Yom and she was whorled into a smoky torrent. It was the same instant her palm landed on something—someone—and she gripped it with all the strength she could muster. She couldn't even see who she had managed to grab a hold of, her vision already clouding into nothingness. Her scream was soundless as Quia pulled through a darkness that reeked of licorice and smoke—a place in between—before reaching a speck of light that exploded around her.

The next second, Yom was thrown against roughly hewn ground. *Panchaian ground*, her mind sputtered as she tried to keep it from dissociating in the shock. Harsh sunlight beat down on her, a surreal change from the flower-threaded night she had been in not one moment ago. The light slanted differently here; the air bit at her cheeks, smelling of dust and foreign fruit. Strange bird calls rang out above her and Yom looked up. Jeweled feathers flitted on the edge of her vision, and hovering over her, an enormous set of stone-fanged jaws loomed.

Everything was different, everything was wrong.

Her hand was clenched around something and she turned to see the back of a blond head, hair pulled into a knot. Lucan groaned, moving stiffly, eyes glazed in confusion. The last glimmer of hope transformed before Yom's eyes like the mirage that it was. In the single second of a chance she had, she hadn't been able to reach Lior. And now, her friend, her lost love, was on the other side of Okeanus. She had failed, well and truly.

Yom whipped to her other side, looking for Quia. She hated him; in that moment she could have pushed him into Okeanus without a second thought. He claimed he cared about her, but it was clear all he cared about was his duty. He had found his precious numenborn, and finally returned home.

All it had cost Yom was everything. Cernunnos's threat rang in her ears, a dirge that would not relent. *If you are not returned to my realm in seven days, I will sever the Bind. Permanently. And then no one will have you.* Quia had, in a matter of seconds, destroyed the hard won bargain Yom had forged for his and Lior's freedom, and Yom would have to pay the price.

ACKNOWLEDGEMENTS

I thought writing this book would be the hardest thing I'd ever accomplish. I was wrong—publishing it definitely takes the cake. This has been an arduous journey, full of anxiety, self-doubt, and far too much coffee, but it would not have been possible without my partner, my love, and my light, Aaron. You have enabled me to chase my dreams, and I will never stop thanking you for it.

Equally integral, though for different reasons, are my parents. Mom, Dad, I love you, thank you for letting me read at the dinner table, and never questioning why your kid preferred to squirrel herself away in her room, scribbling and crying. I was a weird (and moody) kid, and you've always seen and nurtured the best parts of me.

Thank you to the Brodkey clan. Terri, Jason, thank you for being champions of this book even though I am still deeply frightened that you will read it. Max, Sam, I better see this book displayed in a place of honor in your homes. And thank you all for not being weirded out that I took your name to publish under before Aaron and I officially tied the knot.

Thank you to my editor, Kit, for being the first person to read this book and connect with it. Your belief in me and this story pushed me forward during a time when I wasn't sure how to keep going.

Thank you to my early readers, both writers and friends: Tammy, Lexi, Niamh, Andréa, Emily, Kara, Kelly, Stella, Stephanie, Ella, Haley, Mel and Anna. Thank you to those of you who provided detailed beta commentary at a crucial moment for this story. Thank you to my friends who received a completely unsolicited manuscript in their email when they didn't even know I had been writing a book for over a year. And a special thank you to Andrea for talking me off a ledge no less than once a day, whipping my adverb usage into shape, and for being the best critique partner a gal could ask for. I truly feel spoiled by your friendship.

Thank you to the incredible artists who helped me bring this story to life: Emily (@MillyIllus), for illustrating the most gorgeous cover I have ever seen, and Rin (@RinVargaIllo) for creating interior illustrations that feel like stepping into this world.

Thank you to my incredible Street Team—you are this book's village.

And thank you, the reader. For giving this book a chance.

SOUNDSCAPE

Hearing Damage	THOM YORKE
Crush	ETHEL CAIN
Habits (Stay High)	TOVE LO
The Feels	LABRINTH
You're All I Want	CIGARETTES AFTER SEX
Dancing With Your Ghost	SASHA ALEX SLOAN
The Night We Met	LORD HURON
October Passed Me By	GIRL IN RED
Violent	CAROLESDAUGHTER
All The Things She Said	T.A.T.U.
you should see me in a crown	BILLIE EILISH
Believer	IMAGINE DRAGONS
I am not a woman, I'm a god	HALSEY
EVIL	MELANIE MARTINEZ
Nobody Gets Me	SZA
Only Love Can Hurt Like This	LORD HURON
favorite crime	OLIVIA RODRIGO
Way down We Go	KALEO

GLOSSARY

AETHERIUM	A powder created by Bluefingers for recreation. Leaves the user in a state of dull euphoria.
ALBION	A province that neighbors INISFAIL to the south. Domain of Coventina and her BEARS.
AMAUROSIS	A mythical plant that has been lost in ARCADIA since the ANCIENT WAR. It submerges the user in a semiconscious state with hyper-strength. Also known as VICTOR'S ROOT.
ANCIENT WAR	The war between GODS and TITANS that preceded the SEPARATION of ARCADIA and PANCHAIA.
ARCADIA	The Queendom and its network of provinces.
ARDENNES	A mountainous forest on the eastern side of the Arcadian continent, though not incorporated into Arcadia's network of provinces. Location of SYLVEAUX. Domain of Arduinna.
BEAR	Bound servants of the TITAN Coventina.
BIND	An agreement between a human and an Immortal. Bound servants of TITANS bear torcs around their necks, and Bound servants of GODS are tattooed with their agreement.
BLACKCOAT	Colloquial name for a LEGIONARY soldier. Their northern uniform includes a thick blue coat, but legionaries in the provinces are notorious for their corruption, hence the moniker.
CATARACTA	The capital city of ARCADIA, and cultural center of the Queendom. Home of the Queen's palace, the House of Flowing Waters. Also known as the eternal city.
CUT	A cluster of buildings in INISFAIL where Cernunnos's operation is based, and where the STAGS live.
DRESSEN	A province of ARCADIA, whose capital is TRAIANA. Domain of Renos and her EELS.

GLOSSARY

DRIFTER'S METTLE	An old matron's powder made of crushed nutmeg and tea leaves.
EEL	Bound servants of the TITAN Renos.
ETERNAL CITY	A moniker for CATARACTA because of the history contained in the city, both ancient and modern.
GOD	A type of Immortal born of the WORLD TREE. Creator of humans.
GUTTER	An underground keep where Renos and her EELS live.
FERIA	The eight day long festival of spring, first celebrated by the Ancients, now celebrated by modern Arcadians, culminating in LUPERCALIA.
FURORIS	A powder created by Bluefingers that induces mania. It is typically given to fighters before a match or foot soldiers before a battle.
HOUSE OF FLOWING WATERS	The palace of the Queen of ARCADIA, located in CATARACTA.
HOUSE OF OAK	Another name for the domain of Cernunnos.
IBERNIA	A province of ARCADIA, whose capital is INISFAIL. Domain of Cernunnos and his STAGS.
INISFAIL	The WORLD TREE's lifeforce that animated the immortal GODS and TITANS, and then subsequently the world the immortals created.
LEGIONARY	A royal soldier serving the HOUSE OF FLOWING WATERS.
LUMINIX	A powder created by Bluefingers that creates instant, blinding light upon contact.

GLOSSARY

LUPERCALIA A secretive ritual held in the HOUSE OF FLOWING WATERS on the eighth and final day of the FERIA.

MOONFLOWER A plant controlled by the HOUSE OF FLOWING WATERS due to its potency. One of its powers is to leave its user in a state more open to suggestion.

MORNINGSTAR An interprovincial train that runs from INISFAIL to TRAIANA.

NUMEN The lifeforce, originally from the WORLD TREE, that animates gods, titans, and all their creations— humans, animals, and nature.

NUMENBORN A human born with the gift of numen from one of the gods, and with it an echo of the god's own power; or an animal born with the gift of numen from one of the titans, and with it the ability to shift their shape at will.

OKEANUS The vast, enchanted waters that separate Arcadia and Panchaia. No one is known to have sailed it and lived to tell the tale.

PANCHAIA The half of the world that was separated from the Arcadian continent. Little is known about Panchaia and reaching it is thought to be impossible due to Okeanus.

RUTHBANE An old matron's poison created from hogbean and morning glory seeds that kills its victim within a day.

SEPARATION A massive earthquake that ended the Ancient War by splitting the land into two halves, now known as ARCADIA and PANCHAIA.

SOMNARIUM A powder created by Bluefingers that puts someone to sleep instantly.

STAG Bound servants of the TITAN Cernunnos.

GLOSSARY

SYLVEAUX   A city located high up in the trees in the Forest of ARDENNES.

TENEBRAX   A powder created by Bluefingers that creates a cloud of darkness.

TITAN   A type of Immortal born of the WORLD TREE. Creator of nature and animals.

TRAIANA   The capital city of DRESSEN. Location of the GUTTER.

TRIALS   A ritual that a Priest takes a Panchaian child through at the age of seven years, to open the connection to their NUMEN, and assess whether the child is a NUMENBORN.

TRIARII   An elite class of soldier who serves the Queen as a personal guard as well as undertakes special assignments. Known to be the most deadly fighter in ARCADIA.

VICTOR'S ROOT   A moniker for AMAUROSIS that derives from the use of it during the ANCIENT WAR to create warriors endowed with hyperstrength.

WORLD TREE   The great tree that sits at the center of the world, whose lifeforce animated the GODS and TITANS in the beginning of the world.

WACACHAN   The ancient name for the WORLD TREE.

ABOUT THE AUTHOR

Rebecca Brodkey lives in the Chicago suburbs and spends most of her time hunched over a notebook, reading, and eating popcorn. She studied Physics and Mathematics at the University of Michigan and has been a lifelong Latin and mythology nerd. *Darker Than the Starless Night* is her first novel.

Visit her website

RebeccaBrodkey.com

Join her Newsletter

RebeccaBrodkey.substack.com

Follow her on Instagram

@RebeccaBrodkeyBooks